# hot boyz

**By Marissa Monteilh**

HOT BOYZ
THE CHOCOLATE SHIP
MAY DECEMBER SOULS

# hot boyz

Marissa Monteilh

*An Imprint of* HarperCollins*Publishers*

HarperCollins books may be purchased for education, business, or sales promotional use. For information please write: Special Markets Department, HarperCollins Publishers Inc., 10 East 53rd Street, New York, NY 10022.

FIRST EDITION

*Designed by Elizabeth M. Glover*

Library of Congress Cataloging-in-Publication Data

Monteilh, Marissa.
Hot boyz / Marissa Monteilh.—1st ed.
p. cm.
ISBN 0-06-059094-7
1. African American families—Fiction. 2. African American men—Fiction.
3. Los Angeles (Calif.)—Fiction. 4. Brothers—Fiction. I. Title: Hot boys. II. Title.

PS3613.O548H68 2004b
813'.6—dc22 2004041082

04 05 06 07 08 JTC/RRD 10 9 8 7 6 5 4 3 2 1

*To my husband, Ron Allen Monteilh, Sr.—*
*R/I/P 5-31-91.*
*A HOT BOY back in high school.*
*"Through the Years," you never let me down.*

# Acknowledgments

I always give thanks and praise to God for the gift and for the knowledge that it is choice, not chance, that determines your destiny.

Special thanks to: My loving family—Alexis, Adam, Ron Jr., Nicole, Darrien, Greg, Tom, and the Fullers.

Friends—Ollie, Vicky, Annette, Darnella, Darryl, and Tami.

My new agent and confidant, Jimmy Vines. Thanks!

My personal reviewer—Speed reader, Angela Looney.

Bookstores—Bernard Henderson (BlackBooksellers.org) @ Alexanders, Pam Lang @ Barnes & Noble, Carlee and Lynee @ Waldenbooks, Lisa @ Waldenbooks, Marie @ 2000+, Feron @ Phenix Books, Marcus @ Nubian Books, Fanta @ Oasis Books.

The Antelope Valley Writers Group—Bonnie, Lynn, Beverly, the two Brendas, Joan, Gina, Dorothy, Tanya, Antoinette, and Marilyn for their invaluable spirit of camaraderie.

My two VIP "Sisters in Pen"—My mentor, Victoria Christopher Murray, and my spiritual buddy, Cydney Rax (BooksByCydney.com). I love you both!

Media—Twanda Black, Marjorie Coley, and Stephanie Williams @ 104.1 KISS FM. LaShaunda Hoffman @ *Shades of Romance* magazine, Shunda Blocker-Leigh @ *Booking Matters* magazine, Naomi and Patricia @ AV Today, Ryan Chadwick @ AV Press, Penny @ AV Journal, Harrell Carter @ 101.5 Carter & Co., Maxine Thompson @ On The Same Page (VoiceAmerica.com).

Online Reviewers—Nathasha Brooks and Wayne Jordan with RomanceInColor.com, N. Jeffries with Heartstrings.

Book Clubs, Janel Stephensen and the special members of The Special Thoughts Reading Group, Andrea Renee Ransom (R/I/P 5-4-03), Jan Emanuel and The Good Book Club, Oakland.

Fellow Authors—Darnella Ford, Maryann Reid, Nancey Flowers, Nina Foxx, Jacquelin Thomas, Mary B. Morrison, and Evelyn Palfrey.

The impeccable Carol Mackey with BlackExpressions.com.

Warm thanks to Patricia, April, Jim, and Stephanie @ BlueWorldTravel.com for the Soul Cruise 2003.

My Publicist—Lauretta Pierce @ LiteraryWorld.org.

The HarperCollins Family—Carrie Feron, Selina McLemore, Diana Tynan, Lisa Gallagher, and Rockelle Henderson.

The one and only Richard Curtis @ CurtisAgency.com.

And to my readers—thank you for your hunger! You inspire me to keep cookin' it up!!

Marissa Monteilh

# prologue

"*Bang!*" One loud, thunderous sound rang from outside the house just before Thanksgiving dinner was served. The pulsating, resounding boom was followed by an immediate thud against the ten-foot-tall front door to Mason Wilson's Ladera Heights home.

Claude, Mason's younger brother, dashed from the dining room in a panic. He pulled the door open with startled strength. Just as everyone else's panic level started to gear up, Mason yelled for the teenagers, Cameron, Rashaad and Star, to go into the back portion of the expansive house.

With his heart pounding, Claude fell to his knees. His tall, blood splattered woman, Fatima, lay on the front porch, flat on her back, with her flip-phone still in one hand. Fifty-two missed calls registered on the display.

She had a large gunshot wound to her chest. As a pool of warm, vivid red blood spewed from her body, Claude lifted Fatima just under her shoulders. Her body hung limp like a rag doll as he held her in his arms.

"Tima, no," he cried out to the skies above as though God could come down and touch her with His healing hands. Tears rolled down Claude's pained and helpless face.

His family members screamed in disbelief at the ghastly sight. Torino, the youngest brother, hugged his elderly mother, Mattie, holding her tight with a shielding embrace.

"*Bang*," another shot rang out. Mason's wife, Mercedes, ran to the phone and frantically dialed 9-1-1. Mason emerged from his study carrying a stainless steel Glock. He raced past Fatima's body and onto the front lawn, only to find the seemingly lifeless body of a man slumped over the wheel of a burgundy Lincoln town car.

Fatima's best friend and newfound lover, Venus, frozen and stunned, stood over Claude and Fatima with her hands covering her wide-opened mouth . . . in shock.

Barely breathing, Fatima gasped for air. With heavy eyelids, she struggled to give a half gaze, looking up at her friend Venus. She fought to swallow, forcing her own blood and saliva down her throat to make room for her words. Just barely, she managed to part pale lips, and said faintly, "If . . ." The remainder of her sentence never came. She closed her mouth and shifted her glassy-eyed glance toward her man one last time. A calm took over her face. Her eyes shut as her head fell to the side. Fatima lay dead in Claude's arms, on his very own birthday.

The day before, the sun shined brightly. Claude Joseph Wilson, mindful of his appointment with his longtime lady, Fatima Clark, sped down La Cienega Boulevard in his graphite blue CLK55 Mercedes. He had a few stops to make before he made his way toward the beach community of Palos Verdes to meet the love of his life.

His first stop was Magic Johnson's Starbucks in the Ladera Center for his usual cup of their Grenada blend. After all, what would a weekday morning be without kicking it with his neighborhood boyz? But today, it would only be a quickie.

The next stop was an even quicker run by his business, Wilson Realty, right around the corner on Centinela. He'd hired a new, top-selling realtor who he stole from Ladera Realty named Heidi Hamilton. Today was her first day. He wanted to welcome her aboard just before the start of the staff's monthly open house caravan.

The suave, six-foot-four-inch stud's last stop was Dominique's Jewelers in the South Bay Galleria. He'd put a new, eighteen-carat yellow gold and diamond Presidential Rolex on hold over the phone. Today was the day to pick it up. It was, after all, the least he could do for himself on this, the eve of his thirty-seventh birthday.

Just before noon, the always independent Sagittarian stud pulled up to the luxury hotel along the beach. He spotted Fatima's champagne Lexus GS4 parked near the front office.

"What room are you in, baby girl?" he asked, calling from his Motorola three-way as he parked. "I'll be right up, kiddo. I love you," he proclaimed.

Within twenty minutes of Claude's arrival, Fatima's best friend, Venus Ortiz pulled up. And that's when the birthday celebration began.

Fatima's excitement showed, whereas Venus seemed unsure. Toffee-colored Fatima checked out her rigid friend and giggled to herself. She knew her friend well enough to bet that she would soon loosen up.

"Happy birthday, Claude," Venus said softly, with an embrace and a kiss on his cheek as he leaned his NBA frame down to hug her. She blushed and then smiled, looking down at her feet.

Claude noticed her shyness. He smiled back. He proceeded to insert a CD into the portable boom box and it began to play "Freak Me Baby" by Silk. Right away, he removed his clothes all the way down to his birthday suit and started to do a solo cha-cha while Fatima handed Venus a glass of chilled champagne. He watched Venus swallow it in one big gulp.

He danced his lengthy body around while Fatima sang, "It's your birthday," to his soulful but corny striptease act.

Fatima sat on one end of the bed. Venus sat on the other. Venus tried not to stare Claude down but couldn't help but notice his wide, protracted member she'd heard so much about. He dove in between them, onto the bed, lying on his back in the middle of the mattress with his arms spread-eagle and his long penis pointing to the ceiling.

Fatima lay next to her man, kissing the side of his vanilla bald head and snuggling her way under his one-armed hug. She draped her never ending, slender leg over his muscular, hairy thighs as they both stared at Venus.

Feeling a mixture of the bubbly and the heat from the Latino half of her heritage, Venus slowly stood up to take off her hipster blue jeans and then her tube top. She was braless. She stood in front of the couple in her bikini panties, hugging her upper body with her arms.

Fatima smiled and stood up. Venus smiled back. Claude sighed. Venus then dropped her arms and bared her honey-colored breasts. Both ladies removed their underwear in unison. Fatima laid her top heavy, foxy brown, toned butt down again. Venus poured herself another glass of the bubbly and gulped half before she laid down, too.

Fatima took the lead and leaned over on top of her friend, coming down within an inch of her brown, makeup-free skin.

Venus allowed the aroma of Fatima's musk oil fragrance to consume her. Venus looked Fatima dead in the eyes. And they kissed. Crimson lips to crimson lips. Full tongue to full tongue. Face-to-face.

At full attention, Claude noticed them start to grind. *What a show they're putting on,* he thought. But the sight was more than he could take. He pulled Fatima over on her back and went down on his woman's center as though it was familiar territory.

Venus watched in silence. Chill bumps formed on her arms. She couldn't tell if she was cold, scared or turned on. Her head was spinning. The room smelled of spellbinding black cherry. The soft serenade of the Silk CD echoed off the walls as though the group was personally whispering sweet nothings into her ear. She could not believe her senses, let alone her eyes.

All at once, Venus's best friend turned from her back to her stomach, and began to position her mouth smack dab between Venus's inner thighs to bring pleasure to her buddy.

Venus tensed up. Her hips rose slightly. She felt a combination of revolt and surrender. She forced herself to focus on the core of the stimulation. And she was swept away. Venus mumbled through her ecstasy, "It's not my birthday." Venus closed her eyes and her breathing intensified.

"That's right, it's mine," Claude said loudly. He stood up and took a stance behind Fatima who was on her knees. He centered himself, bending down to an exact level for easy access and entered her from behind. Fatima responded with a moan. As Claude pumped away, stimulated by the sight of his woman giving pleasure to Venus's full-figured body, his blood rushed to increase his momentum just as Fatima hit a steady flow of sucking that caused Venus's legs to quiver, pumping a blood-gushing release. Both Claude and Venus screamed together, "Tima."

They sighed fast-paced breaths. Claude threw his sweaty body onto the bed. The three lay through the night, together.

# chapter 1

***Two years later***

Mason Jeremiah Wilson's experienced limousine driver had to fight to make his way through the thick crowd of fans that gathered in front of the luxury hotel in Hawaii. As the driver pulled to a stop, Mason's many admirers waved paper and pen in his direction, hopeful of an autograph. His young, eager-to-please caddy, Winton Hill, and representative from Titleist, Natalie Glenn, did their best to part the seas. Mason stepped out of the long black Cadillac and hurried up to the front door. His caddy led the way through the lobby and up the private elevator to the executive penthouse.

"Are you hungry, Mr. Wilson?" Winton asked as they entered the swank, twelve-hundred-square-foot suite, setting down the luggage.

"Not yet. I just need some time alone," Mason replied.

"No problem. I'll see you in the morning," said the young Creole man with a curly Afro sticking out from the sides of his black Titleist cap.

Mason patted him on the back as he prepared to exit. "Thanks, man. I really appreciate your help today."

"Things will improve. Tomorrow is another day, Mr. Wilson."

"I heard that, Winton. See you later."

Mason closed the door and took off his custom snakeskin golf shoes and then his Sean John golf shirt and pants. He strutted his ebony frame around in his underwear, pacing a trail along the carpet from the front door to the panoramic ocean view and back, over and over again. Mason pulled his titanium putter from his golf bag and grabbed a few balls from the side pocket. He turned one of his shoes on its side and putted the balls right inside, one after the other. Once again he repeated the putt, never missing a shot, never skipping a beat.

*That's what you should've been doing today, Mason. Get your mind right and focus. You made way too many errors out there to be at the level you've fought so long and hard to reach. Be yourself, let go and just get the job done.*

Mental focus was crucial to Mason's game, just as with any golfer. He loved the feeling of each game being different from the previous, each round being perfected, each hurdle being straddled and then stumbled upon. The unpredictable game of golf had him hooked.

He glanced at himself in the dresser mirror and thought he looked unusually tired. His dark brown skin shielded his age well, but today he noticed a slight, horizontal line along the bridge of his nose, right between his eyes. He inspected it and tossed it away to his imagination. Then he stretched his top lip down over his upper teeth to better expose his recently trimmed mustache, which actually had a single strand of gray peeking through just to tease him. He rubbed his finger over the strand and then stepped back to further examine his image. He looked like his dad, a tad over six feet and slightly bowlegged. He was naturally muscular and semi-slender, with a strong, thick neck and a classic jawline. He was pleased with what stared back at him but thought, *I need to relax, just for a few hours or so.*

Mason hadn't had a drink in years. He glanced over at the minibar, gated and locked, awaiting the green light slide of his room key card. It always seemed to call to him, even after all this time. He shook his head to chase away the thought and picked up the TV remote. He turned on the wide, flat-screen television, lay back along the bed and began to channel surf.

He turned to the music station and heard a song that made him think. He picked up the phone and made a call.

"Mrs. Wilson, your husband is on line two," announced Mercedes's assistant.

"Thanks, Vicky." Mercedes picked up the receiver to her desk phone. "Hello, baby."

"Baby, listen," Mason said, turning up the volume.

A smile formed on Mercedes's face. "That's 'Through the Years,' isn't it?"

"That's it." Mason quickly changed the channel.

"What happened?"

"Oh, it was almost over. What's up with you?"

She looked disappointed. "Oh, not much. How are things going with you?" She took a seat in her high back executive chair.

"I've been doing so-so. But, not too bad, considering. Do you have time to talk?"

"I'll make time," she said, aiming the remote toward her office door and pressing the ivory square button with the tip of her manicured thumb. "When will you be home?" she asked as the door closed.

"The tournament ends on Friday. Just a few more days. How's Mom doing?"

"She's fine. Always asking if she can go home though. Seems the only time she even thinks about anything other than back home in Houston is when Star and Rashaad are around. She's crazy about her grandkids. She keeps calling Rashaad your name."

"Is she still getting confused about who's who and what's what?"

"Not so much lately. It just sort of comes and goes. She did ask if you went back home with your dad and when the two of you would be back. I had to remind her that Jesse was not coming back and that you were working. It just breaks my heart to see her go through this senility thing."

"I feel you. All we can do is pray on it and continue to keep her around family. Have you heard from Claude? He said he was going to call you to talk about you referring your client to him."

"He called. That designer Lola Carter wants to buy on the lower side of Ladera. Looks like our neighborhood is becoming quite popular these days. It's that massive corner house on Springpark."

"That should be a good commission for Claude. You think the sale price is near a million?"

"I'm sure it is. I gave him her contact information so they can hook up."

Mason continued to channel surf. "What else was he talking about?"

"Just the same old-same old about how Venus gets mad at him for trying to discourage Cameron from becoming a model. He wanted me to try to talk him out of it. I told him I am definitely not the one."

"Why would you talk someone out of modeling? You hire models and produce shows for a living. I think Claude wants his son to be a basketball player."

"I don't want to get involved in any more family mess. It appears as though things are finally calming down after the drama of Fatima dying."

"That's what family is for, Cedes."

Mercedes rocked back and forth staring out at her office view. "I know that, Mason. And I'm so glad that Claude adopted Cameron after everything he's been through, being that he's not Claude's biological son. But with Claude and Venus, it's an ongoing battle with Cameron and the way he treats his own stepmother. It makes me so mad."

"Just imagine how you'd feel if your stepmom was your dead mom's best friend."

"Maybe so. I suppose that's why Venus is always trying to win him over. It never seems to do any good though. And Claude is so busy with his real estate deals that he's never around to mend fences anyway. Besides, you know how disconnected he can be. He just rides around, usually in that red Ferrari, hanging out at Starbucks every chance he gets. I'm going to start calling it Club Starbucks." Mercedes ceased her rocking motion.

"That's a good one, Club Starbucks," he said, dancing around her comment. Mason scrolled through the programs offered on the hotel's select channel menu. A call waiting beep sounded. "Anyway, they're supposed to be calling me for an interview with ESPN. I've got to go. But, I'll call you tomorrow to let you know how things are going."

"Okay, baby. I love you," Mercedes said, puckering her plump, coral lips to smooch the sound of a smack.

"Ditto," said Mason, and then he clicked over. "Hello?"

"Mace?" A voice asked.

"Yes."

"I'm waiting."

"Where are you?"

"I'm downstairs sitting at the bar area. I'm on my cell."

"Come on up. Room 2301."

"Okay."

"Bye." He hung up the phone and propped up two pillows, placing his left hand behind his head. He pressed start to begin his adult pay-per-view movie and then picked up the phone again. "Please, no interruptions. I need to take a nap."

Later in the week, cocoa brown and beautiful Mercedes Wilson sat at her desk inside of their six-bedroom Bedford Avenue home, located in the upper section of Ladera Heights. Those are the more expensive homes with the best view of the city.

Ladera Heights is a quiet neighborhood of cul-de-sac streets that give safe haven to young children. With immaculate, landscaped homes, the upscale area in Los Angeles is grand.

To a passerby, one would momentarily conclude from the rows of beanstalk-like palm trees that they were in the exclusive area of Beverly Hills. Some call Ladera, BBH, the Black Beverly Hills. But with its suburban feel, you'll find a Fat Burger, Popeye's chicken, and a beauty supply store every quarter mile. Many celebrities have called Ladera home, but most of the residents, mainly African-American, are unknown.

This particular afternoon, Mercedes settled her wide, curvy hips into the comfort of her suede desk chair. Her cognac-colored hair was pulled back into a bun as usual. Plush, newly acquired furnishings surrounded the oversized pine desk in her home office. She'd often search the web for decorator websites, to send e-mails, take care of work issues for her modeling agency, and to peruse her daily calendar. Her Aquarius horoscope read that she needed to shoulder her responsibilities with cheer and efficiency. Cheery and efficient described her to a tee.

She reached over to grab her cup of French roast coffee in one hand, breaking off the tip of a buttermilk donut with the other. Her almond eyes peeked from under her long eyelashes as her attention veered off to meet up with the pop-up television screen. She turned up the volume.

"After experiencing a slump over the past couple of days, PGA star Mason Wilson leads the way in round one of the Sony Open tournament in Hawaii at nine under par. With runners up Tiger Woods, Vijay Singh and J.J. Henry giving him a run for his money at eight, five and two under, respectively," the young Asian-American sports anchor reported.

Without delay, Mercedes picked up her cordless and dialed. "Girl, turn to ESPN. They're talking about Mason's day on the course. He's in the lead again," she told her homegirl, while chomping on her donut.

Sequoia replied casually, "Woman, I'm in the dang car. You amaze me. You still light up like a Christmas tree every time that man comes on TV. He's on that tube damn near every day."

"Yeah, but he looks real good today. All fitted in his black and white looking so sexy."

"You'd think the two of you just met last week. It's like you guys are in high school," Sequoia said, turning up her car radio.

"And that's the way it should be. I just don't get to see him enough."

"Well, that too can cause it's own set of problems. But, to change the subject, as much as I'd love to talk about your perfect husband, why don't you get out on Saturday and hang out with me at your own husband's club? Hey, mister. Watch it," she yelled out in Mercedes's ear.

"I'm not going there, Sequoia. You know that. And calm down before your road rage gets the best of you yet. Anyway, I have an event to go to with Mason Saturday night. Besides, Foreplay is a singles club and that's exactly where you need to be, not me. Ask Colette to go. You know she's always up there checking on Torino."

Sequoia replied loudly as if it was necessary to talk over the sound of traffic. "Colette is way too negative for me. I don't even talk to her anymore. She's always doggin' Venus for marrying Claude after his woman died. Venus is like a sister to me now. Colette needs to mind her own business."

"Yes, she does. But if you need a partner in crime, she's your girl."

"I'd rather go solo."

"Sequoia, I know you're not going to Foreplay to meet a man, are you?"

"Heck, no. I just need to shake my ass. That's how I get rid of my week's stresses."

"But watch yourself up there, girl. That's where all the groupies hang out. That's a lot of competition."

"I can hold my own. Besides, they're only coming up there to meet your man, hoping he's in town," Sequoia said even louder.

"Calm down. They can hope he's in town right along with me. Mason bought that club to make money, not as a second home. Most people who hang out there know he rarely even shows up."

"If you ask me they're looking for just his type—rich, fine, and famous. A whole lot of husband stealers hover around the premises on a regular basis."

"That's why married men need to keep their butts out of those places. Anyway, Sequoia, I know you're tired of holding out, trying to stick to this born again virgin mission, aren't you? Don't you just want to call Bobby and ask him to come by and rock your world?"

"Now Mercedes, if I've waited this long, why would I ruin it by getting freaky with some ex of mine? Being freaky is what I'm trying to stay away from. Besides, I know my future husband is in church, not at Foreplay. I'm just looking to relax and dance, that's all."

"Don't be so sure. Anyway, I'll call Torino and tell him to put you on the guest list, plus one. I'm sure you'll find a friend who'll be thrilled to go with you. Someone who won't mind getting in for free. Have fun. Talk to you later."

Star Wilson's young teenaged footsteps could be heard making tracks down the hallway carpet toward her mother's office. She put on her brakes and nearly stumbled, making a right into the doorway. "Mom, Daddy was just on TV. Did you see him?"

"Yes, Star. I did. He looks good," Mercedes replied with a smile.

"When is he coming home?" Star plopped down onto her mom's camel leather guest chair, taking a yoga-style position.

"By the end of the week."

"Mom, I have a college night event on Friday night. Do you think he can make it?"

"College night. In the ninth grade? That's early."

"They want us to start thinking about our futures a lot sooner than eleventh grade. Plus, colleges look at grades for all four years in high school, not just the last three."

"I know that. But college night for freshmen? I guess things have changed since the days when we'd get a mention of applying for college just prior to our senior year." Mercedes pecked away at her ergonomic keyboard as she spoke.

"Like you said, that was back in the day. It's the new millennium, not the sixties."

Mercedes glanced at her daughter, raising one eyebrow. "I was not in high school in the sixties, Star."

"I know, Mom. I'm just kidding. Really though, I want Daddy to be there. It seems like people always ask me if he's coming to things like this."

"Like who, other students?"

"Teachers, too." Star leaned over to break off a piece of her mom's donut.

"Yes, you can have some," Mercedes said, looking at Star like she was being rude. "I'll bet the teachers are just impressed with the fact that your dad is Mason Wilson. Perhaps they need to be more impressed with Star Wilson."

"I know. They're just starstruck, I guess. It does get tiresome though."

"I'll bet. For now, tell them your mom, Mercedes Wilson, will be there, ready, willing, and able to listen and help you get cracking on your college experience. And would you like a sip of coffee, too?" Mercedes offered, noticing Star making a funny face.

"No thanks, Mom. Coffee tastes like mud. And this donut tastes like one hundred percent sugar. How do you eat those?"

Suddenly, the sound of a loud thump radiated, coming from downstairs, just below the family room. "Mom, come here quick," Mercedes teenage son Rashaad yelled from downstairs. "Grandma fell."

Star and Mercedes bolted down the spiral staircase and yelled to Rashaad, "We're coming. What happened?"

Mattie Wilson sat flat on the floor with her legs bent to her chin. She lifted her face toward Mercedes. "Oh, Mason is overreacting with all of his yelling. I just tried to sit on the bed and missed. I'm not hurt."

Mercedes told her mother-in-law, "You missed? You're about three feet off, Mamma. And you mean Rashaad, not Mason. Mason is out of town. Now come on and stand up so we can help you onto the bed."

"I'm fine." Mattie shooed Rashaad's hand away as he and Mercedes reached in to lift Mattie under her arms. "I got down here by myself. I can get up by myself."

Rashaad retreated and waved his hand like he did not even have to be told twice.

Mercedes motioned for his cooperation. "Come on son, help her up. Her hip has to be sore. Not to mention her butt."

"I said I'm fine," yelled Mattie with her voice cracking. She clapped her hands twice and raised them above her head as if speaking in sign language. "I'm so tired of you all trying to make me feel helpless. There's nothing wrong with me. Just because I misjudged the bed? How many times have you fallen?" she asked, looking at Rashaad.

He replied without missing a beat. "Not since I was about six."

Mercedes slapped him on the shoulder. "Rashaad, stop. Now Mamma, I'm going to count to three and I want you to grab my hands so I can pull you up."

"Come on Grammy," said Star with a sweet, calming voice. "We know you can do it on your own. But we want to help, just like you would help us."

Mattie's face lit up. "Now see, that's my little girl. She's the only one in this house who understands me. I raised three hardheaded boys and Star is the only one who knows her grandma like no one else. Come here angel, give me a hand."

Star reached her own tiny young body down under her grandma's left armpit and helped her lift herself to a standing position.

Mercedes moved in to help her to the bed. "I can walk, child. My goodness." Mattie pushed Mercedes away with her eyes. "You all act like I'm an invalid or something. And when is my Jesse coming home anyway?"

"Mamma, Jesse died ten years ago," Mercedes reminded her for the twentieth time.

"My husband is not dead. You stop saying that. He's just gone away for a little while to work some things out. He'll be back."

"Yes, Grammy," Star replied. "You're right." Mattie gave Star a pat on the top of her head as she sat on the bed and Star knelt to rest her head in her grandma's lap.

Mattie looked down at Star's face and gave her a warm smile. "You want me to braid your hair, little girl? You know you need to oil your scalp and brush your hair every day."

Star replied, "If that will give me hair like yours, Grammy, yes, I do. That would be nice."

Star's hair was thick and long and wavy just like her grandma's. Grandma Mattie's hair was just like an Indian's, dark with a few platinum strands and so long she could sit on it. She always wore it in a braided ponytail. Mattie did not look her age. She swore by Camay and always smelled of White Shoulders.

Mercedes and Rashaad made their way toward the door. Rashaad whispered toward his mother's ear. "Mom, what are we gonna do about her? My friend Miguel's grandma ended up living in a convalescent home because it just got too hard on the family."

"That's something we're never going to do. Not ever. Not if your dad has anything to do with it anyway. We have the room, we have the money, and we have the help right here. We'll all just have to put in our time and be patient."

"But, Mom, Grandma seems so angry."

"She's just in denial because some of her freedom's being taken away. Deep down she's fighting to hold on to her independence," Mercedes said, turning to watch the pair bond.

Rashaad watched as well. "Star sure is good with her."

"Yes she is. That's just her way. Star's always been nurturing and patient and gentle. It's very calming to your grandma. Maybe we need to take notes from Star."

They both peeked into the bedroom as Mercedes grabbed the doorknob. Star sat in between her grandma's legs with her slender body, long face, big eyes, and button nose. She was facing the TV when she took the remote and turned to BET. Her grandma carefully brushed and parted her hair and began to cornrow like a pro. Braiding hair was one thing, among many others, that Mattie had never forgotten. Mercedes pulled the door shut.

# chapter 2

The next afternoon, Mercedes and Colette Berry, who was Torino's girlfriend and also a model with Mercedes's agency, went shopping at the Fox Hills mall. Colette had to be five eleven with a typical lean and lanky model's figure. She was the color of buttermilk. Her eyes were a lighter shade of brown and her lips were stingy thin. Her relaxed, butterscotch hair was the same color as her skin. She wore it cut just above her shoulders, all one length. She was younger than Mercedes by about eight years and they tended to differ on various subjects.

They ran into Venus who was loaded down head to toe with bags from Foot Locker, Men's Land, and Finishline.

Mercedes's jaw dropped. "Wow, girl, look at you. Who's all that for?"

Venus talked fast. "This is just some stuff for the guys. Claude needed some of the new Jordans so I got some for Cam, too. And then of course they needed the gear to match."

"That's nice of you. Girl, my kids have to buy their own stuff. They wouldn't trust me to pick out a toothbrush for them," Mercedes admitted.

Venus laughed. "Well, they don't know. It's a surprise."

Colette simply stood at Mercedes's side, turning right to left to look at the passersby.

"What's the special occasion? Birthday, anniversary, pre-Christmas shopping?" Mercedes asked, still amazed by the number of large bags.

Venus put a couple of them down to rest her right arm. "Anniversary. I just thought I'd give it to them both next week. Kind of a family anniversary. I want to include Cam."

"I know they'll appreciate it. Are you done?"

"No, just one more quick stop at the Silver Hut. There's this silver charm Cam mentioned of a basketball hoop and his number twenty-three."

Mercedes commented. "That should make Claude happy, too. Last I heard Cam was thinking about anything but becoming a b-baller."

"Cam knows he can't deny his skills now. At only sixteen, that boy is already six three and could probably handle a spot on a college team right now. I'm going to support him and his dad's wishes for him."

"You're one helluva lady, Venus. Maybe you should make a stop at your car to lighten your load. Do you need any help?"

Colette cleared her throat.

"I'm cool. I'm just headed straight upstairs and then I'm out the door. You two must have just gotten here, huh?" Venus asked, noticing their empty arms.

"No, we just got through eating lunch. We've been looking for a dress for Mason's big bash at the club in two weeks," Mercedes told her.

"Are both of you going?" Venus inquired, looking at both.

Mercedes answered for them. "Yes. You should try to come out."

Venus replied, "Claude hates stuff like that. You know how he is. But we might."

Colette spoke up, "I can understand if you can't make it. We'll see you later." Colette walked away to peruse the Bath & Body Works store window.

Mercedes spoke right on the heels of Colette's last word. "Anyway, you should try and stop by sometime other than only on Sundays for dinner, even though that's nice, too. I think it would be nice to spend time just getting to know each other better. Besides, I never see you anymore."

"I will. You stop by, too. I'm home just about all day," Venus informed her.

Mercedes leaned in for a hug. "Sounds like a plan. Take care, dear."

"Ciao." Venus picked up her bags and proceeded to the up-escalator.

Mercedes walked over to Colette who was now looking at the Charlotte Russe window display. "Why are you so blatant about showing your distance toward her? You don't have to be so rude."

Colette kept her sights on a slinky pink jumpsuit. "Please, I could care less what that woman thinks about me, running around here doing all of that guilt shopping. Her stank ass marrying her dead best friend's man. That is straight scandalous and you know it." She pointed at the outfit. "I wonder if that's going to be too short for my inseam. My long legs screw me up every time."

"Colette, why are you so judgmental? I personally am not one to judge."

"Probably so. It does look short. I need to go to the Ann Taylor in Century City. Mercedes, that's one thing I hate about you. You're such a damn do-gooder. You always justify each situation based upon the last person's viewpoint that you hear," Colette said as they continued to walk along, strolling and looking.

"And what's wrong with that? That woman is a part of my family. You have to learn to give people the benefit of the doubt."

Colette stopped and looked at Mercedes. "Venus is a cow who still manages to sleep at night. Buying all that shit for those men in her house. Don't you think she's trying a little too hard?"

"Do you think you judge her too much, Colette? You never know what's really going on in her head."

"Yeah, a ball of confusion, sin and betrayal. I could never imagine doing that to my best friend. She needs her ass kicked."

Mercedes placed her right hand on her hip. "You know, I thought I knew you well after I hired you once you started dating Torino a couple of years ago. But you're really starting to surprise me. I think she's being a damn good friend to Fatima to want to look after her family."

"That's a hell of a lot more than just looking after. Mercedes, I say Venus must have had her eyes on Claude way before all of this happened. Didn't they think about how this would affect Cameron? He just ended up resenting her."

"Perhaps Claude will too in the long run, who knows. But that's for them to figure out."

Colette continued to walk.

Mercedes caught up. "Anyway, Colette, what's up with you and my brother-in-law?"

"It's damn serious I'd say."

"Well, when in the heck is that love affair going to be sealed with a marriage license then?"

"Apparently no time soon from what I can tell about Torino. That boy is commitment phobic."

"You'd think after the amount of time you two have been with one another he wouldn't have any doubts."

"Probably no doubts about me, but just about losing his bachelorhood. He's scared he might miss out on something."

"That's ridiculous. I know he didn't say that. His mom and dad taught him about the important things in life, like love and family. Not being out there in the streets without a good solid foundation."

"Torino just seems to be the odd man out when compared to Claude and Mason. He seems so different from his brothers."

"Different in what way? Do you want to go into Macy's?" Mercedes asked, pointing toward the store.

"No, I'm cool. He just doesn't seem like he ever really connects with them. Like he's still trying to find his way, yet they seem to have managed to find theirs."

"Perhaps that's one reason why he's so reluctant to settle down. Maybe he expects more from himself. After all, he is the youngest."

"I suppose so. But he never even wants to talk about our future. He just doesn't seem to have enough time for me."

"Well, you need to think about that. Is that enough for you? But then again he does work hard at that club," Mercedes reminded her.

"It's mighty funny that he seems to manage to spend time with his boy Kyle, or wining and dining all those high rollers that come in night after night." Colette was distracted. "Did you just see that young teenager wink at me?" she asked, turning her head as a young man walked by breaking his neck.

Mercedes didn't even bother looking back. "That's a good sign, girl, please. He was probably looking at your ass."

"Why is it the only asset men see is our ass?"

"Probably because we're always showing it." Colette was wearing a pair of J. Crew stretch jeans that looked like they were spread on with a knife.

"I'm sick of being defined by my butt."

"It's just a black woman thang. Enjoy it while you can before that rear starts dragging to the back of your knees."

"Oh, hell no. Never."

Mercedes asked, "Anyway, what is that like for you just walking into the club, hanging out while you know he's at work, charming the patrons and working the room?"

"I'm used to it by now. But every now and then we get into it when I spy some chick sniffing up behind him. He thinks I don't know that he has this system where I'll be in the VIP area, yet he might have some little honey on the other side, just behind the bar," Colette said while frowning.

"Oh, is that how he does it?"

"Mercedes, please, like you don't know."

Mercedes stopped again. "No, Colette, I don't. Usually when I go in there I sit my butt down and run my mouth with Mason until it's time to go. Maybe I would notice if I were in your shoes."

"Don't tell me you don't even notice all of the groupies hovering around Mason."

"And?"

"And, doesn't that make you feel, I don't know, territorial?"

"I don't think a situation can make you feel territorial. I think you either are, or you're not. And I'm not. I can't afford to be, being the wife of a famous athlete. Groupies will always be out there. It's how your man reacts to them that matters. And that's something you can't control." They started walking back along the other side of the mall. "I trust Mason. Don't you trust Torino?"

Colette blew a forced breath from her nose. "Not really. I wouldn't put it past any man to stick his finger in some woman's coochie under the same table you're sitting at and not miss a beat."

"Dang. It sounds like you just don't trust men in general."

Colette explained her position. "Oh please, my last boyfriend had two cell phones. One for me and one for his hoochies. I busted his tired butt and slapped the hell out of him and moved on. And these freaks out here don't even care if a man's taken or not. They just make it easier for men to play their game. They'd just like to get their hooks in the men we've got."

"Look, you're not going to get very far without trust, Colette. That goes with the territory because we have some hot ones, the Wilson brothers. I will say that."

"Well, I plan on keeping mine, thank you very much."

"Don't try too hard with your emotional self. That's usually the very attitude that makes them run away—you know, holding on too tight," Mercedes said as they stopped at the window of a shoe store.

"Those are nice," Colette said, pointing to a pair of Matori black spiked pumps. "Not holding on tight enough causes there to be enough room for infiltrators. That's not about to happen," Colette said, sounding very serious.

"Okay, Colette. Sounds like you've made it your job to keep up with him."

"Speaking of jobs and to change the subject because you are definitely getting on my nerves, what is my assignment for tomorrow?"

"You didn't get a call from Vicky yet?"

"No. And I've been checking my cell all day."

"Call her in the morning. I don't think you have anything until late afternoon from what I remember."

"Cool. By the way, I'll see you Sunday night at your house for dinner."

"Uh oh. See, now that's a good sign, coming by for dinner for the first time."

"Anyway, I'm about to get going. I'll find something to wear later. Thanks for the lovely conversation," Colette said, walking in the opposite direction.

Mercedes proceeded toward the exit door. "Yeah, you too. Drive safely."

Mason missed Star's college night, but made it home that Saturday afternoon, just in time for the formal affair later that evening at the Meridian hotel. It was an event to celebrate black athletes in tennis and golf. It was a fund-raiser for the YBAA, the Young Black Athletes Association.

Mercedes always tried to be understanding of Mason's relationship with his business partner, Cicely James. But did Cicely have to attach herself to Mason's hip at every function to promote his career and their nightclub?

Cicely and Mason were very close way back in elementary school in Texas. When the Wilsons moved to Los Angeles, so did Cicely and her mother, even moving into a neighborhood near Ladera called Westchester. They both attended Westchester High School and they'd hang out every now and then. Cicely and her mother then moved away from Los Angeles to Atlanta, but Cicely came back to go to college in Los Angeles and she stayed. After she graduated, her mother died of cancer.

Mercedes met Mason in college at USC. She got pregnant one summer when she went away to spend the weekend with Mason while he was on an amateur golf tour overseas. Mercedes was amazed that Cicely called three and four times a day while Mercedes was there, yet Mason never let on that Mercedes was around. It was a known fact to everyone on the outside that Cicely was his main woman even though Mason denied it.

Mercedes was taken aback by Mason's attention at the time, especially his promises and charms. He gave her the impression that he was not interested in Cicely on a romantic level, that they were more friends than anything else, and that her calls were on a friendly level.

Mercedes was satisfied just taking on the role of Mason's lover. When Cicely found out that Mercedes was pregnant, she was actually woman enough to call and congratulate her, letting her know that what she and Mason had was strictly platonic and that she was definitely doing her own thing. Cicely had been seeing a guy whom she met at Pepperdine College in Malibu. He was a promising young basketball player who was considering an offer to play pro ball. But, he died on the court during a pre-season game. He had a heart attack. Even today it seemed like Cicely had never had a real love affair since then. She'd always bury herself in her work at the club, and in her marketing business that she ran from her home.

Cicely was an intense walnut color and she had big eyes, almost the color of dark rum. She wore a naturally curly bob-cut. Tonight she was sporting an elegant, black Chanel dress with a simple gold Christian Dior hip-belt and gold leather slides.

Cicely hooked her long, thin arm along Mason's buffed, brawny bicep. Her dimples were in full effect. She rested her dainty wrist upon his hairy forearm, topped by her other hand, and took him away from his wife without asking. She introduced her business partner to the long line of well-wishers who gathered to meet and greet the well-known, well-dressed, African-American golfer.

Mercedes smiled a fake smile their way. Mason motioned for her to come over and join in on the niceties. She acquiesced in support of her husband. Cicely played with one of her locks of hair and smoothed it behind her ear. She dropped Mason's arm as Mercedes approached. Cicely backed away and gave Mercedes the once-over before she made her way over to another group of guests.

"So, when do you enter the senior's tour, Mr. Wilson? Isn't the age limit fast approaching?" a male, Caucasian guest asked, trying to be humorous.

"No, actually the senior's tour does not start until the age of fifty. I've got a good eleven years yet."

"How about the Ryder Cup Tournament? Is that fast approaching?" his female companion queried, holding a glass of sherry in hand.

"It's next month. I'm looking forward to it. The course is beautiful and the weather in England is always nice."

"You live in Florida, do you?" the male inquired.

"No. We live in Ladera Heights."

"La who?" he asked.

Mercedes said, "Ladera Heights. It's between Culver City and Inglewood."

"Oh," said the woman, turning up her nose. "Near Inglewood, huh?" She took a swig from her glass.

"That's right. Actually it's one main street away from being considered Inglewood," Mercedes replied.

"Oh," the lady responded with a puzzled stare, taking another big sip.

"So, is this the lovely lady who keeps you dressed to the nines?" another male asked, encouraging a chuckle with the nod of his head.

Mason gave one quick titter. "Good one. This is my wife, Mercedes."

"Do you still own the modeling business I read about?" the woman asked, obviously up on the background of the Wilsons.

Mercedes responded. "Yes, I do. It was originally a talent agency but I changed the name to Simpson Models. Simpson is my maiden name. It was a business passed down from my parents when they died."

The woman seemed concerned. "Oh, I'm sorry to hear that."

The other male changed the subject. "That's quite a responsibility, running your own business. How on earth do you juggle being a mother, wife of such a visible man, and still run a business?"

"It pretty much runs itself sometimes. I have great employees who step up and help out a lot," Mercedes said with pride.

Mason added, "And she still manages to be my right arm," offering his right arm to Mercedes as she took hold.

"No, I'm sure you'd be able to handle things just fine, even without me," Mercedes said, looking over at Cicely who was watching from afar.

"I never want to know that feeling, dear. Excuse us," Mason said as he and his wife headed for a cozy love seat near a corner fireplace.

Mercedes spoke close to his ear. "I think your own fans don't really know you're black sometimes." They took a seat.

"Oh they know. They know that above all else."

# chapter 3

Torino Jesse Wilson pulled up to his reserved spot in the rear parking lot of club Foreplay just before seven in the evening. Torino exited and closed the door of his BMW.

Torino was a gifted football player back in high school. He was highly recruited as a tight end. While Claude and Mason got their degrees from USC, Torino played at UC Berkeley. But he was involved in a car accident and broke the fibula and tibia in his right leg just before his last year. He had surgery but didn't get much attention from the NFL after that. The good thing was that he stayed in school and took advantage of his scholarship. One thing Torino was not, was a quitter.

Torino loved the limelight and loved to make sure that his patrons, especially the famous ones, were treated royally, and they knew it. His height allowed him to look some of the taller than average ballers straight in the eye. He wore short dreads and had handsome features. He wore small gold hoops in each ear.

Torino was well-known amongst the professional athletes and actors who either lived in Los Angeles, or traveled in town for a little fun, as the man who could get the job done.

He was a die-hard bachelor and wanted to stay that way. He could make old women blush and young women giddy. On any given evening, two or three of his admirers could show up and make an, "I'm his lady" appearance without warning. So, the guys at the door and the ladies in the booth always let Torino know over their walkie-talkies, who was in the house and what their twenty was. He had a system for keeping them separated, especially from the watchful eye of Colette Berry, the only one who could really claim a legitimate stake to his affections.

Torino knew how to wine and dine people, flashing his bright white teeth. His perfect complexion and big brown eyes were just a couple of his physical assets. Those who didn't know him would have sworn he was twenty-something because of his hip-hop ways and trendy, up-to-date look. But actually, thirty-four was just around the corner.

Torino's eldest brother, Mason, had purchased Foreplay about six years ago. Mason co-owned the club with Cicely, but Torino, who had been the club's manager since its grand opening, was responsible for its success.

The club was always packed, and you could always count on a long line outside. Partially because of Mason's reputation, but also due to Torino's promotional skills. Torino wanted to someday own his own club, but for now, Foreplay was his home away from home.

"Hey, dudes, you need to get that kitchen together as per the inspectors. They're going to be back next week and they aren't gonna let us slide this time. I want it sparking clean and smelling like its deserving of an A grade. I'll check back with you in a couple of hours, now. Don't play with me," Torino warned his kitchen staff.

Foreplay nightclub looked like a juke joint, but with sophistication and elegance. It had a second floor balcony slash VIP area, lined with a chrome banister, overlooking the entire club. Everything in the club was black and red. Mason loved bold red and thought there was no way to get around using black for richness and class.

The oblong bar aligned the entire rear potion of the club. The top of the bar was deep red, veined, solid marble that looked like speckles of brown sugar were thrown here and there. A dozen or so black leather sofas and love seats were scattered throughout with wine-shaded suede throw pillows. The dance floor area was mirrored all around, which made it look twice as big. The large disco ball hovered overhead, shedding triangular bits of light in rainbow hues.

The restaurant area was located through the double doors just to the right of the roped-off, VIP stairway. Restaurant evening hours were only from eight until eleven and usually for the serious dinner crowd. Appetizers were served at the bar until closing time. After eleven o'clock, Torino used the restaurant as a private sanctuary for special, high-profile VIPs who needed to be secluded.

The club was about to be on and crackin'. At nine o'clock it was usually scarce but by ten, double digits, people felt the need to make their way in.

Just around ten, an impeccably dressed Torino, wearing a navy blue Italian suit and black silk muscle shirt, saw Sequoia Smith coming his way.

"Hey, Sequoia. How's it going?"

"Cool. I talked to Mercedes the other evening. She's doing well. She was watching Mason on TV," Sequoia replied, wearing a form-fitting, baby blue velour J-Lo sweat suit with dark blue suede Manola Blahnik Timbs. She was not hurting for money.

"I'll bet. That brotha' is always on TV."

"That's what I reminded her. You running the place by yourself tonight?" she asked, looking all around.

"Yeah. Cicely's been out of town. She was in Hawaii but I think she's back now."

Sequoia paused. "Hawaii. Isn't that where Mason was?"

"I suppose so. I don't keep up with him. But I surely keep up with my boss. She said she'd be back tonight."

"Oh really?"

"Really. And what brings you out tonight?" Torino asked, looking dead at her cleavage. "You're looking all toned and tanned and voluptuous."

"Yeah, kinda similar to Colette's build, huh?"

His heart-melting charm was not working. "Not really. But . . ."

Sequoia put her hand up. "But what, Torino? You are not God's gift to women."

"But, I just gave you a compliment. That's all."

Sequoia started talking loud. "Boy, don't you know after all these years I see you as my brother. You, Claude, and Mason. When are you going to give up and stop trying?"

Torino shook his head and scratched the back of his neck. "I see your ego has grown with age, huh?"

Sequoia put her arm through the tiny round silver handles of her handbag and leaned into Torino as she slid it up over her shoulder. "And so has your big head if you think I've waited this long to find Mr. Right to start playing cat and mouse with you, Torino. Especially with you. Lord knows you've got enough mice running around up in here."

"Hey, Sequoia," said Kyle Brewer. He was Torino's running buddy, the spitting image of Derek Jeter, light eyes and all. Kyle was a fireman and he'd met Torino years ago when they both interviewed for a position with the department. Torino did not get the gig. "You're looking mighty good tonight."

She stood up straight. "Can it, Kyle. By the way, thanks for putting my name on the list, Torino. See you later." Sequoia switched away with extras.

Sequoia was easy on the eyes. Sexy as hell, she was built like a brick house, sort of sturdy and curvy-firm like Serena Williams. Her brown hair was a long and curly weave, but it looked natural. She had a way of accenting her nutmeg skin with just the right amount of makeup to make her look like a movie star, even though her profession was running her aging mother's travel agency.

Torino's eyes were glued to her very being. "That will be the last time her stank ass comes up in here trippin' like she's Janet Jackson."

"You must admit she looks real screw-licious though, dude," Kyle said, sharing the glance.

Torino broke his stare. "There are a lot of other fine women in here who deserve more attention than her spoiled attitude." Torino shifted his focus back to his work. "By the way, can you help me out by getting the VIP guest list from the doorman and taking a copy of it to the VIP bouncer?"

"I'm on it, Tito." Kyle chuckled.

"Tito? Oh, now see. You're trying to get kicked out of here, right?"

"Just messin' with you, dude. Hey, where's Colette? Is she coming in tonight?"

"I don't know. Why you worried? Just help me out." Torino raised the antenna of his two-way radio.

"I'm on it. A nigga' got eyes," Kyle admitted.

"Eye yourself right on out the front door and don't look back if you're gonna start verbalizing about my lady. You can keep that to yourself."

"Okay, calm down. I'm on my way to get the list." Kyle took a step and paused. "Hey, you know what *VIP* stands for, don't you? Very important pussy, right?"

Torino walked away as he replied. "You are one horny brotha, Kyle. I'll check you later." He spoke into his radio. "Where are the VIP wristbands, man? Get them to the front door now."

Later that evening at home, Mason began to disrobe to the warmth of the bedroom fireplace as Mercedes sat on the end of their brass bed atop a white chinchilla comforter with gold brocade pillows.

"So, baby, I didn't want to worry you but Mamma fell a couple of days ago," Mercedes said, scrolling through her calendar for the week.

Mason froze in between stepping out of his trousers. "What was she trying to do?"

"She was just trying to get into bed, or so she said. She's fine though. You'd be so proud of Star the way she handled her grandma. Watching them together is a sight for sore eyes."

He resumed disrobing. "They are quite a pair. Mom seemed fine earlier today."

"Yes, because she was happy that you were back. Whoever you are."

"Now come on, she knows I'm her son."

"I'm not so sure," Mercedes said, turning to answer the cordless phone. "Hello? Hey, girl. How was your evening out?" She whispered to Mason. "It's Sequoia. She went to Foreplay." She returned her focus to her call. "You had fun, huh?"

Sequoia talked loud from her mobile as usual. "No love connections but I shook my ass all right. And that bartender makes a mean apple martini. When did your man get home?"

"This afternoon."

"Is Cicely back?"

Mercedes placed her electronic calendar on the nightstand and leaned back on the pillow to talk. "Back from where?"

"I heard she was out of town."

"So."

"So, I heard she was in Hawaii."

"Oh, she was . . . yes, she's back. We saw her tonight. Now I know why you're calling so late."

"I am not trying to start any mess, so you didn't hear it from me. But wasn't Mason in Hawaii?" Sequoia asked as if she already knew.

"Yes, he was in Honolulu."

"Well, you need to find out where she was. That's all I have to say. Fill in the blanks for yourself."

Mason yelled from the bathroom. "What about Honolulu?"

"Oh, Sequoia just asked about which part of Hawaii you went to. She's going on a cruise later this year—a cruise to Hawaii. Aren't you Sequoia?"

"Yes I am. You know that's a shame that you never lie to that man. Or maybe that's good just as long as all of that honesty is mutual."

Mercedes stood up, resting her feet on the off-white carpet, speaking close to the receiver. "You know something. Why is it always the ones with no man trying to ruin the good thing of the ones who have one?"

"If it were ever to be ruined it would not be my fault. I was not the one in Hawaii with my business partner, ex, okay? Ooh, girl. This is the new Whitney cut." Sequoia increased the radio volume.

"Good night, girl. I've got to go and hop in the shower with my husband. A born again virgin I am not," she said, removing her dress.

Sequoia sounded worried. "Don't you dare say that too loud. I'll bet you tell him all of my business."

"Why not? You're all up in his. Besides, husbands don't count anyway. He's my other half so I can tell him anything."

"You didn't tell him I'm holding out, did you?"

"No, I didn't." Mercedes removed her brassiere and thong underwear.

"Oh yeah, right. You've been lying to me since middle school. You can't keep anything from that man. Especially the bit of news I just broke about him and *her*."

"I call it a bit of non-verifiable gossip. I'm standing here naked, girl. Gotta go. Bye."

"Poof, be gone." Sequoia hung up singing.

Early the next morning, Mercedes stepped out onto the dew-misted lawn to get the morning paper. Kailua, their chocolate lab of five years, ran toward the door but dared not run outside as he barked at his master, waiting for a command. Mercedes hushed him so he would not wake Mattie. She turned back toward the door and noticed a black, convertible Ford Mustang parked in the driveway of the second garage. Once again someone spent the night at Torino's place. Torino had lived in the back house ever since he lost money from an investment gone bad. He lost his home, new Yukon Denali and had to sell most of his belongings. But Mason had mercy on him, allowing him time to downsize. Mason gave him two years to get himself together. It had been three. Usually, it was Colette's mint green Nissan Altima in the driveway. Mercedes walked back toward the door and noticed that Kailua looked at her like she was doing his job. Mercedes had forgotten that Star taught Kailua how to fetch the paper. "I'm sorry Kay-Kay. You can get it next time."

Mason pulled up into the cul-de-sac to his brother Claude's house on Senford Avenue just as Claude closed the front door to his Spanish-style home behind him.

"Hey, Claude," Mason said as he stepped out of his Mercedes SUV. The license plate simply read, CEDES.

Claude opened the door to his Ferrari, tossing his briefcase into the passenger seat. "Yo, brother. Why did you copy me and get your wife's name on your license plate?" he asked Mason, pointing to the vanity plate of his own Lexus parked in the driveway that still read TIMA.

Mason walked up and gave Claude a brotha' handshake. "Mercedes did that. This is her second car." Mason looked toward the Lexus. "Man, you still have that car. Between that, the C-class and this one, isn't that three just for you?"

"I'm saving the Lex for Cameron. And why are you worried anyway? What are you up to?"

"I just thought I'd stop by to congratulate you on your new buyer."

Claude crossed his arms and leaned back against his ride. "Yeah, Mercedes's contact made an offer on Springpark so that's a go. And I'm about to close on a few other properties this week. I can't complain. How's Mom?"

"You should come by sometime and see for yourself. I mean it's not like you have to travel very far. Why do I have to be the one to come down the hill all the time to see you anyway?"

Claude paused. "Oh yeah, like you're ever around anyway. Don't worry. I'll be by tonight for Sunday dinner."

"And how are Venus and Cameron?"

"They're cool. Venus is in there. I think she's on the computer researching some project. I would go back in with you but I've got an early meeting at the office. Go ahead on in and see Venus if you want," Claude removed his key ring from his pocket and put one foot into his car.

Mason walked toward his ride. "Naw, I'm going to head on over to the Bucks for a cup of java."

"Java? You're getting whitewashed more and more everyday, brotha'. Hey, I've gotta go, man. How long you gonna be in town?" Claude asked, taking a seat, closing the door and turning the ignition.

Mason got in and started the engine, too. "For a week or so. I'll see you tonight."

"Later," Claude yelled as he backed out.

Both brothers pulled off in their luxury cars with spinning wheels, revving their engines as they reached the stop sign at Slauson. Claude took off to the west doing about seventy. Mason leisurely turned in the other direction, headed to Starbucks.

Back at Mason's home, Torino walked up to the front house to visit his mother. She was sitting on her bed, brushing her hair.

"Hey there, Mom. Good morning." Torino leaned down to hug her.

"Good morning, son. How are you?"

"I'm fine." Torino sat in her rocking chair.

"Have you made breakfast yet? If not, I can do it."

"No, Mom. I'm about to get going for the day. I'll stop somewhere."

"I sure could use some of your award-winning apple pancakes."

"I haven't made those since I was in high school, Mom."

"I know." Mattie began picking the tiny strands of hair from the brush. She tossed them into her trash can beside the bed.

Torino reflected back. "They were good, huh? I wonder who taught me how to cook in the first place."

"You were the only one of the three who spent time with me in the kitchen."

"And I'm glad I did. I'll get back in that kitchen for you soon enough."

"That would be nice." She resumed brushing her hair.

Torino stood up. "Well, I have to get going. I'm just checking on you."

"I'm just here waiting on your dad. He's supposed to pick me up in his classic car today. You know, the car we named you after."

"The blue Torino."

"Yes. I love your name."

"Me, too. As long as the Tito comment doesn't come up."

"Oh no. You just tell people your name is Torino, not Tito."

"Okay, Mom." He put his hand on her back and then headed for the door.

"If you see him as you leave, tell him to just honk and I'll come out so we can get going."

"I will. See you later."

"See you later sweetheart. I love my baby."

"I love you too, Mom."

Even though he was Ladera's most well-known VIP, some mornings when Mason was in town he'd stop by for his favorite cup of Caramel Macchiatto. Today he was lucky enough to find a parking spot in the very front. All eyes were on him as he walked in.

"What up, dude? We don't see you nearly enough," said Greg, one of the young managers at Starbucks in the Ladera Center. The nutty smell of coffee beans and the sweet smell of cinnamon greeted Mason's every step.

"Hey, I've been on a series of tours lately. Just seems like I don't have time for the things I really love. You know I've got to keep up my routine though."

Suddenly, Mason's baby brother Torino walked in and they patted each other on the back.

"Hey, I saw the car out there. I thought Mercedes was in here. How goes it?"

"Hey dude, it's cool. What you been up to lately?" asked Mason.

"Nothing much, bro. I'm glad you're back."

"How have things been over at the club? You did keep everybody in line while Cicely was gone, right?" Mason asked as they slowly moved up in line.

"Yeah, I've got it all covered. We just need to pass our inspection next week but we'll be cool. Hey, did you go to Hawaii, too?" Torino asked, noticing the many stares directed at his brother.

"Yeah, man, I went. And?" Mason raised his eyebrows.

"And Cicely went?"

Mason turned to face his brother. "What are you saying? That she travels on vacation with me while I work? Man, she just happened to be on vacation in the same state. Not the same city, okay?"

Torino put his hand up. "I heard that. I was just asking."

Mason turned back around. "Plus, it seems like she deserved a break considering all the business you two have been bringing in lately."

Torino made a point of changing his tone. "Man, just about the entire Lakers team was in last Friday night. The DJ was announcing names left and right. Even Iverson was in town and stopped by."

Mason bobbed his head. "That's what I'm talking about. Comp those boys and their guests because they can surely buy the bar." They gave each other fisted taps.

Torino agreed. "Every time."

"Hey, what's up with you and Colette, man? How's she doing?"

Torino took a deep breath. "My girl wants to move on in back there with me. I don't know, though."

"What you need to do is get out on your own in a bigger place and settle down with your busy self. How long have you been seeing her, for a year now?"

"No, more like two."

"That's a lifetime for you. I'd say it's either about time for living together or time for a ring. You know what Mom would say."

"Oh heck no. I'm not even ready for that."

"You afraid that'll cut off your action, dude?"

"I'm so busy with this club that I can't even think straight, let alone make time for sideline action. Well, not much anyway."

"Yeah, I saw some car parked back there last night. Who you foolin'?" asked Mason.

"That was Kyle's new Mustang. I wouldn't have a woman's car parked up in there. Colette is the drive-by queen."

"Hey, bro, I was thinking, we need to talk. Look, Cicely and I are thinking about opening a new club in Atlanta, man. You think you might want to relocate? I'd set you up and pay expenses." Mason looked hopeful.

"Oh heck no. Man you could not pay me enough to leave L.A. Especially lovely Ladera. Just look around at the scenery. It's only eight in the morning and these ladies look like they're going in for stripper tryouts."

"Hi, Mason. How have you been?" asked the girl behind the counter as she handed him his coffee. "Here's your regular, with extra crème." She blushed.

He took the already prepared brew in the sleeved cup and handed her his money. "Thanks, Vanessa. I've been good, and you?"

She continued, giving full-on attention. "I saw you on TV last week. Congratulations on winning the tournament. We're real proud of you here in Ladera Heights. You've got a lot of kids looking up to you. You're like our hometown hero."

"Thanks."

The manager cleared his throat and gave Vanessa the eye and she caught it. "Anyway, I'll see you again real soon, okay?"

Mason gave a nod. "For sure."

"And you're having?" Vanessa asked Torino.

"Just pour a cup of the coffee of the day."

"Sure," she said, still eyeballing Mason.

Mason and Torino took their cups and sat at a tiny table near the window.

"So, you coming up to the house for dinner tonight, man?" Mason asked, taking his seat.

"Wouldn't miss our regular, especially when you're in town. I stopped on through to see Mom before I left and she looks real good."

"Yeah, but I think we need to schedule a family meeting to talk about her condition, bro. Her dementia is getting worse. We need to get her on meds right away to help slow down the process. Mercedes has been doing some research so I think the next step is another appointment with the neurologist."

"I'm cool with that. Do we need to meet at Claude's house then so Mom won't be around?" Torino took a cautious sip.

"No, it's cool at my place. She's pretty much holed up in her room all day and night anyway."

"Let's do that before you leave then." Torino looked around.

"I'll ask Mercedes to check with Claude and you and work it out."

Vanessa came over to their table. "Here you go, Mason. Just thought I'd bring you a banana scone, hot from the oven, just the way you like it. All sticky with honey."

"Thanks, my dear. You didn't have to do that but I appreciate it."

"Anytime," she purred, moon-walking back behind the counter.

"Man, I never get that type of attention. You are one spoiled brotha, brother. Hell, my brother's a pimp."

"You're the one who's been pimping since pimpin's been pimpin, as they say."

"No, you're the one," Torino insisted.

Mason offered the scone to his brother but he declined. "It's all a mirage, bro," Mason explained. "Fake as an acrylic nail and temporary as a stick-on tattoo."

# chapter 4

Mercedes and Star headed off to church just as Mason returned home from his early morning routine. Mercedes waved her hand out of her white Benz convertible and sped away without looking at him. Star turned and waved to her daddy with the ends of her newly done cornrows blowing in the wind.

Mason found his son, now seemingly putting on muscle and a little height, rummaging through the kitchen cabinets for something to munch on. Rashaad, at fourteen, was obviously going through puberty but handling it well. He was good-looking, with his pecan skin and low fade, and he now wore contacts in place of his glasses. "Hey, Rashaad, what's up with you, son?"

"Nothing much," he replied, opening a box of vanilla wafers and reaching his hand inside. "I wanted to go over to the Fox Hills mall and look around but Mom said I have to keep an eye on Grandma."

"Yes, you do. And what if you did go? What would you be looking around for?" Mason poured himself a glass of pineapple juice.

"Just looking." Rashaad popped two cookies into his mouth.

Mason took a long gulp and then asked another question. "What do you need?"

Rashaad chewed as he spoke. "It's not about needing anything in particular."

"Oh, Rashaad, please. Now remember, I used to be a teenager, too. I remember when that dang mall was built. My boys and I used to go to the mall without a penny in our pockets just to walk around and check out the girls. Don't tell me times have changed that much."

"No, Dad. I guess they haven't."

"See, back in middle school, well, we called it junior high school back then, the thing to do was go to the movie theatre and find a group of girls you like, and then you sit right behind them and get your rap on."

"Get your rap on?" After taking a handful, Rashaad replaced the box in the cupboard and stood near the sink.

"Well, you know what I mean. By the time your mom and dad would pick you up from the theatre, you'd have a number or two and wouldn't have watched a lick of the movie at all. Those were the days," Mason reminisced, finishing the other half of the juice and placing the glass in the sink.

"I'll bet that was a lot of fun. Checking out some girl in the dark," Rashaad said with sarcasm. "What would happen if she stood up and she'd be three inches taller than you?"

Mason put his hand on his son's shoulder. "Good question. That would happen at times. Chances are she'd be just as mad that you were shorter anyway so no harm, no foul."

Rashaad went into detail with his comparison. "See, at the mall, it's cool because you can see who's walking around and check them out in the bright light, in shopping mode, eating, chilling, and strolling. These are the days, Dad."

"I guess these are. But, just not today for you, son." Mason looked at his watch.

"Where are you about to go?" Rashaad put two in his mouth again.

"I've got to get over to the Radisson for a business meeting at eleven and then I have to go to the country club to get in some serious practice this afternoon. I'll be back later, in time for dinner, though."

Still chewing Rashaad asked, "When is Mom coming back?"

"Didn't they just go to church? They won't be long."

"Man, Dad."

Mason headed for the kitchen door and then paused. "Man,

Dad, what, Rashaad? You have a problem sharing the weight around here?"

"No, Dad. It's just that the weekend is the only time I have to hang out."

"And the weekend is when we need to chip in the most. Anna is only here to help out with housework, cooking, and watching your grandma during the week. So I suggest you make plans for late afternoons or early evenings or for when your mom is home."

"Okay." Rashaad looked bored with being read. "How long are you going to be around town, Dad?"

Mason walked into the living room as Rashaad followed. "I've been asked that question about three times today. I'm not sure. I might be leaving by the end of the week. I'm just trying to earn a living in a world that the white man has claimed as his. I've got to stay on top of my game and on top of my schedule, unlike most in this business. I can't slip up, son. I've told you that before."

"Dang, Dad, lighten up. It's cool. I just asked." Rashaad thought for a second. "How about if I go with you?"

"Rashaad, who's going to stay here with your grandma? And this is a business meeting, son. You'd be bored to death."

"Not more boring than sitting around here."

"Son, your mom will be back soon and you tell her I said you can go on over to the mall then. Here. Try to distract yourself from the scenery long enough to buy yourself something." Mason pulled out his money clip and extended his hand to offer two, crisp, one hundred dollar bills.

Rashaad's eyes bugged as he wiped the cookie crumbs from his hand onto his pants leg and took the money. His tone was controlled. "Thanks a lot, Dad." Rashaad walked back in the direction of his room.

Mason sorted through some mail and then went into the garage to grab his golf clubs. He tossed them in the back of the SUV.

As he backed out of the driveway, his elderly neighbor waved and spoke. "Hello, Mr. Wilson. How are you doing?" Her husband passed away the year before and Mason rarely saw her. Seems she was always indoors.

"Just fine, it's good to see you," Mason replied.

She picked up her paper from her lawn and continued to converse, raising her cracking, ripened voice. "Got any tournaments coming up soon? You're not leaving town again, are you?"

*That's four,* he said under his breath. "There should be one coming up soon. You take care now."

"You too, Mr. Wilson. Have a blessed day." She mumbled aloud after he pulled off. "I don't know how they stay in that house what with what happened to that poor girl a couple of years ago. Man could live anywhere he wants to. It just doesn't make any sense."

After eighteen holes of golf, Mason returned home later that afternoon.

"Hey, baby. Is Rashaad back yet?" Mason asked Mercedes as he came though the door leading from the garage to the house. He kissed his wife on her right cheek as she chopped onions on the cutting board. "What are you sniffling for?"

"These are the strongest onions I've ever seen." Mercedes squeezed her eyelids together. "Yes, I just picked Rashaad up about an hour ago."

"Good. Did he have a good time?" Mason stood behind her with his arms around her waist.

"It seemed as though he did," she said, wiping her nose with the back of her hand. "You know how quiet teenagers are as soon as you try to ask them something."

"What are you cooking that smells so good?" he asked, peeking over her shoulder.

"I made this Parmesan chicken coated in egg, baby. It's a new recipe. I think it turned out pretty good."

"And scallops?" His eyes bugged.

"And scallops. I'm just chopping up these puppies so I can throw in a few."

"Now you're talking. I'm going to go check on Mom." He backed away. "Did Claude and Torino call?"

"Torino did, and he's bringing Colette."

"Uh oh, he's starting to bring her to dinner. Sounds serious to me."

Mercedes grabbed the dish towel to wipe her hands. "I know, I thought the same thing. That's a trip for him to do that, huh?" She turned to face Mason.

"It's about time, though. As long as she's been putting up with him."

"Baby, I think he's been the one doing the putting up with. Colette's been acting weird lately. She's very insecure if you ask me."

"Your own friend, and you can't talk to her about it?"

Mercedes stepped to the stove to turn over the chicken fillet. She removed a couple from the skillet and placed them on a paper towel. "I don't know her that well. But I think she's not beyond following him after he leaves the club and stuff."

"Uh oh, sounds like a stalker move to me. But I doubt it. I'll be right back," Mason said, sneaking to grab one of the strips on his way out. "Oww, damn that's hot," he said, sucking his thumb and tossing the piece back and forth.

"Here greedy, take this." Mercedes handed him a paper towel. "Always putting your hands on something that might burn you."

"Yeah, but it sho' tastes good."

Mason finished the chicken and walked into his mother's room, wiping his fingertips and his lips. "Hey, Mom. How's it going cutie pie?" He leaned over to kiss her on her forehead.

Mattie was sitting on the edge of her bed, rummaging through her purse. "It's about time you came by here to check on me. When did you decide it was okay to disappear and stay away so long?"

Mason sat next to her. "Mom, you know I've been working."

"Oh, please. You've been up to no good. Are you seeing someone else?"

"Mom, what are you talking about? Seeing whom?" Mason scooted closer to her.

"Don't sit so close. You think I don't know about that woman you've been talking to. I know how you men are."

Mason stood up and smirked. "Mom, I'm not sure who you're referring to but we're about to eat dinner soon. Now go get washed up and come on out into the kitchen. All right?"

"I'll be out when I get good and ready. Just like you don't do what I want you to do. You can't make me do anything just because you come in here telling me to jump." Mattie pulled out an old tube of ruby red lipstick and started applying it to her cheeks, glancing into the mirror next to her bed.

"Mom, I'll see you at the dinner table. That looks nice, Mom."

"Good-bye. I'll see you again in a month or so the way you come and go." She replaced the top of the tube without screwing the stick back in.

Mason stepped toward the door. "Okay, Mom. See you in a second. I love you."

"That's not anything special. You love everybody."

Mason walked down the hallway and reentered the kitchen just as Mercedes finished setting the table. "Baby, Mom sounds kind of irritated."

"She's not coming out?"

"Not without a fight it sounds like."

"Go tell Star. She's in the front room. Star can get her to do anything." Mercedes took a tall pitcher of lemonade from the refrigerator.

"Hey Star, how was church this morning?" Mason asked, walking into the living room taking a seat in his pale green reclining chair until dinner was served. He stared at the television, catching a glimpse of the Lakers game for a second.

"It was good," Star replied. She stopped reading her magazine. "Dad, you gave Rashaad some money today?"

Mason looked at Star as if surprised. "Yes, I did. And?"

"Nothing." She kept turning the pages.

"What? What do you need money for?" he asked, scooting to the edge of the chair to catch a connection with her eyes.

Star did not look up. "I know you're not paying him for watching Grammy. I don't get paid for that."

"Do you think you should?"

"No, and he shouldn't either. We should do it because we want to. Not because we have to."

"Okay then, let's say I gave him the money not for watching his grandma, but for just being my son and because I wanted to show him he deserved something nice."

"Oh yeah, right."

"Can't I do the same for my daughter?"

"No thanks."

"What's with the long chin? Look at me."

Star raised her sights but kept her head in place. "I'm fine. It just amazes me that Rashaad buys that. I mean that you just give him money because he deserves something nice. You give him money because you feel guilty about not spending enough time with him."

"Where did that come from?"

Star sat back and resumed her reading. "I'm old enough to see things, Dad. I'm not a baby anymore."

"No one said you were. And you'd better not forget who you're talking to. I know that much."

"Sorry." She closed her magazine, placing it on the coffee table and crossing her arms.

"Anyway, would it make you feel better if I took the money back from him?"

This time she looked her dad directly in the eyes. "I think he's wearing the money on his feet by now."

"What do you want me to do, smarty?"

"Spend more time at home, Dad. Just try to spend more time at home." Star took the remote and changed the channel to MTV.

"I'm home right now, and see, I can't even watch a Lakers game."

"That's not what I'm talking about."

"Star, things should ease up after next year. But for right now, I'm peddling uphill just to remain focused enough to stay amongst the top players in the world. It's more than a notion to do what I do."

"I understand. Mom tells me that all the time. But why still peddle uphill when you're already there."

"Because the very road I traveled to get here, is the same road I'd have to take back down if I'm not careful. It's like treading water just to stay afloat. Or peddling a bike so it doesn't tip over. Don't ever think you've arrived for good. There's always someone else who's younger, better, and more marketable."

Star was silent.

Mason continued. "Okay, I promise next week, I'll be home for three days straight and we'll do something together, all four of us, okay?"

"Uh, huh," she replied still staring at the television.

"You don't believe me?"

"I believe you, Dad. You've never lied to me." She sat back and crossed her wrists over her head.

"For now, do me a favor and get your grandma to come to dinner. If anyone can, you can."

She sat up. "No problem. Here. I'm turning back to the game for you." Star handed him the remote, got up from the couch and walked down the hall toward her grandmother's room.

"Thanks, Puddin'," Mason said as she walked away.

She yelled to him, "Puddin'! Oh, Dad, I hate that name."

"Okay, so now you're too old for me to call you Puddin', huh?" She did not reply.

"Dinner is just about ready," Mercedes yelled from the kitchen. "Star, did you go get your grandma?"

"Coming, Mom," Star yelled, responding to her mother instead.

Within five minutes, Venus arrived. Mason greeted her at the front door.

"Hey, Venus. Good to see you."

She gave him a hug and took off her sweater, tossing it onto the arm of the living room sofa along with her purse. "You too, Mason. You've been busy lately, huh?"

"Yes, as usual. Mercedes is in the kitchen."

"Thanks," she replied as Mason took his seat again.

Venus walked into the kitchen. "Hey, Mercedes. Can I help?"

"No thanks, girl. I'm just about done. Where's Claude?" Mercedes asked.

"He's on his way from a showing."

"He's one driven man. Almost to the point of being a workaholic."

"I'm not mad at him."

"But that's the Wilson men for you. And how about Cameron?"

Venus took a seat at the long kitchen table. "He's over at his grandma's house. Fatima's stepmother called and asked him to spend the weekend so he's been over there since Friday night. He'll be back later on tonight. How have you been?"

"Cool. I'm just warning you that Colette is coming tonight." Mercedes rinsed out a bowl to place the herb pasta in and dried it off.

"No problem."

"I know she was pretty hard on you at the mall."

"Oh please. She's mild compared to what I get from some of my own friends. Or should I say ex-friends. Even Fatima's family hates me. They only deal with Claude."

"Sorry to hear that. They'll come around."

"Maybe not." Venus picked up a glass, pointing to the lemonade. "Can I pour some? It sure looks good."

"Go right ahead," Mercedes said, placing the pasta and string beans on the table.

Just then, Mason answered the door to welcome in Torino and Colette as Star entered the living room headed for the kitchen with Mattie.

"Hey, man. What's up?" Mason asked.

"Nothing much, bro. I'm just hungry as I don't know what."

"Mason reached for Colette. "Hey, Colette. How are you?" They gave each other a hug.

"I'm great. Thanks for having me over."

He closed the door. "Oh, anytime, anytime. You always look like you just stepped off the pages of *Elle* magazine, especially in that pantsuit. You've got a future in the business for sure."

Colette's cheeks were flushed. "Thanks. Sometimes I wonder." They took a seat on the sofa and Mason sat in his recliner again.

"You've got to know it, and be assured of yourself."

"Torino tells me that all of the time."

Torino put his arm around her. "She could be in Italy or Paris making big money, man."

"Not without you, Torino," she said, snuggling into him with a beaming grin.

Mason replied. "Now see a man can wait. But your youth and opportunity will not knock twice."

"It would have to. I can make it right here in California if it's meant to be." She patted Torino's knee.

"Okay now. Don't let a chance pass you by," Torino said.

"I'll deal with that when it comes."

Mason looked at his brother and winked, and then talked to Colette. "Venus and Mercedes are in the kitchen."

"Oh, I'm fine right here. Oh, the Lakers are playing," Colette said, crossing her long legs.

"Someone's knocking at the kitchen door. I'll get it," Star told her mother as she got up from the kitchen table with Mattie.

Mercedes said, "That's got to be Claude. He hasn't used the front door in two years."

"I know. And he never will, Mercedes." Venus sounded concerned.

"Oh, I can imagine that must be hard on him."

"I know, but he never mentions it," Venus said.

Star opened the side door. "Hey, Uncle Claude. Good to see you." She greeted him with a kiss.

"Hey, shining Star. Is everybody here?"

"Yes, now that you're here," Star replied.

Claude smiled and walked up to Venus and Mattie, giving them each a kiss.

"Hey, Claude," Mercedes said, then looking to Star. "Baby, go get Rashaad out of his room and everyone else, too. Dinner is served."

Mercedes made conversation after Mason blessed the table. "Colette is really getting a lot of attention from the retailers and talent bookers for runway assignments. Did she tell you, Torino?"

"Yes she did, actually. I've noticed that she's been working a lot more lately."

"Congratulations, Colette," Venus said, holding a dinner roll in her left hand and fork in her right.

Colette cut her chicken in half and immediately posed a question to Claude. "So, Claude, how's business going for you?"

"It's great right now. Interest rates are low and home buying is up. We're getting a lot of listings from sellers right now, too."

"That's great," Colette replied as she picked up her water glass.

Claude continued talking. "My wife congratulated you, Colette. You must not have heard her."

"Oh, that's okay, baby," Venus assured him.

"No, it's not okay. Torino, you really need to make sure your woman has better manners. Especially here at the table with our mother. Mom taught us better than that."

Torino spoke up. "Chill out, Claude. I thought Colette smiled at her after she said it."

Claude gave her the eye. "She needs to open her mouth."

Colette spoke while still looking down at her plate. "Thanks, Venus."

"No problem," Venus replied.

Torino swallowed a sip of lemonade and asked, "Anyway, Claude, what's got you going today?"

"Not a thing. I had a great day."

"Seems you're always a little cranky when you're in this house," Torino added.

"What are you trying to say?" Claude inquired.

"Just that it seems like you're never in a good mood at dinner." Torino put a forkful of pasta in his mouth.

Mason spoke up. "Okay now gentlemen, would you mind cutting the arrow throwing in my house. All of this because Colette didn't respond to a compliment?"

"Really," said Torino while chewing.

Venus tried to detour the conversation. "Mercedes, this meal is really good. I've never tried chicken made this way."

"I'm glad you like it," said Mercedes, until she noticed Claude beginning to speak again.

"Dad taught us to respect and support our women."

Torino was calm. "You support yours, and I'll support mine."

Mercedes interposed, "Anyway, people, we do have teenagers at the table. Show them how we can all get along."

"Teenagers pick up on that nonsense, too. That's just why Colette's not welcomed in my house with that crap," Claude stated.

"No problem," Torino replied. "You can rest assured of that."

Mattie could not hold her comment any longer. "I'm about to take the two of you over my knee and tan your hides. Acting like you're still six years old. Wait until your daddy gets home."

Rashaad and Star laughed, obviously getting a kick out of the goings on. Mercedes gave them a look.

"What's all this I hear about your big event at the club on Saturday night, Mason?" Venus asked, feeling a bit of sweat building up over her lip. She dabbed her mouth with her lap napkin.

Mason explained, "It's a tribute from a role models' organization, and I'm also giving a few performers a chance to showcase their music. I've invited a couple of producers so hopefully they can get lucky and work out a deal if they're good enough."

Venus told him, "That sounds like fun."

"You will be there, right?" Mason asked Venus.

"Count us in," said Venus. "Right, baby?" she asked Claude.

"Right," he replied with reserve.

"And you, Colette?" asked Mason.

"I wouldn't miss it," Colette said smiling.

"Well, it sounds like it's going to be a nice evening out," Venus interjected.

"Can we go, Mom?" asked Rashaad.

Mercedes shook her head no. "That club is twenty-one and over."

"Even if Uncle Torino lets us in?" asked Star.

"Did you tell them they could go?" Mason asked Torino.

"As long as they stay in the restaurant area, they'll be fine."

Claude repeatedly shook his head at Torino and continued eating.

Mason said, "No way. No one under twenty-one in that club. I don't want any problems, bro. Thanks for trying to make it work but I'm afraid not."

"Dad," Star begged.

"No." Mason was firm.

"What are you going to wear, Colette?" asked Venus. "Did you and Mercedes find anything in the mall the other day?"

"No," Colette said, looking at her plate. "And how did your family like all of the stuff you bought them?" She looked toward the group. "She was really loaded down at the mall, you know, with Jordans and jewelry."

"We liked it just fine," Claude answered for Venus.

"It was a surprise, Colette," Venus said, looking disappointed.

Colette went on and spoke to Claude like she had cotton in her ears. "Kind of pleases you and Cameron when she does stuff like that, huh?"

"None of your damn business," Claude answered.

"Claude, what is your problem?" Torino asked, placing his fork down on his plate.

"The problem is your significant other who serves no significance whatsoever. Man, I'm out of here." Claude scooted his chair out and put his napkin on his plate. "You really need to shake this one. She's not fit to be at this table, let alone in this family. And just so you know, Colette, my lady is too much of a lady to say this so I will. If you have a problem, be woman enough to bring it up. Don't dance all around it like some chicken." He stood up and walked away from the table. "Let's go, Venus."

Venus got up as well. "I'm coming, baby. Mercedes, I'll talk to you tomorrow. Thanks for dinner."

"Good night," Mercedes said, rubbing her forehead.

Torino looked as though his jaw was firming. "Colette, come on." He told Mercedes, "Were gonna go, too. I'm gonna walk her to her car and then turn in. Talk to you later. Thanks."

Mercedes and Mason sat staring at each other as everyone left and Star and Rashaad got up from the table.

Mattie spoke next. "My boy Claude really loves that girl."

"I'd say he does, Mom," replied Mason.

# chapter 5

Before Mason left town again, and after a little prompting from Mercedes, they decided to hit the town. Mason agreed to hang out but only if they ended the night his way after dinner. And his way consisted of the private, exclusive, champagne room of his buddy's club called *T & A*. Tonight, Mercedes let her hair down, in more ways than one.

The scantily clad dancer worked her moves like a professional. Mason and Mercedes sat at the front row table of the dimly lit, tiny, private blue room just as the stripper began to work her first song. The long, tall, golden dancer stepped on stage and quickly grabbed the steel pole, making it her friend.

Mercedes's eyes were fixed upon the girl's rear end in wonder. "Where in the hell did she get a backside like that?" Mercedes asked Mason. Mason was unable to reply from his dropped jaw.

"Ladies and gentlemen, please welcome our next dancer, Mènage," said the energetic announcer slash disc jockey.

The skimpily dressed waitress, who looked like she could be a dancer herself, placed a glass of orange juice and a glass of non-alcoholic beer on the tiny round table just as Mènage stared in Mason's direction and then she focused upon Mercedes.

Mason spoke to his woman, pulling out a wad of ten-dollar bills. "Here, baby. Give her these."

"Oh, no, you go right ahead," Mercedes replied, staring at the money and then eyeballing the dancer's gyrating rear that was within three inches of her face.

"Put it in her G-string, Cedes," Mason said, handing her the bills and then sipping the juice with his other hand.

"That's perfectly fine, you go right ahead," Mercedes said.

Mason did just that, slipping two bills, folded longways into the thong running down the crack of her ass. The bills disappeared into the depth of the dancer's gluteus maximus.

Ménage decided to make an about face and break down to her knees, moving in toward Mercedes's face with her round breasts.

Mercedes's glance was more full on and deliberate than before. She took in a deep breath and blew her exhale through her mouth. The beer she was pouring dripped onto her hand along the outside of the glass. She stopped pouring but never looked down. She placed the bottle on the table and scooted her butt down into her seat, still managing to lean her torso forward at the same time.

Mercedes inhaled and smelled Mènage's skin drenched with Champagne by Yves Saint Laurent. The words, "You smell great," escaped from her lips without an ounce of knowledge from Mercedes.

"Thanks, sweetie. Is this your woman?" asked Ménage, breaking for a half second to direct her inquiry to Mason.

"That's my wife," said Mason with a full-out hard-on.

"She's pretty. You two look like Michael and Juanita Jordan up in here."

"Compliments will get you everything," replied Mason.

Mènage backed away from Mercedes and gave Mason a bit of breast action himself. "Actually, you look like Mason Wilson, the golfer," she whispered.

"Even more complimentary," he said with a grin.

Ménage moved back into Mercedes's very existence, flipping her curly, jet-black hair over Mercedes's hair for privacy and whispered in her ear, "Mrs. Wilson. How do you like it?" asked Ménage.

"My husband is the one who likes it. But I must say, you are very talented."

Ménage backed away to make direct eye contact. "Can I straddle your husband later on with a lap dance?"

"Now you're trying to take all my man's money, huh." Mercedes took her glass and guzzled a few swallows in one.

"This one would be on me," Mènage said.

"I think I can fulfill that fantasy for him, but thanks."

Ménage backed away farther with both eyes fixed upon Mercedes. She then made her way to the next group of high-profile patrons. Five hot, excited, loud men in business suits who owned a baseball team.

Mason told his woman, "I think she likes you."

"I admire women who can shed their inhibitions and let it all hang out like that," Mercedes replied as "Doin It" by LL Cool J played in the background.

"You know you could dance up there right along with them, baby. Your body is just as good as hers," Mason complimented.

"Mason, please. Compliments are accepted, but I keep it real. Three small facts like having babies, fast approaching my forties, and about fifty pounds rule out any runway dancing for me."

"That's just my opinion."

Ménage's second song was over. She picked up her leather bra and scooped up her dollar bills, picking up quite a few next to Mason and Mercedes. Mercedes reached in her own purse and handed Mènage a fifty-dollar bill.

"You deserve this. Job well done," Mercedes said with a hush.

"Thanks, baby. Turned on for the night?"

"My husband is," Mercedes replied.

Ménage smiled at the couple and exited the stage as another dancer, wearing a rhinestone outfit that looked like dental floss, began bumping and grinding her way down the short runway.

"Girlfriend needs a little more meat on her bones," Mason said, finishing off his juice.

Mercedes looked around the room. "Am I the only woman in here?"

"Tonight it looks like it. I thought we'd have a more private area."

"Let's go Mason. It's time I gave you your own private dance." Mercedes put her Prada purse under her arm and stood up.

Mason agreed. “We’re out,” he said as some of the men glanced their way.

They exited quietly and stood in line for their car.

Mercedes noticed a bright flash. “What was that?” she asked as the valet brought Mason’s Porsche around. Mason held the door open for her.

Mason commented. “Some damn paparazzi thinking he’s slick. I saw that light bulb go off.”

Later that evening, Mercedes was still stuck on the thought of the flashing camera. “Baby, doesn’t that bother you. I mean anywhere but at a strip club.”

“You know I don’t go anywhere I don’t want to be seen. And there is nothing wrong with being seen with my wife.”

“Okay then. If you say so.”

“I say so.” Mason pressed the CD remote and the song “You Sure Love to Ball” by Marvin Gaye played on the surround sound stereo in Mason and Mercedes’s bedroom.

Mason sang along, “Pretty little sexy mamma, you sure love to ball.” He watched his thick, curvy wife work her round hips in a sexy circle while he sat on the end of the bed. She removed her sheer lace lavender robe exposing her nudity and threw it on top of the round brass bedpost. She worked her moves with ease, almost as though she’d learned a few moves watching Ménage, the strip expert.

Mason sang again, “Turn around, I’ll love you night and day.” He started to grab her and she backed away, doing a half turn move of her own, ending up with her ass to his face. “You’re my foxy lady,” he sang along with Marvin as though singing a duet.

Mercedes lowered her body, putting her hands on her knees and stuck her butt out, gyrating it in Mason’s face. “Damn, that must be jelly because jam don’t shake like that,” he said. “That’s just the way I like it.” Mason could not contain himself. “Now you know I’m an ass man, baby. Don’t be so mean. Show ’em what you’re working with.” He grabbed her around her waist and pulled her down as he lay on his back. She turned over and then sat up, gazing into his brown eyes as the next cut from the Bedroom Ballads CD started to play "It's All Right" by Chante Moore.

Mercedes felt Mason's warm skin against her round, wide buttocks and rubbed herself against his pubic area back and forth, accompanied by his hands on her rear end to assist the grind. She threw her arms into the air, closed her eyes and sang, "Hello my love, before the sun rises, after it goes down, I love ya, I love ya, I say it over and over again, I love ya, hey, hey, hey. Relax your mind, we can be free together, take our time."

She silenced herself as she felt Mason's finger exploring deep inside her moist walls while she straddled him and rubbed her P-bone on his hardness.

"Oh, I'm going to take my time all right," Mason said, moving in syncopation with his wife.

After his wetness test, she said, "But I'd say I'm ready for you now, baby. What do you say?" She lowered her torso down to meet her husband's upper body, exacting their chests nipple to nipple.

"No, I think you need some more lubrication," Mason suggested in a low tone.

"Like what?"

"Sit on my face, Cedes. Move on up here so I can taste you."

"Oh, baby, now you know what that does to me."

"Come on. Bring that leg on up over my shoulder," he urged.

Mercedes raised her body upward and straddled Mason's face with her shaven cha-cha that always smelled of baby oil. She looked down between her smoldering legs and could only see his eyes—closed shut. She felt his mouth, warm and wet, accompanied by his long, strong tongue, protruding inside of her and licking her opening.

"Mason, wait. For some reason, I can't take this tonight."

Mason did not reply. He placed his hands on each of her butt cheeks and pushed her middle deeper into his face. Mercedes grabbed the headboard with tight-gripped palms to steady her body and her mind. Her legs began to quiver but she still tried to grind along with his expertise.

"Uuhhhmh, Mason," she groaned through the shivering lips of

her mouth, silenced by the sensation rushing to her tiny point as he flicked her pearl.

Mason pulled his head back to adjust the pillow under his neck and then returned to pleasing his wife. Her licked her diamond and then sucked it, feeling her shudder and then moved down to her hole. He stopped to ask, "You liked Ménage, didn't you?"

"Uh-huh," Mercedes responded.

"Show me how much you liked her. I'll bet she'd do a better job at this than me."

"Oh, I don't think so," Mercedes said, while Mason resumed his shenanigans against her opening.

Mercedes turned to catch her own reflection in the dresser mirror. All she could see was her own plump, dark brown ass, pumping away at Mason's face. She imagined one of Mason's male employees under her, licking her into freak mode, and Ménage sucking his penis at the same time. Her thrust increased as she watched the massive hands squeezing her mahogany backside. She positioned herself more securely and pumped deeper and deeper into her fantasy. She closed her eyes and her moans grew in volume and intensity.

Mason ate it like a vulture, moaning in reply to her ability to escape and enjoy. He moaned, "Uh-huh, uh-huh," to accompany her desires. As he sucked her through her orgasm, Mercedes squeezed her throb into his mouth with force and held onto the headboard again for dear life, lightly banging it against the wall with each forward motion until her wave subsided. She wiped her forehead with her wrist and backed away from Mason's face to expose his full-on smile.

Her man felt proud of himself. Proud for pleasing his wife and proud for knowing after all these years, he still knew how to hit the spot.

"Do you think the kids heard us?" asked Mercedes, suddenly returning back to the present.

"I don't think so. You kept it down pretty well. Besides, they're on the other side of this dang-goned house, woman."

Mercedes carefully slipped down onto Mason's stiffness, still reeling from the strain of her flexed leg muscles, allowing her hot, post orgasm walls to take him in. She closed her eyes again. This time, "My First Love" by Tamia was accompanying their heated vibes for each other.

Mason closed his eyes as well and let her go to work. She leaned down flat upon his chest and rode him like a black pony. Mason moved her up to allow her nipples to fall into his open mouth, while sliding his tongue across her fullness and licking her tawny colored areola. She felt him growing and growing, knowing this throb meant it was about to happen. She lowered herself slightly to find his lips, exchanging tongue with wide-opened mouths. His wand protruded and widened with an increasing motion just as she released herself from their kiss. She sat up straight and took on his full enjoyment, giving steady, full up and down motion to welcome his juices, hearing her own rear flap against his thighs.

Mason was silent, almost holding his breath through his discharge as she then felt him gradually decrease in size. She laid on top of his chest, placing her head along his neck. They fell asleep in that position for an hour or so until Mason turned her over and tucked her in. He turned his back to her and gave in to his relaxation, joining her slumber and satisfaction as if in heaven.

Early the next morning, Mason heard the loud, startling ring of a telephone in his mind. He answered it, yanking it from its cradle, only to have the continuous ringing persist. Mercedes picked it up as he continued to sleep.

"Hello," Mercedes said with a frog in her throat.

"Hi, Mercedes. Sorry to wake you. It's Cicely. Can I talk to Mason, please?"

"He's sleeping," Mercedes said, squinting her eyes from the light of day.

"This late?" Cicely asked.

"Yes, this late."

Mason snapped out of his sleep. "Who is that, baby?"

Mercedes covered the phone with her hand, "It's Cicely."

"I'll take it."

She spoke to Cicely. "Hold on one minute." Mercedes covered the phone again. "Are you sure?"

"I'm cool."

Mercedes handed him the phone, looking back at him as she tossed the silk sheets from her legs and headed toward the bathroom.

He sounded half dead. "Hey, what's up?"

"Late night, huh?"

"You could say that," Mason said, rubbing his eyes.

"I'm glad you had a minute to enjoy yourself because you need to leave again on Monday morning. One of the new investors wants to get together with us in Atlanta to discuss the new club."

"Sorry, but you're on your own. I'm out of here tomorrow night."

Cicely asked, "Where are you going?"

"To the tournament in Orlando. I'll be back next week."

Cicely seemed irritated. "Well, how am I supposed to know what to say to them? I'll just call and reschedule."

"No, don't do that. I've been trying to get him to book a date for a month now. You go ahead and handle this meeting. I'll try to be available via conference call by then. You can do it."

"Mason, I do not want to blow it."

Mason assured her. "I have full trust in you. Go on to the meeting and handle it yourself, Cicely."

"Yes, but I don't know anything about the business plan or the site itself."

"I'll show you all of that stuff before I leave. Are you going to be around today?" Mason asked.

"I'll be here until late afternoon. Heidi and I are going to a party this evening and I don't think I'll be around tomorrow. I have to go over to the club and go over some receipts."

"I'll come by later. Just sit tight," he said, slumping back down into the comfort of the old mattress.

"I'll be here. And I want you to know that if I still feel insecure about this meeting, I'm not going to do it. I do not want to be the reason why if this deal falls through."

"See you in a little while," Mason said. He reached over to hang up the phone.

* * *

Mercedes reentered the bedroom wearing her long robe, tied at the waist. Her hair was brushed back, tied in a bun again. She proceeded to the bedroom door and prepared to exit.

"Hey, why don't you get back in bed for a little while?"

"Not when you obviously have things to do soon. I don't want to get too comfortable."

"Cedes, I won't be long."

"Well, good. I'll just get started on some breakfast then. You'd better get going. Maybe you can spare a little time with Rashaad or Star today. After all, it is Saturday, and I can't remember the last time you were home on a Saturday." Mercedes exited the room and shut the door behind her with a slight bit of force.

Mason stared at the closed door for a second and then turned to his side and began to doze, breathing deeper and deeper into a snore within seconds as though he had no need to get up for the rest of the day.

# chapter 6

"Where's Daddy going?" Star asked, peeking through the plantation shutters in the kitchen. "Isn't he going to eat breakfast?"

"He has a meeting this morning, baby. He'll be back." Mercedes looked in the direction of Mattie near the stove. "Mamma," she yelled in a panic as Mattie walked toward the pan of frying bacon, prepared to place her hand along the side.

Mattie jumped and started stuttering. "I—I—I'm just going to add a little water to these grits."

"Mamma, it's okay. This is a hot skillet full of frying, hot bacon. You'll burn yourself," Mercedes said, using her body to shield Mattie's vision from the stove.

Mattie began to walk to the table, taking short, choppy steps in her bare feet. "Oh, there you go again, never letting me help you. Always trying to keep me from doing what I like to do, like driving."

"Mamma, sit down. You know they revoked your license when that cop saw you run that stop sign last year. Besides, isn't it better now that I take you places? I'm like your very own personal driver," Mercedes said, trying to make things seem brighter.

"Yippee," Mattie replied sarcastically.

Star jumped in. "I feel you, Grammy. I don't want Mom taking me everywhere I need to go either."

Mercedes reacted, "Thanks a lot, Star. Then you don't need a ride to that birthday party today?"

Star was nonchalant. "Actually, I do, but I can always call Asia's mom and she can take us."

"Stop trying to play it off. You need a ride and so does your grandma. I'll take you both around twelve or so. Kinda like killing two birds with one stone."

Mattie looked startled. "Who you gonna kill? I'll bet you all can't wait until I just fall over and get out of the way."

"Grammy, don't talk like that," said Star. "You're going to be around to see your great-grandchildren. That's how long you're going to live."

"You'd better get started now then because I'm going to go get Jesse soon."

"Star is only thirteen and she's not starting soon. Anyway, here, you all come on and eat." Mercedes placed the breakfast on the table. "Where is Rashaad?"

"He's in his room," Star said.

"As always. Go get him and tell him to eat while it's hot."

"Rashaad, come on and eat," Star yelled at the top of her lungs.

"Don't yell, Star. I could have done that. Go get him."

"What?" Rashaad yelled, walking toward the kitchen.

"Time to eat," said Star in a lower tone. "Time for our family breakfast. And standing in for Daddy, once again is Mommy." Star stretched out her arms to each side, looking toward Mercedes.

"Funny. You'd better watch your mouth."

Rashaad said in agreement, "Shoot, Mom. She's right. Why is it that Dad always leaves just when he has a couple of days off?"

"It's his busy schedule. You should be glad he provides for us like he does. How many other kids do you know who have the type of lifestyle and opportunities he's given the two of you? Not many," Mercedes explained, scooping some of the scrambled eggs onto her plate.

Rashaad took his seat. "Maybe not. But they have the opportunity of having their dad home on the weekends, at least."

"Boy, you'd better eat this food and stop complaining. I thought none of the boys your age felt it was cool to hang out with their parents anyway."

"Maybe if I had the chance I could decide that for myself," Rashaad said matter-of-factly.

Mattie chimed in, "Boy, sit down and shut up. And you'd better stop your bellyaching, all this cooking I've done this morning. Thank God I don't have my cane in my hand, young smart mouth." She cut her eyes at him.

Rashaad prepared to respond, "Grandma . . ."

"Don't say it," Mercedes advised.

"Grammy, how many pieces of bacon do you want?" asked Star.

"Give me about five or so," she said, pointing to her plate.

"You are not going to eat . . ." Rashaad said, looking dumbfounded.

Mercedes interrupted. "Give her five or six, Star."

"Here you go."

"Why not give her a dozen pancakes and a dozen eggs," Rashaad joked.

"You know what, Rashaad? You can go to your room. Since you insist on being a pain. Just go and think about what disrespectful, dumb things have been coming out of your mouth lately."

Rashaad stood up. "Why is it that Star can make comments and I can't?"

Mercedes pointed to the door. "Just go. And I do not want to hear a PlayStation or television. Do you hear me?"

Rashaad started to walk away.

"I asked if you heard me, boy." Mercedes voice resounded.

"I heard you, Mom," he said with a downward glance.

Mercedes looked at Mattie. "I'm so sick of him being negative."

"Jesse would have tanned his hide for talking back." Mattie shook her head.

"That sounds like a great idea. He's going to have his butt in church tomorrow."

"Do you think Daddy will be able to go?" Star asked.

"I don't flippin' know. Why don't you ask him yourself?"

"I will, Mom," Star said, staring at her mother in amazement.

"Good. Now let's say grace," Mercedes said, still sounding irritated.

Mattie took over and blessed the food, holding hands with her daughter-in-law and granddaughter. "Heavenly Father, hear our prayer, keep us in thy tender care, help us to be kind and good and thank you for our daily food, Amen."

"Amen," Mercedes and Star said in unison.

Later that morning, Mercedes rushed downstairs with her keys and purse in hand. "We've got to get going." Star was standing by the door but Mattie was coming out of her room, still barefoot. "Please hurry up, Mamma. Go get your shoes. Your CT scan appointment is at one o'clock."

"What are you talking about?"

"Mamma, just come on. Let's go for a ride." Mercedes rushed into Mattie's room and grabbed her ballerina slippers. "Here. Put these on. I'll stop and get you some pistachio ice cream, okay?"

"Why didn't you say so? Let's go," she said, slipping her feet into her shoes.

Mercedes pulled up to the three-story parking structure of the UCLA medical center. She went up all three levels, circling and circling over and over again, trying to find a parking space.

"Mamma, they've got this huge medical facility and there's nowhere to park. This is ridiculous."

"You can just drop me off, I'll go in and get in line."

"No, Mamma. I need to go with you," Mercedes said, distracted as she wound down a ramp a little too fast. She screeched as she slammed on her brakes. "Uh, oh," she said. "I almost hit him." Mercedes rolled down her window.

"Lady, you're killing me," said a black man driving a new blue Navigator.

"I'm so sorry, sir. I could tell you were trying to move over. I just cut it a little too sharp."

"That's okay, just be more careful," he said, rolling up his window.

"I will," Mercedes mouthed, pulling over to make sure her mother-in-law was okay. "You all right, Mamma?"

"This sure is a rough ride today. All this just to go to Newberry's to get some ice cream?"

Mercedes heard another honk. It was the man whose car she was blocking. He was letting her know he was about to back out if only she'd move.

"Oh, good." She gestured by raising her hand and waving to the driver as they both backed up.

She pulled in and looked at her watch. "Finally, we're here. And we're right on time."

"Mrs. Wilson," the nurse called from the waiting room door.

"Right here." Mercedes held onto Mattie's arm as they went into the examining room.

Ten minutes or so went by after the nurse asked a few questions and then left.

"How much longer," Mattie asked impatiently.

"Just a few more minutes." Mercedes stared at the wall clock.

"Mattie Wilson," the doctor said, walking in the room a few moments later.

"Yes," Mattie said, smiling at the doctor.

"I'm Dr. Green."

He looked at Mercedes. "Wallace Green."

"Hello, Dr. Green," Mercedes said.

He turned and stood over the sink, looking down at the medical file. Mercedes noticed the back of his head, with his curly dark hair, well groomed and trimmed along his neckline. "I see you made your way into a parking space without causing injury to yourself or others," he joked, turning to look at Mercedes.

"Oh my God, was that you?" Mercedes asked. "I'm so sorry."

"You apologized already. These parking structures are pretty much crowded all the time. And it's even worse on Saturdays," he said, sitting upon the small, black leather stool on wheels. "So, Mrs. Wilson. How are you today?" He scooted over next to Mattie.

"I'm fine. How are you?" Mattie acted like he was the ice cream man, being so cooperative.

"I'm doing better," he said looking at Mercedes again. "Has she had a CT scan before?"

"Yes, a year ago at Brotman Hospital in Culver City."

"Which doctor?"

"Doctor Maya Turner."

"I know her. She's a great neurologist. Okay, so this is a follow-up to check the status of the dementia. I'll just check your vitals and then ask you a few questions if you don't mind, Mrs. Wilson."

"No, I don't mind."

*My how obliging Mattie is,* Mercedes thought. *I'd be too. What a bedside manner he has.*

Dr. Green checked Mattie's blood pressure, pulse, and heartbeat. Mercedes rolled her huge wedding ring around as she continued to investigate the doctor's features, even the shape of his ears and his baby-fine sideburn hairs.

"Excuse me, ma'am," he said, trying to startle her from her zone. "Your name is?"

"Mercedes Wilson."

"Mrs. Wilson?"

"Ah, yes, Mrs. Mercedes Wilson."

"She's your mother-in-law?"

"Yes, she is my husband's mother."

"I see. Well, Mrs. Wilson, we'll need to have you take her to the x-ray lab right down the hall. I'll meet the two of you there in a few minutes. Is that okay?"

"That's just fine. Thanks, doctor . . ." Mercedes replied, making it obvious that she'd forgotten his name.

"Wallace."

"Dr. Wallace, right. That's just fine. Thanks."

"No, my name is Dr. Green. You can call me Wallace."

Mercedes gave an embarrassed smile.

Mattie watched the doctor as he walked away. "That man looks just like Jesse did when he was young. Tall and handsome and he smelled good, too. Did you notice?"

"I noticed, Mamma. Let's go get this done."

Once in the x-ray room, the technician assisted in getting Mattie onto the table.

"Perhaps we should give her something to relax her," Dr. Green suggested. "Is she claustrophobic?"

"No. She seems to do real well with these type of things."

"Then we'll just see how it goes."

Mercedes watched him talk to Mattie, coming within six inches of her face as she lay on her back about to enter the machine. He explained everything to her and touched her upper arm as he spoke. Mattie closed her eyes and smiled.

"You'll have to wait outside because of the rays. You understand, right?" Dr. Green explained.

"No problem. I'll be right out here when you need me. Thanks, Dr. Green," Mercedes said, making a point of referring to him in a professional way.

He made a point of watching her walk into the waiting room just before he slowly closed the door.

Mercedes tried to keep both eyes focused on the road while licking the sides of her rainbow sherbet cone. Mattie was crunching the sugar cone of her own double dip of pistachio. "Hello?" Mercedes pushed the button to the speakerphone of her cell.

"Mercedes, it's Cicely."

Mattie looked irritated, saying, "You need to hang up and focus on this trip."

"I will, Mamma." She resumed her call. "Hey, what can I do for you?"

"I hope you don't mind me calling but isn't this Mason's old number?"

"Yes, we switched phones a couple of months ago."

"Oh, I see. Well, I'm calling because Mason left his briefcase over here and I think he might need it when he leaves tomorrow. Can you tell him to come and get it?"

"Aren't you in Leimert?" Mercedes asked.

"I'm still here."

"How about if I come by and get it? I'm just coming back from Mattie's doctor's appointment. I'll swing by if it's okay."

"That should be fine. How far away are you? Because he just left. I can try to call him again."

"He didn't answer before?"

"No," Cicely said.

Mercedes licked another drop of melting ice cream. "I'll just run by real quick. You're still on Creed, right?"

"Yes."

"See you in a minute."

Mattie stared out of the window looking angry.

Cicely opened the door wearing casual hip hugger jeans and a tiny white tee with silver lettering that read, "diva". She also wore an unusually warm smile on her face.

Mercedes greeted her. "Hi, Cicely."

"Hello, Mercedes. Good to see you."

"Thanks for telling me about Mason's briefcase. That man is good at this kind of stuff."

"I know. He's always been, even back in the day," Cicely replied.

Realizing that she didn't go back as far with Mason as Cicely did, she replied, "Yes, even back in college." Mercedes peeked in. "You've decorated this place real nice. I haven't seen it since Mason bought it years ago."

"Let me go and get his briefcase. It's right back here."

"Thanks." Mercedes stood still.

"Hey. Let me show you around real quick."

"No, I'd better not. I just had my mind set on running up to your door. I'd . . ."

"It'll only take a minute. My place is pretty small, not like that gorgeous house you live in."

"But it's obvious that you have impeccable taste. I've wanted to get into black art but never really took the time to look into the different artists and styles," Mercedes said, stepping inside at the same time.

"Come on back for a minute. His case is back here anyway. In my office."

"Okay," Mercedes said, still leaving the door open and glancing outside as she looked around the living room.

Cicely had a LifeCycle and Stairmaster in her den. She made a point of going to the gym three times a week. She'd always say her butt needed to be as flat as her chest, and they both were. Mercedes checked her out not feeling a bit intimidated by her body. But feeling something.

"And back here is my little sitting area where I meditate and where I work," Cicely explained.

"Good for you. I noticed your exercise equipment. I have a treadmill and some other machines just collecting dust."

"How in the world would you ever have time, what with all that you've got going on with working, being the wife of a pro golfer, a mom, and taking care of your mother-in-law?"

They walked into Cicely's office and Cicely headed straight for Mason's snakeskin case.

Mercedes said, "Mrs. Wilson is worth looking after. She's been so good to me through the years."

Cicely smiled. "All I have to look after is my cat, Chaka." She pointed to her baby. "But you know how cats are, they just sleep and eat." Chaka was a big, fluffy Calico, all curled up in the middle of her wide-back wicker chair.

"Just like a man I've always said," Mercedes joked.

"Okay?" she replied like a sista-friend.

"She's beautiful. And who's this?" Mercedes asked, looking at a framed photo of Cicely and a woman, obviously on vacation somewhere.

"That's my sister Heidi. Unlike most sisters, we're pretty close. I don't know what I'd do without her."

Mercedes turned her head for a minute and paused. "Did you hear that?"

"What?" Cicely asked.

"The sound of . . ."

Mercedes ran to the front door just fast enough to catch the tail end of her SUV turning the corner on Creed Avenue.

Mercedes yelled, "Oh, my God. Mattie drove off. She started the car and drove off." She placed her hands to her head with a wide opened mouth.

"Mason's mom? I thought she couldn't drive anymore."

"Yes, but she doesn't know that," Mercedes said. "Let me use your phone, please. I've got to call Mason. He's going to kill me."

Mercedes dreaded the call with every digit, even as she pressed talk.

"You did what?" Mason asked loudly.

"Mason, I just ran in for a second and she pulled off," Mercedes explained.

"You left your keys in the car?"

"I guess I did. I turned off the ignition but I don't remember taking the keys out."

Mason got louder. "Obviously you didn't, Mercedes. How could you have done such a thing?"

Mercedes tried to stay calm. "Mason, we need to figure out what to do. Scold my ass later but your mom is out there and we need to find her."

Cicely interrupted, "Let me talk to him, please." Mercedes handed her the phone. "Now Mason, calm down and think rationally for just a second. Let's call the police and get our thoughts together about where she might go and what else we can do. Let's be positive. She'll be just fine."

"Cicely, I cannot believe she left the keys in the car and went inside."

Cicely replied, "Mason, now stop this. I'm going to hang up and dial 9-1-1. You start driving around and see if you can locate her yourself."

Mason began to focus. "Okay, she did like Fox Hills Park and loved to go to West Los Angeles College to jog. I'll try those places. What was Mercedes doing at your place anyway?"

"She came to get your briefcase for you. Good-bye, Mason." Cicely clicked over and dialed 9-1-1.

After the call, Cicely took Mercedes into her arms and hugged her, patting her on the back.

"Calm down, now. Let's do what they suggested and go look for her ourselves for now." Cicely took her cell phone and ran into the house to get her keys. They hopped into her black Explorer.

Cicely called the Wilson house but there was no answer.

"Star went to a birthday party and Rashaad is not supposed to be watching TV or answering the phone, so I'm sure he's pouting in his room."

Cicely reassured Mercedes. "You know we'll find her. Just keep saying that to yourself, Mercedes. We'll find her. Think good thoughts."

They drove around the Leimert area, up and down Crenshaw Boulevard and through side streets, residential and business sections.

Cicely had an idea. "How about if you call your cell phone? Didn't you leave it in the car?"

"That's so smart. Surely she'll answer right?"

"Surely."

The phone rang and rang and rang. "I don't think she's ever even answered a cell phone. I'll try again in a minute."

"Did you have gas?"

"A full tank."

"And does she carry a purse?" Cicely asked, making a U-turn after coming to a dead end street.

"Yeah, but she puts silly things in it like coupons and broken jewelry and tons of makeup. It's more of a catch-all than anything else."

Mason called on Cicely's phone. Mercedes looked at the Caller ID and answered the phone herself without even thinking. "Baby, did you find her?"

Still sounding panicked, he said, "No. I was going to ask you the same thing. Did you tell 9-1-1 that she's my mom?" Mason inquired. "You know I know those cats over there."

Mercedes rolled her eyes. "No, I didn't think to tell them that. Why don't you call them?"

"No, you call them back and tell them who she is. They'll get on it quicker, I promise you. I'm about to pull underground at the old condo she and Dad shared to see if she went back there. I'll call you again." He hung up.

"So, tell them she's Mason's mom, huh?" Cicely asked.

"Yeah. I pray nothing happens to her."

"She'll be fine. Here, I'll call for you. You just keep your eyes peeled while I drive. I'll call them back."

The sun began to set and Cicely drove Mercedes to pick up Star at her friend's house in Baldwin Hills.

Star sat in the back seat amazed. "Grammy did what? No way. She's such a freedom fighter. I'll bet she's having the time of her life, just driving on her own like she's wanted to."

"Let's hope so," Mercedes said.

Cicely pulled down the block on Shenandoah and turned the curve toward Mercedes's house.

"Oh my God, will you look at that," said Mercedes. Her jaw dropped at the sight of her own car parked askew in her driveway. "Mason must have found her and drove my car back here."

"Yes, but he didn't call," Cicely replied. Cicely pulled up, barely into the driveway as Mercedes and Star ran inside of the house.

"Mamma," yelled Mercedes, headed for Mattie's room.

"Grammy," yelled Star, running though the living room and toward Mattie's bedroom door. Cicely was right behind her.

"What the heck is all the noise for," asked Rashaad, wiping his eyes, exiting his dark bedroom.

Mercedes burst into her mother-in-law's room and saw Mattie, jumping to shield her braless breasts from view with one hand.

"Don't you know how to knock, young lady? I'm trying to get out of these clothes. I've had a long day at work and you all can't even let me rest in peace?"

"Grammy, where have you been?" Star asked.

Mattie slipped on her robe. "I told you, I went to work. What is wrong with you all looking at me like you've seen a ghost?"

"Who brought you home, Mamma?"

"I drove like I always do."

"You drove?" asked Cicely.

"Yes. And what are you doing here?" Mattie's frown grew deeper. "You aren't supposed to be in this house," she told Cicely.

"Mamma," Mercedes said to her statement. She forced herself to divert her attention from Cicely's hurt feelings to walk over to give Mattie a big hug and kiss.

"What's for dinner?" Mattie asked.

"Whatever you want, Mamma," Mercedes told her.

Rashaad stood outside of the door still in a fog. "She got lost today. How did that happen?"

"Don't ask," Mercedes replied.

Suddenly, Mason ran through the door followed by Claude and Venus. "Is she here?"

"Yes, she drove herself here," said Cicely.

"Oh my God, Mom, are you all right?" asked Mason.

Mattie replied with a glower, "What is all the fuss about? Now leave me be and close my door until I'm ready to make dinner later on. You all must be starving."

"No problem, Mom," said Mason as he exhaled and exited her room, leaving his mom to herself.

"Shouldn't we have her checked out to make sure she's okay?" Mercedes asked Mason with no reply. They all headed toward the dining room.

Claude remarked, "You know what, Mercedes? That was irresponsible. This is the second time something has happened to my mom when she was supposed to be under your watchful eye. The first time you let her put fingernail polish over her eyes."

Mason spoke for Mercedes. "Now wait a minute, Claude. I've been thinking. I was mad, too, but this could have happened to any of us. At any time she could just walk out of this house and leave, walking, driving or whatever. It's not Mercedes's fault."

Mercedes explained. "Claude, I treat her like I would treat my own mother. Actually, I treat her just like I did treat my own mother. I love Mattie and I think the amount of time that I put into caring for her is more than anyone else in this family, with the exception of Anna during the weekdays. I try my best."

Cicely interrupted, "Mercedes, I'm going to go now. I'll leave you all to talk about this."

"Good-bye and thanks," Mercedes said. Cicely walked out, leaving the four of them in the dining room to continue their disagreement.

Star went into her room and Rashaad went out into the backyard. He opened the side gate and Kailua came running out, jumping up and down around him in circles.

# chapter 7

Claude looked sternly at the group as they sat at the extended table in Mason's formal dining room. "I think now's a good time for that family meeting."

Leaning back in his chair, Mason looked purposefully at his brother. "Claude, I don't think I like what you're trying to suggest. No one is better at taking care of Mom than Mercedes."

"Are you saying that Venus couldn't do it just as well? I'll bet there wouldn't be anymore mishaps like this."

"You know what, Claude? I don't like what you're saying about my wife."

"It's not so much about her. You're never here to help out anyway. I'm just saying maybe Mom should come live with Venus and me. At least I'm home in the evenings and Venus is home all day."

"No, Claude. Mom has always lived with me since Dad died, and she is staying right here." Mason was unwavering in his conviction.

Venus interjected, touching his forearm, "Honey, let's not jump to conclusions. We're still in the heat of the moment here. Let's take a few days and think about this."

Claude refused to listen. "No. I say we vote now. Another day here and who knows what might happen."

Mercedes asked, "Oh, now, Claude, you're overreacting a little bit, don't you think?"

Mason went on. "Oh, he's overeating all right. Besides, when was the last time you took the time to come by and help out or check on her other than coming to dinner? You avoid this house like the plague."

"Maybe that's true, Mason. But perhaps you should ask yourself that same question. After all, she lives in your own home. What's your excuse?"

Mason tapped his fingers on the cherry wood dining table. "I have no excuse for making sure that family, and not some nurse at a convalescent home who doesn't even know her, takes care of my own mother. No one said it would be easy, but we need to prepare for her future. From what the doctor tells us, this dementia only progresses."

Mercedes agreed with a whisper, looking back in the direction of Mattie's room. "True, and the reality of it all is that soon she won't be able to walk, feed herself, or go to the bathroom on her own."

Claude rubbed his goatee with his thumb and forefinger. He looked across the table at his older brother as though he was feeling aversion. "We're so far away from that point. We need to focus on how well she's doing now and enjoy her mental and physical abilities now. After all, look at what she was able to do. She was well enough to drive back to her son's house. She knew the way, she arrived safely, she came inside and she went to her room."

"That's a miracle if you ask me," Venus said.

Mercedes added, "That was probably your dad who guided her here. Did you even think of that?"

Venus agreed. "Mercedes is right. And he will continue to guide us. We need to pray and stick together and not let anger and premature decisions drive a wedge between us."

Claude was stubborn. "Well, starting next week I want her to live with me and Venus and Cameron. We deserve as much time with her as all of you have had."

Mason had an idea. "Obviously our vote is going to be split. Let's wait for Torino and see what he wants to do."

"Oh please, Torino's so damn partial to you, Mason. I mean he's living behind your home and working for you at the club. Who do you think he's going to vote for?"

Mason scooted his chair back and stood over the three of them. "You know what, Claude? Fine. You get a room ready and you take care of her starting on Monday. How's that?"

Claude nodded his head in agreement. "That's just what I think she needs. We'll keep an eye out for her just like you all have done. It's the least we can do after you've had her around for all of these years."

Mercedes was not convinced. "Mason, I don't know."

"Baby, let's let him do this."

"Don't you think we should ask Mattie first?" she inquired.

Claude stood as well. "No. The time has come for us to start making decisions for her. She doesn't know what's good for her anymore. I say we just do it."

Mason spoke. "Like I said, it's fine, especially since you two are fine examples for deciding what is morally and spiritually right for mankind, huh?"

"Pardon me?" said Claude.

"Forget it. I have to get going." Mason walked toward the living room. "And maybe you two should get going to start getting things in order. Mercedes, where's my briefcase?"

Mercedes sighed. "Oh, with all of the confusion, it's still at Cicely's house."

"I'll go get it. I'll talk to you two later," Mason said without looking at his brother or his sister-in-law.

"We'd better get going too, Mercedes." Venus hugged Mercedes. "Thanks for your caring and attention with Mattie."

Mercedes returned the embrace. "I'm just glad everything turned out okay. I'll see you later."

Claude walked out of the side door without a good-bye. He mumbled to himself, "I hate this damn house."

"Are you two coming for dinner tomorrow?" Mercedes asked as Venus put one foot through the doorway.

"I'll call you," said Venus, following behind her husband.

Mercedes attended church with Star and Rashaad the next day. Mason wanted to stay home with his mom to get in some bonding time until he left later that evening. After service, crowds of people gathered to talk and greet each other.

Outside the church, the Reverend stopped Mercedes and the kids. "Mrs. Wilson, you are going to be able to chair our shelter for the homeless event scheduled for next year, right?"

"As usual, I wouldn't miss being a part of it."

"How's it going anyway?" the Reverend asked.

Mercedes seemed reserved. "Pretty good."

The dapper-looking Reverend was being his regular exuberant self. "Pretty good. You're supposed to say, outstanding."

"Outstanding," Mercedes said unconvincingly.

"It didn't sound like you meant that. Is everything all right?"

"Yes, everything's outstanding, Rev."

"Where's Mr. Wilson. Is he on the road?"

"No, he's at home with his mom, just spending some time with her."

"How is Mrs. Wilson doing? I haven't seen her in a month of Sundays." He looked to Mercedes for signs of a happy face.

"Good one, Rev. She's one strong woman. We're praying her disease doesn't spread too quickly."

"Pray that it doesn't spread at all. Have faith and know that all is well. It's all in God's hands."

"Amen to that. She just had a scan done and it confirmed that it is Alzheimer's because it's gotten worse since last year. But they have this new medicine that can slow down the progression."

"That's a blessing. How are you guys handling the caregiver aspect of your mother-in-law's situation?"

Mercedes noticed other parishioners standing by, anxious to talk to their pastor as well. "We take turns. We have a housekeeper who's real helpful while I'm at work. She cooks during the week and helps out a lot. I only go in to the office a few days a week. But my brother-in-law is going to take over with her for a while. I'll let you go. It was nice talking to you."

"Mercedes, if you ever need our Angels group to come by and help out, wash clothes, do anything at all, just ask. And I really think it wouldn't hurt to have a family session with you and Mason as well as the kids."

"Thanks, Reverend, but Mason is real private when it comes to that. He has an image, you know," she said in a low tone.

"That's one reason why I'm suggesting it. Sometimes the image can cause people to live according to what's expected of them on the outside, as opposed to what's needed on the inside. Most importantly, God."

"I admit we've been spinning in all directions lately. I appreciate your offer. I'll keep that in mind," Mercedes said, giving him a good-bye hug.

"Hey there, Rashaad," the Reverend said, noticing Rashaad's maturing face. "My, you have grown so much over the past few months."

"I know. Good to see you, Reverend."

Star reached out for a hug, too. "And you, little lady. You're looking more like your mother every day."

"Thanks," said Star, as she fidgeted with her scrunchie, reaching back to secure her long braids into a ponytail.

Mercedes started to take a step toward the car. "Well, Rev, take care and make sure you tell your wife Robbie we said hello. We'll see you next week."

"He's a real special man," Mercedes told her kids. "We're blessed to have him in our lives. He seems like he really cares."

"Uh huh," said Star, as Rashaad eagerly took the keys from his mom so he could drive her car.

Mercedes placed her hand out for him to give them back. "Not so fast, mister."

"Oh, Mom," he replied, handing them over with reluctance, slumping his shoulders.

"Do you want to go eat at Dinah's Restaurant or Pann's?" Mercedes asked.

"I say Pann's," said Rashaad, suddenly perky again.

"Are you okay with that," Mercedes asked Star.

"Uh huh."

Mercedes imitated her. "Uh huh? Let's just go."

* * *

At Claude and Venus's house, the stepmother/stepson drama started to heat up.

"Dad, where are you?" Cameron called his father from the guest room where Venus was getting the frilly queen-size bed ready for Mattie.

Claude spoke from his mobile, keeping his tone down. "I'm showing a house in Windsor Hills right now. My client is right here. What do you need, son?"

Cameron stepped into the hallway, trying to talk without being heard. "Dad, I asked Venus a simple question about my Spanish and she told me to look it up next time before I asked her. Dad, she always has an attitude."

"Put her on the phone, son." Cameron walked back into the room and handed Venus the cordless, standing right beside her, scratching the parts between his cornrows. "Hey, Venus." Claude excused himself from his clients. "When I'm done with this showing that I'm smack dab in the middle of, I'll be right home. But do you think you two can get around this without my help?"

Venus looked up at Cameron with a sharp stare and paced a few steps toward the bed. "Claude, I'm sorry that Cam bothered you while you're working. I don't mind helping him out, really. But I think he takes advantage of the fact that I'm half Spanish. He gets lazy about studying. Actually, I think this is a take home test and he just keeps coming in here asking me for the answers."

"I think it's a big advantage for him to have you around to help. Okay, honey? Please?"

Venus was firm yet she spoke in almost a whisper. "You've got to support me on these type of things, Claude."

"I do. I just want both of you to try."

"Try. Okay." Venus hung up and walked over toward Cameron, who glanced down at his textbook. "What do you need to know, Cameron?"

He put his book under his arm and turned to walk out. "Forget it."

"Cameron, hold on," she said firmly. He turned toward her. "I know you didn't go to such extremes to tell on me to my own husband and then you have nerve to act like you don't want my help after all. What did you need to know?"

Cameron's eyes met hers in a piercing stare. He opened the book and flipped through the pages with rapidity. "There is one thing I can't find in here." He looked her square in the eyes. "How do you say, 'You're not my mom,' in Spanish?"

Venus responded immediately, staring him down. "*Usted no es mi madre.* How's that?"

He stared back. "*Usted no es mi madre!*" He repeated the translated sentence, word for word, with conviction and certainty and authority. She heard the exclamation point at the end of his last word.

Venus was unwavering. "Anything else you need to say?" She waited for his answer.

He returned the look, then broke their stare and closed his book. "No, that just about says it all."

"Good, Cameron. And don't forget that your grandmother will be staying with us starting tomorrow night." Venus turned around to resume her preparations.

"*No problemo,*" Cameron said, walking back to his room, slamming his door.

Venus continued to make the bed. Under her breath she said, "*I am not going to let that boy run me out of here. Anyway, it's no un problema.*"

Mason was running in place, wearing his brown Sean Jean sweat suit as he waited in front of the house as his family pulled into the driveway. Mercedes did end up letting Rashaad drive down the street from the main intersection to the house. Mason walked up to the driver side and leaned in. "I need to go for a run, baby. I'll be back in an hour or so. You look good behind the wheel of that spaceship, boy," he said to Rashaad.

Rashaad locked the car door with the remote after they got out. "Dad, we brought the chicken and waffles you like."

"Keep it warm for me, son. I'll be right back." He turned and started to jog.

"Hold up, baby. I can throw on my jogging suit and go with you," Mercedes suggested with anticipation. "Mason!" Mercedes yelled as he ran on down the street with his headphones to his ears. He waved and disappeared around the curve.

"He's leaving again?" asked Rashaad, staring toward his dad.

"He's always going in a different direction from us anyway. What difference does it make?" asked Star. She paused and looked at her mother and then went on into the house, shaking her head from side to side.

Rashaad went through the side gate and started to play with Kailua.

*I'm going to go catch up with him*, thought Mercedes, rushing upstairs to change her clothes.

Star went out into the backyard and tossed the waffles to Kailua.

"Don't give him the wings, silly. He'll choke," said Rashaad.

"I'm not. I'll eat those," she said, taking one in between her teeth and biting the chicken with a frown.

Mercedes hopped in her car. She drove for maybe thirty minutes, but could not find Mason. After a few minutes more, she returned home.

"That was fast," said Star as her mom walked through the front door.

"I didn't find him. I don't know what course he had mapped out, but it wasn't the usual one, that's for sure."

"That's strange. Maybe he ran to Starbucks. Did you check there?"

"That wouldn't make sense." Mercedes placed her keys on the kitchen island.

"But, knowing Daddy . . ."

"Yes, you're probably right."

After dinner, Mason walked into their bedroom with a tall mug of coffee in hand.

"What's this?" Mercedes asked as she exited the bathroom and he handed it to her.

"Coffee."

"Oh, Mason."

"Just for you, baby." He kissed her forehead.

Mercedes looked delighted. "Wow. Thanks, Mason. That was very nice of you."

It was time for Mason to begin packing his bags, just before his driver picked him up. He was an expert at packing light. Mercedes sat on the end of the bed watching him do his thing. She sipped on her perfectly prepared coffee and then asked, "Where did you go today?"

"When?"

"When you ran off to jog by yourself."

"I jogged down the street and around the neighborhood."

"Did you go through the park?"

"No."

"Which street did you take?"

Mason paused for a moment, looking perplexed. "Why are you asking me that?"

"Because I went looking for you. I was driving around and couldn't find you."

"You went looking for me? Mercedes I simply turned at the corner of . . . at . . . Slauson and then down to Chariton. I think. Heck, I don't know. I never take the same path twice. What's up with you?"

"What's up with you?" She sipped her coffee again.

"Mercedes, when I get back we can go jogging together. I just went running alone. I was fired up and ready to get it over with. Is there a problem?"

"No problem. You didn't hear me say I was coming?"

"Dad, the limo is here," Star yelled from downstairs.

"No I didn't. I had on my headphones. Now can we drop this? I've got to get going." Mason yelled, "I'm coming." He rushed down the stairs and out the door. Mercedes put down the mug and followed behind him.

"I'll call you guys tonight," he shouted from where he stood as the driver held open the car door. "It'll be late by the time I get into Florida. Star, I know your brother ate my take-home plate."

"Uh huh," she replied.

"I love you," he said to his wife and daughter as they waved from the front porch.

Mercedes replied, "Have a nice flight. Be safe."

"Oh, so no ditto this time?"

"Ditto," Mercedes said, blowing a kiss his way.

He got inside and the driver closed the door.

Star stood, leaning against the doorway, without saying a word.

"Star, are you mad because your dad ran off to jog without me?"

"Whatever, Mom. You just always let him get away with stuff like that."

"No, I don't actually. I already talked to him about it."

"Yes, but the point is, even though you discuss it, he never changes. I'm never going to let my husband be so selfish."

"Star, you don't know what type of boundaries you're going to have once your married. It all depends on how the relationship is structured and what your individual professions are. Things like that. And you can't make people do things."

"Well, I already know I'd never put up with that. For all you know, he has a girlfriend around the corner."

Mercedes face reeked with impatience. "Star, that's enough. You'd better watch your mouth, young lady. Sometimes I go with him and sometimes I don't. Your dad works hard and he simply jogs in the neighborhood to keep in shape, alone or not. Stop pouting."

Star uncrossed her arms and walked away.

Mercedes was firm. "And head straight to the kitchen to put the dishes in the dishwasher."

Star was silent, yet she headed for the kitchen.

"Did you hear me?"

"Yes, ma'am."

Mercedes closed the front door as the limousine turned the corner. Star's sentence repeated in her head. *For all you know, he has a girlfriend around the corner.* Mercedes reopened the door and sat on the porch in deep thought.

# chapter 8

Claude picked up his mother the next day to get her situated in what he hoped would be her permanent home. Once Mattie got settled into her new room, Claude retired to his bedroom suite.

The elegant, enormous room, decorated with leopard furnishings and cherry red accents, opened up to blend into the fifteen-by-twelve bathroom. No door separated the two rooms, except for the private commode and bidet, and his and hers walk-in closets.

He'd brought Venus a glass of chilled champagne and poured himself a tall glass of cranberry juice and then ran the water in his roman tub with thoughts of unwinding with his wife. He wanted to celebrate the fact that his mother was now living under their roof. He opened the balcony door to their bathroom, looked out and lifted his head toward the dark sky. He enjoyed the feeling of relief.

After taking a few deep breaths, he closed the sliding door behind him and came back inside. "Would you care to join me?" he asked Venus, standing over her as she lay in bed reading.

"I'll leave you to yourself so you can totally unwind. I'll be waiting right here," she replied, momentarily taking off her reading glasses and giving him a peck on the lips as he leaned down toward her.

Claude disrobed and got in the deep Jacuzzi tub. He lay back, thinking about how much he liked to bring out Venus's wild side in bed.

He kicked back and soaked for a good twenty minutes. As he got out and dried himself off, he looked over at the bed to see that Venus had set the book aside. She lay on top of the brown covers, on her stomach, wearing only a silk teddy. She was watching his every move.

He walked toward her with a black towel around his waist, placing a kiss on her flushed cheek. She sniffed his fragrant chemistry and said, "I love you." He kissed her again, this time with tongue. Claude stood up to come around and lie on his back while Venus turned to face him. She started to lick his left nipple and made a beeline down to his private parts to bring him pleasure. She kept her hands free to massage him.

No matter what type of day Claude and Venus had while vertical, their horizontal moves seemed to be pretty much in sync, both usually willing to get intimate as if the stresses of their daily lives had no effect.

Claude turned Venus over to lie on her back. He hovered over her and entered her slowly. Claude liked to get her into the "L" position where one leg was bent to the side and her other leg was pointed straight up. The angle of that position always seemed to hit the spot just enough to send Venus's sounds of ecstasy into repeated revving resonance. Claude then knew it would be his turn to reach his climax.

But Venus was sure he noticed that the lubricating came far and few between lately. This particular night, it did not come at all. Maybe Claude was too into the moment to notice that Venus was totally dry. As he moved her leg back even farther, she caught a faint glimpse of something, or someone, lying on their leopard lounge chair to the left of their black granite poster bed. Venus closed her eyes and refocused, realizing the image was even clearer. Venus felt Claude's pounding and repeated penetration hitting her very soul. She could hear him sigh, but all was a blur, all except the sultry, frozen image of her best friend, Fatima, watching them make love. Venus's breathing pattern increased and she shut her lids until it was over. Before she could even fake her usual orgasm, Claude released inside of her. She opened her eyes and the image was gone. Venus lay still while he turned over and collapsed.

Thirty minutes later, Venus moaned in her sleep, tossing her head back and forth, but Claude was too knocked out to notice. Venus jumped straight up in the bed and threw her eyes open as if in horror. Sweat beaded from her forehead. Her honey-colored hair was soaking wet. She placed her fisted hands deep into the mattress, almost in anger. Venus glanced over at Claude as he lay on his stomach. His face was toward hers as she watched him sleep. Venus closed her eyes and took a deep breath, feeling a jittering motion in her stomach. She started to gag and swallow at the same time. The swallowing reflex caused her to gag again, and she sprang to her feet, running into the bathroom where she stood over the ebony commode and threw up.

She fell to her knees, waiting for the next violent expulsion. But it never came. Venus sat on the gray tile floor with her back to the wall, wiping her mouth with tissue paper.

*What did I do?* she asked herself. *Why in the hell did I agree to this?*

The night before Mason was set to come home, he sat in his hotel room after losing the tournament in Florida. A young, unknown golfer won at twelve under par. Mason felt like he'd totally lost his focus. He was disappointed in himself. *Did he use the right club?* he wondered. Would that have made a difference on the seventh hole? He switched his attention from his golf bag to the minibar. He looked around for his room key. Next to his key was the hotel phone. He made a phone call instead.

"What are you wearing?" he asked.

"That's so corny."

"No, really, I want to know."

"All right, I'm wearing a white baby doll."

"Describe it," Mason prompted, lifting his rear to make room for him to pull his gray boxers down to his knees.

"It's a sheer, short, sexy number."

Mason used his right hand to stroke his stiffened wand. "What are you wearing under it?"

"Nothing," she whispered.

"Do you like the way you look in it?"

"Yes."

"What do you think I would do if I saw you in it?"

"You would probably start kissing my hard, pink nipples through the sheer lace fabric."

"And flick your nipple with my tongue."

"Yes, and then you'd pull my arm through the sleeve so you could taste my breasts. First one sleeve and then the other."

"And then?" Mason asked with his eyes closed.

"And then you'd stand me up to let my nightgown fall to the floor and you'd stand back and stare at my firm, trim body while I'd watch your nature rise through your shorts. You'd take them off, standing at attention at the sight of me, just waiting to get in my body."

His hand stroke quickened. "Oh yes, and then."

"And then I would raise my right arm upward to the ceiling, rubbing my own breasts as you approached. You know how much I like it when you lick my armpit, right?"

"I know that drives you crazy."

"And then you would insert three fingers inside of me just to see if the licking under my arm was working. I'd get so hot that I'd beg you to lay me down on my back and try your best to insert your entire hand inside of me until we were only able to see your wrist as you stroked me with your fist."

Mason had to slow himself down. He took a deep breath and then resumed. "Oh, now you're talking. When do I get to put my dick inside of you?"

"When I remove your hand and lick my own juices from your fingers, only to beg you to turn me over and enter me from behind."

"Then I can put it in?"

"Only after you kiss my back, gently with your hot tongue and then kiss the nape of my neck with your thick, sexy lips. I'd poke my rear end toward you and slowly raise my leg to assist your entry."

He felt sweat building over his eyebrows. "Do I get to push into you while I'm up against your round ass?"

"Yes, you'd find your way into my body, feeling the thrust of my swollen ass bumping up against your stomach and thighs. You'd push yourself deeper and deeper while I grab hold of the pillow with one hand, bracing myself along the edge of the bed to secure my place."

His imagination grew more and more colorful. "Am I grabbing your titties from underneath you?"

"Yes, your hand is squeezing them, feeling them bounce as you reach around to hug me along my waist and I feel your pulsating penis about to let go."

"Am I pounding you like you've been a bad girl?"

"Yes, like I've been a very bad girl. And then I lower my torso so that you can get all the way inside." Her breathing started to get shorter and shorter. Her moans accompanied his next question.

"I pull your hair from the back as you look upward toward the headboard, screaming for me to hit it harder and harder, right?"

"Yes. And you pull my hair so hard that I scream."

"Let me hear how that pussy sounds right now."

She put the phone to her wetter than wet opening and inserted her middle finger, letting him hear the sweet sounds of the moistness he'd created.

She returned the phone to her ear. "Do you like that," she asked.

He was deep into the moment. "That sounds so good. Now I want you to picture me in there, banging you into the mattress, plummeting you with my stiff dick. I feel your juices run like a river while you squeal for me to keep going."

She agreed, "Yes, just like that, just like that."

"And then just as I get a glimpse of you in the dresser mirror, I spank you so loudly and so hard that you scream again."

"You slap me again and I scream again and again. I get so excited that I reach back to slap my own ass and you demand that I do it again and again."

Mason put the phone between his chin and chest and started squeezing his left nipple with this left hand, focusing the thumb of his right hand back and forth over the tip of his hard rock. "And just when I grab your cheeks as they spill in between my fingers, bouncing up and down to accompany my stroke, I feel my blood start to flow with more and more force. The flow starts to rush up my thighs, to my hips, to my ass, and all through my dick as I yell, shit, I'm coming, and shoot my cum deep inside of you. Just like that baby, just like that." Mason slowed his words as he opened his eyes, looking down to find his own juices spewing over his fingers.

He panted deeply as he asked, "That was good, girl. Was it good for you?"

"It was really good for me, honey," she said as though she was totally satisfied, too.

"Good night." Mason told her.

"Sleep tight, Mace," she said to a click.

The next Sunday, Mason returned home from Orlando and was bombarded by meetings. He also had an appearance that took up half the day. He decided to take a nap before dinner was served.

Mercedes and Venus sat in the backyard on the wrought iron chairs, overlooking the beautiful surroundings. It was time to spend that quality time with each other that Mercedes had mentioned at the mall. The conversation became real and honest.

"Venus, you cannot possibly think that this family feels indifferent toward you for marrying Claude."

"I think they resent me for marrying my dead friend's man, yes."

"I can tell you that I do not. That's for sure."

Venus crossed her legs toward Mercedes. "Yes, Mercedes, but you can't speak for your husband, or even my stepson. I always feel like the black sheep tramp of the family. Before I knew it, Claude and I were in Vegas saying I do."

"I think you and Claude have a great marriage. Maybe Fatima and Claude never got married for a reason. We all know she was into her own thing."

"Don't I know it. Fatima was an only child. Her mother was on welfare and had trouble trying to support the two of them. When Fatima was in middle school, she found out that her birth mother was selling her body to put food on the table. And her mom was doing it right in front of Fatima's face. Sometimes with Fatima right in the same room of their single apartment. She'd pretend to be sleeping when a strange man would crawl right into her mother's bed. She'd wake up the next morning and her mother would hand her a few bucks for lunch. She hated spending that money, and eating the food, and wearing the clothes that her mom's Johns provided. It really screwed her up at a time in her life when she was very impressionable. She almost dropped out of school after one night, while her mother was sleeping, one of her mom's tricks tried to climb in bed with Fatima but she whacked the hell out of him and ran out the door, never looking back. She ended up living with her birth father who had remarried. Those are Cameron's grandparents who are so supportive of him now. He tried his best to get her back on track. She lost touch with her mother after a while. Her mom didn't even come to Fatima's funeral."

"Dang, I never knew that."

"I grew up down the street from Fatima. I'd let her come and stay with me and my mom and dad. That was until my mom left my dad for another man right after I graduated from college. Even in my early twenties, it turned my life around so badly. I vowed to never, ever divorce once I got married."

"So you and Fatima had always been close, huh?"

"Oh yes. For a long time. My mother ended up moving to Chicago. I used to visit her more, before I got married. But her man and her, I mean my stepfather, never come out here to see me. My real dad has always been around though. He just refused to ever commit to a woman again. I sort of felt the same way about commitment. That's why I wasn't really in a serious relationship until I met Claude. But with him, it was like falling in love with a friend."

Mercedes had a lightbulb moment. "That explains a whole lot, Venus. Life is such a trip. What happens as a child really does relate to how we treat ourselves as adults. I mean, our parents' actions really do affect our adult relationships, don't they?"

"They seem to."

"And with Fatima going through all of that, it sort of explains the whole promiscuity thing. Women always complain about absent fathers, but it really hurts when a mother doesn't make a child the priority. Her mother didn't save her. I mean mothers are supposed to nurture and always be there. But at least Fatima grew to be close to her real dad. It seems like both of you had your dads around."

"We did."

"Do you ever feel bad for not being able to convince her to leave that crazy guy alone? The one who killed her."

Venus massaged her temples as she spoke. "I tried, Mercedes. I knew Owen was fucking crazy. But Fatima was so monogamous-phobic. She had to have variety. And it was like she was trying to protect him or something. She seemed so reluctant to really break it off one hundred percent. Maybe she had some deep dark fear of him really hurting her. He'd threaten her all the time. And he did it, just like he said he would."

"Just like he said he would? I remember you telling the police about that," said Mercedes. She was all ears.

"He told her if she ended it, he would end it for both of them."

"Dang. But Venus, tell me, why in the hell didn't she just go to the police herself?"

"Maybe because she just plain old didn't believe him. And I think it was because deep down, she really liked him. But not as a husband. She never wanted a husband. Just as a lover. Fatima was insatiable to say the least. From what she'd tell me, the two of them had crazy sex. I guess he really knew how to hit her spots."

"That's what those damn orgasms can do, impair your freakin' judgment. She must have been too tired to please Claude half the time."

"First of all, after she hooked up with Claude she didn't have to work so she had plenty of time on her hands. But I doubt that Fatima would have had trouble pleasing even four men. I'm sure her appetite allowed her to please both of them. It's just that Owen wanted more than she could give him."

"Venus, there must be so much pressure on you, being that you were the only one she ever really talked to about what was going on with her and other men. Especially what was going on with that psycho. But one thing you must keep reminding yourself is that what happened to them was all a part of their experiences in their lives. You could not have saved her if her day to die was Thanksgiving afternoon. Don't beat yourself up about it. It was God's will."

Venus rocked back and forth in her chair. "I beat myself up because I'm now the wife of the love of her life. She needs to be here with him, not me. She needs to be here raising her son, not me." She banged her forehead with the palm of her hand. "Why would she ask me to go ahead with something like this? And why did I agree? This all started that night she asked me to do her a favor. She asked me to share her man for a night."

Something nudged Venus's memory and she recounted what happened. She sat back and crossed her legs.

*I can picture Fatima stepping out of the Olympic-size pool in La Jolla like it was yesterday. I watched her sashay around in her rainbow string bikini as we walked inside to a private indoor area near the Jacuzzi and sauna.*

*"This is the life," she said, walking over to pour water over the hot rocks. She took such great care of herself and I know she enjoyed being the woman of a successful man like Claude. They each did their own thing and they never sat still. Not even for a minute.*

*She said to me, "Venus, you know what? I'm going to tell you something and I don't want you to get offended or feel shocked by it so I'm warning you, it's pretty wild."*

*"What?" I asked. By this time, all I was wearing was a green bath towel.*

*She admitted, "Sometimes, actually quite often, Claude and I fantasize about you in bed."*

*"Oh, thanks for telling me. That, I really don't need to know." I remember laughing nervously.*

*"True, but after all this time, I think I need to just throw this out there for you to swallow, or spit out."*

*"Okay." I waited.*

*"Claude's birthday is next week. Actually it falls on Thanksgiving day."*

*"And?"*

*"And, I thought it would be a great idea to ask you to be his present so to speak. You know, to ask you to be part of a ménage à trios so to speak."*

*"A threesome? Oh, I'm spitting that out for sure," I told her.*

*"Venus?" It was like she was begging.*

*"With you and Claude?" I asked.*

*"Yes, with my Claude and me. I'm willing to share."*

*"Wow." I was awestruck.*

*"Venus, come on now, I think I know you pretty well after all these years. I know you're not the saint you try to pretend you are. You're nowhere near as curious as I am, but I know you think about certain things every now and then."*

*"Oh, you just know it, huh?"*

*"Venus, tell me you've never fantasized about being with another woman."*

*"Okay, I've never fantasized about being with another woman."*

*"Oh, can the act. I see the way you look at women when they walk by looking all good. You always turn around for a second look."*

*I explained the difference. "That's just women checking out women, making sure they don't have more than we do. That doesn't mean I want to lick them."*

*"Well, I get hit on so much that I think I must be giving off some type of gay-dar or something. But I don't feel gay. I just feel curious. A lot."*

*"Well, that's you. I know I'm not gay, that's for sure."*

*"So, you think you have to be gay to be with a person of the same sex?"*

*"Duh, I think so."*

*"I don't." She was dead serious.*

*"Well, we differ on that. I can't imagine going down on any woman. That's nasty."*

*"How about if they went down on you? How could that be any different from it being a man? It might even be better."*

*"Because the woman would still have a vagina between her legs when she was done, that's how. Then what?"*

*"See, that's when women like you need a man around to finish off the job. That way you can get licked by a woman and fucked by a man. No harm, no foul." She amazed me with her openness.*

*"Foul, it is. I'm not even into that."*

*"How do you know?" She leaned in closer. "Claude is six foot four all over," she sang like a tease as if it would titillate and make a difference.*

*"Whatever. I just know."*

*"Venus, try it with us. Just this once. Please. If you don't want me to touch you, I won't."*

*"Fatima."*

*"I'm serious. I just want to watch Claude fulfill his fantasy."*

*"That doesn't threaten you?"*

*"Not in the least. If anything it just helps to spice things up," she said. "It's not like you're seeing anyone who would mind."*

*"Thanks for reminding me. But, what if he seems like he's enjoying himself a little too much?"*

*"That's the point. Would you want your man to not enjoy himself?"*

*"You trust Claude that much?"*

*"I trust you that much. I can't think of another woman I would rather share a special evening with like that than you."*

*"Have you two done this before?" I just had to ask, because Fatima had never mentioned it to me before.*

*"Once before, in Vegas. We hired one of those girls who came to our room and did me. He just watches. Okay, twice before. But this is his birthday. His special day. You will have fun, I guarantee you, girl. Come on, lighten up," Fatima said. She even reached over to hold my hand.*

*I pulled my hand away and folded my arms along my waist. And then I asked a dumb question. "What if I like it?"*

*"You are so damn stupid. If you like it, we keep on doing it. If you don't we won't."*

*"That kind of thing can ruin a friendship."*

*"Trust me. It won't." She gave a half smirk. "Venus, I love you so much that I know I can trust you with my man for one night. Even if something ever happened to me I'd trust you to be someone he could turn to. Actually, I would want the two of you to be together. That way, I'd know what he was getting. You love me and you'd love him, I just know it."*

*I had to ask her to clarify that statement. "You mean, you wouldn't mind if your best friend got with your man if you died. That's creepy."*

*She still went on to explain. "What better person to share your man with? Someone who you know is loving and trustworthy and caring. And Cameron loves you to death."*

*"Let's not even talk about that. You're not going anywhere," I told her. Little did I know her fate.*

*She still insisted on continuing on about her wish. "Venus, let's get real. You know how crazy Owen's ass has been talking lately. I'm just going to say this. If something were to ever happen to me, I would want you to look after my Cameron and Claude like they were your own. Promise me."*

*And then I actually helped her to underestimate what Owen was capable of. "Owen isn't going to do anything to you. He just talks shit. But you really need to leave his dumb ass alone."*

*"Girl, just promise me?"*

*I just wanted to shut her up. "Fine, Fatima, I promise to be with Claude if you die. How's that? He probably wouldn't even want my ass after being with your open-minded self."*

*"Yeah, right. Good, so we have two deals. One for next week, and one for . . . well. Let's just call it the* if *deal," she said.*

*"The* if *deal. Yeah right. Hopefully, I'll be married and have a man of my own one day. And I sure as hell won't share him. I want babies too you know."*

*She actually kidded about it. "This way, you'd have an instant family."*

*I was not amused. "Fatima, stop."*

*"And I saw you checking out my titties through my bikini top. You're going to have a ball."*

*I was in denial, but she did make me laugh. I swatted her back with my hand. "I did not. They're so damn big it's just hard to miss them."*

*"We're going to get you out of that closet yet. That's a promise." Fatima was a damn fool, that's for sure.*

Venus snapped back into reality. "I miss her."

Mercedes gave her sister-in-law a direct look, with her jaw slightly dropped and her eyes fully expanded. She caught herself and gave a quick blink, snapping back from Venus's story. "Wow. All this time I had no idea."

Her shock was apparent to Venus. "You know what, Mercedes? I know all of that sounds weird."

Mercedes played it off. "No, it just comes as a surprise, that's all."

"And Mercedes, I'm not gay. I was just curious. I felt safe with Fatima."

Mercedes put her hand up. "I didn't say a word."

Venus glanced up toward the sky. "It's haunting sometimes, Mercedes. I made a decision to go forward with that evening. But one thing that Claude never did was touch me. We just did it for him. And then I ended up going forward with my other promise."

"Yes, you did. And you lived up to it. I guess one shouldn't knock others for what they do. Unless you're put in that situation, you really cannot judge anyone."

Venus seemed to be in a daze, as though she no longer heard Mercedes's response. She fiddled with the gold bangle on her wrist. "At times, I can still smell her scent. She had this earthy, Egyptian musk oil she'd wear morning, noon, and night. I think it kind of seeped into her brown skin like maple syrup in a pancake. I smell it in the house, in our bed, in her car, on the towels, even on Claude sometimes. It's the weirdest thing."

Mercedes still could not hide her taken aback look, but seemed understanding. "Wow, girl, that's pretty deep. I'm sorry you're having a hard time. The two of you just need to get away and talk this out. I know Claude doesn't have any regrets, not about marrying you anyway."

"Mercedes, you know he misses her. He won't admit it but, I'm not even sure he sees me as someone he loves. I think since I'm the next best thing, he tolerates me. And I think he feels comfort in knowing that I knew her so well, unlike anyone else. I think it was easier for him to marry me than to start dating and looking for a new woman. But I know he's not happy."

Mercedes's supportive, understanding nature shifted into fifth gear. "I agree that he hasn't been the same since she died. I also think that Claude's not happy with himself, or with me and Mason more than anything. He just wants his way with his mom. That's the only dilemma I think he's been working through right now. But now that she's living with you two he should be a little more satisfied."

"I hope you're right."

"You two need to just drive down to Laguna Niguel or San Diego and stay in a hotel for the weekend. If Claude is cool with it, I'll watch Mattie and Cameron. Just do something to get this whole thing out and discussed. Especially so that your relationship with Cameron can heal. Maybe even take him along. But to be honest with you, I don't think Cameron would have liked any woman his dad ended up with."

"I'm not so sure. I think he just despises me because I was like his auntie before. Plus, I know that every time he looks at me he sees his mom. He's going through a hell of a time."

"He'll be fine, Venus. A lot of kids hate who their mom or dad marries. And I'm sure he's going through puberty, you know. That's the real trip."

Venus mustered up a smile. "That gangly boy is growing like a weed, isn't he?"

Mercedes returned with a smile of her own. "Tall and thin just like his mom."

Rashaad, with a basketball under his arm, entered the backyard with Cameron, running until they stopped just next to Mercedes's side of the patio table.

"Speaking of," Mercedes said.

"Mom, can we walk up to the park and shoot hoops for an hour?" Rashaad asked.

"Sure, baby." Mercedes glanced at her watch. "Be back by six-thirty though so we can eat, okay."

Rashaad hugged her. "Okay. Bye, Mom. Bye, Auntie Venus."

"Bye."

"Bye, Aunt Mercedes," said Cameron. The two ran out the side gate from the yard, exiting to the sounds of a dribbling basketball.

Venus glanced at Mercedes as if to prove her point. "Enough said."

"Shoot, girl. You guys had better get that boy straight. I should have told him to ask you."

"No. It was up to him to ask. It's cool that you gave them permission. I'm almost oblivious to his disses. It's like I'm invisible."

"One day, he's going to do something that will get on your very last nerve and you're going to go straight off on that boy."

"Yeah, well, in the meantime, I'll let his dad check him."

"Oh, no. You will surprise him one day. I can see it coming. I say you belt that little nigga in his belly and make him respect you." Mercedes laughed.

Venus denied it. "Oh, no, I would never hurt that boy."

"So you run around being hurt and disrespected instead, huh? Wake up, Venus. You need to put your foot down."

"Thanks. Who knows what will need to happen to make him come around. Maybe one day he just will."

After dinner, Rashaad approached his dad who had made his way to the living room sofa. "Dad, can Cameron spend the night after we go to a movie, please?" Cameron walked out of the kitchen with Star.

Mason replied, "Sure son. Make sure it's okay with Venus though."

"Thanks, Dad," Rashaad said.

Cameron remarked to Rashaad, "I'll call my dad and ask him."

Venus and Mercedes joined Mason and Star in the living room.

"So Claude is keeping an eye on Mom, huh?" Mason asked Venus.

"Yes. I think maybe I'll make dinner next time if it's okay," Venus said.

"Fine with me," Mercedes replied.

"Me too," Mason agreed without making eye contact.

Star snuggled into the sofa, hugging a yellow throw pillow. She stopped her channel surfing at an episode of *Friends*.

"Hey, Star. How about an after dinner song?" Mercedes suggested.

"Oh, Mom. I'm stuffed, I can't move anything, even my fingers."

"Oh, Star," Mercedes urged, "come on and play that new song you learned last week in school."

"Which song was that?" asked Mason.

"It was the 'Toreador Song' from the movie Carmen Jones, wasn't it?" Mercedes said.

"I love that song, please play it for us," said Venus, who could sense her reluctance. "If not now then later, okay?"

Mason told her, "Girl, you know you need the practice. Get on over there and play that piano. All of those lessons you've had. One day you're going to beg people to come and hear you play."

"Hopefully she'll have a full house. Go ahead, baby. It'll just take a minute," said Mercedes.

"Oh, okay, Mom." Star strolled over to the piano with her head hung low. She pulled out the seat to the white upright and positioned herself smack dab in the middle. She cracked her long fingers and looked down to view the position of her feet over the pedals. Star placed her fingers in position, took a nice deep breath and then began to play.

Mercedes, Mason, and Venus sat in complete silence, absorbing every keystroke and each sway of Star's shoulders. She moved along with the melody as if she were one with the piano. Star swayed left to right, hitting high notes and low notes, looking like she was part of a symphony at the Hollywood Bowl. Her gift was obvious, yet perhaps unappreciated in her own eyes. But to those on the outside looking in, this was a gift from God, the essence of one making use of talents and abilities sent straight from above. Her skill could not be denied. Star had a true future as a professional pianist.

Star finished the last few notes with a good, strong pounding of the keys. She immediately stood up and headed straight to her room.

"Hold on, baby," Mason said as the family began to clap. "You must give your audience a chance to show their appreciation for your hard work. It is only right that you turn to them and bow."

Star stopped with her back to the applause. "Daddy, it's been a long time since you've heard me play, huh?"

"Yes, it has and you've improved so much. That was perfect, baby girl."

"Thanks," she said, turning around with a fake smile, looking at her mom and Aunt Venus. She proceeded to her room with her mom on her heels.

"What's wrong with you?" Mercedes closed the door.

Star threw herself down on the bed. "Daddy acts like he's the reason I'm so good."

"No, he doesn't. He just wanted you to enjoy the accolades."

"No, that's his style. He has no idea how I got so good because he's never around. Now he's going to try to teach me to stand around and take in the fake attention like he does."

"Star. Your dad gets that attention all right, but that's part of his profession."

Star sounded like she wanted to cry. "I'm not doing this for appreciation from the outside. I do it for my own satisfaction. It's an escape for me. It just felt weird playing for him, or playing for anyone. I don't mind when I'm with my teacher, or around you. But Mom, please don't make me do that again."

Mercedes sat next to her and gave a one-armed hug. "I'm sorry, honey. I didn't realize you felt that way. But if you want to make a living at playing the piano, you're going to have to get used to playing in front of groups of people. Those are the people who are going to pay to hear you play. Those are the people who will determine how much money you make depending upon their demand for your music."

Star stood up and looked up at the ceiling. She didn't shed a tear. "I don't want to do this professionally. I do it because I've been playing since I was three. Because Grammy taught me and it was fun then. Now it's not."

"Are you saying you want to stop playing, Star?"

She took a step toward her mom and gave an eye lock. "I want to go away to college, to Spellman or Howard. I want the piano to get me there. I want a scholarship."

"Even if that doesn't happen, you know you will go to college. Your grades are excellent and you know the money is never going to be a problem."

"I don't want Daddy to pay for me to go. I want to earn my way."

"Star, now come on. I thought you wanted a scholarship to the Shepard School of Music at Rice University. You said you wanted a Doctor of Music Arts degree. At least that's what you told your music teacher last year."

Star sat back down next to her mom. "Mom, I told her that because I want them to help me get offers. I want to be a clothing designer like you were."

Rashaad yelled from the hallway. "Mom, we're about to leave now. Venus is taking us to the movies and then we're coming back home."

"Why isn't your dad taking you?"

"He said he'd be right back."

"See how he is," Star said, leaning back and hugging a large stuffed animal. "And I miss Grammy already."

"I'll ride with you guys," Mercedes yelled to her son. "Star, we'll talk about all of this later."

"No problem, Mom. I've got a good three years before I graduate."

"Stop it." Mercedes stood up. "Star, you start thinking about whether or not you're really set on what you say you want to do. When I was your age, my plans changed every month. I'm behind you in whatever you choose. We'll give you guidance, but it's your life, baby. I'll be back in a minute."

"Okay, Mom."

"Bye, Star," Cameron and Rashaad yelled together.

"Bye," Star yelled back.

Mercedes met up with the boys in the hallway. "What was that all about, Mom?"

"Just go on ahead. And who said you could go to the movies?"

"Dad did."

"Then he should have taken you," Mercedes said, walking ahead of the boys.

Mercedes called Mason on his cell and told him to pick up the boys at 10:45 from the Magic Johnson's theatres in Baldwin Hills. By the time the fellas all got home, Mercedes was in her office, surfing the net and answering e-mails. Mason went into the study to talk on his cell phone. The boys chilled in Rashaad's room, which was filled with Lakers memorabilia, lava lamps, and black light posters.

Cameron looked around the room before picking up the video game control. "This house kind of reminds me of my mom. I think because this was the last place she was alive."

"I wondered about that. It doesn't bug you to be here?"

"No, it's cool. I'm not trippin' off of that."

Rashaad gave a look as though be wasn't buying his cousin's answer. "Man, what's up with you and your stepmom? You two just don't talk or what?" Rashaad asked Cameron as he turned on the Madden game.

"She's not my stepmother. She's just my dad's wife."

"I thought you two had it cooler than that."

"She doesn't feel like a mom to me. No one can ever replace my mom." Cameron pressed the buttons of the controller to set up his team.

"I'm glad I don't know what it's like to have to deal with a new mom or dad. It's bad enough just dealing with the ones I've got."

"You're lucky. You live with both of your real parents."

"Do you ever hear from your real dad?"

"Man, I never even met him."

"Do you look like him?"

"I don't know. I've never even seen a picture, dude. I think I look like my mom."

"Did he just not even try or what?"

"Mom told me he spent some time in jail for grabbin' her and then when he got out, my mom said she had to relocate so that no one knew where we were. We got a place and it seemed like Mom worked all day and night while I had this baby-sitter named Puddin'."

"Puddin'?"

"Weird name, huh?"

"Man, that's what my dad calls Star. She hates it."

"I hated her. But then after a while Venus started coming around and staying with me while my Mom worked."

"You've known Auntie Venus that long?" Rashaad asked.

"Yeah, my whole life. I still can't believe you call her Auntie."

"She is my auntie. Was she cool back then?"

Cameron explained, "She was always cool until Mom died. Since then, she's been smothering me and treating me like a baby. And then for her to marry my dad was too crazy, man."

"When did you meet Uncle Claude?"

"I was little, man," Cameron stopped for a second, putting extra energy into scoring a touchdown. "Now what, dog?" he taunted his cousin. "But, it's been about maybe ten years or so. Me and my mom, we were always hanging out, just the two of us. We'd go for ice cream every day, sing in the car, and play checkers before bed. We had our little routines. I know she had it kinda hard because she was struggling with trying to keep a job back then. We moved a lot and I changed schools all the time. But Claude took us in and we moved into his big house. We had fancy cars, designer clothes, food, and video games. And we traveled all the time. He moved my mom and me from the ghetto to Ladera like it was nothin'. It was like I'd died and gone to heaven."

Rashaad warned, "I'm 'bout to score again real quick. Has he always felt like a dad to you?"

"Always, I can't imagine having any other father."

"What would you do if your father showed up out of the blue?"

"I'd tell him to get to steppin'. He hasn't been a father to me in all this time."

"Don't you feel like telling Auntie Venus that sometimes. To get lost, I mean?"

"Not really. I just wish sometimes she'd back off and just be my dad's woman, not my mom. I don't need a mom."

"If that's the way you feel, it's cool." Rashaad stopped playing for a minute, pressing PAUSE. "Hey, isn't my mom's friend Sequoia fine, dog?" He put his hand up for a high-five from Cameron.

Cameron slapped him back immediately and then gave him a look. "I've noticed. But, aren't you a little young to be checking out grown women?"

"Don't tell me it's cool for you and not me. You're only a little bit older than me," Rashaad said.

"No, I ain't mad at you, though. She's got a big old ham hock booty, huh?"

"A big old juicy booty." They both laughed and resumed playing.

Mercedes yelled from the room next door, "Rashaad, when are you two going to go to bed?"

Rashaad froze as he replied. "Soon, Mom. But there's no school tomorrow because of faculty meetings."

"Still, you need to go to bed. All I hear are your deep teenage voices in there. I'll give you until midnight. I think that's enough."

"Okay Mom," Rashaad laughed under his breath, bumping Cameron with his elbow.

"Good night, you two," Mercedes said.

"Good night," they replied.

Cameron asked. "Do you think she heard us, dog?"

"Please, my mom? If she did, she'd have been in here so fast."

They resumed again, speaking lower.

"But yeah, Sequoia is a hottie. How come she couldn't be my stepmom?" Cameron asked.

"Even Colette is a serious honey, too," said Rashaad, with a gleam in his eyes. "She could be my auntie any day."

"Uncle Torino, oh, he's always getting the ladies. How'd he get so lucky? He's all old and stuff."

"He's not as old as my dad," Rashaad said.

Mercedes's voice bounced off of the wall and into Rashaad's ears. "Rashaad, make that eleven thirty with your loud mouths."

Rashaad looked stunned, like he thought she'd gone into her bedroom.

Cameron whispered to him, "She's still right next door, man."

She spoke again. "Change the subject and tone it down."

Cameron looked at Rashaad with his mouth open.

"Yes, Auntie Mercedes," said Cameron, speaking for his cousin. "Just one more game and then let's go to sleep," he suggested. Mercedes's footsteps could be heard walking out of her office and down the hall.

Rashaad spoke low. "That's bound to come up again. My bootie is grass. I say we do it now." He turned off the game and the boys called it a night.

# chapter 9

It was time for Mason's big night at his club. Everyone was dressed to the hilt and ready for an evening of fun, dancing, and celebrating.

"I see Claude decided to get himself out of the house tonight, huh?" Mercedes asked Venus. Mercedes wore a knee-length jersey dress. They were seated at a private bar table.

"Yeah, he was actually acting like he was looking forward to the celebration with his brothers. He's really so proud of Mason."

"Who's with Mamma?" Mercedes asked.

"Cameron. He's good at keeping an eye on her. But she's really been keeping to her room and staying out of places where she can get into trouble."

"That's good."

Suddenly, Colette walked up sporting a black halter cat suit. Venus spoke first. "Hey, Colette."

"Hey, I really thought you and your husband weren't going to be able to make it."

"Well, Claude had it on his calendar after all."

"I see," Colette said, looking over at Claude who was near the bar.

Mercedes looked over, too. "Claude looks especially handsome tonight."

"I shaved his head this morning. I just love doing that. It's such a turn on," Venus said with a smirk about as sexy as her mini-dress.

"Okay?" said Colette, sounding like Venus was simple. She

switched her sights to Mason, who was talking to one of the record producers. "Mercedes, your muscular man is a stud. He just rules the world right now."

"He's doing okay for himself."

Colette told Mercedes, "I think it's such a trip that every young girl and boy in the country wants to be just like Mason Wilson."

"Oh, Lord. I can't imagine that," Mercedes joked.

"Hey, baby." Torino came over and gave his woman a hug.

Colette responded. "Hey there, cutie. You sure have this place looking good." She rubbed the back of his neck.

"Well, when the owner gets honored, it's pretty serious. I don't want to miss a step. Hey, Mercedes. Hey, Venus. How's it going?"

"Just fine," Venus replied.

Mercedes hugged him. "I'm cool. You really do have this place together."

"I see you ladies are representing the Wilson men well," Torino complimented.

"Thank you," said Colette all by herself.

Sequoia approached. "Hey there you all. What's happening?"

"Hey, Sequoia," said Mercedes.

"What's up Torino?" asked Sequoia. Her low waist pants and cropped top matched her skin color exactly.

Torino looked surprised. "Oh, you're speaking to me tonight, huh?"

"I'm fine thanks," she said, being facetious.

Colette inquired, looking puzzled, "You two weren't speaking before?"

"No, he's tripping. Where's Kyle?" Sequoia asked.

Torino asked back. "Why?"

Sequoia explained. "I need to check with him about the guest list for Wednesday night, that's all."

"I'm the one who approves the guest list. Not Kyle."

"Well, approve me on that list with two of my girls. Please?"

"I'll think about it." He turned to face Colette.

"What's with the attitude, Torino?" asked Sequoia with a sour look.

Colette peered around her man. "What's with your attitude

with my guy, Sequoia? You're trippin' and then acting like he should do you a favor."

"Nobody was talking to you." Sequoia informed Colette.

"Well, I'm talking to you."

Torino turned to face Sequoia and blocked Colette with his back. "Cool it now. I've got you for Wednesday." He turned to Colette. "I'll be right back, baby. I see Cicely." He walked away without looking back.

"I'll come with you," said Colette, keeping one eye on Sequoia.

"Who made her his watchdog?" asked Sequoia as Colette switched away.

"Sequoia, ask yourself why you talk to him like that," said Mercedes.

Sequoia reached in her purse for a stick of Juicy Fruit. "Oh, he loves it. I've known that booty since I was in middle school. He can handle it. Want a stick?" she offered.

"No thanks. Maybe that's what you really want, is for him to handle it," said Venus. "Did you ever think of that?" Venus looked around to check for Claude's whereabouts.

"Yeah, right. That skinny little dude. I likes my men four inches taller than me and six inches wider. I'd hurt him."

"Please, Torino towers over you by a foot," Mercedes commented. "Either way, when Colette's around, nobody gets anywhere near Torino's butt. That girl is on him like white on rice."

"I noticed. When did that start?" asked Sequoia.

Mercedes glanced over at them. "I'm not sure. I don't remember her being like that before either. Maybe something happened to damage the trust, who knows."

Sequoia guessed. "Maybe she just knows what a dog he is."

"You don't know that," Mercedes replied.

"Oh, please. I see him up in here running his game in the name of promoting. That boy gets coochie like Oprah gets paid. And with Kyle by his side, they are double trouble."

"If you say so," said Mercedes.

"So where is the man of the hour anyway?" Sequoia asked, smacking the sweetness out of her gum.

Venus answered. "He's over there, surrounded by the cheerleader-looking women and the businessmen."

Mason peeked over the heads of a few of his guests and pointed at Mercedes, giving her a just-one-minute gesture.

Mercedes nodded to confirm. "He'll make his way over soon. He's just doing what's required of his profession—being sociable."

It was time for the emcee to speak to the club goers. "Ladies and gentlemen, please welcome me in honoring a man who is gifted beyond imagination. A man who excels in a sport rarely thought of as one that African-Americans could or would succeed in. He has, to say the least, succeeded.

"Mason Wilson started his life in Houston, Texas, living in a rural area surrounded by acres upon acres of land. His dad took him out into the fields where he practiced putting with a baseball bat and tennis ball. When his family moved to Los Angeles, Mason asked his father if he would take him to the driving range to hit some balls. After five or so buckets, his dad was tired, but Mason was not. Not being able to afford lessons at the time, his dad taught him all he knew. After a while, Mason was eating up the game of golf, and his dad had to admit that he did not know enough about the game to teach his son any longer. By the age of ten, Mason was playing eighteen holes like it was nothing, sometimes beating grown men."

Mason stood next to his wife looking humble.

The emcee continued, "One day, Earl Woods, Tiger Woods's own father, caught a few of Mason's strokes and suggested that he call one of his instructors to be evaluated. The result was that Mason Wilson had a gift. The fourteen-year-old dazzled the instructor, almost to the point of reminding him of the talents of little Tiger Woods at that time. The instructor contacted PGA scouts who tracked Mason's progress for the next five years.

"After graduating from high school on a golf scholarship, Mason attended the University of Southern California, where he met Mercedes, who he later married just as his career was starting to take off."

"Who wrote this bio?" Mason whispered to Mercedes. She grinned.

"For the next fifteen years, Mason Wilson set records and excelled at a level that stunned the golfing community. Even some who had downplayed Mason's potential as a minority golfer soon had to give it up to him and his A-class game. Mason has won just about every title there is and he's still going strong.

"Children of all ages, races, and faiths know of Mason Wilson's accomplishments and his motto of striving for greatness. Mason speaks at schools and churches and is a true example of a man who has made it, against all odds, with determination, practice and focus. Mason Wilson lets all of us know that whatever our skills in life, goals in life or trials in life, we can make it with determination as long as we have faith and we believe. His hard work has paid off and we want to thank him for showing us that we, too, can excel with hard work. Mason Wilson, the African-American Role Models Association would like to honor you with our humanitarian award in the field of athletics. Mason Wilson, we present you with the Arthur Ashe award of excellence."

"Finally," Mason said out of the corner of his mouth.

The club members clapped and whistled as Mason approached the stage. The head of the AARM Association gave Mason the twelve-inch statue of Arthur Ashe and handed him the microphone.

Mason looked it over, and then put his mouth to the microphone. "Wow, who is that man you speak of? I'd like to meet him." The crowd laughed. "I'd like to thank the AARM Association for this honor. It has been a long road, and yes it has taken a ton of faith to stay on this road. But I could not have done it alone. As for my parents, I pray that all young people have a special parent or parents that they can look up to. I thank Jesse and Mattie Wilson for making me feel as though I was good enough to be somebody. They took the time to teach me and encourage me and love me and I appreciate that. To my dad, who is looking down from heaven not only now, but every time I step onto the fairway. Thanks, Dad. Everywhere I go, I take a piece of you with me.

"And to my brothers, Claude and Torino Wilson, who are here

tonight, thanks for the love," Mason said, nodding to them. "They are my best friends and confidants. There is nothing like the bloodline that exists between family. I'd do anything for you two." His brothers nodded back.

"And last but surely not least, to my beautiful wife, Mercedes. None of this would have been possible without you. You stood by me, forgave me, loved me, inspired me, had my babies, Rashaad and Star who I love so much. And you had my back so many times I can't even count. Thanks, baby, for standing by my side no matter what. And I do mean no matter what."

Mercedes blushed and blew him a kiss.

"Now I say we get this party started and fill these walls with the sounds that this club was built for: partying. Thanks again, everyone, and thanks to my fans. Good night." The crowd put their hands together and showed their love as he handed over the microphone.

"Shake it Fast" by Mystikal started to play just as Mason made his way off of the dance floor, with antsy couples exchanging places with him to get their groove on. Mason went over to his wife after shaking hands with a few more people.

Mercedes gave him a huge hug and kiss. "That was great, baby. Speaking of writing, when did you write that acceptance speech?"

"I didn't. I just said what was in my heart."

"Mason, that was wonderful," Cicely said, leaning into Mason's ear and grabbing onto his left arm.

"Yes, it was. Very nice speech," said a woman standing behind Cicely.

"Thanks, Heidi," Mason replied.

Heidi extended her hand, "I don't think we've met," she said to Mercedes. Heidi's tongue was pierced with a gold stud.

Heidi was no baby. She looked to be in her late thirties and was thick and curvy. She had a butterscotch complexion and long, Cherokee red hair, all one length that hung midway down her back. Her keen features and golden brown eyes added to her striking aura. Her ginger lips looked as though they were painted on with precision. Her previous coworkers at Ladera Realty called her

Miss Beverly Hills because she exuded such class. Some of them even teased her and called her Beverly. She'd say, "Miss Hills to you," just to play along.

Mason did the honors. "Baby, this is Heidi Hamilton, the realtor who works for Claude."

"Hi, nice to meet you," Mercedes replied. Mercedes put her hand behind Venus's back. "And this is my sister-in-law, Venus."

Heidi greeted her. "I know Venus. How have you been?"

"Fine, Heidi. Good to see you."

"Hello, Mercedes," said Cicely. "How's your mother-in-law doing?"

"She's fine. All of that drama over her getting lost is behind us now. Thanks again for all of your help."

"No problem. I'm just glad everything turned out okay. Mason still needs to come and get his briefcase. In all of the confusion, we forgot what you came over for in the first place. Well, we'll see you later. Have a great night. And Mason, save a dance for me, okay?" said Cicely, walking away in her conservative black pantsuit.

"I'll remember that."

"Nice to finally meet you, Mercedes," said Heidi, following Cicely wearing all white.

"And you as well," Mercedes said.

Heidi turned back, remembering Mason, "Good-bye, Mace."

Mercedes watched her walk away.

Heidi seemed to follow Cicely's every move, allowing her to lead the way tonight, walking behind her and peering over Cicely's head due to her own six-foot stature with heels. She nodded to each group of guests as though she'd rather be in the background. Yet, she managed to turn her head to check out the scene behind her and to each side, just to take in her surroundings.

"You never told me about her," Mercedes said to Mason. She looked at Venus. "And you either."

Venus replied, "She's just one of Claude's realtors at his office. I saw her at one of his office parties a couple of times."

In deep thought, Mercedes said, "She sure looks familiar. That's all I know."

* * *

Sequoia was seated at the bar chatting it up with one of the bartenders. Colette managed to find an available seat two bar stools to the right of her just as the bartender was bringing a small bottle of Bollinger champagne over to Sequoia.

"Ma'am, this is from the manager," he said, placing the ice-filled chrome bucket and a glass in front of her.

"Oh . . ." Sequoia began to say.

"From who?" asked Colette, banging her thick beer mug on the bar, springing to her feet and standing behind Sequoia's stool.

The male bartender spoke. "Excuse me, Colette. It's just a drink from Mr. Wilson."

"Where is he?" Colette looked around.

"He's right over there." The bartender pointed as Torino was coming around from the other side of the bar.

She yelled, "Torino, what is your problem? Buying her a bottle of champagne. What is that all about?"

"Colette, come with me." Torino forcefully took her by the arm.

"Ouch, let go of me, that hurts," she complained.

Torino tried to speak quietly. "Shut your mouth and come with me."

Colette looked back at Sequoia, pointing in her direction, "You'd better not drink that or your ass is mine."

Sequoia pulled the bottle from the ice bucket, poured the bubbly into her fluted glass and held up the glass in Colette's direction. And then Sequoia looked at Torino. For the first time, her eyes sparkled back at him. She then started a conversation with the bartender as if nothing ever happened.

Colette spoke within two inches of Torino's face. "I'm not going anywhere, Torino. That was so damn obvious it's not even funny. And you want to make it seem like I'm trippin'. That was disrespectful."

"Woman, it was no big damn deal. I just felt bad for being so abrupt with her earlier and it was a gesture of peace. But you had to blow it way out of proportion as usual."

"Please, you never send me a damn glass of water." She rubbed her upper arm where he'd grabbed her and made a pouty face.

"Colette, you know that you can have anything you want in this place. Everyone knows you. But you came up here tonight on my brother's big night just looking for a fight. I'm sorry but you can't start anything tonight. I'm not having it, Colette. Now go home." He pointed toward the door.

"No." She put her hands on her hips.

"Colette, I will have someone drive you if you've been drinking."

"Drinking? I haven't had a sip yet. But I'll start up in a minute. Besides, you can't just make me leave. Is this how you handle misunderstandings with your main woman and your peripheral ho'?"

"Peripheral?"

"You make the main one leave so you don't run off your safety net. Because I guess you think I'm so in love with you that I'll just forgive you and hang around, huh?"

"Forgive me for what?"

"For trying to kick me out tonight."

Torino looked around as he felt people's stares. "Fine, don't go. But if you so much as blink wrong, I will leave with you and then it will be on, do you understand me?"

"Oh, it's on now anyway. But I'm not even tripping over your triflin' ass ho'. Sequoia is not half the woman I am." She smacked her own self on the ass and stared him down.

"Colette, just find a seat and chill out. I'm about to go check on my family and make sure they're okay. And I've got some serious VIPs here tonight, rappers, producers, and investors. So don't blow it for me. Now can you please go somewhere and just chill out?"

"I will do just that, Torino. You just go do your work. But do me a favor. Don't buy another woman a drink while I'm here, please?"

"Just go, Colette." Torino walked away toward the VIP area and left her standing there.

Colette kept an eye on him for a minute and then she spotted Kyle chumming it up with Cicely and Heidi. "Yes, it's on all right."

* * *

Mercedes and Venus sat in a cozy VIP area on a leather sofa, eating appetizers and drinking Merlot.

"I haven't seen you drink in a while, Mercedes."

"I try not to. But tonight is a special night."

"That Mason is so damn fine, I can't stand it," a group of girls said walking away from Mason and his agent.

Mercedes continued talking to Venus. "So, I figure if I limit myself to a thousand calories per day . . ."

Venus interrupted. "Did you hear them?"

"Yes."

"And?"

"Venus, you know me better than that. Those young girls don't threaten me in the least. Mason gets that all the time."

"But after a while it has to wear on you," Venus said.

"No, after a while you start to get used to it. I used to be just like Colette when it came to Mason. Always wondering what he was doing and why the women in the mall were staring at my man. I don't have time for that. If he wanted to leave me, he'd have left a long time ago. The years make you more secure, not less secure. Especially those young and skinny ones. They don't even faze me." She took a sip of her wine with one hand and dipped a French fry into some catsup with the other. She then looked over at Heidi.

Venus spoke. "You deserve an award. No wonder he hasn't left you for anyone else."

"I spend more energy trying to make him happy and trying to support my black man. You know what I mean?"

"Yeah, girl. I support Claude all right. Maybe too much actually. I need to really get on him, though. He undermined my authority with Cameron the other night. Things won't get any better if Cameron thinks Claude and I aren't getting along."

Mercedes gave her the hush look as Claude walked up.

Venus had to ask, "Hey baby. Where have you been?"

"I was at the bar sipping on some orange juice and making my way around a bit. Hey, Mercedes. You look nice tonight," Claude commented.

"Thanks Claude. So do you. Nice suit."

"Thanks," he said, tugging on his lapel.

Mercedes asked, "I met your realtor, Heidi. Have I seen her before?"

Claude took a seat as Venus scooted over. "I'm not sure. She's been working at the office for a couple of years now. She's one of my top sellers."

"And how does she know Cicely?" Mercedes asked.

"She's Cicely's sister, I think."

"Oh, that's right. That's where I know her from. I saw her picture at Cicely's house."

Claude's eyes got slightly bigger, but not much. "At Cicely's house?"

"Yes, you know the day Mattie got lost. I was picking up Mason's briefcase from her house." Mercedes looked at Venus. "I can't believe she said that briefcase is still there. Mason said he was going back over there the same day to get it, remember?"

"I think so. Maybe he got sidetracked." Venus said.

"Obviously."

Venus bounced in her seat at the "Hot In Herre" cut by Nelly. "Come on, baby. Let's go cut a rug."

"Cut a rug? You're showing your age," Claude actually joked.

Mason walked up and grabbed Mercedes. "Come on, baby. Maybe we can do some of our stripper moves and confuse the hell out of them."

"Mason," Venus said, looking surprised that he would talk that way.

Mason and Mercedes left Claude and Venus behind.

The crowded dance floor was rumbling from the excited dancers simulating removing their clothes, "I am getting so hot, I wanna take my clothes off," yelled Mason.

Venus got up and joined in next to Mercedes and Mason, leaving Claude to sit and watch.

"Watch her," Claude yelled to Mason and Mercedes as he smirked a goofy grin.

And Torino walked over to the floor hand in hand with who else but sexy Sequoia as she yelled, "I think my butt's getting big, hey."

Torino was interrupted from his smooth dance moves by one of his bouncers. "Mr. Wilson, we have a problem at the door, sir."

He stopped in mid step. "What's up?"

"A few people seem to think they've already paid to get in."

"Paid when?"

The bouncer talked directly into Torino's ear. "The door man, Josh, can explain it to you better than I can, sir."

"Excuse me for a minute. I'll be right back," he said to Sequoia, who gave him an approving nod and joined in with Mason, Mercedes, and Venus.

Torino and his bouncer approached the front door in a hurry.

"Torino, these ladies seem to not want to pay the cover charge," said the lady at the cashier's window.

One lady with a Brooklyn accent got irritated. "Excuse me but, why are you talkin' for us? We're the ones who asked for the manager."

Torino's ticket girl remarked like she wanted to go off. "Torino, these chicks are trippin'."

"Trippin'? And who you callin' chicks? You need to see your way out of this," one of the other girls threatened.

"Hey, now calm down. There's no need to get heated. Step over here for a minute," Torino instructed them so the other patrons could pay. "What's going on?"

The third girl started to explain. "See, me and my girls came all the way up here from Orange County. That's about an hour or more drive time. And we're being treated like we're criminals trying to get away with something. We don't have to lie to get up in no club."

"Tell me what happened, please," Torino told them again.

"See, Roslyn here hooked everything up so that all we had to do was show up and give our names."

"Which list were you supposed to be on?"

"I think it was Kyle's list."

"Kyle only has a guest list authorizing before ten o'clock. It's already midnight so it would be full price, which is twenty-five dollars. Tonight is a special event, ma'am," Torino explained.

The first girl spoke again. "Twenty-five dollars, bunk that.

That's what Mr. Swole here tried to sell me." She pointed at the bouncer. "I'm not gonna party for just two hours for no twenty-five dollars."

"Wait a minute," the second lady said. "We already paid ten dollars in advance to get in here. That would be thirty-five dollars. I don't think so," she said, snapping her fingers.

Torino told them, "Sorry but we don't have advance ticket sales or any discounts like that."

The calm one continued, "I paid this guy thirty dollars for three people late last night at club Déjà Vu in Upland. He said our names would be on the list."

"What guy?"

"This Kyle guy. He was promoting and taking names all night."

Torino looked confused. "Kyle took cash from you?"

"Yeah, he did. I gave him a twenty and a ten," she said.

"And he promised to add you to the list?"

"Yeah."

"Did he give you a pass or a ticket stub?" Torino asked for clarification.

"No, just told us to show up. He said he was part owner."

Torino got the picture. "Ladies, I see what happened. Josh, go ahead and let them in and have Shannon hook them up in VIP with a bottle of champagne. I am so sorry you had to go through this. Please accept my apologies. Be my guest for the remainder of the evening if you would. And make sure they get their money back, too. The thirty dollars."

The first lady spoke again. "Cool. You'd better check brotha' with the green eyes, though. He's shady."

"I'll do that. Don't you worry about him. Enjoy yourselves and if you need anything, let me know."

"We'll do that," she said, cutting her eyes at the cashier.

Torino stepped back as Josh said to the ladies, "Come with me."

Kyle was near the food table in the VIP area, surrounded by two model-type babes.

Torino approached him. "Kyle, get over here."

"What's your problem? I'm busy in case you didn't notice."

"Now." Torino was firm.

Kyle excused himself and walked over with an attitude.

Kyle looked confused. "Dude, why you gonna front me like that in front of those honeys. What in the hell is wrong with you?"

"You. I can't believe you had the nerve to stab me in the back, bro," Torino said firmly.

Kyle backed up and threw his hands up. "How in the hell did I do that?"

"You charged for the VIP comps. What the hell do you think you're doing?"

"Look, Torino. I don't know what you're talking about. I'd never do anything like that. I just had maybe six people that I know on my early list. And even that's more than I usually have. I would never do that to you, dude. You know that."

"What did you do last night?" Torino asked suspiciously.

"I went out," Kyle answered like it was no big deal.

"Where?"

"Where I always go. To my spot in Upland."

Torino continued to inquire. "And were you promoting Foreplay?"

"No, man, I'm not gonna go up into another club and promote somebody else's gig anymore than I'd do that to you guys up in here."

"You didn't take ten dollars per head for a spot on my master list?" Torino asked.

Kyle seemed insulted. "Hell no, man. I can't believe you would even ask me this. Actually, it sounds like you're accusing me. What's up with that?"

"I'm basically telling you that it's not hard to believe, Kyle."

"What's hard to believe is that you would doubt my word, dog. Especially after all these years. Who the hell told you this crap?"

"Don't worry about it. I don't want you confronting anybody in here. I'll deal with you later." Torino started to walk away but Kyle put his hand on his shoulder. Torino stopped.

"Oh, so this person is here?"

Torino turned toward him again. "Don't worry about it."

"And I'll bet you let them in for free, right? You did that instead of calling me to the door, huh? Brother, you just got played. Somebody scammed your ass. You've been in the game too long for that." Kyle shook his head in disbelief.

"Kyle, I have seen it all, but this one seems very possible to believe. For them to pick the one person who has been newly assigned to the guest list. Why would somebody set you up like that?"

"You got set up, not me."

"You set yourself up. You're slippin', dude. You should have kept your list tighter than that and not left any names off. I noticed you've been rolling lately."

Torino finally raised his voice. "What are you trying to say?"

"I'm saying you need to break." The bouncer stood nearby and Torino motioned for him to step up. "Escort his ass on out of here."

Kyle turned toward the exit. "I'm gone. And get your hands off me," he said as the bouncer touched his elbow. "Torino, I've had you covered for too long for this."

"Don't get it twisted, I've had you covered. But no more." Torino watched as Kyle reached the door with the big, burly bodyguard on his heels. Kyle looked behind him most of the way, staring at Torino in disbelief. Torino stood silent, noticing a few people giving nosey stares. He headed back toward the DJ booth to get ready for the night's entertainment.

*There must be a full moon tonight.*

Torino got his mind right and made his introductions from the DJ booth.

"Tonight, at club Foreplay, I'd like to introduce the producers of RAM, Rapp All Mighty, Byron and Brice are you in the house? Please give them a hand."

Byron and Brice came onto the dance floor to greet Torino. Brice took the microphone.

"Thanks, big time brotha'. Tonight at club Foreplay, we'd like to debut one of our newest artists, Lady Di. The baddest female rapper in the nation. She's the youngest in our camp and she bites hard. In honor of Mason Wilson and his skills on the golf course, we translate that onto the field so to speak, as Lady Di will perform her debut release, "Playin' the Field." Ladies and gentlemen, please welcome Lady Di."

The beats heated up the surround sound speakers and the short, female rapper stepped up, pounding her petite feet with each sound of the base. She was barely five feet tall, dressed with saggy jeans showing her pink boxers with a hat to the back.

She yelled with a rough, deep raspy voice. "Yeah, y'all. I'm Lady Di and tonight we 'Playin' the Field.' "

*Can't be groovin' with no one-on-one,*
*Got to ball 'til the morning sun,*
*Need some lovin', thuggin', them and me,*
*I can't get down with no monogamy,*
*I'm playin' the field.*

Lady Di continued her rap as Mason tapped his foot and bobbed his head to the beat with a glass of pineapple juice in hand.

Mason noticed the semi-frown on Torino's face. "Lighten up, bro. You've done a great job tonight."

Torino stood by him not quite feeling the same vibe. "Thanks, man."

"Where's your girl? I only saw her from a distance one time all night." Mason looked around.

"Who knows? She's around here somewhere."

Mason patted him on the back and continued to groove. "Well, you hooked it up. Keep up the good work."

Torino took a moment to respond, nearly spilling out the goings-on about Kyle, but he stopped himself. "Thanks, man."

All of a sudden a guy walked by eyeing Mercedes as she stood next to Mason. By accident, the brother bumped into Torino.

"Excuse me, dude," he said to Torino. "There are some fine ass hotties in here tonight."

"No problem, man." Torino found a way to laugh for a second. "Hey, Mason. You'd better keep an eye on your lady in here. You never know."

"I got that. I'm not even worried," Mason said, taking a sip and admiring an oblivious Mercedes who bounced her head and waved her hands in the air.

# chapter 10

By the end of the evening, Mason and Claude and their ladies had gone home. Sequoia snuck out around the same time. Torino was so busy running around, he didn't notice when anyone left.

He asked Josh, "I wonder where Colette is, man. When did she leave?"

Josh was walking by to escort the female cashier to the back room. "She left a long time ago," he said.

"Oh, really?"

"Yeah, I saw here walk out during the rap show."

"Thanks."

"She's a trip," the cashier said as if she knew firsthand.

Torino caught a case of deafness.

Later, Torino drove across Centinela to head home, yet he made a right turn to cruise along La Tijera Boulevard. He did one of Colette's numbers, pulling up just in front of her duplex. He got out of his car and then stopped to make sure his eyes were not deceiving him. Parked just across the street was Kyle's new mustang. Torino stood against his own ride for a few minutes, and then turned to look upstairs toward her unit.

He dialed her number on his cell. "Colette, what's up?"

She was smug and matter-of-fact. "What's up with you?"

"I'm downstairs."

"And?"

"And, is this Kyle's car out here?"

"Torino, like you always tell me, please don't come by without calling again. I'd really appreciate it."

"Colette," he said with urgency as she hung up the phone.

Torino got back in his car and sat for a moment. He was surprised that his heart actually felt like it had skipped a beat. He even felt a little short of breath. Should he go up there, or bash in Kyle's windshield? Should he call back, or just sit there all night until Kyle left?

Looking out of his passenger window, he peered upstairs again. This time, the living room lights were out.

Torino screeched off, burning rubber. He headed toward Slauson. He stopped at the light, talking as if someone was in the car with him. "It's cool. I'm glad. She was a trip anyway, and now I know for sure that she's a ho', too. She and Kyle deserve each other." He backed up and then made a three-point turn, heading back toward Colette's apartment. He sped down the street behind Kyle's car, coming to an abrupt stop. He just barely tapped Kyle's rear bumper. The smell of burnt rubber was potent. Kyle's antitheft alarm went off, ringing in Torino's ears. Again, he looked over at the dark apartment just as the porch light came on. He took a deep breath and backed up just barely enough to pull around the mustang. He drove slowly down La Tijera, back toward his home.

"Hello, are you up?" he asked from his cell phone.

An awakened female replied. "Yes, did you just get off?"

"Yes."

She said softly, "You looked so handsome tonight. I saw you."

"Thanks."

"Why don't you come on by, baby? It's been a while. I'd love to see you."

Torino paused. "I'll be right over."

*Booty-call payback is a dog,* he said to himself, turning back down Centinela and onto Canterbury Drive in Fox Hills.

* * *

Torino arrived back home at ten in the morning. First, he stopped by the front house to talk to Mercedes who was in her office. He let himself in and went upstairs.

"Hey, hey, hey," he yelled as he walked in.

"Hey, there. I'm surprised to see you after the night you had last night." She gave him a look and then glanced back at her computer.

"What do you mean?"

"I mean being the host, getting everything handled so well. It all went off without a hitch."

"Yes, without a hitch." He plopped down onto the love seat.

"You look tired. Why don't you go back to sleep? Or did you even get to sleep? Isn't that the same shirt you had on last night?"

He returned her questions with a question. "You got any coffee?

She stood up, coming around, reaching out for his hand. "I'll make you a cup. Come on. Let's go into the kitchen."

Torino held her hand until they got downstairs. He took a seat at the kitchen table.

He asked, "How's Mom been?"

"She's fine. I miss her though."

"And where's my boy?"

Mercedes poured water into the top of the coffeemaker and slid the pot underneath. "Mason? He's gone for his morning walk."

"He's got more energy than I do. You'd think he was the youngest."

She took a seat. "He keeps spinning like a top all right. Was he always like that?"

"As far back as I can remember. He always had homework, practice, exercise, somewhere to go, and something to do. That's Mason for you."

"I think he'd rather die than slow down. He's an overachiever. But Claude is like that, too."

"I guess that's better than what I've got going on." Torino rubbed his eyes.

"Torino, I don't know what you mean by that. You're moving and shaking, too. And you have such a great way with people. You really should think about a job in public relations or marketing.

Or what about real estate like Claude?" Mercedes pulled out a box of chocolate donuts and put two on a small plate, placing it on the table.

"I hate real estate. There's no way I could do what he does. I'll just leave that up to the professionals. I don't wanna promote inanimate objects. I wanna promote real people. That's my strength."

"Like at the club? They swarm around you like bees to honey."

"I mean like being a record producer or maybe even owning my own club one day. Something that will bring in more money than managing my brother's club."

"I know Mason pays you pretty well," Mercedes said, standing by to prepare Torino's cup.

"Not well enough to buy my own home and get back on my feet. I've been saving but it's just not enough right now."

"It'll come. Everything in its own time. Just be patient."

"I will." Torino ate most of the donut with one bite.

"I noticed Colette wasn't being so patient about your charming ways last night, huh?"

He shook his head. "When is she ever? But that's history."

Mercedes asked like she knew better, "Are you sure? I've heard that before. And then next thing I know her car is in the driveway."

"Not this time. I'm ready to move on."

Mercedes poured the straight black coffee into a tall mug and placed it in front of Torino. "Do you want cream and sugar?" she asked.

"No. I need it just like this. Thanks," he said, taking the mug into both hands.

"So the night was that bad, huh?"

"The night wasn't too bad I guess. I learned a lot about her."

"She is a jealous one, I'll say that. She just wants you all to herself." Mercedes took a seat and picked up the other donut.

"Holding on that tight just caused her to lose out. I'm about ready to break out. You cruise, you lose, as they say."

"Sorry to hear that."

He ran his fingers though his dreads, scratching his scalp to chase an itch. "I'm *so* ready to move on, Sis, that I need Sequoia's phone number."

She started to take a bite and then stopped. "Sequoia?"

"Yes, Sequoia."

"You want to call her and tell her you're interested after all these years?"

After taking a sip, Torino replied sounding sarcastic. "That's what I'd do with the number."

"To like, ask her out?" Mercedes asked.

"Exactly. Very good."

Mercedes blew a long breath between her lips. She put the donut down. "I'm just shocked. You two have been at each other's throats ever since I met her."

"But she's all grown up now."

"Yes, but I thought you two got on each other's nerves nowadays."

"She's just been fighting the feeling."

"I was wondering why she always showed up at the club. I tease her about that."

"I kind of like the fact that she's always treated me like I had the plague. It's been a challenge. But last night, something was different," he admitted.

"Different how?"

"She was more . . . more responsive."

Mercedes chuckled. "Responsive to what?"

"To my glances, my smiles, my energy."

"Okay," Mercedes remarked like he might need to think twice.

"I mean it. Even after I sent her a drink and the cock-blocker intercepted my pass."

"That's funny. So you *were* trying to be shady, huh?"

Torino kind of grinned. "No, just sending an old friend a drink." He ate the last piece of the donut.

"Yeah, right. I see now. Well, I'll tell you what. How about if I have her call you?" Mercedes offered.

Torino looked betrayed, still chewing. "You don't trust me with her number? You don't think she'd want me to have it?"

"I have a feeling she'll be cool with it."

"So, you're being truer to your buddy than to family, huh?"

Mercedes replied. "Torino, that's not it. Look, no matter what the path is to get you two to talk, I think it will happen. She's ripe right now anyway."

"Meaning?"

"Meaning if you treat her right, like a lady, and play your cards right, you just might end up getting at least a date out of her."

Torino remarked, "I hope so because she seems different. These women out here are so quick to just hand over everything they've got. I guess there's a shortage of men, huh?"

"That's what I hear. I'm glad I've got mine," she said, finally taking a bite herself.

"Mason is the devoted one. Can't say that I blame him," Torino said, giving Mercedes the once-over.

Mercedes stood up, "Here, boy, take your coffee and go get some sleep. I'm about to take Star clothes shopping."

He stood up with his mug in hand. "And don't forget what your dear brother-in-law asked you."

"I won't. I'll make that call today. I promise."

"Thanks, Cedes. Isn't that what Mason calls you?" he asked, headed for the kitchen door.

She replied, "Yes. Tito."

"Damn, what's up with that? Okay, Mercedes. Have fun with Star."

"Thanks, Torino."

That Monday night, Mercedes met Sequoia at the popular, always crowded, two-story gym called Spectrum. Sequoia was serious about her workout even though the gym was known for men who were always on the make. Sequoia and Mercedes dressed down and dumpy just to remain unnoticed. They were not in the mood.

Mercedes looked around at the facility while working up a tiny sweat. She did not sweat easily though, so she must have been feeling it. "Thanks for having me as your guest. I really do need to join."

"Girl, you have more than enough exercise machines in your own home."

"Oh, I never go in that room. All of that stuff is in Mason's study that he rarely even uses. Plus I need to be motivated by having other folks around me. It's just the fitness-type energy you get from a gym."

Sequoia spoke from a treadmill beside her buddy. "Mercedes, you do not need to lose weight anyway. You have it going on in all the right places."

"I need to at least get in some cardio for a few minutes. I can't even walk up the stairs at home without breathing heavy. I can't have a man who's all athletic and who can run for miles, and my ass can't even walk up a hill."

"I'm grateful for the company, so I'm just jazzed that you came." Sequoia wiped her forehead with a towel. "By the way, thanks for giving me Torino's number last night. He's usually clowning and being tacky with his player remarks. I can't believe that man wants to try to put a real move on me after all this time."

Mercedes pushed the electronic control to slow down the pace. "I can."

"He needs to put them on someone. I think Colette has straight lost her damn mind. He can do a whole lot better than that bug-a-boo."

"Like you?"

Sequoia skipped over her question. "Anyway, I will say one thing. These brothers out here are a trip. You need to count your blessings, sitting up in Ladera with a famous husband. Mercedes, you are a damn millionaire."

"Oh, and I suppose that's all that's important, huh?"

"It helps. Don't give me that 'money is nothing without someone you love to share it with' crap. You have one of the finest and richest black men in the world to share it with."

"Sequoia, I really don't have much to complain about other than wanting more of Mason's time."

"And we all know you trust him," Sequoia remarked like it was all too familiar.

"You know that's right. I've never really doubted his fidelity. It's my own that concerns me."

"Wait, don't tell me—you've got a young stud muffin on the side that you're holding out. Why don't you just go ahead and admit it?"

"Girl, okay, yes, you're right. I have a young stud on the side who hits it from the back."

Sequoia looked eager to hear more. "I knew it."

"And an old sugar daddy who sucks my toes, and a doctor, my own mother-in-law's doctor mind you, who lets me play nurse, and a bouncer at Foreplay and the stripper at Ebony's, and one at *T & A*'s and . . ."

Sequoia turned down her machine as well and leaned toward Mercedes to interrupt. "A stripper? Have you lost your cotton-pickin' mind?"

"That's exactly it. My mind is lost in a sea of infidelity. I can't stop fantasizing about people when I make love to my own husband."

"Mercedes, now that might not be so bad." She looked to the side in thought. "Actually, I think all of that is pretty normal, except for the stripper. And Bo, the bouncer?"

Mercedes looked around to make sure the man next to her was deep into his headphones. "Normal, huh? Well, it seems like I can't control it and it's getting to the point where I don't even want to have sex because I never know who's going to pop into my head and into our bed." Suddenly, Mercedes looked at Sequoia like she was the *National Enquirer*, noticing the nosey look on her face. "I don't think I should even be telling you any more, judging by the way you're looking at me. Sequoia, this is a problem. Not just some gossip you heard about at the beauty shop. I need help."

"When did this start?"

"I think a couple of years ago, Dr. Smith," Mercedes teased, calling her by her last name.

"That long ago?"

"I think so. All of a sudden I've had this vivid ass imagination that I can't control."

Sequoia just stared.

Mercedes noticed her silence. "I'm not getting anywhere telling you about this. I'm actually getting more frustrated." She turned up the speed.

"No, come on now. I want to help you. I'm glad you wanted to share it with me. Have you told Mason?"

"No. I think he knows I zone out, almost into another world when we make love but shit, so does he."

"Damn, the two of you could be screwing everybody on the block in your heads."

"Not."

"Let's give this workout a rest," Sequoia said, stepping off of the treadmill. She walked toward the locker room, wiping the sweat from her face and swigging her bottled water. Mercedes stepped down, too, and walked beside her, wiping her forehead with her wristband.

Sequoia continued, "Okay now seriously, I think some of this is very normal. I mean I've done that before myself. I had this man who liked me to lay flat back along the end of the bed while he would go down on me. He liked to be on his knees on the floor and he'd just go for the gold. So all I could see was the ceiling. I'd have to imagine him being all kind of people, even my boss one time."

"Ooh, that's really naughty," Mercedes said with sarcasm. She opened her locker.

"You should have seen his Herman Munster face. You would have done the same thing. But damn, he could munch the carpet."

"I ain't mad at you."

"Mercedes, some people think about an ex or even fantasize about being watched. Believe me, there are kinkier things out there than what you're worried about. But I don't think it's abnormal to do that at all. Especially if your own man's stimulation isn't enough."

Mercedes said, "Oh please, girl. You actually think that's it? Oh, I don't think so. Mason is definitely enough. But I hear what you're saying. You're saying I'm just semi-weird, not totally weird?"

"No. Actually, I'm going to check this out on the Internet. There have to be books out there or focus groups, something."

"This sounds like some *Sex and the City* episode. I can picture Samantha sitting at a seminar saying, 'My name is Samantha and I'm addicted to sexual fantasies.' Oh Lord, help me," Mercedes cried.

"That's a start. Pray." The ring of Sequoia's cell interrupted them. She reached into her locker to grab it.

"I'll bet that's Torino," Mercedes teased.

"Just might be." Sequoia flipped it open. "Hi there. Sure. Eight o'clock is fine. I'll see you there." She hung up. "He wants me to come by the club early for dinner on Wednesday."

"Damn, you didn't waste any time calling him, did you? Just take it slow," Mercedes warned.

"Why?"

"He's rebounding from crazy Colette."

Sequoia got loud to make her point. "Who gives a shit? It's been so long since I had sex. I say Torino can rebound his ass off with me. All of a sudden that brotha turns me the heck on."

"Okay. Go for it." Mercedes peeked around the corner to make sure no one was around and then walked away with her towel around her waist and her major breasts hanging. "Sequoia, I'm about to go take a shower. And then I need a Cinnabon. You want to go?"

"No, I'm going to go home and get cleaned up. I need to go make some calls and check on some airfares for that NAACP event. I'll see you later." Sequoia put on her hooded sweatshirt.

"Okay," Mercedes yelled. "Let me know what you find out. Otherwise, I'm checking myself into the Calabasas Center for the treatment of sexual addiction."

"We'll get to the root of it soon." Sequoia stopped as she turned the corner of the aisle, realizing that an older woman was on the other side seemingly in shock from their conversation. Sequoia pulled her hood over her head as she exited the locker room.

Early that Wednesday night, Torino and Sequoia met at the club for dinner. They sat in a booth in the rear section of the dining room. Her skirt was short and tight. She pulled at it to get comfortable as they prepared to get cozy over an intimate meal together. Within two minutes of the waiter handing them their menus, Torino's door manager approached.

Torino spoke before he could say a word. "Man, I'm trying to have a meal here."

"I know, sir, but the combination to the safe isn't working."

Torino thought for a minute, glancing at Sequoia.

She gave a green light smile. "Go ahead, Torino, this is your place of business."

Torino was a little surprised by her kindness. But he refused to be interrupted. He looked at his doorman and said, "Just give me an hour. That's all I ask. I know you can handle this, man."

Sequoia encouraged him again. "Torino, go ahead and tend to your business. I'll be fine, really. I need to make a couple of calls anyway."

He almost felt like he was asking for permission but he asked with a smile. "Are you sure?"

She pulled out her cell phone. "I'm sure."

He gave in. "Just order whatever you want and I'll be right back."

His doorman seemed to rush him. "Sir, the club opens in thirty minutes."

Torino stood up. "I'm coming. I thought you were the assistant manager, so assist my ass." His manager stared at him and looked at Sequoia, lowering his eyes as he walked away while Torino leaned over the table at Sequoia, preparing to excuse himself again.

"Torino, obviously this club can't run without you. That must be a good feeling."

"Yeah, right. Please go ahead and order. I'll be right back."

An hour later, people started to infiltrate the bar area just as the DJ began to set up his sounds. Sequoia made her way from the dining room to the bar and took a seat. She watched Torino run around, racing from the kitchen to the front door, and greeting groups of people, directing them into the VIP area and escorting them to various sitting areas. He walked over behind the bar with his assistant and looked up at Sequoia.

"Baby, I am so sorry about this. I should have known better than to plan something private at the club during business hours."

A younger gentleman walked up to Sequoia and offered to buy her a drink. She looked at Torino and replied, "Sure, that would be nice. I'll have an Absolut Mandarin, straight up."

Torino spoke to the man. "What up, man?" The tall, athletic-looking gentleman nodded his head in return. Torino then spoke to his bartender while pointing his head in the direction of the young man. "Miguel, you have a customer over here." He spoke to Sequoia. "I'll talk to you later," he said, backing away before being pulled to the side by a waitress.

Sequoia chatted it up with a few men throughout the night, danced a couple of times, and hung out with her hairdresser who showed up with a group of ladies celebrating a wedding engagement. As the night wound down, she said her good-byes and made her way toward the ladies' room before calling it a night. As she came out, Torino was standing at the door, waiting like he was standing guard.

He asked, "Did you have fun tonight?"

"Yes, I always have fun here. One day you'll be able to enjoy your own club and not have to work so hard."

"I hope so. Perhaps it is better to be running around than sitting around, trying to pull patrons in off the street."

She reached in her purse to find her valet ticket. "I guess so. Anyway, Torino, thanks for inviting me. I'll talk to you later." She leaned in to give him a hug and he put his hands on each side of her waist to stop her.

"Sequoia, I really am sorry about dinner. Did you get to order anything?"

"I had a Thai salad and some great Chardonnay. Thanks a lot for taking care of that." She noticed Torino's frown. "What's wrong?"

"Next time . . ."

She interrupted him, almost as if she didn't want him to answer her question after all. "Torino, I have to get going now."

"Okay, but will you do me a favor?"

"What?" she asked, prepared to step away.

"Just would you?"

"What, Torino?"

He touched her arm as if to direct her eyes to his. "Come home with me."

She broke the glance. "Torino, please. You have got to be kidding."

"Sequoia, I'm not kidding. I just want to spend some time alone with you. I really need that tonight and I'm sorry we didn't get a chance earlier. Please."

"You don't want to be alone tonight?"

"No," he said with his voice, his eyes, and his touch.

She waited for a second, and then answered almost as though she was still unsure. "Okay, Torino, I'll bite. What time do you get off?"

He shook himself out of doubt mode and replied. "I'll be leaving in about twenty minutes. Will you wait?" Now both of his hands embraced her hand.

She pointed. "I'll wait right here by the door."

He suggested, "Or at the bar. Order whatever you'd like."

She shook her head. "No more bar for me. I'll take a seat right here. Just let me know when you're ready."

"I'll be right out. Thanks, Sequoia. You can follow me in your car, right?"

"No problem," she said, taking a seat on a red high-back chair near the entrance. She placed her tiny gold bag in her lap, crossed her legs, and smiled as Torino walked back toward the kitchen door. He looked at her for a moment, his glance on her never-ending, firm-looking legs, and smiled back. He disappeared through the double steel door just as the DJ announced the last song for the evening, "Hot Boyz" by Missy. Sequoia looked around at all of the die-hard clubbers who started to exit, bobbed her head without even realizing she was mouthing the words and sang along, "Where you live, is it by yourself? Can I move with you, do you need some help? I cook boy, I'll give you more, I'm a fly girl, and I like those Hot Boyz."

# chapter 11

At nearly two-thirty in the morning, Sequoia pulled up behind Torino's car in Mason and Mercedes's long driveway. She got out and walked with Torino as he led the way, holding her hand while they quietly headed toward his door. They stepped inside and she took a seat on his tan sofa. She wondered what the heck she was doing there. "So, now what?"

"Now what, what?" he asked, turning on a couple of lights.

Sequoia tried to figure it out, as if she didn't know. "Did you invite me over to watch a movie, talk, play checkers? What?"

Torino placed his keys on his bar and took off his suit coat, hanging it up in the hall closet. "I invited you over to spend a little time together."

She looked around at all of his burned-to-the-quick candles and half-burned incense. "Is this how you get all of your honeys to come back with you after work? You offer them breakfast and then tell them they should sleep at your house since it's getting late?"

"First of all, I did not offer you breakfast." He turned on the stereo. The smooth Hiroshima CD was number one.

"Oh, you know better than to play game with me. Or maybe it would have been better than 'follow me,'" she mocked.

He ignored her attitude, almost used to it by now. "Would you like something to drink, Sequoia?"

"Like what?"

"What would you like?" he asked, walking toward the tiny kitchen.

"What do you have?"

He opened the refrigerator door, peeked in and told her, "Water, orange juice, Kool-Aid, red wine, rum and Coke, brandy, whatever."

She was still acting suspicious. "Alcohol, huh?"

"And non-alcohol."

She took off her pointy, golden ankle-strap shoes. "Torino, let's just get it over with."

"What?"

"Give me a break. You know you want it as much as I do."

He walked toward her and stood near the television, turning it on as well. "What? Some Kool-Aid? Yes, that is exactly what I'll have. A nice, tall, cold glass of grape Kool-Aid. And I'm pouring one for you, too, just so you can cool off. "

"Screw the Kool-Aid, Torino. Come on so we can get the fucking over with."

"Sequoia, why do you always have your guard up? Why do you always think somebody wants something from you? Why are you so damn angry?"

She sat back, leaning on a round sofa pillow. "I'm not angry. I'm just hip to the game."

"And how many men have run this so-called game on you that made you so hip?" He stood over her.

"Why are you worried?"

"Because you give me the impression that you've been used."

"Used up?" she asked. "Is that what you're trying to say?"

"No, damn it. I mean taken advantage of by some men who think they need to add you to their list of conquests because you are so damn fine. But what they don't see is that having a woman like you on a regular basis is worth more than having you for one night. I'm not interested in a one-night stand with you."

She actually lowered her volume a notch. "What do you want from me, Torino?"

The phone rang. It rang three times. Sequoia looked to Torino. He looked back at her.

"The machine will pick it up."

"I didn't say a word. I know why you get calls this time of night."

He didn't reply. He sat on the love seat, making sure to not sit on the sofa she was on. He sat on the edge, trying to lean toward her. "Here's what I want you to do. I want you to calm down and relax around me. Stop fighting the feeling and just breathe. I'm not gonna hurt you. We've known each other too long for that bullshit."

She looked him dead in the eyes. "Torino, do you consider yourself a player?"

"I've been in a relationship for a couple of years. Does that sound like something a player would do?"

"Were you true to her all those years?"

"No," he admitted without hesitation.

"Why didn't you marry her?"

"Because I didn't want to."

"Oh, you didn't want to. But she was good enough to call your woman, just not the mother of your kids."

"You could say that."

"And what separates a woman who's good enough to just screw from one who's good enough to be the mother of your children?"

"I feel like I'm being interviewed by Barbara Walters."

"I'm just trying to get to the core of what your intentions are."

"Fine, Sequoia, let me see." He leaned back, looking like he was searching for the right answer on the ceiling. "Probably a woman of virtue who would inspire a man to give up his bachelorhood, not make him do it. How's that?"

Sequoia paused and then spoke. "Do you love her?"

"I think so."

"You think so?" she replied loudly.

Torino stood up. This time he got louder. "Calm down, Sequoia. Your feisty attitude must have scared the shit out of many a man through the years. But you're not gonna scare my ass away. I know you."

"What do you know?"

"I know that you're hiding something behind all of these questions and this mean exterior. You've been hurt, probably a few times."

"Oh, like you don't know."

"What makes you think I know?" This time he sat on the arm of the sofa.

"Mercedes has told Mason about how Bobby dogged me. Mason told Claude. And Claude told you."

"My brothers and I have a lot better things to do than gossip about which dude tripped out on you."

"It takes a tripped-out dude to know one. Like your ass was ever faithful to Colette."

"I admit I've had to use my B list from time to time. And I've met some women who I thought might be able to move Colette out of position. Yes, I've had my share. But that crap gets tiring."

"Your share of what?"

"My share of pussy. I always say, pussy is like eating cheesecake all the time, day after day. It tastes good but it's too rich."

"So, you're tired of the cheesecake?"

He said it in her words. "I'm tired of the cheesecake."

"What are you in the mood for?" Sequoia scooted over to lean toward him this time.

"Something different. And I'm warning you, that's your last question for the night."

"So now you're into something different. Something so different at a time when I bring my big ass to your place after all these years, ready to let you rock my world. And that was a comment, not a question." She smirked.

"That's what you came here for?"

"Duh, nigga, it's three in the morning. I'm not one of those women who come up to the hotel room and then say, I didn't want to give it to him, he just took it. Bunk that. I'm a grown ass woman and you're a grown ass man, Torino. You know why I'm here."

He stood up. "I'm here to eat some pizza and drink some Kool-Aid. I have these slammin' Wolfgang Puck frozen pizzas. The barbeque chicken one is about to get devoured. I'm sure you brought your hunger along with your horniness."

"I am not horny."

"Okay."

She grinned again, seeming to lighten up. "Okay, I am horny. But I can cure that with one phone call."

"And so can I. I didn't ask you over here for that. Let's just chill."

"Just chill. And that was not a question either."

"Whatever you say. I say yes, let's just chill, Sequoia, and talk, and eat pizza and drink purple Kool-Aid."

She looked up at him with wondering eyes. "And drink purple Kool-Aid?" she asked.

He gave her a look.

She rephrased her words. "Okay, I mean, let's drink purple Kool-Aid."

"Yes, purple."

She let out a powerful breath. "I am sort of hungry, Torino."

"Cool." He went back into the kitchen and removed a cardboard box from the freezer, placing the pizza on a cookie sheet. He set the temperature on the oven and put it inside. Within forty-five minutes, they were eating and drinking, seated on his sofa, together, talking over the volume of the Dave Koz CD playing to a volume-less, old *Martin* episode on his wide screen television.

As the sun started to rise, Sequoia yawned and rested her head back on Torino's soft, cushiony sofa and closed her eyes. Torino took his chenille cover and placed it over her, rotating her head around to rest on a bed pillow.

He proceeded to his room, keeping one eye on the vision of her surrender, and closed the door. After that night, Sequoia basically, never left.

After an evening of hot, passionate sex where Mercedes's fantasies were racing as usual, she lay on her back, wearing only a black lace thong. She fanned herself with her hand to cool and dry her sweat and propped the pillow behind her head.

Mason laid down butt naked. He turned on the TV to watch the golf channel. She remembered to tell him about Sequoia. "Mason, Torino broke up with Colette."

"I'm not surprised. She's a hot head."

"And, you are not going to believe it but Torino actually asked me for Sequoia's phone number."

"For what?"

"That's what I wanted to know. You'd think so they could sign up for a WWF match and beat the hell out of each other."

"I'm telling you. That boy admitted that he likes her."

"He sure did."

Mason scooted up to lean back against the headboard. "Man, I was blind to that one. They're pretty much the same age but I've just never even noticed an actual spark between them. Only darted stares. If they ever got together, there'd be a 5.0 earthquake in Los Angeles."

"Well, perhaps he had this lightbulb moment about her and wants to give it a shot. I gave her his number."

Mason spoke his opinion. "You women are so protective of each other. You could have just given him her number."

Mercedes replied with spunk, "He asked me, not you. Can I please handle it the way I want to?"

"No problem." Mason continued to stare at the television.

"Mason, do you think Torino is a cock-hound?"

"A cock-hound? Where did that come from?"

"It's just that he's so fickle and he never seems satisfied. I'm just worried about my best friend."

"I think if anyone can handle Torino, Sequoia can."

"True. But I've seen Torino with a whole lot of women. He goes through girls like a starving man devouring a Krispy Kreme donut."

"He's not that bad. He was with Colette for a long time."

"Like I said, I've seen him with a whole lot of women, even while he was with Colette. Sequoia's like a sister to me. I don't want her to get hurt, baby."

"I can't guarantee that she won't now. That's on her. But she's known him long enough to know what she'd be getting into. Why did you tell him you'd give her his number if you have this much doubt about him?"

"I was just hoping that he's gotten all of his running around out of his system like you and Claude did years ago. After all, he's not getting any younger. He needs a good woman."

"You're right about that. Even the woman-crazy brothers eventually get tired of one-nighters and cheap thrills."

"Do me a favor, please, and ask him what his intentions are."

"I'm not Sequoia's father, Cedes. That's not my place."

Mercedes stood up to go into the bathroom. She still looked concerned.

Mason watched her strut her rear end in front of him. He checked her out from the waist down. "All right, I'll pry a little."

"Thanks, baby."

He stood up and stepped into his pajama bottoms. "Do you want anything from the kitchen?"

"Just a few graham crackers," she yelled his way.

"Sounds good. I'll be right back. And I say go ahead and hook them up."

"I already did," Mercedes informed him.

"Good".

Little did they know Sequoia was sleeping just a few yards away.

Since Mason promised Star he would spend time with her when he had a few days to be home, he decided it would be nice to drive her to school, which he had not done since she was in the fourth grade.

They drove as slow as snails in the single lane of cars to the main drop off area in the front of her high school. Cars seemed to come to a stop as they looked over to peek inside of the tinted windows of Mason's black-on-black convertible Porsche Boxer.

"Daddy, why do people always stare at you?" Star asked, watching the other parents break their necks to ogle her famous father.

"I think maybe they recognize me."

"I know that. But why do they stare? I mean, I think that's so rude to just be all up in somebody's face like they're from another planet."

"It's human nature, Star. They see someone on television, and then when they catch them in person, it's only natural I suppose."

She felt the sticky eyes from the outside but tried to look preoccupied, zipping up the front pouch to her denim backpack. "I would never stare if I saw someone famous. So what."

"If you saw Justin Timberlake you wouldn't stare?"

"No."

"How about Bow Wow?" Mason asked, looking over at her like he was getting somewhere.

She waved her hand toward him. "Oh, please. I don't care who it is. It's just an invasion of privacy to watch someone eat or talk in private, or drive their daughter to school," she said loudly, looking the driver of a car dead in the eye.

"I don't even notice anymore."

"Well, I do," Star said. Mason prepared to stop in front of Star's school along with the other parents dropping off their kids. Star panicked. "No Daddy, just pull up over there, down the street," she pointed up the street about a half a block.

"But you'll have to walk farther," Mason said.

"I'm okay. I don't want everybody peeking in and being even more nosey as I get out."

Mason pulled up. "Fine. How's this?"

"This is good." She bent over to pick up her lunch bag from the floor. "I'm surprised you're home this morning. I thought you'd be on the course or jogging by now."

"Well, I'm not. I'm here taking my gorgeous, talented daughter, who is growing up so fast, to school. Don't I get a kiss?"

Star leaned toward her dad and stopped in mid-reach. "Oh my God, Daddy. Oh my God."

"What, Star?"

She sat back, pressing her back against the seat. "Daddy, take me home right now."

Mason turned to face her. "Why?"

"Daddy, I need to go home to Mom right now. Please, Daddy, just go," Star insisted as she held on to the side of the seat for dear life.

Mason shifted the car into gear. "Star, are you okay?" he asked, pulling out again into traffic.

"No, Daddy," Star said, reaching her hand under her rear end and holding her breath.

"What is it?"

She pulled her hand from underneath her skirt. "Dad, I've started my period."

"Your period?"

"Yes, and it's all over my skirt and the seat and everything."

"Wait, I have a towel in the trunk," he said, starting to pull over.

"No, Daddy. Just get me home to Mom, please. Hurry up."

Mason began to speed along as he called Mercedes on her cell phone but there was no answer. "Where is she?"

"She was going walking with Aunt Venus."

"Aunt Venus? Okay, when I pull up, I'm going to run in and grab a towel or sheet or something, and you go inside and head to your mom's bathroom. I'm sure she has some tampons under the sink."

She turned up her nose. "Tampons? No way am I using those."

"Well, don't you have any pads just for this very occasion?"

"Mom and I thought this day was at least a year away. Daddy, hurry and get me home and then go get some pads from the store."

"I'm hurrying," he said, taking the short route back to their house.

When he arrived and put on the parking brake, Star flung the door open. "I'll be right here. Go," she told him.

"Hold up a minute," he insisted. "Sit tight." He ran inside and then ran back out with a dark sheet as Star scooted along the seat, stepping out. She stood up, draping the sheet in between her legs and behind her butt. "Hurry, Daddy. I'll be in the bathroom."

"I'll be right back," he said, throwing a towel over the passenger side seat.

After making his way to the grocery store, Mason noticed people staring at him with the box of Kotex in the ten items or less line as he handed the cashier his debit card.

"Just slide it through, Mr. Wilson."

"Okay," he said, seeming nervous.

"You act like you've never done this before."

"I have. It's just that my, well, thanks. Can I have a bag, please?"

"Paper or plastic?"

"Paper."

Mason arrived back home in two point two seconds. He ran inside to Mercedes's bathroom where he found the door locked.

He knocked. "Star? Do you know how to use these?"

She took the bag and locked the door again, speaking from the other side, ripping the box open. "Yes. But isn't there a belt or something I'm supposed to use?"

"I don't know. You'll have to ask your mom on that one."

"Daddy, can I just stay home from school?"

"Sure, baby. Just take care of yourself."

"Is the seat of your car okay?" she yelled from the bathroom.

"It'll wash off. Anyway, it's black leather. Nothing will damage that. What's important is you right now."

"Good answer, Daddy," she teased.

He smiled and shook his head, heading back outside to clean off the leather seat.

"What a day already, and it's only eight in the morning," he said aloud.

Mercedes was at the jogging trail at Fox Hills park. She bent over to stretch her legs out just as Venus walked up.

"Thanks for meeting me," said Mercedes, giving Venus the once-over. "You look good, Ms. MexiBlack."

Venus snickered. "Thanks. What's been up with you?" she asked, tying her sweatshirt around her waist.

"Not much. Just handling my business with the agency and the family," Mercedes said, turning from side to side.

"It must feel great to have some place to go other than staying home all day. I keep thinking about going back to work. Like it was before I married Claude."

"You mean teaching?"

"Yes. At least part-time," Venus replied, stretching her fingers to the sky.

"Why don't you?" Mercedes asked.

"Claude is so old-fashioned. He said no woman of his is going to work. He wants me at home."

"Some women would kill for that chance."

They started to jog while Venus explained. "Yes, but I think not working robs you of your desire to grow and utilize your gifts and talents. I love kids and my job wasn't so much about the money, obviously because I wasn't getting paid a whole lot, but it was rewarding."

"You can always come and help me out dealing with those childlike models I have to play mother to. Those girls are so dang immature. I need to run an agency for mature, plus-sized models. Maybe then they'd show up on time and confirm their appointments and not be such prima donnas. These girls will cancel a booking if they break a damn nail."

"You're so silly, Mercedes."

"I'm serious. I'll hire you. Just say the word and it's done."

Venus declined. "No thanks, but I think I am going to work on a volunteer basis for some worthy cause that helps kids who are terminally ill or who have AIDS."

"That's nice of you, Venus. We're doing a benefit for the homeless at church if you want to help our committee. We do it every year and it brings in a lot of money for shelters and medical care organizations and food resource centers."

"Now that, I'd love to do," Venus said, looking inspired.

"What do you say we do about twelve laps? That's a few miles," said Mercedes.

"I'm game," Venus replied.

After about twenty minutes, they slowed their pace down to fast walking. A couple of women walked by, leaning in toward each other after giving Mercedes the once-over. Their attempts to muffle their voices wasn't working. "Hey, isn't that Mason Wilson's wife? She'd better stay out here if she wants to keep that fat from chasing away that man of hers. She doesn't look as young as she used to."

Mercedes's head followed their movement as they passed. "What the hell did you just say?" she belted out within a split second of their comment.

"Excuse me?" one lady asked, looking like she was interrupted.

Mercedes put her hands on her hips and turned back to face them both. She began to blink a mile a minute. "I overheard what you said, with your scrawny self. You need to put on a few pounds from what I can see. Shoot, I will hurt you up here in this park. You need to work on your whispering skills, or could it be that maybe, just maybe, that comment was meant to be heard?"

Both women stopped a couple of yards away. "No, ma'am. I apologize if I offended you. It was a private conversation."

"She's sorry," said the lady's friend. "She meant no harm."

"Well, harm was taken." Mercedes walked on at a slow pace. "Venus, let's go. My own people doggin' me out while I try to walk along the same trail in the same park that I've been walking in for most of my life. People never cease to amaze me."

Venus tried to console her. "Mercedes, just ignore them. You look good and more importantly, Mason likes you just the way you are."

"I ain't about to lose my ass for no stranger who thinks that sexy is what they see in *Elle* and *Glamour*."

Venus agreed. "I'm with you on that."

Mercedes took a deep breath. "Now that I'm all worked up, I'm going to go right on over to the Serving Spoon restaurant for some grits, chicken sausage, cheese eggs with onions, and biscuits," Mercedes said out loud toward the two women as they walked down the track. "Come with me. My treat and then I'll bring you back." She looked back at the ladies again. "People made me work up an appetite. I've gotta work hard to keep all this wagon I'm dragging.

And besides, you could stand to eat a little anyway," she said, looking at Venus's slender hips.

Mercedes got back in her car and noticed the missed calls on her cell while Venus got in the passenger seat for a ride. She called Mason immediately.

"Sorry I missed your calls. Baby, can you believe these two so-called ladies, sistas, had the nerve to insult me at the park today. Talking about how I need to work at losing weight to keep from losing you."

Mason spoke in a low tone. "Baby, I'm sorry that happened but Star started her period today."

"And then when I confronted them they were all apologetic like . . . What did you say?"

"Our baby started her period?"

"When, in school?" Mercedes asked, with her eyes opened the size of quarters.

"No, in the car with me on the way to school."

"Mason, no. How is she?"

"Just come on home, baby, she needs you. I see there's no one quite like Mom," Mason admitted.

She looked at Venus. "See, this is what life is all about. I'm on my way," she told Mason.

She dropped Venus off at her car and said her good-byes.

That weekend, Mason went to church with Mercedes and the kids. Mason got a chance to sport his new charcoal Ralph Lauren suit. And Mercedes wore the off-white mandalay dress given to her by the designer, Marc Jacobs. Rashaad tried his best to wear his suit, but he always seemed to leave his jacket at home and his tie in the car. And Star looked sweet, wearing her new peasant dress she and Mercedes bought from Forever 21.

The Reverend pulled them aside after service. He excused Mason and Mercedes from the teenagers and took them into his private office. As soon as they sat down he hit them with a direct question. "Now what is going on with the two of you?"

Mason replied for the couple. "What do you mean, Rev?"

"I mean I've gotten word from the teen group that Star and Rashaad are withdrawn and nonsocial and I know that's not like them. So I like to start with the parents and see if they know what's going on. I hope you don't mind."

Mercedes commented, "No, I'm fine with you asking. I know Star has been a little defiant about her school plans."

"Oh, really?" asked Mason.

"Yes," Mercedes said. "And Rashaad is just moody."

"That's true," said Mason.

The Reverend asked, "Where did he get that from?"

"Not me," Mason replied.

"Not me," Mercedes replied.

Mason said, "I thought moody means sometimes you feel good and sometimes you've got a lot on your mind. That's everybody."

"Why don't we ask them?" Mercedes suggested.

"Why don't we. I'll be right back," said the Reverend.

Star and Rashaad came inside looking like they'd just been arrested.

"What's wrong, Mom?" asked Star. Cautiously, they took a seat around the Reverend's desk.

"Nothing, dear. We just want to talk to the two of you for a minute."

"About what?" asked Rashaad.

Mercedes explained. "About the four of us as a family. Your dad and I want to know what we can do to make things better."

The Reverend added his comments. "And the first step is talking about what some of the concerns or issues might be. There's nothing too deep for God's arms to reach. I just want all of you to be able to communicate. Now I can leave the room if you'd like," the Reverend offered.

"No, Rev, that won't be necessary," said Mason.

The Reveremd spoke directly to Star and Rashaad. "Or, if the two of you would prefer to come back another time, that's fine too."

Rashaad asked, "What do you want to know exactly?"

Mercedes replied, "How can we make things better? What, in your opinion, can be improved?"

Rashaad looked at Star. "Well, I don't have any problems really." And then he looked at the Reverend. "I just know that I worry about Cameron. He's cool and everything and I know sometimes he feels bad coming by the house after Aunt Fatima got killed."

"Has he told you that?" asked Mercedes.

"I asked him and he just plays it off."

Mason was understanding. "I'd understand if Cameron did still have bad feelings. I'm sure our home reminds him of her. And the same for Claude."

Star added her thoughts. "I agree. She was killed on our own front porch and we act like it's no big deal."

"It was a big deal. It'll always be a sad time but we have to move past that. There are memories of Fatima in our home that are good, too," Mercedes added.

Mason spoke directly to the Reverend. "And we've talked about this before. We all had a family meeting and decided that we could handle it, but I see that it still needs to be discussed."

Rashaad added, "I'm fine, I just worry about Cameron."

"That's commendable. And what else? What about you, Star?" asked the Reverend.

"I want the four of us to have a normal life and be together. Sometimes I hate being the daughter of a famous man. That's all I have to say." She crossed her arms in her lap.

Mason looked concerned.

The Reverend spoke up. "Okay. That's something that needs to be looked into further. Is there anything else? Not that that's not a lot right there."

Rashaad looked at Star again who simply stared at her own hands. "No, that's it," he said.

"Do you think that you worry a lot?" the Reverend asked Rashaad.

"No," he replied, shrugging his shoulders.

"Do you think you are as social as you could be?"

"Yes," Rashaad answered again.

The Reverend summed it up. "See, I always believe in talking things out. Every concern is valid if one feels that it is. What I think we need to do is pray on it, and then the four of you need to continue talking and verbalizing your feelings. Rashaad's concern for his cousin shows a great and healthy level of caring. And Star's obviously very loving. She desires something that she feels she does not have. That needs to be worked on."

"Rev, I appreciate what you're trying to do, but we'll work this out amongst ourselves. Thanks for getting us together for this discussion. Your time is much appreciated," Mason said, sounding very formal.

"No problem at all, Mason. Now let's all hold hands and bow our heads and pray."

Venus waited for Claude to come home while she checked on Mattie to see how she was adjusting to her new surroundings.

"Mattie, can I get you anything?" Venus asked. "I'm about to hit the sack."

"No, baby. I'm fine."

"How's your room? Is your bed comfortable?" Venus asked.

Mattie sat on her bed stroking the sheet with her flat hand. "You know, these white cotton sheets are just like the ones I used to use when the boys were little. Somehow, white sheets make you sleep better, you know?"

"I agree with you on that."

Mattie buttoned the last couple of buttons of her pale flowered sleeper and then unbuttoned them again, looking down toward her knees. "And that Mason was always off with his dad, running up behind him, wanting to do and be everything his dad was. I always wished I had a daughter to help me with all that laundry and those dishes and such. But, I know how men are. They are the breadwinners and we do the domestic stuff."

"Yeah," Venus said, standing over the bed, smiling.

"One day, I'm going to move back into my house and you can come over and stay with us. When you met Claude he never brought you over much, but we knew about you," Mattie said to Venus, settling into her bed.

"I was never around that far back, Mattie."

"Oh yes, you used to wear that yellow and green sundress when we went to the functions at church back then. I always liked your long hair and beautiful skin. I always told Claude how pretty you were. You've always been nice to me."

"Thanks, Mattie. You've always been nice to me too. Well, you sleep tight." Venus turned on the side lamp and turned off the bright ceiling light.

"And don't let the bed bugs bite, right?" Mattie asked, looking up at Venus.

"Right. You wouldn't want that. See you in the morning," Venus said, starting to close the door.

"See you in the morning, Fatima."

Venus froze. She looked straight ahead, closing the bedroom door in slow motion. She pulled the door tight to make sure it shut all the way, and then leaned her back against it. Mattie was just mixing things up, she told herself. But the bottom line was, Mattie had fond memories of Fatima and missed her very much. Mattie thought Venus was Fatima all this time. Fatima was part of her mother-in-law's memories, not her.

During sex with Claude that night, Venus was fairly quiet, once again feeling as though she was being watched while her husband did his business with her for what seemed like forever. His drenching sweat dripped onto her hair and into her eyes. It stung as it hit her eyelids. The room was spinning with each pound of his midsection against hers. After about forty-five minutes, Claude was finally done and he dismounted only to succumb to the exhaustion of his grinding. He crawled off of her and onto his side of the bed.

She turned on her right side to lay behind him. She looked at Claude's back while he snored, recalling her mother-in-law's words. She could not get Fatima out of her head. Finally, she gave in to shutting her heavy eyelids. Yet she tossed and turned every couple of hours, all night long, waking up hot and sweaty, trying to find a comfortable place and peace of mind.

The next morning Venus awoke to Claude phoning from his car just as she had finally fallen into a deep sleep.

She snatched the phone from its base and he spoke. "Baby, I was showing a house today and met this housekeeper whose sister is a live-in nurse. She's in between gigs and available if we need her. Why don't you give her a call and interview her?"

"Okay," Venus said, her eyes still adjusting to the light of day.

"Her name is Gloria Sanchez. She lives in Inglewood so she's close. I'll call back and leave her number on the message center."

She squinted her eyes, realizing it was nearly ten o'clock. "Is she supposed to be a live-in for us?"

"No, you can handle most of the hours. We just need her around maybe five hours per day."

"What about at night?"

"Mom sleeps well at night," Claude said as if he knew.

She sat up. "Claude, sometimes she gets up and wanders around, you know."

"Yes, but never enough to interrupt anything."

"She could get into anything, like turn on the stove or even leave."

"I thought that's why we left the alarm on."

"It is."

"This housekeeper suggested those locks at the top of doors so Mom can't get them open. You've been doing fine with her, right?"

"Yes, I have. But she needs to have her bedding changed, stuff like that. Sometimes she wets herself, and she just needs a lot of attention."

"That's what this woman would be for."

Venus suddenly felt wide awake. "Claude, I want to go to night school over at West Los Angeles and take some notary classes or volunteer for the Make-A-Wish Foundation. So I think we need her at night, too. Maybe even live-in."

"It's up to you, Venus. Just get in touch with her and check her out before she accepts another assignment. Make it open-ended, and don't offer her more than ten dollars per hour."

"That's only like fifty dollars per day."

"That's all housekeepers make," he said.

"But we don't need a housekeeper. We need a trained nurse and they get paid more than that, honey. Especially if she lives in." Venus heard people talking in the background.

"Baby, I have to go. Just get going with it and let me know."

"I will. I'll call her today," Venus assured him.

"Good girl. I'll see you later tonight at dinner. Gotta go, bye."

"Love you," Venus said.

# chapter 12

After hiring Gloria, Venus was able to focus on planning dinner herself so she invited everyone to their home for Sunday dinner. Her lavish gourmet kitchen opened up into a huge room, which included the breakfast nook, dining area, kitchen, and den.

"Hey, Venus. Look at you, getting down with a serious meal," said Torino, walking in the den entrance with Sequoia, hand in hand. "I hope you don't mind that I brought Sequoia."

"Sequoia is family anyway. Hey, girl, how are you?" Venus and Sequoia kissed on the cheek.

"I'm doing fine. What can I do to help?" Sequoia asked.

Venus pointed to the counter. "Maybe you can rinse that lettuce and throw together this dinner salad. Just a few tomatoes and shredded carrots."

"You got it," she said as Torino went into the den to talk to Claude and Mattie.

"Hey, Mom. Good to see you," Torino said, taking a seat on the sofa next to his mother.

Mattie told him, "Hello, boy. You walked in here smiling like you got an A on your homework."

Claude pointed toward Sequoia. "That would make me smile, too." He gave Torino a high-five.

"I should have known you'd be happy to see me with anyone but Colette."

Claude chuckled. "Man, you've got to admit, she was a case study."

"If you'd just have let me handle that on my own. I knew it wasn't gonna last," Torino said, looking relieved.

"All is well. I see you're smiling now." Claude leaned in to whisper, "I thought about that myself one day."

"You did, huh? With Sequoia?" Torino asked.

"Yeah, back in the day. But Mercedes wouldn't let me get near her back then."

"Me, too. But more than that, Sequoia wasn't game either," Torino admitted.

Claude told his brother, "I see no one's blocking right now."

Torino leaned back and stretched his arms out. "No, man. Not now."

"You know what I think?" Claude asked as though he had a valuable answer. "I think these ladies start getting older and then start thinking twice about the standards they've set for the perfect man. Their list of thirty turns into a list of three. Breathing, working, and hung."

"And sometimes just breathing," said Torino.

Mattie chimed in, looking at Claude, "What do you know about getting older?"

"Mom, I was just talking to Torino."

"Okay now, watch your mouth. I'll show you old," Mattie said, raising her cane as she sat.

"Okay, Mom. You're right," said Claude, giving Torino the eye.

Torino laughed. "She gives new meaning to the term, raising cane."

"You too, boy," she warned Torino.

"Come on in," said Claude, after hearing a knock at the front door.

"Hey, you all," said Mercedes, walking in with Mason and the kids. Rashaad headed straight for Cameron's room, giving a wave as he passed everyone. Mason headed straight for his mother.

"Hey, Mom. I miss you," he said, giving her a bear hug.

"You, too. Where have you been?" she asked.

"Looking for you," he joked. "Can I take you to breakfast one day next week?"

"I don't mind as long as you're here early because I have a meeting at noon during the week."

"I will make sure it's early, Mom," he said, not letting go of her. Mattie seemed irritated and pushed him away, reaching for her purse alongside the couch. Mason helped out by handing it to her.

"What's up?" Mason asked Claude.

"Not much. What about you?" Claude stood up and they hugged, too.

"Just loving this getting out for dinner thing. I can get used to this," said Mason.

"Hey, Star. Come on over here," said Mattie.

Star beamed. "Hi, Grammy."

Mercedes said her hellos and then excused herself. "Let me go see if Venus needs any help. Oh, and I see Sequoia too, huh?" Mercedes said, glancing into the kitchen.

Torino smiled.

"Come with me, Star," Mercedes told her daughter.

"Oh, Mom. Can I watch MTV Road Rules in Cameron's room with Rashaad."

"No, leave the boys to themselves. You come in here with the ladies," Mercedes said noticing Star's frown. "Come on now."

"Dang, Mom. The boys always get to hang out and I never do." Star followed like she was walking the green mile.

Mercedes and Star walked into the kitchen. Mercedes greeted her best friend. "Hey, Sequoia. Torino brought you to dinner, huh? Sounds pretty serious to me."

"Don't jump to conclusions. We're just hanging out."

"Okay, hanging out." Mercedes offered a kiss on Venus's cheek as Venus rinsed off a few tomatoes. "Hey, Venus. Girl, you trying to outdo me, or what?"

Venus looked happy. "Just trying to hold up the standard you've already set."

"From what I see and smell, you're doing it all right. What can we do to help?" Mercedes asked.

"Nothing, we're done. Let's just call the guys in here so we can get started."

Star looked relieved.

"Star, please go get the men, sweetie. Thanks," said Mercedes, patting Star on her head. Star sauntered off expressionless.

Sequoia commented, "That slender girl is filling out in a couple of places, Mercedes. You'd better keep an eye on her. She looks at least sixteen, not thirteen."

Venus asked, "And she's in the ninth grade?

Mercedes said with pride, "Yes, she started school early even though she was born in January. They tested her and went ahead and approved her for admittance way back in first grade. So she's only thirteen and already a freshman in high school."

"She got a great education at Parent school, huh?" asked Sequoia.

"Very good," Mercedes replied. "How's Cameron doing in school, Venus?"

"He's doing well in Spanish, I know that much."

Mercedes laughed while pulling up a chair. "I guess living with a teacher is like home school, huh?"

"You could say that. If we could just break through that wall, I'd be so happy." Venus shook her head while placing the napkin holder on the table.

Mercedes said, "Keep cooking like this and you'll break through. You know what they say, the way to any man is directly through his stomach."

"Let's hope so," Venus said, looking hopeful.

Things seemed much more calm and everyone seemed more amenable as they ate and laughed and told jokes. They used to have a routine of mentioning the highlight of their day at dinner. Claude reminded them of that tradition and family members reflected on their individual highlight. Mattie cracked everyone up when she said her highlight was passing a gallstone.

The ten family members and friend had an enjoyable meal of shrimp spaghetti, garlic bread, and a salad, while a few of the adults sipped on White Zinfandel. Venus made a lemon cake that was the hit of the evening.

Torino scooted his chair back and took his plate to the sink. "I hate to eat and run but we're about to go. I need to get to the grocery store before it's too late."

Sequoia followed behind him, noticing a slight buzz. "His cupboards are typical of a bachelor. Not even paper towels in the kitchen."

"Oh, it's not that bad," Torino rebutted.

Venus said, "Thanks for coming, you two."

"No, thank you, Venus. Everything was lovely," said Sequoia with a hug.

Claude stood up to walk them to the door. "Thanks for coming. And come back again Sequoia."

"She will," said Torino, speaking for her.

Mercedes took each of her family members' plates and rinsed them in the sink, placing them in the dishwasher. "We're right behind you. We're about to leave, too."

Rashaad and Cameron looked at each other as if they had other plans. Rashaad said, "Mom, can we all play Scategories first? Just one game."

Mercedes glanced at Mason who shook his head affirmative and then acquiesced, "Okay, just one game."

"Good night," Torino said, exiting the front door.

Sequoia and Torino entered the grocery store to pick up a few things. They held hands and talked like two teenagers. She responded to his every word and seemed a little more demure, a little calmer, and a little more relaxed.

"What's with all the canned food? Can't we make it fresh?" Sequoia asked as they walked down the wide aisle in Ralph's Superstore.

"You're right but canned is faster and just as good." Torino placed two cans of string beans in the cart. "Now I can get down with the fresh ingredients when I want to."

"I believe you." And then she told him as though she'd made a mental list, "Okay, now. And you need face soap, toothpaste, Ajax, and paper towels."

"I'm on it."

"I'll get in line," Sequoia said, after noticing only one checker open on a packed Sunday evening.

Torino came back with a small version of everything, and a small box of condoms. He threw them into the cart on the sly.

"What's that?" Sequoia asked, knowing good and dang well she knew.

"Just a few condoms."

"For what?" She even blushed as she inquired.

"I always keep those around. It's just a habit."

"I'll say that much. I'll bet you've come here before just for that one item, huh?"

"It is a necessity. Almost like a staple."

"A staple?" she ragged on him.

"Yeah, no single man should be without it."

"Or single woman, I suppose."

"Oh, I guess you stay supplied, too?" Torino asked.

"Yes, it's just that mine are probably expired by now. But yours keep disappearing, huh?"

"Funny how that is."

"Yeah, funny," she teased him.

Sequoia reached up toward the top cabinet in Torino's kitchen, realizing that like most men who are tall, Torino liked to stack things high. She stretched up, high on her tippy-toes as her heels rose from the base of her three-inch mules. She struggled to balance two cans of creamed corn, trying to push them back, all the way in.

Torino smiled as he walked up behind her, checking her out from the bottom of her flexed, elongated calves to the tips of her raspberry painted fingernails. "Let me help you," he said, touching her back with his right hand. He scooted the cans into place with ease. She slowly lowered her heels, feeling herself pressed between him and the counter as she tried to turn around.

"Thanks, dear," she said, feeling his pants zipper in her lower back. She leaned back, resting her head on his chest and brought her right arm back to wrap around his neck.

Torino put his left hand on her stomach and pressed her into him even more. She rested her left arm over his.

"This feels so good," she said, sounding comfortable and safe. "Feels like I'm in good hands."

"Yes, you are," he said, turning her around to face him.

He drew her eyes to him. She looked up at him and studied her own reflection in his eyes.

She moved in closer and kissed him with a soft peck on the lips. He wanted more. He took her lips to his, opening his mouth to meet her tongue. Moaning with each movement of their tongues, he sucked her lips and pulled away again with a gentle peck.

In silence, Torino guided Sequoia to the center island of his kitchen. He took the box of condoms from a plastic bag and then back-armed any items that remained, scooping them off and onto the floor. He lifted Sequoia to sit on top of the tile countertop, unbuttoned her blouse and removed it, leaving it to fall to the kitchen floor. He passionately squeezed her ample breasts together while they peeked through her underwire bra. He undid the snaps and took both of her saluting nipples into his mouth, breathing like a man who'd not had a meal in years. Sequoia leaned back on her hands and looked down to see him enjoying her. Her bottom half squirmed with excitement as if it was finally about to happen. He released her breasts and slipped her out of her blue jean skirt, sliding it to the side.

Torino laid her flat on her back, at the same time parting her legs right in front of him, bending her knees upward and removing her high heels, placing her bare feet flat against the edge of the white tile.

He puckered his lips and kissed the outside of her panties. He licked the outlined shape of her vagina until she started to groan in anticipation. He flicked his tongue up and down along her middle and licked the cotton fabric, teasing what lay beneath. He almost ate her tangerine panties with his teeth, finding a way to move the thong aside just as he slipped the tip of his tongue around the outside of one lip. She jumped and squirmed for more. He licked both lips, side to side, finally pointing his tongue inside of her, tasting her excitement with a tongue screw. He noticed her coils of dark brown hairs, long and unshaven and wild, just the way he liked them. He raised his attention to her clit, touching it lightly and then sucking it and licking just below. His mouth devoured her. Sequoia began to buck like a wild pony yearning to be tamed by his talents. She started to rub her own breasts and moved her hips in cooperation with his strokes. Her legs were now pointed straight out into the air above his back. She had a leg lock on his head so tight that you could only see the top of his dreads.

Sequoia felt a rush that was different, it was intense, it was powerful, and it was coming fast. She held back for a second and then gripped the back of his head, giving him all that she'd been saving. She became so dizzy and so foggy, that she started to cry. Tears rolled down her cheeks while she gave in to the rush.

Torino rose and noticed her emotions. They were spelled out in her dreamy, teary eyes. He came up to wipe her cheeks, while she turned her head almost feeling ashamed that she'd let him get to her like that.

"Don't cry, baby. Are you okay?" he asked.

"Yes," she said softly.

"Are you sure?" he asked, looking her dead in the eye.

"I just lost control."

"I'm glad you did," he said.

Torino took a condom from the box. He bit the foil end with his teeth, taking out the lubricated rubber and securing it on his long, dark, stiffness. He then pulled down Sequoia's thong and pulled her to a standing position. He bent her over the island, laying her tummy flat on the counter. She rose up on her tiptoes so that her hips exacted the height of the edge of the island. Cautiously, he inserted his wide, middle finger into her moist opening. Sequoia tightened up for a moment, and then exhaled deeply, relaxing so as to enjoy his penetration.

"Are you ready?" he asked.

"Yes, I am," she said. She looked back at him and caught a glimpse of his girth. She was surprised and impressed. She braced herself.

Torino took hold of his own penis and guided himself into her, careful to sense her physical reaction as he worked each inch into a full entry within a matter of seconds. He pumped his way into her and listened for her groans of pleasure with each gradual motion.

Indeed she did moan upon his entry. He was deep and his size took up all of her.

"Sequoia?"

"Yes."

His heartbeat mirrored her rhythm. "I think I'm in love with you, baby. I think I've been in love with you for a long time. Just say you'll never leave me."

"I'll never leave you."

"Say you belong to me."

"I belong to you, Torino. Nobody but you."

His face was within an inch of her long hair, flowing down her back. It smelled of sweet orange as he took in the aroma, almost feeling dizzy from the sensation of being inside of her. "Can I come inside of you?"

"Yes."

"Can I come inside of you?" he asked again.

"Yes, you can," she replied louder.

He looked at her, spellbound by her flagrant sexuality, hoping to catch eye contact. But Sequoia's head was bent down with her eyes shut.

"Sequoia, I've wanted you for so long. I watched you when you danced and I watched you when you walked. I've been wanting you for so many damn years."

"Well, it's yours now."

"There's no turning back, baby. I'm coming for you now."

"Give it to me. Give mamma all of your stuff," Sequoia said, finally looking back to watch him work it.

Torino saw her brown, sultry eyes looking back at him and exploded before he could release his next word. He pumped and then froze, tightening his glutes and allowing his shooting juices to pulsate into his new woman.

He spoke while still grunting. "That's what I'm talking about, right there. That's how it's supposed to feel."

All Sequoia could say was, "Torino. I love you, too."

He kissed her back softly and then removed himself, grabbing the base of the condom. He then rested his chest on her back. Both breathing in exact unison. Both drained. Both having released their emotions for the other. Both collapsing through a slow, lasting exhale.

Mercedes left for work in the morning. She decided to go in a little later after dropping off Star and Rashaad at school. Just as she pulled out of the garage, Sequoia was strolling down the side walkway from the back house, prepared to start her day as well.

"Hey, girl. I'm going to have to start charging you rent, too," Mercedes yelled out of the driver side window.

"I wouldn't blame you. Even my mom is starting to trip. She says I'm never home. I moved her in with me and now I'm gone all the time."

"You're still paying for that duplex in Culver City?"

"Oh, come on now, I haven't been around for that long." Sequoia was running her fingers through her hair. "I need to get him some new mirrors in that tiny bathroom. I need to be able to see the back of my nappy head."

"Your hair looks fine. I'm surprised Colette hasn't come by trying to start something. Check your tires now," Mercedes kidded.

"She calls every now and then, but for the most part I think she's been pretty quiet."

"Where are you headed anyway?" Mercedes asked.

"I have to stop by IBM and set some travel arrangements for one of their executives."

"And that's it?"

"So far."

"Shoot, I'll be at that office all day trying to book these models for a show Eve is doing next month."

"If anyone can do it, you can," Sequoia said, glancing at her wristwatch. "Maybe I'll see you later, okay?"

"I'm sure you will."

Sequoia started toward her Jag when Mercedes called her back. "Sequoia?"

Sequoia stopped and turned around. "Yes, girl. What?"

"You really like Torino, don't you?" Mercedes asked.

"Yes, Mercedes, I really do. He's just different. It's like we have a history together. We seem to know each other so well. Nothing shocks either one of us."

"That's important. Just be careful, Sequoia. Take it slow and make sure this is what you want."

"Mercedes, we're just dating."

"It seems like you're living together, almost," Mercedes said with a wink.

"Well, we're not. But, we are spending a lot of time with each other. Believe it or not, Torino is a man who is generous in spirit and sex. I am really happy."

"I can see that."

Sequoia sounded as if she was hypnotized. "I've been alone for so long, I just can't describe the feeling. It's like we just fell into sync with each other."

"Like I said, be careful and ease into it."

"I think I'm beyond easing into it. Why do you keep saying take it slow? What's up with you?" Sequoia asked.

"Just that he's fresh off of dealing with Colette. You never know what his feelings really are about her," Mercedes explicated.

Sequoia sounded assured. "He's over her, believe me. She's the least of my worries. Look, I've got to go."

"Okay, girl. Call me later if you can. I want to hear more," Mercedes said as she prepared to put her car in reverse.

"Sure. I'll give you a buzz."

"Okay, girl. Have a good day. I guess I can't call you the born again virgin anymore, huh?" Mercedes joked.

"Born again, yes. Virgin, hell no," Sequoia said with a melody. She threw her hands up to the blue sky and sashayed away.

Sequoia had Colette on her mind most of the day, without even knowing why she was really bothered by her. It was not like Torino was giving Colette the time of day or anything. Sequoia barely made it into her two-bedroom home that evening when she sat down to pour herself a glass of white wine. She called Mercedes at home and found herself inquiring about Colette.

Sequoia told Mercedes, "She's just a trip, that's for sure so I don't feel sorry for her. And I must say that she's no fan of mine anyway."

"Colette doesn't like too many females. And you're saying that you don't feel sorry for her about what?"

"About breaking up with Torino. She smothered him like gravy on a pork chop."

"That she did."

"And about being pregnant."

Mercedes replied, "Oh, she's not really pregnant."

"Yes, she is."

"Please. She's just trippin'. With her vain and shallow self, she's not *even* going to ruin her figure or her career trying to get a man with the I'm *pregnant* game."

"The pregnancy test has two pink lines, Mercedes. She mailed it to Torino."

"She what? She mailed the test kit to him? I wouldn't be surprised if that was probably somebody else's test. But I must say that I don't know if she'd stoop to borrowed pee or not. What's she gonna do about it?" Mercedes asked.

"She wants it, so she says. But Torino doesn't buy it."

Mercedes seemed understanding of Torino. "Hell, he doesn't even know if it's his, or if she's even pregnant at all. Why do women always play that card? Like having a child with the man is going to make him leave his woman?"

"A lot of men do just that."

"Torino won't. That much I know."

"He'd better not," warned Sequoia.

"Wow, look at you. You're playing for keeps. When are you going to make your way back over here to your man's house?"

"In a minute. I'll talk to you later, girl."

"All right now. Be careful and be happy," Mercedes admonished.

"I will."

Within a few hours, Sequoia was preparing to make it on over to Torino's place. She knew he was about to leave and that he'd probably be gone when she got there. But she had the key to his place anyway so it didn't matter. She was secure in knowing that when his night was all said and done, he was coming home to her. And she'd be waiting.

After nine o'clock that night Torino was in his car. He answered his cell while on his way to the club.

Kyle greeted him. "Hey dude."

Torino was casual in his reply. "What up?"

"I need to talk to you."

"Talk."

"Man, chill out."

"Talk." Torino repeated himself.

"Colette is pregnant."

"She told me that hard-to-believe news. But, if she is, it's yours."

"Torino, man."

Torino signaled to turn into the parking lot. "Anything else, bro? I've gotta go."

Kyle sounded apologetic. "Man, I want to explain."

"No need. You thought with your dick. I ain't mad."

"No, I mean about the comps at the club, Torino. Let me explain."

"Talk."

"I was wrong. I was wrong about that and about kicking it with Colette."

Torino turned off the ignition and prepared to exit his ride. "Well, as far as Colette is concerned I guess it couldn't have been too wrong. You're about to be a papa, bro. Anyway, I never got a piece of that without a glove, man. I'm out."

Kyle gave up. "Peace."

Click.

* * *

Venus spent the next day on the telephone, looking for volunteer work either as a cuddler with a baby adoption service, or placing children who were in foster homes. She had not heard back from the Make-A-Wish Foundation, which was the gig she really wanted.

The in-home nurse, Gloria, came into the den and handed her the cordless phone.

"Thanks, Gloria. Hello?"

"Hello, is Claude there?" a woman asked.

"No he's not. Who's calling?"

"It's Heidi from the real estate office. Is this Venus?"

"Yes it is. How are you, Heidi?" Venus turned off the television that had been watching her.

"I'm fine."

"I'll tell him you called. Is there a message?" Venus inquired.

"Well, just that I have the rent check for this month and I'm about to go out of town. Can I bring it by?"

"How about if I run by and get it. Is that okay? I'm about to leave anyway."

"Sure, that's fine," Heidi said.

"Which property are you in?" Venus asked.

Heidi replied, "I'm on the northwest corner on Sixty-fourth and Garth."

"I'll be right over."

Venus walked up to the door, noticing a new white Infiniti parked in the driveway. She knocked three times and then Heidi opened the door.

"Hello, Venus. Thanks for coming by. I just didn't want to send it being that it would get to him late."

"It's okay. I wasn't doing anything really important. I have the time," Venus said, standing at the threshold.

"I'll go get the check. Have a seat."

Venus sat in the chair by the bay window. "How long have you lived here?"

Heidi walked back with her purse. "Oh, not that long. I really should buy my own home, especially since I'm in the business. I should be able to do that by next year. I moved in right after Claude and his ex-wife bought their new home. I guess it's a lot larger, huh?"

Venus corrected her. "That was Fatima. They were never married."

Heidi signed the check. "Oh, I'm sorry. I got it wrong."

Venus looked all around. "It's okay. Yes, I think our house is quite a bit larger, but I like the style of this home. The high ceilings are very nice."

"Thanks," Heidi said, handing Venus the check for six hundred dollars.

Venus looked at the amount. "Is that all you pay?"

"Yes, they've never raised the rent on me."

"Who's they?" Venus asked.

"Claude and Mace. His name is on this house now, too."

"How long have you known Mason?"

"Pretty much ever since I met Cicely. Probably back in college. He's the one who asked Claude to rent it to me," Heidi explained.

"Oh, I see. It's just that I thought you and Cicely were sisters. At least that's what my husband told me."

"Oh gosh, no. Whatever gave him that idea?" Heidi pointed to a framed picture of her and Cicely. "No, she's just my best friend in the world, that's all. You know how we are, always claiming our best friends are family, like a second cousin or something. That's black folks for you."

Venus stood up. "I guess so. Well, I'm going to get going, Heidi. I'll make sure to give Claude the check."

"Thanks for stopping by. I could have given it to Claude at work but like I said I'm on vacation this week. Cicely and I are going to Mexico for ten days. Cancun you know."

"That should be lovely. Enjoy yourself, Heidi. I'll see you a little later."

"Okay. Tell Claude I said hello for me."

"I will." *What the hell is this all about?* Venus asked herself.

# chapter 13

Just before dusk, Claude pulled through Holy Cross cemetery to a street called Resurrection. He parked his fancy red sports car along the curb and stepped out with two bouquets of white roses for his first love. He stepped onto the curb and walked over toward the statue of Mary that watched over Fatima's graveside. "Fatima Clark," read the gray marble stone, "Always in our hearts."

He removed the dirty, metal flower vase as ants scattered for cover. He headed toward the water fountain to rinse the dirt and grass to fill it to the rim and returned to the tombstone and neatly arranged each bouquet in the vase. He took a deep inhale to the fragrant, rich petals, replaced the vase and stood back to admire the way the long stemmed roses spread out from left to right like wings spanning along the direct width of the stone.

The warmth of the hot wind blew across his face. He kneeled down on one knee and began to speak.

"Fatima. My dear Fatima. I pray that you know how much I miss you. Not a day goes by that I don't think about you. These flowers are from Cam and me. He talks about you every now and then but I know what's up with him. Actually, he hates it when I bring you up because it makes him have to face too many feelings. I refuse to push him, but eventually he will need to get it out and face it. But what kind of role model am I when I have trouble facing it as well?"

Claude looked toward the nearby hillside, sloped, and green

blades of grass and tall headstones lined up in a row. He recalled a telephone message he'd heard on Fatima's cell phone the day she died. He replayed it in his mind as if he'd memorized it.

*Fatima, It's Owen. I'll tell you one thing, you want to end it, I'll end it for both of us. I'm not going away this time to just leave you to your happy little family. You run to me every time that sorry ass nigger of yours decides he needs to work late, probably fucking his secretary. Unlike him, I won't share you with your best friend like you said he wants to. I don't understand why you won't just leave him. Just when I go away, you trip out when you see that I've started to move on.*

*I give you one week to get your ass free and meet me in Vegas. I'm not playing, so you'd better call me by noon today so we can make plans to meet and talk in person. This has been going on for far too long. I'm not waiting any longer. And I'm not going to just disappear. And if you think I'm playing, try me. I will not let him have you. Without you, I have nothing to live for anyway. You don't want to be my enemy, Fatima. Don't make me start trippin' out. I love you. And I suggest you call me right now. And don't even think about having Thanksgiving dinner with him. Good-bye.*

He sighed and talked toward Fatima's headstone. "Look, Fatima, I know that you loved me. I really do forgive you for getting involved with Owen. I have to forgive you, otherwise I'll go crazy. I know you intended to cut it off. You must have been scared to death. And I'm sorry that asshole was sick enough to do what he did. He deserved more than what he got. But you didn't deserve to die.

"Venus is okay. At times I can't figure out where my head is with her. Sometimes I hate her for agreeing to marry me. Sometimes I hate her for loving me. Sometimes I hate her for desiring me. Sometimes I hate her for being in that house with me. A part of me respects her for taking on Cam and me. I respect her for dealing with the shame and the guilt and the gossip. But she is a good woman and I made the choice to say I do, so I must deal with it. I got myself into this situation and by the grace of God, I'll get through this.

"I love you, Tima. Maybe being married would have made a difference, I don't know. But I thank you for Cam. I thank you for bringing him into my life when his jerk of a father abandoned both of you. I thank you for being our angel and watching over us. And I thank you for the many years you gave me, being my woman and making me happy. It must be a glorious feeling to be able to rest in peace. Tell Daddy I said hello. I'll see you both again some day. Good-bye."

Claude continued to kneel and then gave the sign of the cross. He stood and shook away the loose grass from his right knee. He stared at the large, shady trees all around him and reached down to pick up a tiny branch with thin stems that extended outward. He bent two of the stems into a curved shape and tucked the tip into the base of the branch. It resembled a heart. Claude placed the heart on the stone just above the word "heart." He blew a kiss toward her name and turned to walk away. He stepped inside of his car for a few moments, eyes shot with fine lines of blood, and pupils wet and cloudy. He started the engine and honked two quick times as he pulled off.

*I can no longer play this game. I've got to know more. I've got to put this to bed,* he thought. He exited the cemetery and got onto the 405 freeway. He reached into his glove compartment and pulled out a piece of folded paper. On it he'd written Owen's old address, which he'd found on Fatima's computer. He drove the long distance south to San Pedro.

Claude drove up the street toward a run-down, weather-beaten home in the middle of the block where weeds and dead grass grew wildly. He parked across the street and looked over, imagining Fatima's car pulling up into the driveway.

He walked up to the broken picket fence. A man exited the front door and walked out onto the porch.

"Can I help you?" asked the young man. He looked to be in his mid-twenties.

"Are you Owen's old roommate?" Claude asked from the sidewalk.

"Who's asking?" the man asked with caution, trying his best to make his voice carry.

"I'm Claude Wilson. Fatima's, I guess you could say, husband."

The man greeted him with a blank face. "Hello, Mr. Wilson. What can I do for you?"

Claude walked through the front gate and up the dusty walkway. He stood at the base of the steps and looked up. The closer Claude got to the guy, the more the man smelled of gin.

"This might not make sense to you but . . ." Claude looked away for a moment and then back up toward the young man. "I need to know something about him. I need to see pictures of him doing normal, everyday things. I need to hear you say he was normal, just like you. Just like me. Just a man in love who went too far."

The young man's eyes were bloodshot and he looked tired, unkempt and in need of a long hot shower. "Mr. Wilson, Owen was hurting but he didn't want to lose Fatima. I think he felt he no longer had control because he couldn't get her to do what he wanted her to do. Which was to settle down with him."

"Did he talk to you about it? Did you see this coming?" Claude asked with an angry edge to his tone.

The young man pulled out a pack of Marlboros from his pocket. He flicked a Bic lighter and lit one up, putting the cancer stick in his mouth yet still talking as it bounced about. He squinted his eyes as the smoke slowly rose toward the sky. "He talked to me and said he was having trouble letting go. I didn't interpret that to mean he was capable of murder. I saw no signs that he would buy a gun and go off. He had other women here all the time. But I know no one compared to Fatima. He was very popular, but he never got into other women too deeply. And believe me, there were a lot of them. He even has a new daughter. His daughter has to live her life without him."

"And? Hell, my son has to live his life without his mother."

The man spoke hauntingly. "And I, Mr. Wilson, have to spend the rest of my life without my father."

Claude stood motionless.

The young man took the cigarette from his mouth and blew a long puff of smoke, flicking the ashes onto the porch. He took another long drag, blew smoke again and reinserted the cigarette between his lips. "My name is Owen, Jr."

Claude blew out a deep breath while his thoughts simmered. "You lived with your father and saw all of the womanizing and then to top it off you had to deal with what happened two years ago?"

"Yes. It's been hard on me, too. But he was not himself, Mr. Wilson. He just snapped."

"I hate to tell you this, boy, but I really think your father had to have been crazy to begin with. People like that usually have problems way before an incident like killing someone."

Owen, Jr. tossed the cigarette onto the porch and stomped on it with his black vinyl house slipper. "He'd just lost his job, and my grandmother, who was his birth mother, had just died. He needed Fatima and he was losing her, too."

"That's just too damn bad." Claude tried to force himself to keep his cool, but it wasn't working. "I tell you right now, I feel a little bit sorry for you, son, but if I'd found out that your dad was screwing with my woman, I'd of found his punk ass and pulled the trigger dead in his fat mouth."

"I could stand here and curse you out, or ask you to leave, Mr. Wilson. But I understand. Believe me I understand. And I'm sorry." He sounded very, very tired.

"No disrespect, but you mean to tell me you saw him running game with pretty much a married woman and you said nothing? Let's just hope I don't end up in a mental hospital and then escape just so I can come after you." Claude paced a few steps toward the gate and then turned back. He shrugged his shoulder and then decided to speak reverently. "Man, I don't mean that. This all seems like a bad dream that just won't end. Where the hell was I when all of this was going on?" he asked himself, shaking his head toward the ground. "Owen, tell me something. Did they meet here sometimes?"

The young man took another cigarette but this time he did not light it. He simply put it behind his ear. "Yes."

"Did you know her well?"

"Yes. Never like a mother figure or anything like that. But I never got involved as far as giving him advice. After all, I'm the one who needed advice from my father."

"Well, in spite of that you should have done something."

"I wish I would have. If only I'd known what was going on in his head."

"If only I'd known I was sharing her with a damn lunatic," Claude said, looking down at his feet as he kicked a few bits of trash away from the concrete pathway. "Well, anyway, thanks for your time. And you know what? I don't need to see those photos after all. I'm about to go see him myself."

"Good-bye, Mr. Wilson. And good luck."

"Claude."

"Claude. Take care."

The next morning, Venus noticed Claude was quiet. He did not check on Cameron or on Mattie as he usually did before he made his way out. He passed on breakfast and walked out the door, nearly forgetting to say good-bye to her.

"Are you going straight to the office, baby?" she asked, pulling his arm back as he took a couple of steps past the threshold.

He leaned back and replied, "Baby, I'll be home late tonight. I'm going to drive on out to Lancaster and visit the men's prison there and then head to work."

She eyed him like he was speaking French. "What?"

"Venus, I have to."

"Claude, don't tell me."

"I just have to, Venus. I can't go on like this."

Her mouth hung open while she watched him walk away, get in his car and then pull off, driving slower than usual. She just stared out the door, leaning against the doorframe in her robe with her legs crossed at the ankles.

"Neither can I," she said out loud.

The long line of visitors stretched around and around, wrapping its way from under the aluminum awning, which blocked out the morning sun all the way to the middle of the parking lot. The line moved slowly, full of people who looked fairly upbeat, some even full of anticipation, excited to see their dads, husbands, boyfriends, brothers, and sons. But Claude was not having anything but answers today.

He filled out his visitation paper, writing the inmate name Owen Chambers. The lady behind the bulletproof glass entered his name into the computer. Owen had not had any visitors that day so Claude was allowed to proceed. He passed through the security detectors and took the filled-to-capacity county bus up the long hill to visit the maximum-security inmates on the north side of the prison.

After about ten minutes of sitting in a sterile room upon a dingy bench, they called Claude's visitation number.

He was instructed to sit at window eighty-three. He took his seat on the low, cold metal stool and waited. He noticed the many faces of the inmates wearing their prison blues. All of the inmates with visitors around him had arrived. Yet the seat on the other side of the thick glass was empty. Then, he heard the sound of rattling chains approaching as a guard escorted a prisoner to the opposite seat. He looked up and their eyes met. It was Owen, Fatima's murderer.

Even though Owen's ankles were chained, his hands were free and he had the nerve to carry a big black bible in his right hand. He even had a gray plastic rosary around his neck. His neck was small, he was small, and he looked old. He took a seat.

Owen reached for the receiver as the guard walked away. Claude stared at him, just examining his face as if his eyes had the ability to snap pictures, or shoot bullets. He saw Owen's lips move. Owen tipped his head toward the receiver. Claude picked it up, grabbing the base with all of his might.

Owen spoke first. "Don't tell me."

*The exact same, weak ass voice from the cell phone message,* Claude thought. "You got it, it's me."

"It's about time."

Claude shook his head in disgust. "You are one punk ass muthafucka, dude. You are really one poor excuse for a man."

Owen shook his head as if in agreement. "That's your opinion."

Claude was choking the phone with his tight fist. "You should be dead."

"I will be, soon enough," Owen said as if dying was routine.

"Yes, but to die while incarcerated ain't shit compared to what you did."

"Don't forget, Claude. I'm insane, you know."

"That you are, or just one slick, tired ass nigga. Which one?"

Owen was smug. "You came here to make yourself feel better, I see. Get it out."

Claude leaned back, as far away from the glass as he could get. "You don't even have the decency to tell me you're sorry."

"For killing my woman? Why would I owe you an apology for that?"

Claude's eyes narrowed. "You killed the love of my life."

"Oh, spare me. I couldn't get her to marry me. But why didn't you, bro?"

Claude spoke with a deeper voice. "That's none of your damn business. And I'm not your bro."

"I'll tell you why. It's because you were too busy doing your thing. She used to tell me how busy you were."

"You know what? I heard your tired ass message that the police took into evidence. That's some fucked up shit to threaten a woman like that."

Owen smirked. "I don't think they needed your tape, considering I was sitting in a car outside of where she was shot with a bullet in my chest. I confessed."

"You couldn't even kill your damn self right. Next time aim for your big ass head."

"Believe me, if I could, I would."

Claude sneered as he spoke. "I hope the rest of your life is a living hell, because mine sure is."

Owen sounded like a prophet pimp. "Heaven on earth, or hell on earth, it's our choice."

"This was not my choice."

"You asked God to be here in this life. He gave you life and all that goes along with it"

Claude leaned closer. "I didn't asked God for shit."

"Oh, certainly you did, that's why you're here."

"Oh, so now you're the mystic spiritualist, huh?" He sat up straight as a board. "Why is it that every man in jail suddenly finds God?" Claude asked, looking around and behind himself. "Where is he?"

"He's in my life, that's all I can say."

Claude looked at Owen's hands, examined each grubby finger. His unkempt pinky fingers had extra long nails, and dirt had collected underneath. He looked at his tired, tiny, beady eyes, with his cloudy, gray eyeballs. His Afro was a mess, in need of a serious haircut, with gray at his temples and sideburns. His aging skin was medium brown and he was unshaven. He had bad, yellow teeth and chapped lips.

"I don't know what the hell she saw in you," Claude said with malice.

"What she saw you can't see right now, brother. But I'll show you if you'd like." Owen grabbed his crotch with a naughty stare.

"No, keep that Vienna sausage tucked away for your new woman on the cell block. I'm sure you're used to bustin' asses with it by now."

Owen acted like that was a compliment. "That I am."

"I just want you to know one thing."

"What's that, chief?" Owen replied as if it was all a joke.

Claude clenched his jaw. "You are one sad excuse for a man who is in need of every word that Bible has to offer you. You had no respect for my relationship with Fatima Clark and you took her life because you couldn't control her. I despise you for that. My son despises you for that. And her family despises you for that."

Owen almost grinned. "Speak for yourself. I know for a fact that Cameron does not despise me."

Claude raised his voice. "Don't you dare speak his name. You don't even know that young man."

"Oh, but I do. I met him a few times but around him she always referred to me as Bobby Cujo, her old friend. And ask Venus about how well I knew him. You did end up marrying her, I understand."

"News travels fast behind bars, huh?"

"Shit, you're a prominent figure. You're a hot ass boy, right. News around here doesn't travel as fast as you, putting a ring on her finger when Fatima was still warm in the ground. I guess that makes you a fine one to judge. Is pussy that hard to come by nowadays?"

Claude slammed the phone down, without replacing it on the hook. Visitors nearby gave him their full attention. He sprang to his feet and started to reach for the receiver again, but instead spoke by mouthing the words, "Fuck you."

"Anytime," Owen mouthed back, laughing while he pushed the buzzer for the guard, hanging up the phone.

Claude watched as Owen was escorted away, looking back, taking choppy steps with a haunting smirk. Claude's legs and heart gave way to his pain as he sat back down and cried.

Claude's voice was shaking as he phoned his wife from the car. "Venus, I'm on my way home. We need to talk." Claude disconnected the phone without even hearing her reply. He raced down the freeway and off at the Howard Hughes Parkway exit. He pulled into the driveway and entered the front door two seconds later. He sat on the leather recliner in the den and called out for Venus.

Venus ran downstairs, rushing up to her husband as if he were in trouble. "What's the matter, Claude?"

"Is Cameron home?"

"No, he's at his grandparents' house. They came to pick him up."

"Sit down," he instructed her like she was a child. She did just that. "Bobby Cujo? What the hell do you know?"

She cursed under her breath. "Bobby who?" You could hear a pin drop.

He studied her, knowing she was playing dumb. "Venus, I want to know now."

She felt her stomach contract. "Claude, calm down. Your mom is down the hall."

He spoke louder and more defiant. "You start talking. Now!"

Venus looked uneasy, eyeing the floor. She crossed and uncrossed her legs as if she was trying to get comfortable with herself and her words. She raised her gaze and went for it.

"Claude, Owen is Cameron's father."

He snapped his fingers loudly. "I fucking knew it. Dammit, Venus. And you knew all this time and didn't tell me?"

"Fatima made me swear that I wouldn't."

Claude struggled to put two and two together. "She knew him that damn long?"

"Yes."

"So when she told me Cameron's father abused her and that she didn't know where he was, that was a lie."

Venus tried to explain. "He abused her back then and swore he would stop. And he did. After that, the two of them just always managed to keep in touch. They had some sort of chemical bond or something. She just couldn't seem to really get him out of her life. And at times, it was like she really didn't want to. Maybe because he was Cameron's father."

"Oh please, it's not like he ever got to know this fool. I still can't believe that she brought him around Cam without telling that boy he was his own father. Cameron's been thinking his dad is out there lost in the wilderness. She could have at least told him who he was instead of bringing him around and calling him fucking Bobby Cujo. I won't even ask why that name was her choice other than the fact that Owen is a damn dog himself. How confusing for Cameron."

"Cameron was so little, I'm sure he doesn't even remember meeting Owen. Anyway, Claude, those were not my personal decisions. These were choices that Fatima made. She knew that Owen wouldn't be the best father to Cameron. And she knew that eventually, she had to get away. But she never did."

"Fourteen years of never did. And now you have the nerve to wake up every day in the very house that Cameron wakes up in, knowing his own father shot and killed his mother. How do you live with that?"

Venus looked empty. "I ask myself that very question every day."

"At least you have some conscience," he snarled.

"Claude, I don't think Cameron needs to know now."

"No, the time to tell him was years ago. It would kill him now. That boy has a crazy-looking, grown half brother and a new sister he'll never know. It was hard enough with him just dealing with the two of us marrying each other. I thought I was doing the right thing."

"So did I. Claude, we both wanted what Fatima wanted. She asked me to look after the two of you if anything ever happened to her and I agreed."

"Oh, so you married me on a promise? Like some sort of agreement?" he asked.

"Something like that. But Claude, I really fell in love with you after Fatima died. It seems we had so much in common, so many similar memories and we each knew her so well. It just felt comfortable to grieve with you. But on a daily basis, I wonder about myself. What kind of woman falls in love with her best friend's man? That's a hell of a secret to keep."

"You've been keeping a lot of secrets lately, huh, Venus?"

"Yes I have."

"So now what?"

"I don't know."

"Venus, all of this allegiance to Fatima is tearing our lives apart. She's just as powerful in death as she was in life."

"I agree. But my concern now is about us. Can you love me the way I need to be loved after all that's happened?"

"I don't know?

She looked stunned. "You don't know?"

"You know what I do know? I know that I need to be alone."

"So do I," Venus said, standing up to walk out. She thought for a minute and then just decided to put it out there again. "Claude, Fatima fooled around on you. I didn't. One day you'll stop being so angry with everyone around you, and try to figure out why you've never been angry at her."

Claude was silent. He squinted as he looked at his wife. "Did Fatima love Owen? Was she only with me for my money?"

Venus paused before she replied, "Those are two questions I'll never be able to answer. I surely don't need your money. You know, one day, you're going to have to be okay with perhaps not having the answers to those questions about her. One day, you're going to have to let her go so that you can tend to your marriage, Claude. But let me ask you a question now. Are you still in love with a dead woman?"

"Are you?"

Venus gave him a piercing look of distain. His expression mirrored hers. She exited the den and slammed the double doors together behind her.

Cameron arrived back home late. Venus greeted him at the door while Claude stayed in the den where he slept all night. Venus lay in bed alone, unable to doze off. She felt sick, she felt depressed, and she felt to blame. Tears were swimming in her eyes until the moment she finally shut her heavy lids, frowning as she slept.

Later that evening, Torino was winding down the last hour at the club. He stood back for a minute, watching the partygoers shake their butts off, meeting and greeting and engaging. From the corner of his eyes, he could see a woman coming toward him, walking at a fast pace. It was Colette.

"What are you doing here?" he asked.

She sounded excited. "I need to talk to you."

"Don't make me call Bo to escort you out. Who let you in, anyway?"

"Torino, why are you so angry with me? I just don't get it. I'm carrying your baby." Colette touched her own stomach.

"I'm not gonna get into that." Torino talked into his two-way. "Bo, please come here now."

"I want us to talk. This pregnancy happened for a reason. It's a sign that we need to be together." She began to reach for his arm.

Torino moved away. "It's a sign that you're a ho'. Now get out of my face."

"Mr. Wilson, are you okay?" Bo asked, standing behind Colette.

"How did she get in?"

"Sir, we have a new girl at the door. Colette paid the girl just as I turned my back to resolve another matter."

Colette interrupted. "Torino, I am not leaving until you talk to me."

"Oh, you think so?"

"Are you seeing Sequoia?" Colette asked.

"Bo, will you see Miss Berry out of here, please?"

"Yes, sir," Bo replied, extending his hand toward the door.

"You're really going to kick me out of here? I've been here by your side for all of your events for the past two years."

"Not anymore."

"You'd kick your own baby's mom out?"

"I'm kicking Kyle's baby's mom out."

"Torino you know for a fact that there were times that we didn't use a condom. I'm way too far along for it to be anyone's but yours."

Torino turned his back. "Bo, don't let this happen again."

"Yes, sir," he said, after placing his hand on Colette's elbow. She walked toward the door, looking back the entire time.

"Faggot," she yelled with vengeance in her voice.

Torino simply spoke into his two-way again. "Let's meet in the kitchen to count the drawers. Out."

# chapter 14

Venus pulled up in her Montero and parked in the driveway. She called Cameron from her cell to come out and help her remove the bags from the back of her SUV.

"How many bags are there?" he asked as if she could do it herself.

She insisted and raised her voice. "Cam, come out now. I need your help."

He hung up and ran outside thirty seconds later looking half dressed and undone. "All right. Here I am."

"Here, I'll take a few and you can take the rest." He peeked inside of a bag from Robinson's May. "What did you buy? Anything for me?"

"Not this time, Cam. Just something for your grandma."

He pulled a box from the bag. "She needs this pillow?"

"Yes, if you must know. It helps her to secure the back of her neck. She's been having aches in her neck and back lately."

"You sure spend a lot of money," he commented.

Venus threw her head back as if he had the nerve. "Excuse me?"

"You just buy things almost every day," he commented, taking two bags under his right arm and three into his left hand as he led the way.

"Oh, like groceries so you can eat and clothes to put on our back and shoes for our feet, stuff like that?"

"Yes, and things for Grandma. I'm just saying you must like shopping."

She looked displeased. "Cam, I can think of a lot of other things I'd rather do. Oooh." Venus suddenly gasped and dropped a small bag.

Cameron immediately turned back toward her. "What's wrong?"

"Uumh," she said, grabbing the side of her stomach.

"What's happening? Are you all right?" Cameron put the bags down and reached around her back with one arm.

Venus fell to one knee while Cameron leaned down on the concrete walkway with her.

"What's going on? Are you okay?"

"Cameron, I think I'm just hungry. I think I need to eat. I'm just feeling a little dizzy."

"Are you sure that's it?"

"Yes, I'm sure. I think I have a cramp from . . . Ooh," she said, panting loudly.

"Let me get you into the house."

Cameron grabbed her under the elbows and helped her stand. She took a few steps, almost reaching the front door when she stopped and said, "Oh my God."

Venus looked down and saw dark red blood running down from the inside of her legs to her feet. Her black sandals were soaked.

"Venus, oh no. Gloria, come here quick," Cameron yelled, while holding Venus's hand.

"Go get her, Cameron. Leave me right here. Just go get her." Venus buried her head toward her knees.

Cameron stared at Venus without taking a step.

"Go, Cameron," she hissed under her breath. Her mind raced. *This has got to be all about karma.*

He ran into the house yelling, "Gloria, come quick. My mom is sick. Help us please. She's outside."

The next evening, Claude and Venus arrived back from the hospital. Venus got out of the car on her own, realizing that the walkway had been washed down. No sign of the blood from her miscarriage.

Cameron hurried outside to greet them just as they made their way to the front door. "You look good, Venus. Are you feeling better?" he asked.

"Much better, physically, Cameron. I'm sorry you had to see that."

"No, I'm just sorry you had to go through that. I was scared for you. I'm glad you're home."

Claude questioned him, "Cameron, did you do what I asked you to do?"

"Yes, Dad. I changed the sheets and cleaned up your room."

"I didn't want you to do it. I told you to ask Gloria."

"But, today is Sunday and she's gone. It only took a minute."

"Thanks, Cameron," Venus said.

"And where's your grandma?" Claude asked as they all walked inside the house.

"She's sleeping."

"So, she doesn't know what happened?" Venus inquired.

Cameron replied, "No, she didn't ask me anything about where you were anyway."

"Good. I'm going to go lie down. Thanks for your help."

"No problem. Do you need something to drink or anything else?" Cameron offered.

"No, I'll be fine."

"I can help you upstairs," Claude said, while heading for the kitchen.

"Really I feel good as new. You two just order a pizza or something. No family dinner tonight, okay?"

"Of course not, baby. Get yourself some rest," Claude said, passing through the kitchen door.

Venus took each step slowly, but made her way up the double flight of stairs and into the master bedroom. She closed the door.

Cameron joined his dad for a drink of Sunny Delight. "Dad, was it a girl?" he asked with a hush.

Claude looked surprised. "Cameron. She was not far along enough to be able to tell something like that. She couldn't have been more than a couple months."

"How come you guys didn't tell me she was pregnant?"

"I didn't know, son. I'm not even sure she knew."

Cameron was full of questions. "Has this ever happened to her before? Because I read some women have trouble like that all the time."

"Apparently not. If you must know she's been on the pill forever, so she tells me. You read up on it already?"

"Yeah. Wow, that was a trip. I really felt scared for her," Cameron admitted.

"She told me you did, son. And I appreciate your help and concern." Claude looked at Cameron for a second, trying to see any resemblance to the man who killed his mother. He saw absolutely none. "Thank God," Claude said out loud before he knew he'd released the words.

"Thank God is right," Cameron said in agreement. "We need to keep an eye on Grandma and Venus, huh Dad?"

"You've got that right, son. At least for now."

Mason and Mercedes decided to take a nice, leisurely drive in his Porsche, down the coast from Ladera toward Malibu and Santa Barbara, just like they used to years ago. The top was down and Mercedes had her face to the breeze as they conversed like two teenagers along the way.

"Got that hair blowing in the wind like you did back in college, huh?" Mason commented.

Mercedes leaned her head back, brushing her bangs to the side. "Oh, it feels so wonderful, so exhilarating, Mason. We need to do this more often."

"Where do you want to end up?"

"How about the beach like we used to do, honey. Remember how we'd drive out to the Palisades and fool around on the sand. Let's go to that spot. Please?" she asked, feeling energized.

"Okay, baby. Don't start to beg. I'm not sure we can even park near there now. Things have changed so much what with all of the floods and mud slides along the coast."

"Let's just go check."

Mason put the pedal to the metal as they drove along Pacific Coast Highway toward Chitagua Boulevard. It looked different, yet it was still the same stretch of beach. They could see it from the highway.

Mason pointed. "See, we can't even park over there anymore. We used to be able to drive right onto the beach. It looks like we're not getting any farther than this guard gate these days."

"It's okay, Mason. Let's just get out and walk."

"Baby, that would be nice, but how about if we just sit here and enjoy the view from the car." He parked the car facing the ocean.

"Eighteen years ago you would have been game."

"Eighteen years ago, I would have pulled the car right up to the sand and we would have laid out in front of the headlights, getting freaky."

"I remember. Nowadays you can't even sit out there without someone coming up to rob your butt."

Mason pulled Mercedes closer, cupping his hand over her right shoulder as she scooted over. He leaned his seat back to extend his body.

"This is nice," Mercedes said.

Mason brought up a subject that had been on his mind. "Mercedes, you know I came from a household where my dad was always gone. Mom held down the fort so to speak."

"But I'll bet you guys had a choice to be out there with Daddy if you wanted to be."

"Sometimes we did."

"See, Star and Rashaad can't just tag behind you on trips out of town. Your line of work is much more demanding and high profile."

"Why can't they go with me? Especially now that Mom is with Claude. You can all go."

"You're right." Mercedes said, looking animated. "Whatever happened to us doing that anyway? I remember going from hole to hole, walking along the ropes, cheering you on."

"Things changed when the kids came along. But we need to plan to go together again. You know what? I think I'm going to sell my interest in the club. I'd like to sell it to Torino."

"How can he afford it?"

"I don't mind helping him get a loan now that I can see he's maturing and trying to do right. He seems different since he met Sequoia."

"I've noticed. But don't base your decision on the fact that he and Sequoia are together. That has nothing to do with his future. Base your decision on him and his ability to pay you off."

"Sounds like you don't have much faith in Torino?"

"I do, really I do. And I must admit it would be nice to not have to worry about Foreplay anymore."

"I just love the name of that club," Mason said, placing his hand on his own crotch area.

"Very funny. Mason, do you know how much it means to me to be able to say that you are my first and only love?"

"I feel the same way."

"Oh, so I'm your first love?"

"Yes, Mercedes, and my only love. I've never been in love with anyone else, ever," he proclaimed.

"But you had others before we met. I didn't."

"Let's not go there, Cedes."

"Anyway," Mercedes said, looking out along the shore, "years ago, we'd have been down there on the sand, deep into round two by now." Mercedes kissed his cheek. "We can start with round one right here."

"Are you crazy?" Mason asked, checking out the surroundings. "The top is down and these attendants seem a bit too busy for my taste."

"Oh hell, honey. Make it fast like you used to," Mercedes said, looking eager.

"I can't believe you're asking me to make it fast for once."

"It was fast that night we came home from the strip club. Did you see me complain?" she asked with a gleam in her eye.

"No."

"Okay then, come on."

Mason still looked uncomfortable. "Damn, but what's my motivation?"

Mercedes's tone became seductive. "Knowing that the woman whose mouth is pleasing you is your lady, your wife, and the woman who loves you. Is that something you want?"

"Say no more," he said as she felt his bulge start to grow. He leaned the seat back all the way and unzipped his dress pants, pulling his penis out. She licked the tip with her stiff tongue and took him deep into her mouth.

"Oh, yeah. That's it, let it hit the back of your throat."

Mercedes positioned herself so that she could use her left hand as well, stroking the bottom and bracing it upright, easing it into her mouth with rapidity, adding her warm saliva for lubrication.

"Do you love me?" she asked, breaking away for a verbal tease.

"Yes."

"You don't want me to leave you, do you? Not the pussy that has only had you inside for eighteen years. The pussy that is virgin to anyone but you. You wouldn't want me out there giving your stuff to someone else would you?"

"No. You're my woman, baby. This dick belongs to my wife," he said, raising his pubic area closer to her mouth for continuation.

Mercedes barely got two licks in when she felt his veins pulsating and his penis thicken. She closed her eyes and moaned him through it as he expelled his secretions into her mouth.

Mercedes took every drop, licking his tip and then kissing it.

Mason jumped. "Okay, now that's not fair."

"That's what I like to do, please my man."

"I can see that, baby." He pulled the flap of his underwear back over his penis and secured his pants, glancing around the car for spectators. There were none.

Mason's phone rang. He could feel Mercedes give him a glance that spoke volumes. "Don't get that," she said, taking a mint out of her purse.

Mason looked at the display of the phone number that flashed from his dashboard. "It's Claude." He let the call go.

Mercedes leaned over against his shoulder and continued looking out at the water. She enjoyed the peace and quiet and serenity. The phone rang again.

"It's Claude again with a 9-1-1 page. I've got to call him back."

Mercedes scooted over and handed him the phone as he pushed automatic callback.

"What's up, man? Is everything still on for dinner?" Mason asked.

"Mason, Venus left us. She left me. She left a note. That's all. Just a fucking note." Claude sounded dejected.

"Venus left you? When did this happen?" Mercedes sat up in her seat.

"She just came back from the hospital and I thought she was taking a nap."

"The hospital?" Mason asked, sounding extra concerned.

"Man, she had a fucking miscarriage yesterday."

Mason looked at Mercedes who looked alarmed. "A miscarriage. Oh, I'm sorry, man."

Mercedes eyes bugged.

"Cameron was in his room and I went over to the office for a minute. When I came back her car was gone. All she left was a note on the refrigerator."

"What prompted that?" Mason asked.

"I don't know, man, I was just about to take her away for a while so we could be alone and now she's gone."

"Bro, calm down. Mercedes and I are on our way."

"Let's get going, Mercedes," said Mason, starting the car, not saying another word as he hung up.

Mercedes called Venus from her cell phone as she and Mason drove to Claude's house. Mason was quiet as a mouse.

"Sister, girl. What happened over at that house? You left Claude and Cameron?" Mercedes asked.

Venus was driving. "I knew he'd call you guys. I had to, Mercedes. I had no choice. It was just too hard."

"Why didn't you talk to me first? I had no idea you were that fed up."

"I didn't either. It was an impulsive move at first, but I really think I made the right choice. That's Fatima's house. Her everything. Not mine."

"Venus, you seemed to fit in just fine. I just never saw it as that bad for you. Even when we talked."

"Mercedes, I lost my baby yesterday. I've always wanted a baby. I thought maybe that would have made a difference, but it just wasn't meant to be either."

"How far along were you?" Mercedes asked as Mason pressed the button to lower the ragtop.

"Not long. I didn't even know it myself. I don't even remember being late," Venus said gloomily.

"I'm sorry you went through that. But that must have been hard on everyone, even Claude."

"He just up and went to work after I came home."

"You know how Claude is, Venus. He isn't as direct about expressing his feelings like his brothers are. Even so, I'm sure he just doesn't know what to say to you."

Venus was not sounding very understanding. "He's just fine at saying what he needs to say when he wants to. But, it's not like he could have even said the right thing to make it all okay. It was a mistake from the beginning."

"But Venus, didn't you even try to talk it out before you left? You told me you never wanted to divorce."

"I know I said that. But Claude knows as well as I do that this is best."

"I don't think so. He seemed pretty shook up. I think Claude is crazy about you, girl." Mercedes looked to Mason who nodded his head in agreement.

"Believe me, he's not."

"Have you ever thought that maybe all of this is just in your head? That your guilt is one of the reasons why you're internalizing this so much? You're beating yourself up way too much."

"Mercedes, imagine yourself in my shoes. In your case, you married for the love of a man. In my case, I married a man I fell in love with because of the love of a friend. I loved her, too. It's easy to judge but this is some crazy shit."

"I'm not trying to judge. At least I hope I'm not sounding like I am. But I've never heard Claude say one bad thing about you."

"Maybe so, but it's not like he and Fatima just broke up. I feel her ghost every day, Mercedes. It would be better if she could show up and kick my ass or call me and threaten me. She's dead. The silence in that house was so loud that I thought I was going to go nuts. And then the voices started, and I'd imagine her everywhere, in our bedroom and in his car. Everywhere. Even Mattie called me 'Fatima' the other day. And Claude and I argued about some serious stuff recently. He'll never forgive me. It just weighs too much for me to take. I tried, but I just can't do it, Mercedes."

Mercedes asked, "He'll never forgive you for what? Plus, you know Mattie was just confused. She calls me Star half the time. Sometimes we can be our own worst enemy. You're putting yourself through this major guilt trip. That's the real problem."

Venus was quiet.

"Will you just stay still for a while and take time to think about your decision? I'm not saying go back, but don't make any rash plans too prematurely. Let this sink in for everyone. Will you do that?"

Venus sounded tired. "Yes. I'll be at my dad's house until I get a place."

"You know you don't need to find a place, what with all of the property that Mason and Claude own. That's the least of your worries."

"And that's another thing, Mercedes. You need to check out your neighbor, Heidi. For some reason, Claude and Mason have her all hooked up in a house around the corner."

"Okay, I will," Mercedes said, looking at Mason but not letting on.

"I just don't want the confusion. I want to start working for the Make-A-Wish Foundation and start over. I want a new beginning."

"You know Claude was just about to take you away on a vacation. He just told Mason that today."

Venus's mood did not change. "No, I didn't know."

"Wouldn't that have helped?"

"I don't know, girl. I think it's a little bit too late. Claude's not even sure if he can love me the way I need to be loved. This takes work. Dealing with a dead ex-girlfriend and a dead friend is more than a notion. Claude doesn't know how to handle me and he can't deal with my emotions. There is a way to love me. He just doesn't want to know how. Maybe we got married too fast. I never spent time in that house and we didn't have any premarital counseling. We just jumped at an impulse after we bonded over the loss of Fatima. I'm not Fatima. I'm not a clone. I'm Venus."

"Wow. Girl, I really don't know what else to say. It sounds like you've thought it out and I support you. But I just don't know what this family would be like without you. You've been around for so long. Just promise you'll call me and let me know what's going on. And I really think you should consider some type of counseling. It really can make a difference."

"I will."

"I'll call you to check on you. I'll try you tomorrow night on your cell. And Venus?"

"Yes."

"You can't run from this. I hope you change your mind."

Venus sounded grateful. "Thanks. I'll talk to you later."

"Good-bye. Keep your head up." Mercedes gave Mason a questioning eye.

"I will."

Venus disconnected her cell phone and then turned off the power, filing her phone in her purse. She exited the freeway at La Tijera Boulevard and drove through the business section of Ladera. She pulled her SUV up to a traffic signal, stopping at the red light. She tapped her finger along the leather-padded steering wheel, looking around at the familiar surroundings. She noticed a young, teenaged couple walking together in the crosswalk, hugging and laughing as if they did not have a care in the world. She smiled. As she watched them step onto the curb, she caught a glimpse of a bus bench on the north side of Centinela near Fat Burger. It was an advertisement for Wilson Realty, with her husband's smiling face underlined by their slogan, "You could be home by now." Her brief smile turned to a frown.

The song "Wasting Time" by Faith Evans came on her radio. She turned it up. "Life's not that important if you don't have love," she sang. She changed the station to an all-news program. Venus drove on down toward La Brea and through the streets filled with apartments in Inglewood. She parked in the back in her dad's space. The sofa would be her bed for now.

That night, Mason and Mercedes took the time to go for a walk together. They threw on their sweat suits and headed down the street for the two-mile trek to the park and back.

Mason said, "Seems like we've been so worried about Claude losing his woman, that we neglected the fact that Venus lost a best friend in Fatima. That's got to be a big part of what she's feeling. It can't be all about Cameron not accepting her." They turned the corner onto Green Valley Circle.

"It's Claude and his distant ways as well." Mercedes took a sip of her bottled water. "Will you promise to keep this under wraps if I tell you?"

"Cedes, you've never given me that intro to anything you've ever told me. Come on now."

"The three of them were together the night before Fatima died."

"I know. Claude told me just before she got shot. Just before she arrived at the house."

"And you didn't tell me."

"Well, you didn't tell me."

"I just found out. Was he bragging when he told you?"

"No, Cedes."

"Mason, would you ever . . . ?"

"No. I would never want Sequoia to join us."

"Are you sure?"

"More than sure. How about you?"

"No way. Venus was braver than I would be. That's wild."

"Tell me about it."

"But apparently Fatima asked Venus to be with Claude if anything ever happened to her."

"I knew that. Claude already told me that, too."

"He knows?"

"Venus told him a couple of days before she left."

"About the *if* promise?"

"Whatever it's called."

"You men talk more than we women do."

Mason asked, "Did Venus ever tell you what she knew about that dude Owen?"

"That he'd been threatening and stalking Fatima for a long time, yes. She didn't want to break it off with Claude so this guy started acting more and more weird. Right before he killed her, he'd asked her to spend the day with him in Vegas, actually to get married. She told him she was coming over to our house for Thanksgiving and couldn't talk to him. Owen said if he couldn't have her, no one could."

"Damn, that was one sick brotha," Mason said, shaking his head.

"See what can happen when you bring a third person into a relationship. You never know how they're going to behave."

Mason nodded in agreement and then looked around the neighborhood. "Baby, do you think we should move away because of the memory of what happened to Fatima?"

Mercedes started to sound winded. "Sometimes I wonder. I don't know."

"Those new homes up the hill are a lot bigger and newer."

"Well, our house is paid for. And I really don't need anything bigger. Do whatever you think is right, honey. I trust you."

Mason explained, "I didn't say move out of Ladera. I said the new homes on the north side." A car honked as they made their way back home. Mason waved.

"Who's that?" Mercedes asked, looking at the white Infiniti as it drove by.

"I don't know," Mason replied. He picked up his pace even more.

Mercedes managed to keep up with him while returning to the topic at hand. "Like I said, I trust you."

# chapter 15

Mason got his chance to spend quality time, one-on-one, with his aging mother Mattie. He picked her up from Claude's home at eight o'clock sharp and took her to her favorite place for breakfast, Dinah's Restaurant.

She beamed as they walked in, almost as if she was on a date. The other patrons were staring at Mason and leaning into each other for a whisper as if Michael Jackson had just walked in. Mason held her arm. They followed the young waitress to their window table. Mattie shuffled along in her ballerina slippers, taking small steps yet making her way at a fast pace. She scooted her hips along the burgundy vinyl booth seat just as the drink girl took their order.

"Just coffee for me," Mason told the girl.

"And for you?" the young girl asked Mattie.

Mattie looked at Mason with a question mark.

He answered for her. "She'll just have cranberry juice." The girl gave an immense grin and hurried off to get their refreshments.

"You look really pretty, Mom. With your hair all done up like a crown."

She smiled, patting the top of her head to make sure it was still in place.

A patron came over and asked Mason for his autograph. He obliged. Again, Mattie looked proud.

Before they could really peruse the menus, the main waitress came over to take their food orders.

"What can I get for you ma'am?" asked the nineteen-forties-looking waitress, removing the pencil from over her ear, poised with pad in hand.

"Uhh," Mattie looked around the restaurant at the other patrons' plates, even though she had the menu in her hand. "What's good?" Mattie asked the waitress.

Mason interceded. "Mom, you like scrambled eggs and sausage, right?"

"I just had that this morning." Mattie spoke as though it were so.

"How about a BLT sandwich?" he suggested, knowing she hadn't eaten yet.

"Okay, I'll have that. Oh, and some water please."

"Your water is right here, Mom," Mason said, pointing to her glass.

"More water?" asked the waitress. "No problem," she said,winking at Mason. "And you, sir?"

"I'll have the apple pancakes."

"All right." She took the menus. "Your drinks will be right up."

"Thanks."

Mattie smiled at her eldest son, looking upbeat and proud.

"So Mom, how are you feeling?"

She looked down into her purse, rummaging through it. "I feel fine. I think Claude took my drivers license though, so I had to take it back."

Mason asked, "Claude took it? Where is it?"

"It's in my purse," she said. "Along with my jewelry he hid from me."

The drinks girl placed their glasses down and then moved along to the next group of customers.

Mattie voluntarily handed her large black leather bag to Mason.

Mason looked inside, taking the license into his hand. "Mom, this is Claude's license."

Mattie looked puzzled. "Is that why he took it?"

He checked out the contents further. "And this is the strand of pearls I bought for Mercedes for our one-year anniversary."

"Boy, please. I've had those ever since you were born."

"Mom, that strand is worth a lot of money. I'll make sure to put it in a safe place." Mason placed it in his coat pocket. He looked around the room at the full house, and then back over at his mom who was folding a plain white napkin into two pieces, and then four, and then eight. "Mom, what do you think about not being able to drive? How does that make you feel?"

"I don't think it was right of you all to take my Seville away. I have appointments. It's like everyone tries to keep me in the house. Why are you all so against me?"

"Mom, I noticed that you were stopping at green lights and running stop signs. That's not safe for you or for others."

"The only time I do that is when you all are in the car. You all make me nervous."

"Mom, do you know that an officer reported you after he gave you a ticket for running a red light? He was concerned about your safety. He asked that your license be suspended until you saw a doctor."

"And the doctor said I was fine. You and Mercedes hired that guy to help take my car away."

"We have your car stored away, Mom. Blame it on me if you'd like, but I think it's best," Mason told her, taking full responsibility.

"Well, maybe you just don't know what's best for me after all. Everyone thinks they know but they don't. I can take care of myself. Jesse and I were doing just fine until he went away."

"That's why we're taking care of you in his absence."

Mattie gave a look. "You all taking care of me? I'm a prisoner."

"I know it may seem that way but I want you to know that we do what we do because we care. And I can only imagine how difficult it must be for you to have your independence and freedoms monitored. I want you to continue living a dignified life. You're a classy lady and you deserve to feel as though the things you do won't change too much. But you're still loved for who you are, Mom."

Mattie replied with a glimmer of understanding, "I know that. But it seems that sometimes you all don't understand me."

"Please be patient with us as we adjust, just like you need to adjust." Mason waited for a brief moment while she sipped her water and then he continued. "Mom, do you know that you have Alzheimer's?"

She quickly put her glass down. "Watch your mouth, boy. Do not claim that upon me. I do not have that word."

"Yes Mom, you do."

Mattie was not having it. "Boy, I have never gone to a doctor in my life other than to birth my sons. And I have never, ever been sick. But all of a sudden you all keep taking me to see these greedy doctors who look for things to find. I say if I don't feel sick, why be paranoid and get checked up every second? God guides my life, not some money hungry doctor who labels me with a big word and you all buy into it. I'm not going to buy into it and I mean that."

"But Mom, we have to be proactive just in case the diagnosis is correct. There's this new trial medicine that might halt the progression of the disease right where it is so that you won't get any worse."

"No. I'm not anybody's guinea pig. You all had better not give me that medicine. I mean it," Mattie said adamantly.

Mason leaned in closer. "Mom, it can only help."

"How do you know that if you say it's new? It hasn't even been proven yet."

Mason looked impressed by her comments. "That makes sense, Mom. But it doesn't get to the trial stage unless it's been tested."

"No. Now that's that."

After a while their food was brought to the table. Mattie took her knife and cut her sandwich instead of biting it. She poked each piece with her fork. Clanging silver was the only sound for about five minutes, and then Mason decided to take a walk down memory lane while his mom still had her ability to recall in tact.

"So, Mom. Tell me. What is your most wonderful memory of your childhood?"

Right away she had an answer. "Probably back when I was in high school. That agent spotted me at a basketball game and asked me to dance in the movie *Carmen*."

"I remember you telling me about that."

"I worked with Diahann Carroll, and Harry, ahh."

"Belafonte."

"Yes, and that other lady who killed herself."

"Dorothy Dandridge."

"Yes, she was so pretty. She looked like an angel. And Pearl Bailey, too."

"I know your family must have been so proud of you," Mason said, fully attentive.

"My brothers were but I think my sisters were jealous. One of them found a note this boy wrote me that I hid in my shoe and showed it to my mom. I got my butt beat but good."

"He had a crush on you, huh?" Mason asked with a big smile.

"It was your dad and we were doing more than crushing back then."

"Mom." Mason looked like he wanted to blush for her.

"It's true."

"I see you remember a lot of good times from back then. I love hearing about your early years."

"Yeah, those days make me smile."

"You miss Dad?"

"Sometimes. I think he left to be with that lady around the corner. The one he had that baby with."

Mason paused. "What lady?" The waitress cleared their empty plates and they resumed talking.

"The one whose daughter you became friends with. That was going on for a long time even before you were born."

"What was?"

"Your dad and her. I was no fool, boy. He took good care of you and me, and then we had two more sons and he was a great father to them, too. I'm not sure I want him back. Maybe he should just stay gone."

Mason decided to question her further. "So, Mom, you know about Cicely?"

"I know about Sissy, I thought that was her name."

"Okay, Sissy. You know who she is? Is that why you pulled off the other day from in front of her house?"

"I know who she is and I know you brought her home that day. Don't you do that again, letting her into our house after all this time."

Mason stopped playing dumb. "I won't, Mom. But have you ever wondered about her? She is my half sister."

"Heck no. I could care less. And don't you ever, ever betray me like that. She is not a part of this family and never will be." Mattie started tapping her straw in and out of her glass of juice.

"Mom, her mother died back when Sissy graduated from college," Mason said as if it would matter.

"So that means your dad is with one of the other women then."

"What others?"

"I know about all of them. The tall, dark-skinned lady at the post office, the waitress, and I think there was even an Asian stewardess recently."

"Are you sure?" Mason asked his mom as the waitress placed the bill on the table.

Mattie sat back, starting to look restless. "Oh, please. Your papa was a rolling stone and you know it, just like you. Where's my purse? I'm going to pay the bill so I can go home and call him. He's going to have to come home and come clean with me."

Mason handed Mattie her bag and she unzipped it quickly, reaching into a tiny coin purse. Mattie pulled out a one-hundred-dollar bill. "Keep the change," she said to the waitress as she walked up again.

"Mom, no, you keep that. I'll pay for it," he said to the lady, taking the bill back from her. "It's my treat, Mom. Let's go up to the counter and I'll take care of it. This has been really special for me. Did you enjoy yourself?" They stood up and walked toward the exit.

"You sure do ask a lot of questions."

"I just want to know as much as I can about my mom and my past."

"Well, now you know."

"Yes, I guess I do. You know how you always told me to work my butt off and be somebody?"

Mattie looked frustrated. "Another question."

"Well thanks, Mom." He stood next to her at the cashier, handing his credit card to the cashier while Mattie took a handful of lollipops out of the bowl near the register. Once again, all eyes were on Mason. He smiled back at the gaping faces and asked his mom one more question. "Mom, where did you get that money?"

"Claude's wallet. You need to keep an eye on him. Do you want a green one?" she asked, putting the rest of the suckers in her purse.

"Yes, Mom. Green is my favorite color."

She remembered.

Mason asked Torino and Claude to meet him at Starbucks to hang out for a bit. Torino arrived first and then Mason pulled up in his new platinum Mercedes jeep that Titleist gave him. He and Torino sat at an outside table in the corner.

"That's a nice one, man," Torino said, admiring his brother's ride.

"It was either that or an Escalade EXT, but you can't go wrong with a Mercedes, I always say. It rides like I'm on air, man." Mason sported a Wilt Chamberlain throwback jersey, Sean John jeans and blue Chuck Taylors.

"You bite hard, dude. I'm gonna have to roll that to the club one night this week."

"No problem."

Torino looked around at all of the people coming and going. "This place is like a Black Falcon Crest," he said, looking around at the sights and sounds of Ladera.

"Hey, true life is stranger than fiction. We should write our own soap opera just based on our little community. Hey, what's up with you and Sequoia, man?" Mason asked, leaning back in the dark green patio chair.

"Brother, Sequoia is one hell of a lady."

"I won't disagree with that. Even though she can be a little nosy. But I know she means well."

"She sure helped me move along from Colette, I know that."

"Hi Mason," a woman said, strolling by, shaking what she was working with.

Torino said, "Man, you've got every damn opportunity out here. How have you stayed out of trouble all these many years?"

"No comment."

"And you walk around by yourself. It's not like you have bodyguards or an entourage everywhere you go."

Mason explained. "You know I'm not down with all that fake shit. People like that just hang out trying to get in your business and in your pockets. I can take care of myself."

"I don't know if I could do it. I mean resist all that pussy thrown your way."

"You've got enough on your hands just dealing with the women from the club. You'd better slow your roll, though. I hear Colette was acting pretty damn stupid up there the other night. Cicely told me. They say don't mess with a woman's mother, her money, or her man. You'd better watch yourself, bro."

"Especially a crazy woman. I'm just glad I fired her. She's acting like she's fatal and shit."

"Normally I wouldn't recommend hiring another one so fast, but if anyone is cool it's Sequoia," Mason said.

"I know she got on your nerves. She'd always prompt Mercedes to do fidelity checks through the years, right?"

"Oh, she's just looking out for her friend. I can't say that I blame her," Mason said like it was no biggie.

"Anyway, about moving on. Some people need the time in between women and some don't. I don't."

"And you're sure that baby's not yours?"

"Positive"

"Okay now. Do the right thing if you have to," Mason warned, sounding fatherly.

"I'd step up if I needed to."

Mason noticed Claude walking up, headed for the front door.

"Hey, bro, what's up? Come on over here and have a seat, man." Mason shouted, pulling out a chair.

Claude greeted them both with handshakes. He had stubble on

his chin and looked a few pounds lighter. "Hey, I didn't see the two of you sitting over here. I had to get some fresh air. That office is driving me crazy. Seems like no one can do anything without tugging on my jacket."

"I know the feeling," said Torino.

Mason added, "Both of you need to hire some better help. You shouldn't have to work that hard at this level."

Claude took a seat. "Just because you have all of those flunkies running all up behind you. You don't even have to pick up a phone."

"Yeah, but I sure as hell pick up a golf club and work my ass off in that way."

"I'm not downplaying your gig, dude. You are serious," Claude said.

"Are you okay, man? You look a little tired," Torino asked.

"Yeah, like I said, that office is going to be the death of me."

"You don't want any coffee?" Mason asked.

"No, just some fresh air."

A woman walked by wearing a short, tight business suit. "Hello, Mason. Good to see you," she said with a girlie voice.

"Hey, how are you doing?" Mason said with a smile. She walked away.

Torino remarked, "Damn, man. It's like all of the women in here stopped at the beauty shop and nail salon and then came out dressed like they're going to the club. How do all of the fine ass women end up right here?"

"Looking for men like us," said Mason.

"Well, here I am," Torino said, holding up his right hand.

Claude left him hanging. "You don't want any of these women. Most of them have husbands at home who ignore them so they stroll on in and order a venti something so we can boost their egos with our stares. We're just falling into their trap, phone numbers or not."

"Well, trap me," Torino said like he meant it.

"Hi, handsome," one lady said to Claude.

He nodded.

"See now, Claude, don't tell me you don't want to get to know that," Torino told him.

"Do you mean do I or will I?" Claude replied.

"Both."

"Yes, and no."

Torino examined his brothers. "You two are sitting up here acting all faithful."

Claude said, "Try getting married, Torino, and you'll see. You'll find that you don't have to order anything just because it's on the menu."

"You're both ordering, just like I am, or was."

"Speak for yourself," Claude warned.

"Sounds like you're wavering in your fidelities already, Torino," Mason said.

"It's tough, man, but I don't think so. Not this time. Sequoia is wearing my ass out. That girl can ride it all night long, any way I want it."

Claude looked amazed. "Sequoia? I can't even imagine that. She seems so demure and reserved."

"Sequoia? Shit," said Mason. "Mercedes used to tell me about her." He noticed Torino looking at him funny. "Okay, now, I said used to."

"She's wild, huh?" asked Claude.

"Big time, until the break of dawn," Torino volunteered. "It's cool as long as she's a freak in the sheets with me and class in the streets."

"It's all good then," Mason agreed.

Another hottie walked by. She took off her leopard-patterned Foster Grants. "Well, if it isn't the million-dollar hot boyz. Hi, Mason," said the young, sexy woman, as if she knew him personally.

"Hey, what's up?"

"You, baby. My name is Craylonte." She approached the table.

"Hi, Craylonte," Torino said for Mason, looking everywhere on her but her face.

"Can you sign this napkin for my son? He's nine years old and he's been to the driving range a dozen times already. Wants to be just like you."

"Oh wow, sure, what's his name?"

"Jesse."

"That's my dad's name," Mason said, taking out a pen and writing a quick hello to Jesse.

"And my middle name," added Torino.

"Hey imagine that. His middle name is James. I call him J. J."

"That's good," said Torino, trying not to notice the large breasts when she leaned down.

"He's named after his father. Trick ass Negro. He ain't good for nothin'."

"Sorry to hear that," Mason said, handing the napkin back to her. "Make sure you take good care of little Jessie."

"I will. It would be better if I had a man around. Like a role model."

Mason advised, "Not all men are role models. Take your time and find a good mate. Then he can be Jesse's friend once you're sure he has the traits of a role model."

"Are you still married?" she asked, looking hopeful.

"Yes. Happily," Mason replied.

"But is your wife married?" Craylonte joked, and then looked serious as hell.

"Funny."

She looked at Torino and Claude. "How about you two chocolate drops?"

"No, I'm taken," Claude said, almost wondering if he really was after all.

"Me, too," said Torino.

"Oh well. You all be good."

Torino watched her switch her double-dutch butt on to her blue Honda Accord.

She yelled back to them. "And if things change, I'm here every day around this time. Look me up."

"Will do," said Torino, enjoying the humor of her statement.

Mason changed the subject. "Hey guys, on a serious note, I want you both to know something."

"Yeah," said Torino.

"I've got both of your backs, no matter what, bros. I just want you to know that. I've been wanting to say that for a while now."

Claude spoke up immediately. "And we've got yours, Mason. And we've got yours."

"Brotherhood on a real way," Torino added.

Mason answered the home phone in the kitchen just as he walked in the door from his Starbucks run.

"Hey, Mason. It's the Reverend."

"Hey, Rev, how are you?"

"I'm glorious, and you?"

"I'm good. Doing all right, I suppose." Mason replied, leaning back against the wall.

"You know, I was able to connect with an old friend of mine named Dr. Ron Little. He's a real cool brother who works wonders in marriage, family, and child issues. I told him you would give him a call."

"Oh, Rev, I know we talked about this, but I'm sure we don't need anything like that. We're working things out through prayer and faith. And we're spending a lot more time making a point to bond and just do things together whenever we can."

The Reverend replied, "I know you are and I hope you don't mind my intervention, but I've talked to many people who were helped in learning the how-tos of working through issues inside the home. There's nothing wrong with seeking guidance from a counselor. Our kids have counselors on-site in schools all the time, but as adults, we seem to think we can handle it without the knowledge that a qualified therapist can bring. And this guy, man, he's like a black Dr. Phil. He breaks it down and doesn't waste your time trying to make you think you have every right to feel and think whatever, blah, blah, blah. He will call you on it, wake you up and send you on your way to work on it together, with God's guidance and protection of course. Don't say no, Mason. I'm telling you, you won't regret it."

Mason felt the easiest thing to do would be to wave the white flag. "I'll ask Mercedes to set it up. What's his number?"

Mercedes walked along with the packed crowd of onlookers in Mexico as Mason approached the ninth hole of his tournament. Because it was a weekday, Star and Rashaad stayed home to go to school. Anna, the part-time maid, stayed home with them. Mercedes wore a matching golf hat, the same color as the Titleist shirt Mason was sporting. Silence was in overdrive, not even a whisper or clearing of a throat.

If Mason made the long putt for birdie, it would mean one hundred thousand dollars for the day at thirteen under par. He'd had two eagles so far in this tournament and felt he was on a roll.

Mason's caddy, Winton, handed him his putter. Mason eyeballed the distance between the ball and the cup, envisioning his stroke and the angle of the ball, imagining the exact trail of the ball necessary to make this a birdie. His fixed, brown eyes looked down toward the ball, and then to the cup, down at the ball and again at the cup, and over again until he sealed the next move in his head. He pulled back his club and gave a good solid putt, all the while keeping his head down toward the green. The ball rolled with a curve and then cut back toward the exact location of the cup. His caddy raised the pole with the blue flag blowing in the generous wind, and even without touching the circumference the tiny ball sank right inside and disappeared.

Mercedes jumped up and down with excitement. Mason looked over at her and tipped his black golf cap in her honor. She gave him the peace sign and he returned the gesture with a loving smile.

The crowd cheered and followed Mason and Winton toward the tent where he and the other players went over their scorecards. A reporter from ESPN approached Mercedes.

"Mrs. Wilson, you must be thrilled to death that your husband was able to pull off this win."

"Yes, it was pretty close for a minute. Vijay Singh is an excellent golfer and he gave Mason a run for his money. I'm happy he was able to keep his concentration and win by a stroke."

"Yes, that's all it takes and he did it. His game has improved so much recently, especially since you've been on the sidelines I'd say. Am I correct?"

Mercedes was humble. "You are correct that his game has improved. I'm not so sure that it's been because of my presence. I won't take that much credit. I think all of the elements must be considered—the competition, the course, the weather. This is just a really great time for my husband and we are definitely going to celebrate."

Mason walked back toward the crowd with his caddy at his side. He whispered to Winton and then made a beeline back toward Mercedes, greeting her with a hug.

Mercedes smothered him with kisses. "You go, boy. You hit that with precision. I'm so proud of you."

Mason looked fairly reserved, considering. "Thanks, baby. By the way, do you know what today is?"

"Today is the day you won your seventh tournament of the year, that's what today is."

"And?"

"And today is the day . . ." Mercedes paused with her mouth wide open while her eyes spotted a gentleman walking up behind Mason.

"Mason, do you know who that is?" she whispered.

"Yes."

"Mercedes?" the distinguished gentleman said.

"Yes, oh my goodness, Mr. Rogers. It's so nice to meet you."

"I understand today is a special day."

She disbelievingly responded. "Oh, yes it is. Do you know my husband?"

"Yes, and he tells me it is your sixteenth wedding anniversary today. Is that true?"

She rushed her words, sounding very confused. "Well, actually it's eighteen years together, but, oh yes, it is today. Why?"

"Because this one's for you, Mrs. Wilson."

The gentleman who was in on the little greeting set up by

Mason was Kenny Rogers himself. He began to sing, "I can't remember when you weren't there, when I didn't care, for any one but you." Mercedes's jaw dropped.

He continued to sing the entire song, "Through the Years", all the while he held Mercedes's hand while Mason stood next to her.

He wound down the final note and gave Mason a nod and Mercedes a smile. Mason turned to hug his wife. The crowd cheered and clapped for them.

Still in shock, Mercedes said, "Thank you so much. That was beautiful. I will never forget that."

"I guess that really was your song, huh?" asked Mr. Rogers.

Mercedes said, "You can say that again."

"I'm glad I could be a part of your celebration. And congratulations, Mason. Hang in there now."

"We will. Thanks, Kenny."

"No problem," he said, walking away with a couple of security-looking men.

Mercedes looked dreamy. "Baby, I was not ready for that."

"I know. You deserved it though. You're always there for everyone else. Happy anniversary."

"Happy anniversary, Mason."

At home on a Sunday, a couple days later, Sequoia actually got Torino to go to church with her. They went to her Catholic church, St. Jerome's, for the noon mass. But when they got back home, Torino needed a nap, having been up late after working the night before. While he lay on his stomach, barely into his much-needed shut-eye, Sequoia decided to engage in a little love in the afternoon.

She pulled down his dress pants and underwear. She firmly rubbed her hands along the shape of his rump, pressing her fingertips into his brown skin, giving deep tissue strokes with penetrating pressure, kneading his firmness all the way from his lower back to the curve of his butt cheek. Her pleasing touch and massaging expertise awakened him and caused his nature to raise him right on over to his back. He looked up at her as if she'd started something.

"Out of those clothes," he demanded, and she obliged.

Right away, he took over and turned her on her stomach. She rose up on all fours. He mounted her. And he did not hesitate to enter her full on and deep. She was in for it now.

"Baby, that feels so good," Sequoia said immediately, bucking her hips.

"Keep it up," Torino demanded.

"I am," she acquiesced, moving to his sexual demands.

"Oh, yeah, you like that, huh?"

"Yes, Torino, I like that."

"Is this your favorite position?"

"Yes, baby." Sequoia purred and worked her hips until she felt Torino about to build up. She reached behind herself and behind him to grab his firm, muscular butt cheeks and pushed him deeper inside. "I want to feel every inch of you," she squealed as he penetrated her deepest point.

"Oh no, not yet," he said. He pulled out and put his face in between her legs, eating her with his pointed tongue from her front door to her back door as she poked her rear in the air.

"Ohh, yes," said Sequoia, with her face buried in the pillow. Her rush flowed like warm molasses.

Torino came back up and entered her again with his rigidness. "This feels so good, baby. I've never had it like this. I just want to disappear inside of you and . . . damn it, Sequoia," Torino screamed, grunting and groaning as he pumped up against her firm rear end. His peak sounded like the build-up of a sneeze. And then he let it out, loud and strong, squeezing his eyes closed and jerking his head.

"Oh damn," Sequoia exclaimed through her own orgasm. She braced herself to come down from her high and regain her senses but another wave pulsated through her soul. The sensation of her multiple orgasms had grown to be very common when it came to Torino. She fell onto her stomach, no longer able to prop her body upward.

"Get yours, girl," Torino panted as he excreted his last bit inside of her. He froze to allow the extreme muscle tension to subside. He lowered himself and lay on her back.

A minute or two later she looked to the side toward his digital clock. "Damn, I think it's time for us to get up and head outside for the party," she reminded him.

"Hell, I'm ready and raring to go now," Torino said, hopping up, heading toward the shower. "That was better than a nap."

"We are quite a pair, aren't we?"

"You're damn right, woman. I just don't know why it took us so long."

# chapter 16

Mercedes had planned a pool party for their wedding anniversary. She and Mason arrived back from Mexico that morning, worried because the weather was overcast. They rushed about to get things ready.

The oversized backyard looked like paradise. Like being in the country but with a formal feel. One end of the yard had twin tennis courts with a forest green blacktop and bright orange nets. Palm trees and hydrangea bushes surrounded the walkway from the courts on up the hill to the regulation-size basketball court.

A tree house and a huge rock waterfall aligned the outer edge of the Olympic-size, black-bottom swimming pool.

Guests started to arrive and began to mingle, sitting upon the champagne-colored patio furniture with purple swirled umbrellas shielding the sun. Tuxedoed waiters and waitresses served the catered food and fancy drinks. The Kenny G CD *Paradise* played over the speakers.

Cameron immediately ran back to shoot hoops with Rashaad. Torino and Sequoia came out to see if they could help. Star stayed inside, reading in her room and listening to music, waiting for her friend Asia to arrive. A few of Claude's employees joined the group, in particular, Heidi, as well as Claude's assistant.

Mercedes knew about their closest friends, coworkers and family coming, but one guest she was surprised to see was Dr. Green.

He greeted her. "Hey there. Good to see you."

"Hi. I didn't know you knew about the party."

He explained. "I called you, or I should say I called the house last week to talk to you about your mother-in-law but your husband answered. I told him who I was and he invited me to stop by."

"Oh, I see. That was nice of him. And you called to tell me what exactly?" Mercedes asked as if confused.

"I called to tell you about the new electronic bracelet for Alzheimer's patients. It's great to keep track of loved ones so they don't get lost. I didn't even know that Mattie had gotten lost until Mason told me."

"Oh, so then you told Mason about the bracelet?"

"Yes I did."

"I see." Mercedes took in the entire vision of Dr. Green, from his curly hair to his bowlegs. He was long and lean and it was hard not to notice. "I usually don't get my messages for some reason. I left my office number on my mother-in-law's profile just in case you ever need to talk to me about her progress."

"Will do." Dr. Green grinned. He then looked around the backyard. "You have a lovely home. You know, I live right across Slauson on Holt Avenue."

"Oh, you do. So we're neighbors, huh?"

He replied, "Yes, we are after all."

This time it was his turn. Mercedes watched his eyes roam downward, examining her waist area and then looking up toward her chest peeking out from her button-down linen dress.

Her words interrupted his glimpse. "I hope you enjoy yourself. If you need anything, please let us know."

"I will do just that." He started to walk away, just as she did. "And I just want to wish you a happy anniversary, Mrs. Wilson."

Mercedes stopped and turned. "Thanks, Dr. Green. I must go check on the caterers. Enjoy."

They walked away in opposite directions, but one second later Dr. Green ran smack dab into Heidi. He accidentally bumped her elbow and she spilled a bit of her red wine. They laughed it off while Heidi dabbed her arm with a napkin. She wore three-inch heels with her Burberry string bikini. Her hips were barely shielded by a short, tiny white wrap. Dr. Green continued to talk to Heidi, no longer glancing Mercedes's way as he was now fully distracted by a new flavor.

Cicely made her grand entrance as though Diana Ross herself had arrived. She ran to Heidi with a spectacular, dramatic, smooches-type greeting and they disappeared with Dr. Green into a corner near the wet bar. Cicely's sheer pantsuit showed off her hot body in her hot pink one-piece underneath.

Mercedes spoke to the bartender and the waiters and made sure everyone was well taken care of. Mason approached after talking to a few women who Mercedes had never seen before.

"Who are they?" she asked as Mason approached.

"That's Traci and Candi. They're marketing representatives for the Sean John line." Both scantily clad, Traci and Candi, smothered in glittery sun tan oil, decided to sit on the edge of the pool and get their feet wet, sipping on chilled bottles of Jack Daniel's Original Hard Cola.

"You'll have to introduce me later," Mercedes said, giving them her attention.

"Yes, baby. I will do that. What is wrong with you? Are you okay?"

"I'm fine. I just wish Venus were here. And I want this party to be a success."

Mason looked up at the sky. "Well, the weather is turning out to be pretty nice. See, the sun is shining through." He checked out his woman. "And even better than that, you look as beautiful as ever, I'll say that much. Baby, I just remembered. When I took Mom to breakfast, she had your string of pearls in her purse."

"Mamma did? I've been looking for those."

"I took them from her, so not to worry."

"What was she doing with them?"

"Don't ask. She had everything in that bag but the kitchen sink."

"Where are they?"

"They're in my briefcase."

"Oh, you finally got your briefcase from Cicely, huh?"

"Yes, but I left it in the car. I'll go get it while I'm thinking about it."

"Right now?" Mercedes asked.

"I'll just be a second."

"No, I'll go. I need to go in the kitchen anyway and check on things. I'll be right back."

"Look in my blazer pocket hanging in the backseat if you don't see it in the case. But it should be right on top."

"Okay," Mercedes said, going into the house as she greeted more guests, taking the kitchen door into the garage.

She did not see a blazer hanging from the backseat hook, so she looked in the backseat then toward the front seat of his Benz. She found the case on the passenger side on the floor. Strangely, Mercedes noticed a few long, thick strands of hair along the butterscotch-colored carpet. There was one on the palomino leather passenger seat, too. She picked up a strand and ran her fingers along the length of the piece of hair. She held it up and thought it could have been thread or something, it was so thick. It was a cherry red, and it curled when she scraped it with her fingernail.

Shaking her head to shake loose some of her thoughts, she opened the briefcase. Her pearls were right on top. She took the pearls and started to close the case when she spied a stack of photos tucked in the upper sleeve to the left. She pulled out the photos and noticed they were shots from Mason's tour in Hawaii. Mason was smiling with his caddy and a few fans. A couple of shots were taken while he was on the course. And the last two were of Mason, Cicely, and Heidi, all hugged up and smiling for the photographer. It must have been a windy day because Heidi's long red hair was blowing from her back to her side, topped by her red baseball cap.

Mercedes tucked all of the pictures back in the slot, all except for one. She threw the case on the floor of the car and slammed the door, walking heavily back into the house. She made a beeline straight to Mason who was talking to Torino near the tennis court.

"Excuse me, Mason. I need to talk to you."

He noticed her scowl. "What is it? Did you find the pearls?"

"I need to talk to you now," she said, looking at Torino.

"I'll be right back," Torino said, picking up on the urgent need for the two of them to be alone. He walked away and greeted a few of the artists from the night at the club.

"What's going on with you and Heidi?"

"What is *what?* What brought this on?" he asked, lowering his voice.

"This," she said, shoving the picture toward his face.

Mason snickered. "That's just a shot of them and me when they stopped through for the tournament in Hawaii."

"But you said they weren't in Honolulu with you."

"They weren't but they stopped through either coming or going on their vacation. I don't remember. Mercedes, what are you trying to say?"

"I'm saying that this woman is in my own backyard, and her strands of hair are in my husband's car. I'm trying to say that I'm about to go off right now unless you explain yourself quickly." Mercedes was fast losing patience.

Mason did not want to cause a scene. He looked around at the guests to check for stares. "Mercedes calm down. Let's go inside."

"Good idea. Follow me," she said abruptly, storming her way into the house and on upstairs into their bedroom. Torino kept an eye on them.

Mason closed the door behind them.

Mercedes's look was direct. "Mason, what do you have to say for yourself?"

"The same thing I told you a minute ago. Nothing is going on with Heidi and me."

She threw the strand of pearls down on the dresser. "I go looking for a strand of pearls and find a strand of hair. And here I was worried about Cicely all this time."

"Baby, believe me, Cicely is the least of your worries. And so is Heidi."

She rolled her eyes. "Screw this. Obviously you're not going to admit to a damn thing, Mason. You've been busted and you're still playing Mr. Innocent. It makes me sick to see you so damn smug, standing here lying to me after all these years." She paced the length of the room.

"Cedes, I'm not lying."

With irritation mounting, she demanded, "Tell me the truth, now."

"I am," he insisted.

She stopped in her tracks. "I don't believe you."

"Then why don't you ask them for yourself?" he said casually.

"Fine, I will."

A concerned Sequoia and Torino were waiting downstairs for the at-odds host and hostess to show their faces. Mercedes raced downstairs, right past them, leaving Mason standing in place in their bedroom. Mercedes saw Cicely and Heidi in the corner by the bar taking to Dr. Green. She approached like she was in no mood to make nice. Sequoia stood nearby as Torino went back into the house to check on Mason.

"Dr. Green, will you excuse us for a minute?" Mercedes asked abruptly.

An unsuspecting Heidi said, "I didn't know you knew Dr. Green, Mercedes. He lives right down the street from me."

"Oh you live in Ladera too, huh?" Mercedes asked with her toe tapping.

"Yes, right around the corner. What a small world."

"Yes, it is," Mercedes replied. "Dr. Green, we'll just be a moment."

"No problem. I'll be right over here," he replied, getting the obvious drift that something was up.

"Okay," said Cicely. "Mercedes, what's going on?"

"Did the two of you go to Hawaii with my husband on vacation?"

Cicely answered. "No, we went to Maui, but we stopped in Honolulu on our way home. We left early because the weather was so bad. Why?"

Mercedes shoved the photo toward their faces. "What's with all of those cozy pictures of the three of you?"

"The pictures we took on the golf course? Oh yes, I gave the second set to Mason last week. I wouldn't call those cozy. We were just spectators while he played. We were only there for like six hours. What's going on with you, Mercedes?" asked Cicely, trying to be nice.

"Yeah, what's the matter?" Heidi asked.

Mercedes spoke to Heidi. "What's the matter is that I've found your hair all in my husband's car. And you have the nerve to come to my home?"

"Mercedes, I don't know what you're talking about," Heidi said cautiously.

"I think you do," Mercedes said as if challenging her.

Cicely spoke again. "Mercedes, there's something you need to know. Obviously you're having trust issues with Mason, and I'm not one to judge a woman's intuition. But believe me, he is not seeing Heidi."

"What other black woman have I ever seen with long red hair, other than her?"

Cicely went on, "I don't know what you saw, but you need to know something. And I'm surprised Mason hasn't told you."

"What is that?"

Cicely smoothed her surly hair behind her ear. "Heidi is not my sister, she's my lover."

"What?" Mercedes was dearly surprised.

"Mercedes, I've been with Heidi for as long as I can remember. Heidi is not into men. Trust me."

"There's no chance?" Mercedes asked, much more calmly.

Cicely spoke again. "Mercedes, there's no chance that I've been sharing my lover with your husband. Believe me."

Mercedes looked at the photo again. "I feel like a damn fool. Ladies, I'm so sorry."

Heidi remarked, "Mason should have told you."

Mercedes said, "He's like that, trying to keep people's business their own. I apologize."

Heidi explained, "It's okay. You're not the first woman who thought I was after her man. I think because Cicely and I are feminine, we get hit on even more. It appears that we threaten wives when we're really just kicking it with their men because we really like men, as friends."

"Well, it doesn't help that you two label yourself as sisters," Mercedes told them.

"I do that more than she does. Plus we're together so much that people would start to wonder," Cicely said.

Mercedes advised, "One day, I think you two might want to just let it be and damn what people think about you."

"Maybe one day we will," Cicely said.

"Anyway, have a good time and again, excuse my paranoid, insecure ass today. It's really not like me."

"No problem," they both said together.

Dr. Green walked back up with a Mack Daddy strut, eyeballing Heidi as if he wanted to sop her up with a biscuit. Heidi moved in even closer to Cicely.

"Mercedes, are you okay?" asked Sequoia. "I heard what happened. I've seen explosions more subtle than that, girl. That's not like you."

"I must have looked so damn stupid. I must be deep into PMS."

"Never mind that. Are you all right?"

"I'm okay, Sequoia. I've got to go apologize to my man."

By then, Mason was downstairs in the house shooting pool with Winton, his caddy.

With his eyes fixed on his game he spoke to his wife. "You satisfied now?"

"Why didn't you tell me?"

"I just wanted you to know how ridiculous that was."

Mercedes stood with her arms crossed. "Okay so I feel ridiculous, Mason. Are you happy now?"

"Not really."

"Well, I'm sorry."

Mason said nothing.

Mercedes continued, "But why didn't you tell me about Cicely before now?"

"I just found out not long ago myself."

"So, you still should have told me."

"Cedes?" He said her name while sizing up his next shot.

"Yes," she answered, suddenly sounding like a rational woman.

"If you'd have been paying attention instead of snooping, you would have seen this in my briefcase." Mason pulled a pink velvet box out of his pants pocket, handed it to her and continued sizing up his game as if it was golf.

Mercedes stood with the box in both hands and asked, "What is this?"

"Open it," he replied, putting chalk on his cue. Winton took his shot.

Mercedes was almost afraid to catch a glimpse of what was inside as though maybe she didn't deserve it. Lightly, she brushed her fingertips across the top and flipped it open with her thumb with caution, finding that to her surprise, tucked inside the white satin slot was a platinum anniversary ring with three, one carat, princess cut, baby pink sapphires. She inhaled and exhaled a major breath and then placed her flat hand over her heart. Her jaw dropped.

"Happy anniversary," he said as he prepared to take his shot, not even looking back at her. He hit the yellow ball straight into the corner pocket.

Mercedes didn't bother to look at him either. She took the ring out of the tiny box and slipped it on the middle finger of her right hand. She held her hand out for a full viewing, giving approval of its brilliance through her admiration-filled eyes. "Thank you, Mason. It's beautiful." Just as Mercedes prepared to take a step toward him with a pucker, she heard a crash. "What was that noise?"

"It sounded like a car wreck," said Winton, placing the cue on the pool table and taking a few hurried steps toward the door.

Winton, Mason, and Mercedes ran outside to see that Star was behind the wheel of Mason's Porsche, looking shocked and traumatized. She had decided to take the sports car for a drive and she ran smack dab into the small sycamore tree in the front yard. She got out crying, limping toward her mother looking stunned.

Later that evening after all of the drama of towing the car away and filing a police report, everyone arrived back from the emergency room. Mercedes sat in Star's room. She took a moment to console her and help her through her trauma. Star had an ace bandage on her knee. She bruised it on the steering wheel column. Mercedes wanted Star to know that what she did by driving her dad's car without permission was wrong, but that they were indeed grateful that she was not too seriously hurt, nor was anyone else. Mercedes had also gotten in an accident when she was a teenager. She had taken her cousin's sports car for a joyride in the rain and plowed right into the back of a police car. She told her daughter about that day and suddenly her own dilemma didn't seem to bad.

Mason was grateful that all of the commotion was over for the evening. After the guests left and the caterers cleared out, Mason sat in the backyard under the stars and had a conversation with Claude. Mason had had enough.

"I'm putting this house up for sale, man. I'm leaving," Mason told Claude while looking up, examining the glittering big dipper.

"I think that's the best decision you've made in a while, man. You know how I feel about this damn place."

"Go ahead and put a sign up tomorrow. List it for whatever you think it's worth, maybe even less. Just sell it."

"Okay. Where do you want to buy?"

"You know people act like they don't even know I own property all over the country, man. Las Vegas, Martha's Vineyard, and even in Tampa. I'm just talking about living where I want to live. In California."

"Yeah, but where?" Claude asked.

"Perhaps Bel Air, maybe even Beverly Hills, I don't know," Mason muttered with uncertainty.

"You can get a lot more house, but it will probably cost three or four times more. Besides, you need a golf course in your backyard anyway. No more going to the local course or country club to practice. That doesn't make any sense to me."

"Whatever, man. I just need to start over."

"With the family, right?" Claude asked to get a sense of exactly how much of a change he intended.

Mason looked at him as though there was no doubt in his mind. "With the family. Even though I don't know what the hell has been up with them lately. Especially Mercedes."

"I think the ladies in this family trip more than we do. They're all over the place."

Surprise was written on Mason's face. "How is Venus all over the place? She's probably the very one who stays out of trouble the most."

Claude looked surprised. "You're sticking up for Venus?"

"I've never had a problem with her. You need to go get her and stop all of this pride crap, bro."

"Maybe so."

"You know, Claude. All I ever wanted to do was provide for my family like Dad did. He got us straight up out of poverty and wanted nothing more than to do well by us," Mason said, picking up an abandoned, capless, half-bottle of liquor.

Claude reacted, "Man, you need to put that down. Your answers are not in there. I can tell you that."

"Coming from a man who's never had a drink in his life." Mason sniffed the mouth of the cognac bottle, taking in a whiff of the fragrant, potent eighty-proof hard liquor. He gave a look of both repulsion and delight. "All these many years of sobriety would be down the tube."

"After I saw what it did to Dad, tearing up his liver and shit, you'll never get me to try it. It sent him to his grave."

"As much as I respect Dad for all that he did for us by teaching us the value of hard work, in a lot of ways, I refuse to be just like him. Dad solved his problems in a bottle. I grew up thinking that's where all of the answers were supposed to be, right inside of here." Mason squinted his right eye and peeked inside of the brown bottle. He raised it to the sky, trying to see if he could find any quick-fix answers that might be hiding deep inside. He set it down on the table, clanging it with strength as it met the beveled glass top. "There's nothing in there that would help me deal with my stress. I've been there, done that."

"Generational curses, man. It's too easy to keep repeating the patterns of our parents. I refuse to."

"I hear you. The old stuff of our parents and the new stuff we bring to our own kids."

"The buck needs to stop here. I've got my own set of issues."

The two were silent for a minute. Mason thought about his own brother's problems, wondering how in the world he dealt with what happened to Fatima over the years. But he just had to know one thing. "Let me ask you something, bro."

"What?"

"Why is it that you never asked Fatima to marry you?"

Claude looked forward without even a blink. He opened his mouth and then closed it. He licked his lips and then spoke. "I don't know. I think maybe deep down I always knew she wasn't wife material. She always seemed to need time to be alone, so she'd say. Now I know what that was all about. She was spending those alone times with a madman."

Mason perused his surroundings, looking up at the tall palm trees and then up to the dark endless sky. "Yes, life is deep. My own daughter doesn't get enough attention so she takes my car on an excursion and wrecks it."

"Oh, she's just being a teenager. She probably drove by her friend's house and thought it made her seem cool. Surely she didn't mean to wreck it."

"Whatever she meant to do, I've got to make some changes."

"And what's up with Mercedes confronting Heidi tonight?" Claude asked.

"She found some pictures in my car."

Claude looked like he did not need to know the details. "I won't ask. And of all the nights, on your anniversary. You know Venus asked me why I hired Heidi. She thinks I hired her because she's your lover or something. Plus, I think Venus told Mercedes that you and I own Heidi's house."

"Sometimes I really can see how Venus would have suspected something. But Mercedes has never been the type to be insecure. Not like this," Mason said.

"She still doesn't know about Cicely?"

"You mean about her being Dad's child? No."

"And you're not going to tell her?"

"After all of this, I think that's something I'm definitely going to have to do. And it won't be about exposing Dad's secret at that point, it will be about why it took me so long to tell her."

"I'll give it to you. You've held steadfast to your promise to Dad to keep that from Mom."

"Oh, please. Mom has known about his love child all along. She thinks her name is Sissy."

"Damn. I guess Dad wasn't the slick ass player we thought he was."

"Mom was the slick one. She knew every step he made before he made it."

Claude uncrossed his legs. "Well, bro, I'm about to call it a night. I'll get that sign up out front as soon as possible."

"Thanks for having my back."

"That's what brothers do." Claude stood up yawning. He stretched his arms up high.

"Right, right. And by the way, if you're looking for your driver's license, Mom had it in her purse. And some of your cash too, dude."

"Oh, so Mom's been snooping, huh? I thought I was missing some cash. I'm going to have to keep a closer eye on her," Claude replied.

"I'm telling you she's a busybody."

Claude shook his brothers hand and then left, leaving Mason to himself.

Later that night, Claude drove to his deserted office to get going on listing Mason's house. He stepped inside without turning on the lights and sat at his large, circular desk.

He turned on his computer and logged onto the Internet. The light from the screen shined directly upon the wooden-framed family pictures on his desk. Each photo included an image of his wife. One with him, one of Venus and her dad, and one with Cameron after one of his basketball games.

Claude gazed at his missing lady. He took a moment to notice her, picking up each photo and examining it closely, as though she were a stranger. He took a moment to feast his eyes upon her unique beauty, seeing her as an outsider would. He saw her contagious, pretty smile, her wavy hair, and her flawless redbone skin. He admired her style, grace and stature. His stomach churned with a longing for her as a woman and as a friend. He saw this prize as something he'd lost out on. Claude put the examined photos down, and then leaned over to pick up the office phone. He called Venus on her cell phone but there was no answer. He then called her dad's number.

"Hello, Mr. Ortiz. How are you? Long time no see. Listen, is Venus there? She's not. Well, do you know where she went? No. Please ask her to call me when she gets in. I'd really appreciate it. Thanks."

Venus's father's one-word answers convinced Claude that he was bothered. Bothered that the very man who vowed to love, honor, and cherish let his daughter get away. Claude felt his father-in-law's distance was understandable. But he was about to try to fix things.

Claude made another call to her cell phone. Again the machine came on.

"Venus, I don't want to have to show up over there unannounced, but I will if I have to. I'd like to hear from you. Eventually, Cameron will be going off to college, you know. And then, one day, I'm going to have to face the fact that eventually, Mom is going to pass away. I've lost so much, Venus. I can't lose you, too. I just can't. At times I don't know what to say or how to say it. See, I admit that I've spent many, many days trying to deal with my own pain. I apologize for trying to blame you for all of the secrets Fatima kept from me. I know that you were just being a friend. Venus, please call me so that we can work this out. All I keep thinking about is the first time we went for Mexican food to talk about our pain over losing Fatima. It was like you completed my thoughts. We felt everything the same. And then when we met up in Vegas to hang out, my proposal just sprung from my lips, as if it was so natural, as if it was just meant to be." The voice mail cut him off. He called again. He hoped Venus would answer by some stroke of luck, but she did not.

"Venus, I got cut off. Like I said, it seemed to be so natural. We said our vows at the chapel and came home as husband and wife. It felt so right. I don't know what went wrong. I suppose I didn't take the time to notice the signs that you felt like a replacement. But I get it. You will always be Fatima's friend. And I want you to always be my wife. Because you and me, we live on and we must be happy in spite of what people think. That is why we're here. To be happy in love. This feeling I'm feeling right now is not happiness. I feel alone and broken. Please reconsider your decision and come home. Please. I'd really appreciate it. I love you. And I can love you exactly the way you need to be loved. Show me how. And one more thing, in case I didn't say it before; I'm so sorry we lost our baby. I'd like to try again. Good-bye."

Claude logged onto the multiple listing site and added the Bedford Avenue home for 1.2 million. He took a FOR SALE sign from his office, shut down the computer, and exited his place of business. He headed to Mason's house to hammer the sign into the front lawn. And then he leisurely drove home to Cameron, glancing down hoping that his cell phone would ring. It did not.

# chapter 17

It had been almost two weeks since the anniversary party and Star's fender bender. Mason and Mercedes agreed that it was the perfect time for family therapy.

Dr. Little, a distinguished-looking man in his mid-fifties with a classic jaw and hazel eyes, sat in his sofa chair while Mason and Mercedes sat on the dark sofa across from him in his luxurious Westwood office. His many framed awards, accreditations, diplomas, degrees, and family portraits filled the walls. He gave Mason and Mercedes a friendly smile, put on his reading glasses and began to run down his plan.

"The first thing we need to do is agree that whatever is said here is adult conversation for your benefit as parents and spouses. It is not to be used against your children or each other at any time. Is that agreed?"

"Yes," Mason and Mercedes said in unison, nodding their heads toward him and one another. Mercedes rotated her new ring back and forth without even realizing it.

"Now, because I've talked to your son and daughter in detail, I've taken these conversations and converted them into an outline for healing. I want you to know that children, subconsciously, and to their own detriment sometimes, internalize your behaviors as being their fault. They tell themselves that if Mom is sad today, it must be because I was on the phone past my curfew. If Dad is distant, it must be because I did something to irritate him. Do you follow me?"

"Yes," Mercedes responded.

"Good." He repositioned himself in his chair. "Now, I need to know what each of you sees as the biggest dysfunction in your household."

"As parents or spouses?" Mercedes asked.

"Whichever is bigger."

Mason answered. "I see the biggest dysfunction being that I have a high-profile job, exposing me to a high level of visibility and stress."

The doctor took notes. "And how does that affect your wife?"

Mason crossed his leg over his knee. "I think it causes her to take up the slack when I'm not around and sometimes when I am around."

"How do you think that makes her feel?"

"Surely she must feel pressured and weighed upon."

"Would you agree, Mrs. Wilson?"

"Absolutely," Mercedes replied looking pleased.

"How does it make you feel? You tell him yourself."

"I agreed to take up the slack a long time ago. I knew it would be like this. But, once your young children get older and more aware as teenagers, sometimes their concerns are so serious and so real that the answers that used to work no longer do. And when that happens, my response is anger."

"Anger at whom?"

"Anger at myself for not having the right answer, not having the ability to have my husband home more and have him at the PTA meetings, recitals and tournaments."

"Would you say you're angry at your husband, though?"

"At times," Mercedes admitted, looking at Mason as though she awaited a reaction.

Dr. Little asked, "What would cure that anger?"

"More focused quality time with me and the kids. It's just that simple."

Mason countered, "But it's not that simple, doctor. I have obligations and demands that I have to work in between family time."

Mercedes replied, "Sometimes I think you work *us* in, in between work time."

"Wow. Did you hear what she just said?"

"Yes, but—"

Dr. Little interrupted, sensing a denial coming. "Now, with all due respect, I asked did you hear what she said? That is her opinion and not hearing her invalidates her. Did you hear her?"

"I did."

"What did she say?"

"She said it feels like I fit the family in between my career, as if they're second."

"Is that right, Mrs. Wilson?"

"Yes."

"Mr. Wilson, what do you think about that?"

"I can see how that would be her opinion. And I apologize. It's truly not my intention and I didn't know that she felt that way. It makes me feel bad because of course my family comes first. I work for my family so that I can provide for my family."

Mercedes interjected. "And he's done that. A darn good job of it, too. But to nurture relationships takes true, dedicated, devoted, focused time."

"And time is something I don't have enough of."

Dr. Little looked content. "So, I can see that we're getting somewhere. We'll work on that. But now, Mrs. Wilson, what do you see as the biggest dysfunction in your family?"

"Probably that we live this rich lifestyle with the Lynx meetings, golf club memberships, magazine covers, jumbo accounts and fancy cars and homes. Yet behind closed doors, I see two unhappy kids and a so-so-marriage. As a wife, I think I overcompensate the emptiness with food, shopping, and even with sex."

"Oh really?" Mason asked, looking extremely surprised.

"Yes, even though the sex has never been a problem."

Mason remarked snidely, "Okay, so we're in sync on something."

"But also, we've been caregivers for my ailing mother-in-law who I love dearly. We take care of her a little less now that Claude, Mason's brother, has taken her in. But with jobs and responsibilities, I'd almost give anything to have my husband with a normal job, as ungrateful as that may sound. Some women would think I'm nuts for saying that."

"Do you agree, Mr. Wilson?"

Mason crossed his legs in the other direction. "Agree that we have a so-so marriage? No. But, damn, I'm starting to feel guilty for being successful. This life we live is anything *but* so-so. If I wasn't a professional golfer, Mercedes wouldn't overeat, the kids would be happier and my mom would be healthy. I can't take the blame for everyone's problems."

"Now, do you really believe that?" the doctor asked.

"It's like if I had a normal job this family would be normal. It's not that simple. I know plenty of people who work nine-to-five and have more problems than we do. Abnormal schedules should not equate with abnormal family members."

"You're right, Mr. Wilson, but everything in moderation." Dr. Little looked at Mercedes. "Do you see how he feels?"

"Yes," she replied, smiling at Mason.

"What did he say?"

"He said that he feels to blame and that even a different job would not be a quick fix."

"Is that close?" he asked Mason.

"She gets it." Mason kept his eyes fixed upon the doctor.

"Okay, now. Let's me explain this. Dysfunction is normal and is also very common. It's not the level of the issues that makes a family less dysfunctional, it's how you handle the crises that matters. Since you're here in the flesh, I think that's evidence enough that you want to fix it. I can see that you want to learn how to deal with the issues. And so here we are. So far we know that time is a big issue and relieving pressure from Mrs. Wilson by having quality interactions with all family members in a balanced way should help. The diet and anger could possibly be relieved once the relationships start to gel. It sounds like emotions are at the root, not the food itself.

"And from the teens' point of view—Rashaad seems well adjusted. He's just growing into young adulthood. And Mr. Wilson, you're walking in the very shoes he's going to fill. Remember that. As far as Star is concerned, I think she's borderline genius. I know you know that. I think you should get her tested."

Mercedes nodded her head in agreement. "Yes, we're very aware of that. She always scores off the charts on placement tests."

"Well, she's definitely an old soul, I'll say that much. Now dealing with Rashaad's issues, even though they're minor, will be our topic in two weeks. And Mr. Wilson, I want you to make a focused commitment to be here every Wednesday for the next six weeks like clockwork. Is that a deal?"

"Yes."

"So next week we'll deal with Star and her conflict about the attention that being famous draws. She wants and needs to be individual. She looks forward to a future of anonymity. Then we'll talk about how Mrs. Wilson's needs can be met. And the fourth week we'll discuss how Mr. Wilson can give more time to the family."

Mason remarked, "Shoot, I'll just retire from the circuit and we can save ourselves six weeks of psychotherapy."

"Mason has really been trying," Mercedes said, placing her hand on his back.

Dr. Little leaned forward toward Mason, who looked up with a blank stare. "No, no one is saying that, Mr. Wilson. There is room in between the passive and the aggressive choices. That would be overly aggressive and much too impulsive. The fifth week we'll talk about caregiving and the future over the next five years as parents. The sixth week we'll bring in all four of you to tie things together. Allow twice as much time that evening. Are we clear on our goals and outlook?"

"We are," Mercedes answered. "What can we do in the meantime?"

"Work on being there for each other—both of you, with a hug, a smile, a phone call, an e-mail, a wink, a surprise, a touch. Just show some kind of attention. Focus on what really matters in life—*love*."

"It sounds like we have our work cut out for us," Mason replied in a low tone.

"Yes, you do. Both of you do. And it goes deeper than what can be covered in a few sessions. It's a lifestyle change and a life commitment. And one can't do it alone."

Mason responded after Mercedes and the doctor gave him a look, as if awaiting a reply. "Don't look at me."

"You have to be there mind and spirit, willing to do the work."

"I'm willing," Mercedes said.

Mason agreed, coming to his feet as if he wanted it to be over. "So am I."

The doctor and Mercedes stood as well. "Okay then, I'll see you both next week. Oh, one more thing. Your homework is to recall a pivotal moment in your life that changed you forever. I want it in writing so that it takes up at least one complete page. And I want you to read it aloud next week."

"A moment about each other?" Mercedes asked.

"Whatever moment you want it to be."

She shook the doctor's hand. "Got it, Dr. Little. Thanks so much."

"Call me in the meantime if you need me. Good luck." He handed them both his business card.

Mason nodded his head and led the way out.

The next Saturday, the house smelled of cilantro and Mexican spices.

Mercedes walked from the kitchen to the living room and passed by the tall, exquisite vase of colorful tulips that Mason had sent the day before. She sniffed them and then proceeded to take a seat on the sofa.

Mercedes and Star watched Mason's last shot at the twenty-seventh hole at Torrey Pines. The previous day he'd shot a sixty-seven and was ahead by one stroke, leading into the final round.

Star was seated on the floor, leaning back in between her mother's legs. Usually they'd watch highlights or check in for the latest updates from time to time. But today, they sat and watched in silence, almost as if they were watching a tournament with players who were complete strangers. They did not react any more to

Mason's play than they did to the play of other golfers. They just watched quietly, enjoying the game itself, almost as if Mason's achievements had suddenly become routine.

As usual, Mason was now ahead by a few strokes. The last hole was a close one. The runner up came within one stroke, but their husband and father pulled it off and won. The Fox interviewer chased Mason down for an interview.

Mason looked relieved, yet cool. He spoke, sounding a little winded and very rushed. "I had to master my mind, just as my father taught me so many years ago. You can't allow yourself to be distracted. You have to stay in control."

"You seemed to get every break, I mean you escaped the sand and nailed the fairway woods like you were on a mission."

"That's exactly how I felt," Mason replied. "I could not allow myself to slip up. I had to stay focused."

"Looks like your win has qualified you for a spot in the five-million-dollar World Golf Championship event in Ireland this month. Are you prepared for that?"

"I can't think that far ahead right now. I'm not even sure if I'll enter that one. I really want to spend more time with my family for a while. I've got to go, thanks." Mason rushed up the hill with a peppy Winton at his side.

The reporter pulled aside one of Mason's representatives from the Titleist company. Mercedes's eyes bugged.

"Natalie Glenn, what is the Titleist company's stance as Mason Wilson just mentioned that he's probably going to spend more time with his family and might not go to Ireland. What do you have to say about that?"

Natalie seemed elated, yet her voice was very soft and calm. "I think our stance is and has always been evident. Mr. Wilson is and has been a very important individual to us. He has represented our company and our products with class and we are very proud of him. He is a stellar athlete and a warm human being."

"Miss Glenn, what will happen if Mason Wilson decides to take time off, or better yet retire?" Mercedes sat up, leaning in toward the fifty-five-inch flat screen.

"We don't know anything about that. I don't think he said retire. If and when Mace, I mean Mason decides to do that, we will discuss our options. We'll support him in whatever he does."

Star reacted. "Mace?" she commented, giving every ounce of her attention to the interview.

Natalie continued, "For now I think it's a little premature to speculate."

"Okay, Miss Glenn. Thanks for taking a moment to speak with us."

Natalie smiled and hurried up the hill in her tight-fitting, knee-length skirt. Her long, candy-apple red hair was blowing and bouncing as she took each fast-paced step. But to Mercedes, it was as if she was walking at a snails pace. Natalie met up with Mason and shifted her long mane to the left side just as she stood to pose for a couple of pictures while Mason made his acceptance speech. She then continued to stand directly behind him in the winner's circle as he was presented with the trophy and given his check.

Almost like a zombie, Mercedes moved her leg from around Star's body and simply stood up. She went into the kitchen to check on the pan of enchiladas she'd made for the kids.

Star still sat watching the closing moments of the event. Then she changed the channel to BET, sitting in her usual yoga position on the floor with her back against the sofa.

"Mom, when is Dad coming home?" asked Rashaad, draped by a towel at his waist, running inside from his afternoon swim.

"He'll be back in a couple days, son."

He grabbed a drink from the fridge. "I have a golf tournament that the school entered me in. It'll be on Saturday morning. Do you think he'll be able to catch it?"

"I assure you he wouldn't miss it, baby." Her mind was divided.

"Cool."

"Now get washed up for lunch," she said, sounding as though she was speaking in monotone.

"I will, Mom. It sure smells good." Rashaad gave his mother a look of approval, savoring the aroma.

"I'm very proud of you," Mercedes said to her son as he was halfway down the hall.

Mercedes picked up the kitchen phone and dialed. "Sequoia, where are you? Are you in the back house?" Mercedes sounded frantic. She grabbed a snack from the top of the refrigerator.

"No, I'm just running errands. Why? Are you okay?"

"No, I'm not. My intuition told me something was up. I just figured out who Mason has been seeing."

"Who?" Sequoia asked.

Mercedes unwrapped the snack package, taking a seat at the kitchen table. "A girl he travels with on tour. A white girl who reps the company he promotes."

"A white girl. Oh, Mercedes, how do you know that?"

"I just know. I just saw her on TV. I know it's her."

"You've gone on tour with him recently. You never saw her there?"

"No. I've never seen her before in my life. He's usually only with his caddy."

"Is this about that red hair in his car you were trippin' about at the pool party?"

"It's her hair. Just as bright red and it is long."

"That's not enough proof, Mercedes. Does Mason know that you still suspect him?"

"Not yet."

"Are you going to let him have it?"

"Would he really admit it anyway?"

"Why don't you call her and tell her you know? Or better yet, set him up next time."

"No, that's not my style."

"Well, it needs to be." Sequoia could be heard disarming the alarm to her car. "Maybe you should just tell him you already know, just like you told me; he'll probably think you know more than you really do."

"I already confronted him at our party and I was wrong."

"So? Confront him again."

Mercedes looked at the oatmeal cake and decided she did not want it. She stood up and threw it in the trash. "Anyway, I've been bringing people into our bed for a long time now, with my fantasies and wild imagination. I guess all of that imagery in my head turned out to be true."

Sequoia started her engine and immediately spoke over the volume of the radio. "Mercedes, if he is banging this white chick, he's doing it in reality. There's a big difference."

"Damn, girl. This makes me so freakin' mad. And I'm always the one claiming how much I trust him."

Sequoia replied, "Sounds like it's time for you to take back that trust and get him to come clean for real."

At the session with Dr. Little the following week, Mercedes spoke first.

"Baby, I know."

"What do you mean? You know what?"

"Okay, here's a hint. What's red, white, and all over black?"

Mason looked at Mercedes like she'd lost her mind. "What's *what?*"

"Mace, may I call you Mace?"

Mason looked lost.

"Mace, I know. I know you're an admired, desired, wealthy, popular stud and it's difficult with all of your options, right?"

"Cedes," he said, scooting forward without looking at her, glancing at Dr. Little's face for help.

"I knew the rule, I just thought you'd be the exception. But, I guess we wives of famous men need to go ahead and resolve ourselves to the fact that we need to put up with the womanizing and appreciate what we have. We need to just get over it, huh? The bottom line is if you and I are ever going to stay together, I need to come to terms with the fact that I'm going to have to share you, right?"

"Share me? Where is this coming from?"

"Your redhead."

"Are you trippin' off of Heidi again?"

"Your white, redheaded business companion whose been assigned as your Titleist representative for the past year. I'm sharing my husband with her. Actually she is a little sexy but I thought I knew your type better than that."

"Mercedes."

Dr. Little took off his reading glasses. He decided to play referee. "Okay, now let's slow down and get to the truth here."

Mercedes kept her focus on Mason, noticing him fidgeting with his own fingers. "I am right at the truth and there's no better place for Mason to admit his goings-on, next to the church or divorce court, than here and now."

"Mason, are you prepared to get to the heart of this now?" the doctor asked.

There was a long pause and no reply.

Mercedes repeated herself. "Like I said, there's no better time."

Mason sat back. His gut panged with guilt. He spoke. "Natalie was just sex to me. She was convenient and available. She was no drama, no expectations, no requirements, and no emotions. She was just sex." His own voice echoed in his head. He took a deep breath.

Mercedes voice remained the same, but her jaw grew tense. "She's your out-of-town sex partner. My replacement?"

"No."

Her voice grew louder. "So, I fuck the hell out of you in California, and she fucks you in the other forty-nine states, and abroad, right?"

"Cedes. It was only maybe every other month. It stopped before you started traveling with me last month. I told her it was over and that this past week's tournament was her last with me." Mason could not believe he was even agreeing to admit that. He looked around at the walls of the office as if the place was known for promoting the truth in people.

Mercedes grew more and more annoyed. "Oh, so that comes out to, let's see, Mason, about a half-a-dozen times? How dare you use the word *only.* Once is still too much to use the word *only.* That's my husband pleasing another woman."

"Cedes. Please." Mason realized that his confession did not feel cleansing in the least.

Mercedes's brows arched with disdain. "Please, my ass. If pussy was all you wanted, I could have met you in every city when you were lonely, or sent you a *Hustler* magazine. I wouldn't have hesitated if it meant saving my family. But here's how it works, see—my husband is never supposed to have sex without me. After all, I never have it without you." She looked to Dr. Little, sounding very fired up. "Doctor, did you know that? I have never fucked any man but my husband? I am a virgin to anyone but Mason Wilson, who took my virginity and put a ring on my finger when he promised to honor and cherish me until death do us part . . . or until he gets fucking horny."

"I realize that I'm the only one, Cedes."

"How about if I go and fuck Dr. Green? He wanted to, you know. Or how about your own brother, Torino, or his friend Kyle, or Dr. Little here?" Mercedes pointed to the doctor who stared back in complete silence.

"Okay, Cedes, that's enough," Mason said, feeling dejected yet defensive.

"That's for me to decide if it's enough or not. Not you. Maybe you can buy me a six-carat ring this time, huh? Do you think that will fix it? I was feeling lonely many times and I didn't let some strange penis enter my body."

Dr. Little found the strength to clear his throat. "Mrs. Wilson. This is a very critical crossroad in your relationship and I do think this is just the place to release this energy. I understand your anger and hurt. It is natural and expected. But revenge solves nothing and I know you don't mean that."

Mercedes gritted her teeth before she spoke and squinted her eyes. "I want him to know what it feels like to be betrayed. I go around proclaiming my husband's fidelity—that I trust him no matter what. It feels like I've been stabbed in the heart."

"What's happening is that the two of you have come to terms with an issue that most couples deal with way before now. You've been married this long and now you find that infidelities have occurred."

"Who knows when the first time was."

"There was never a time before this."

"Dr. Little. Maybe you can tell me. Why do men cheat?" she asked sarcastically.

"Well, usually for men it's about sex and empowerment."

Mason looked at him as though he was a traitor.

"Sex and empowerment, huh? After all this time he decided to look for sex and empowerment. Like he doesn't have enough of both in his life."

Dr. Little worked to bring clarity to the couple. "Sometimes it's even harder when so many years have gone by. But, one thing is for sure; it's not a reason to go your separate ways. Not when your family is making major breakthroughs toward improving relationships. Mason, do you realize it was a smart thing for her to wait until she got here? It must have been hell for her to keep this inside. I'll be very honest with you, Mason. You screwed up and you've got to fix it."

"I agree and I have fixed it."

"What do you mean?" the doctor asked.

"I told you I already talked to her and told her that it can never happen again. Also, because I'm seriously thinking about retiring and severing ties with Titleist altogether."

Mercedes looked sickened by his words. "Oh, please, spare me."

"Cedes, she means nothing to me."

She pointed her finger directly at his nose. He turned away. "Wrong. She meant about as much as our marriage did, and I would think that was a hell of a lot to risk. Besides, Mason, she's only seven numbers away. What happens next time you catch a case of the hornies or some beautiful woman starts chasing you down? It's just too easy for you to trip up again. You have way too many opportunities to pass up a cheap screw. You're an adulterer."

"I understand how you feel and I'm willing to do whatever it takes."

Dr. Little continued to run it down. "Mason, you mentioned that you've already fixed it. I want you to know that your work has just begun. You need to fix it with your wife; not just by telling her that the other woman is out of the way. You need to clear the clutter you've accumulated. You need to be accountable, loving, and understanding of her insecurities, even when it drives you nuts, and you need to be patient when she's feeling jealous. You have a long road ahead of you. Both of you. The big question is, does Mercedes want to stay?"

"You mean can I live with the fact that a rich, powerful man can never be faithful to one woman? Because that's the real question. It will never stop. Doctor, should I settle for a broke ass faithful man, or live with a rich ass player?"

Dr. Little corrected her. "No, should you live up to the vows you made to your spouse before God?"

"Ask him that," she said, pointing to her husband.

"Mason, can you?" asked Dr, Little.

Words tumbled through Mason's mind. He didn't want to say the wrong thing, yet knew exactly what he was feeling. "Yes, I can. I got married to grow with you, not grow our separate ways. Mercedes, I'm sorry."

Mercedes looked betrayed. "You should have told me at the pool party instead of denying Heidi so tough. That's some sorry ass shit."

Dr. Little asked, "After all of this, Mercedes, can you live up to your vows?"

"I don't know, maybe after some serious revenge fucking. Dr. Little, let's go for a drink and talk about it."

Mason looked stunned and discomfited. "Cedes."

She continued painting a vivid scene for Mason to imagine. "I just don't know. I'll think about it. Picture some dick inside of me while you work though your own guilt. You put my health in jeopardy, you asshole. I hope you at least wore a condom. I feel no pity for you whatsoever." Mercedes looked at an open-mouthed Dr. Little and said, "I'll see you next week, Doc." She stood and switched past them both. She headed to the door with weighted, yet quick-paced steps. "I hope she's worth half of your money," Mercedes yelled while entering the hallway.

Mason got up, shaking the doctor's hand, and strode quickly to the elevator to catch his wife.

Later that day at home, Mercedes felt compelled to call Dr. Little for a one-on-one, just to hopefully hear him give her that glimmer of a lecture that she might need to deal with the new little awakening in her life. Dr. Little answered his office phone.

"Dr. Little here."

"Hello. It's Mercedes Wilson. I feel like I'm about to lose my mind." She sat on the sofa in her home office with her bare feet propped up to the side.

"Mercedes, I'm glad you called. I was just thinking about your situation. You know, you're going to have to decide one thing. Do you want to stand by your man or not?"

"I'm not sure. I just don't think I can ever trust him again. Doctor, these are feelings I never thought I'd have."

He tried to sound calming. "Mercedes, you need to be careful in your case because it is very common for some wives to normalize stressful situations by virtue of being married to successful men. It's not normal to cheat on your spouse, no matter what."

Mercedes placed her hand behind her head. "I agree, but those women have to take responsibility for allowing these men that luxury. I have to be able to trust my husband. And you say 'successful men' as if because they have money they have a different set of allowances in life. Mason's fortune is his wife and family, not his bank account. His incentive should be to make sure he doesn't ruin what we've built together. I'm not okay with his career coming first and his wife second."

"I understand, and all of your feelings are normal. There's a process of trying to cope with being the primary parent in the family, handling finances, the possibility of having to relocate at the drop of a hat, and coming to terms with the possibility of one being unfaithful. It is true that most wives of celebrities reconcile with their husbands when they're famous athletes."

She tucked her knees into her chest. "Yeah. Well, he can have this house and these sorry ass rings if he thinks that all of these material possessions buy my tolerance. How can you buy someone when all of this infidelity creates these intense feelings of betrayal and confusion. Diamonds won't make me stand by my man."

"What will?"

"I don't know. I just don't know."

"Until you do some more figuring out, I suggest you talk to Mason one-on-one. Bring it up and deal with it now before things get further along. You two need to do this in privacy, calmly, and you need to both put a vision together of how you want your life to be. Expect great things and know that your life can be better after something like this. Sometimes, infidelity is not the greatest reason to break up. Physical and mental abuse, financial improprieties and other issues are usually nonnegotiable. Is this negotiable in your eyes?"

"Like I said, I don't know. I'm at a loss right now. I'll see you next week."

"Be strong. And know that it's not all about you. It's about a family."

"Thanks."

# chapter 18

The kids were fast asleep. Mercedes closed the door to her and Mason's bedroom and leaned her body up against it. She turned the lock from behind her. "You're an asshole."

He looked at her like he'd been expecting her attack. "Mercedes, I know how you feel." Mason sat on the end of the bed. He took the position of the thinker.

She walked over and stood in front of him. She struggled to keep her tone low. "No, you don't. Don't even make that dumb ass statement. You've never had your spouse fuck around on you, Mason. You have no idea what I'm feeling."

"I made a poor decision."

"That's what happens when you think with your dick, fool."

Mason felt his own anger start to build. He stood up, walked past his wife, and then headed for the door.

She turned to face him. "Where are you going?"

Mason stopped. "For a walk."

"No. Don't you cop out on me now. You neglected to commit all the way already. So you have to be a man and deal with me being in your face, on your case, in your head, on your nerves, asking questions, yelling, feeling fucked up, slapping you, being disgusted with you, and crying like a baby. You have to fix this. You fucked it up."

He turned back toward Mercedes. His eyes were full on. "How do I do that?"

She stepped up to him, nearly toe-to-toe. "By doing exactly what I just said. You have to help me regain my self-respect and identity. I don't know who the hell I'm married to. My parents never told me about how to deal with a philanderer. Oh, excuse me, a philanderer who's a professional athlete. But I'm one tough woman, in case you haven't noticed. I won't crack. And I can't afford to be naïve again. I have a tough spine, Mason. You didn't fool around on a doormat, so you deal with me. Deal with one hundred percent of my full strength feelings of being fooled around on by my husband of nearly twenty years. Fucking deal with it."

He did not blink. "I'm committed to you, Cedes."

She wagged her finger in his face. "Oh, you are, huh? As of today? As of last week? When was the last time you fucked another woman?"

Mason looked away. "It's been a while."

"How long is a while?"

"Three weeks."

"Three weeks. So that makes it just before we went away for our anniversary and you had someone sing to me?"

"Around that time."

"So that red hair in your car was from when? Since you only fool around with her on the road. Why was her hair in your car, in *our* car?"

"I drove her to the airport when she was in Los Angeles last month."

"Why was she here?"

"She had a layover for a few hours."

"And you fucked her in between flights?"

"No. We just had lunch."

"When? Was that one of the days you ran out when Rashaad and Star and I needed you to be available. You spent three of your rare, unavailable hours having lunch with her?"

"It was my chance to break it off with her."

"Break it off over a meal?"

"Yes. Over a meal."

She gave him a pissy growl. "You jerk. You should have called her and hung up the damn phone in her face after you told her ass to get lost."

"I wanted to do it in a way that I thought would be best, considering the Titleist connection."

"Oh, that was a sticky kind of thing, fucking someone who's in your business circles. You didn't want to piss her off because she might what? Tell her boss and they'd drop you?"

"I wanted to do it face-to-face."

"You went from pussy to face, and dick to face, to face-to-face, huh?"

Mason shook his head and crossed his arms.

She stepped back and nodded furiously. "Mason, you were into this woman enough to share meals?"

"We'd never eaten together before. It was only sex. A quickie here and there. No hugging, no spending the night. We did not fall for each other. Not in the least."

She mocked him with a bitchy edge. "*Not in the least.* Oh, well thank God for that. At least I don't have to worry about her being a hormonal stalker who bonded to your dick and refuses to give up her married lover."

"It was very infrequent and very casual."

"There is nothing causal about extramarital sex, Mason Wilson. What part did I play in you being such a ladies man? Is it that I'm too heavy for you lately? You know, like those ladies said in the park, I need to keep myself in shape in order to keep a man like you. Was it her slim and trim, flat-ass, pale-skinned, thin-lipped self that turned you on more than my fat butt? Gain ten pounds and your man starts feeling up on new panties?"

"It wasn't any of that. It wasn't about you not being good enough. You know how I feel about your body. I love your body."

"Oh, I guess it was because you've just got it going on so tough that they just throw themselves at you, huh? Do you really think your prowess on the course entitles you to bend the rules off the course?"

"No."

"Oh, yes. Obviously you do. You know, when a man cheats, it's the ultimate sign of disrespect. I feel so damn disrespected. And what if this were to have hit the media, it would have been all over America. What if someone saw you two during your cozy little lunch appointment last month? Hell, I'm going to write a book called, *Rich, Famous, Beautiful and Cheated on. It's a real fucked up ride.*"

He lowered his hands down to his side. "Baby, I'm sorry."

"Don't get me started on how sorry you are. And I know you didn't get this type of behavior from your dad."

Mason's heartbeat quickened. His brain wanted to just walk away from the heated emotions of the conversation, but his heart told him to continue talking it out. After all, he thought to himself, *Dammit. I brought us to this mess. I have to get us through it.* "Look, I messed up. I want to do whatever it takes to repair the damage, Cedes. I'd give all of this up, the house, the money, the career, the fame, just to keep my family."

"All you've really had to give up so far is your hoe. Your white hoe. Anyway, why the fuck a white woman, Mason? Why make it even more insulting by going for what's considered the prize once a black man 'makes it.' How embarrassing and insulting. You picked a horny white woman trying to get some big black dick up in her."

"The fact that she was white had nothing to do with it. I didn't end up with her because of her race."

"Don't give me that bunch of crap about how women are women. Like you didn't even notice that she was white."

"I was down and she was just . . . there."

"I could kick her bitch ass."

"That wouldn't help."

"Don't you dare tell me what would help. A nice foot up her ass would sure give me a rush right about now. So who's going to be there next time you're down about a tournament and you get a hard-on?"

He counted to ten under his breath. "No one."

"Yeah right. How do I believe a word you say anymore?"

"I get what you're saying. I'm not saying that I understand how bad it hurts. But I get it. I slept with her—"

Mercedes interrupted him with contempt. "Say her name."

"Natalie. I slept with Natalie one night after a bad day on the course. She came up to my room and we talked about the game that day. And then it happened."

"What happened?"

"She hugged me and then she kissed me good-bye. We walked toward the bed and the next thing I knew, we we're . . . together."

"You were together because you had a bad game?"

"Yes."

"A bad game so you turn to another woman?"

Mason looked disgusted with himself.

"And then?"

"And then, she left."

"There's so much in between the she kissed me and then we were together, that I could puke. But you know what? I don't even want to know the gory details. Knowing me, it'll only serve to replay in my head every waking moment of my life."

"I want you to know this. We got together again a few more times." He thought about the times they had phone sex but didn't dare reveal that to his scorned woman. "It was wrong and I know it. It was . . ."

"What, exciting?"

"Yes, it was exciting and distracting and, and . . . cheap. It never made me feel better. It always made me feel worse. But it's like she knew which golf matches were bad for me, and she appeared."

"So it's all her fault, huh? She seduced you?"

"No. It's all mine."

She rolled her eyes. "If you wanted excitement and a distraction, you could have rented a fucking Matrix movie, you wimp. Or maybe you could have just fallen off the wagon and had a drink. Even that I could handle."

Mason sucked his lips and then turned to look away.

"You committed to a marriage and you just stopped working at it. You vowed to take me for the rest of your life and so that means all other women should have been off-limits. You should have been on lockdown from any other sex than with me. Look at me when I'm talking to you. You at least owe me that much," she said cuttingly.

Mason zeroed in on her direct stare.

"I feel like I went through life with blinders on. I mean, I knew there were groupies, but I never thought you would let one come between what we had. Oh, but there's that old devilish word, temptation. You let temptation get the best of you, in spite of the fact that I sang your praises everywhere I'd go. Not my man, no, not Mason. I never wanted to have a short leash on you and look what happened. So next time you're on the road, it will be another open invitation for you to stray again, won't it? There's no way I can stay."

"No it won't," he begged.

"Yes it will. Your lifestyle is an invitation to stray, Mason. You can get easy sex with pretty women who shut up just to be with you. And then you have this narcissistic attitude like you just happened to put yourself in a bad situation and you're sorry. See women like her let you get in, it's clean and there are no attachments. She just wants bragging rights. And don't think she hasn't told all of her friends every detail about how you are in bed. Now please tell me you didn't have oral sex with her, Mason."

He responded immediately. "I didn't."

"Did she?"

Silence.

"You're breathing hard, Mason." Mercedes watched his chest rise and fall. "You know, it's a husband's responsibility to be true to his wife, not my responsibility to keep you in line. I don't want a man I have to track down and spy on like Colette did with Torino. I can't be on the road with you and baby-sit your ass. And did you ever think about what would happen if she sued you or got pregnant? How dumb can you be? Dammit, you put all of us at risk, not to mention bringing all of her sex partners home to me. What was so wrong with our sex life? Please tell me because I missed that, what with all of the strip club hoppin', wild ass slapping and sitting on your face and stuff."

"Not a thing."

She studied him in silence, staring him down.

His stress lines grew. His guilt owned him. The uncomfortableness of him living in his own skin was evident.

The air was thick. But she spoke again. This time she lowered her voice. “This relationship dishonors me. You’re no role model, Mason. You are foul. Get out of my face.”

Mason did not. He stood in place while she simmered. Sweat covered her nose. She bumped his shoulder with hers, took heavy steps, and banged open the bedroom door as she stormed out.

# chapter 19

During the next week, Mason and Mercedes said few words to one another. If anyone spoke or tried to make conversation, it was Mason. When they were alone, he never got up the nerve to bring up his own infidelity again. He seemed to be dancing around it. But always in the back of his mind he was wondering what Mercedes planned as far as wanting to hang in for the long haul, or not. And yet he also had to decide whether or not to bring up the fact that Cicely was really his sister. He felt uncomfortable, almost praying for a tour date so that he could escape the thick, foul air between them.

They both arrived back at Dr. Little's office to discuss Star, more for her good than theirs. They both drove separate cars.

Mason asked, "Why would a teenage girl wreck her dad's car?"

Mercedes replied for the doctor. "Oh, please. It was an accident. She'd gone to pick up Asia because she couldn't get a ride. She's a normal teenager."

The doctor interjected. "I don't mean to sound overdramatic, but absent dads scar their daughters for life. I'm not saying you did scar her, but she sees you as absent. At least that's what she says she's feeling. She doesn't know how to heal those scars so she thinks that getting attention by any means necessary will draw you to her. That incident was not about the car. It is much deeper than that."

Mason replied, "I thought so. And for the record, I am far from absent."

The doctor explained. "You are the first man in her life and she can forever entertain powerful feelings of being unworthy and incapable of receiving a man's love if your busy schedule includes everything but her."

"It is far from intentional."

"Little girls cannot determine intentional from non-intentional. Just like when a parent dies, that's non-intentional but the bottom line is, they're not there physically."

Mason still tried to justify his involvement. "Emotionally, we connect well. I'm around a couple days per week."

"And what happens on those days?"

"I'm at home and I try to make sure we all have dinner together."

"But how often does that actually happen?"

Mason replied, "Maybe twice per month."

"And aside from that, what else do you do to make her feel important?"

Mason sat forward, his elbow to his knee and his fist to his chin. "Doctor, back in the day, parents didn't have to make a point of making kids feel special. There wasn't all of this psycho-analyzing. I pay for her private school education, piano lessons, clothes, and shelter, meet her every financial need, show love to her mom, and basically provide a good home. How many men can say that?"

"Not many," Dr. Little replied.

Mercedes admitted. "She's far from fatherless."

The doctor tried to clarify. "Yes, but is she a priority? Do you take time to help her develop confidence in herself by complimenting her and bonding with her? Maybe taking her to get her nails done, to a movie, to the library, to breakfast."

"Not recently. Do people really go to the library anymore?" Mason asked, looking at Mercedes, who gave him no reply.

"Mason, when was the last time the two of you spent an hour together without your son and wife?"

Mason thought back. "When we . . . that was . . . well, I took her to school the other day. The day she started her period but at that time she asked for her mom."

"So maybe that was an important moment but still it was a time when she needed her mother. It doesn't mean you didn't try."

"Right. And I also drove my car home from San Diego and she rode with me. We followed her mom back in her car after they met me down there for a tournament but she wanted to ride back with me."

"What did you talk about?"

"I think, oh my God, I was on my cell most of the time handling business and then I called Mercedes and we talked about my schedule while we drove."

"Mason, you can still help Star develop a healthy sense of femininity and help her shape her view of the external world. You're shaping her view of males in future relationships where she could have fear of abandonment and/or issues of sexual promiscuity. Some girls overcompensate by being top of their class, breaking all of the glass ceilings—all as a clever shield so that no one sees the despair. And then there's an overcompensation of food, drugs, alcohol, sex, and work. I'm not saying this will happen but it can."

Mercedes looked like she'd been putting the doctor's words to good use. "She is a bit of an overachiever."

"Other aspects are rage and depression. The rage can be a sign of a fierce desire to succeed. Depression and rage turned inward."

Mason looked overwhelmed, "What are some signs that you've noticed?"

"Star, in my opinion, is angry. But mainly when it comes to talking about you. She is very bright and believes that she has you all figured. And you know what? She does. And that means she's caught on long enough for you to be predictable. You need to be unpredictable. Surprising her with altered behavior can help jerk the energy in the right direction."

Mason admitted, "It sounds like I really need to work on it."

"Actually, the hardest part is getting someone to show a desire. You have that and you don't seem to be in denial."

"Denial won't help my family," Mason said, looking like he was suddenly growing tired of the conversation.

"Acknowledging that there is a problem leads to forgiveness so you can move on to the future. Apologize, Mason. Just say I'm sorry and I want to do better. Ask for a chance and see what happens."

The word forgiveness motivated Mason to glance Mercedes's way, but she turned her head to look out of the window.

As reluctant as Mason was feeling about the doctor's new-age remedies for dysfunction, Mason went to Sav-On in the Ladera Center to buy a card for Star. "It couldn't hurt," a voice inside of him said to the wind as he stepped out of his car.

"What up, Mr. Wilson," a stranger asked as he entered the store.

"Not much," Mason replied without looking in their direction.

He was looking for a basic "Just because" card that would say what he felt about his daughter. He searched and searched through all of the humorous ones, the ones with a million words, the ones that were Afro-centric. And he decided on one that said it all. It brought a smile to his face upon reading the words.

*In some ways it may seem like you've never had a father—but you do. You are loved. Forgive me.*

That evening after dinner, Mason entered Star's dimly lit room. He handed her the card while she sat on her bed, writing in her purple journal. Her left leg, bandaged at the knee, was stretched out on the bed as she kept it elevated. He bent down to turn on the dainty Tiffany lamp next to her bed so she could see better.

"Thanks," she replied as the extra light kicked in. "Is this for me?" she asked, looking up at him. She flipped the envelope from front to back. Her heartbeat sped up.

"Yes. It's just a little something."

"Thanks," she said, tucking it in between the pages of her notepad, almost appearing shy.

He looked surprised that she did not open it in front of him. But he did not push it. Instead, he bent down and braced his body so that he could sit on the floor.

Mason was eye level with her leg. "How's your knee?"

"It's fine. It's just a little swollen still but the bruising isn't bad. I'll be good to go in about a week."

"That's great." They were silent for a few long seconds. "Star, what do you think a father is?"

She kind of smirked at the sight of him sitting so casually. And she raised her eyebrows as though she wanted her brain to kick into reply mode. She calmed herself. Excited by his question. She took a deep breath, and then responded, "A father is someone who plays with a kid. Dads talk for a minute and then Mom goes on and on. Dads teach girls how to relate to boys and that we are love worthy. Dads are protectors from strangers and violence. A dad is a provider, a role model, and a disciplinarian." She surprised herself. All that she had read about just spewed out of her mouth as though she were a guest therapist on a talk show.

Mason looked impressed. "Wow, I didn't expect you to come up with that so quickly."

Star bent down and took the book called, *Whatever Happened to Daddy's Little Girl—The Impact of Fatherlessness in Black Women,* from next to her nightstand. "I've almost memorized this stuff." She reached over and handed it to her father. "I suppose I could recite it in my sleep."

He turned it over and looked at the back cover. "I suppose so. Where did you get this?"

"I bought it after I saw it discussed on a talk show last month."

"I had no idea."

"Daddy, some of the things that book covers are you—in different ways. As a provider role model, you are a ten. But I've tried to think back to us playing and talking and you teaching me, and it's hard to remember. I know you started playing amateur golf before Rashaad was born and you went pro when I was little. I was born just when you really got going. But I also know you haven't been on tour every day of every month for all those years, have you?"

"You know what, Star? I really can't recall going two days straight without something to do. I'm sorry."

"Daddy, it wouldn't be fair to you to say that you abandoned us. My friend Asia doesn't understand what I'm feeling. Her dad left years ago and she hasn't seen him at all. She says at least you've been in the house and we've been together as a family. And one thing I've always known you as is a disciplinarian. I just know Rashaad and I never wanted to deal with you whenever we did something wrong. Because Mom would threaten us with telling you every little detail."

"I guess spankings don't equate to quality time, huh?"

She continued, sounding like a therapist again. "No, but showing us how a man provides and spoils his family is. And even with all the time that's gone by with your career, I still want a man like you, Daddy. I just don't want you to think that a few bucks replaces a few minutes of your time."

Mason now looked stunned. "Who's the adult here, huh?"

"I've just had more time to figure this out than you."

"How about if we go . . ." he thought twice about letting her make the choice. "Well, where do you want to go? Just you and me, no one else around. We'll have the whole day to ourselves."

Her head rambled with ideas at the drop of his suggestion. "Well, I'd like to go to the Botanical Gardens in Malibu and walk around, and then have lunch on Pacific Coast Highway and maybe walk on the beach, once my knee heals that is. And then go to a music store so I can buy some new music sheets. And how about getting pedicures together?"

"Pedicures?"

"Yes, Daddy, pedicures. That would be a blast." She seemed excited.

Mason laughed at the thought. "With my golfer feet?"

Star managed a grin. "Daddy, come on."

"No problem."

"So, it's a date?"

He stood up. "It's a date." He left the book on the floor.

"You can take that if you want."

"Yes, ma'am, I will," he said, leaning over to pick it up. "See you in the morning. Good night, pud, ahh, babe." He caught himself.

"You can call me puddin'. Just only when it's the two of us," she assured him.

"Okay, only when it's the two of us."

"Okay."

She glanced down to open the card and read his message. Warmth owned her face. "Daddy?"

"Yes, puddin'?"

"I forgive you."

"Thanks," he said with a wink and a big smile.

She resumed her writing.

"And Star?"

"Yes, Daddy."

"Don't drive my Porsche anymore."

"I won't."

The next morning, while driving Star to school, a still half-asleep Mercedes asked if Star wanted to skip school and go to the office with her just like she used to do a few years ago. She wanted to see if Star's designer dream was real or just temporary. Star declined, seeming more interested in going inside to talk to her counselor than anything else.

In slow motion, Mercedes went back home to get dressed and then proceeded on to her office, strolling in late in the day. She made a slow path past Vicky with a brief hello, as though she was preoccupied.

"Those flowers in there are for you," Vicky said.

"Thanks." Mercedes did not react to the bouquet, but instead she logged onto her computer to check out her phone list and e-mails. She had one from Sequoia with an attached article called, "Sexual Fantasies." Sequoia wrote:

> *See, it depends on what you do with them. Fantasies live in the realm of our thoughts. If it increases your desire for your partner and increases arousal, it is trouble-free. Your sexual thoughts tell you what is erotic, Mercedes, not that you are some dangerous person. Relax, woman. Escape, and do what you can to cop that fucking orgasm. And don't throw away your relationship. Just a bit of advice from your girl. Love, Sequoia.*

Mercedes managed to smile at the screen and then buzzed her assistant on the intercom.

"Vicky, will you make sure I'm not interrupted. I have homework tonight and I need about an hour or so."

"No problem. Are you in school?"

"You could say that."

"Oh. By the way, you had two calls from a Mr. Green," Vicky said.

Since she said *mister,* Mercedes wanted to make it clear to Vicky who he was. "Oh, my mother-in-law's doctor. Did he leave his number?"

"It's on your call sheet."

"Okay, thanks."

"Dr. Green, it's Mercedes Wilson returning your call."

"How are you, Mrs. Wilson?"

"Just fine. Is everything okay with Mattie?"

"Yes. I just wanted to check in with you and see if she's made a decision regarding new meds. I didn't get a chance to ask you at the party."

Mercedes scrolled along, pecking at her keyboard as she spoke. "We're leaning toward passing on it. She's not going for it. It seems like she really does understand that it's a trial medication. She actually said she doesn't want to be a guinea pig."

"It is a trial med but it has been proven to cease the progression of this disease, too."

"Not reverse it or repair the damage?"

"No."

"Wow, I'll have to talk to Mason and Claude. But I really think it's not going to work for us."

"Okay. Just let me know if things change. But after a while if she progresses too far along, she'll no longer be a candidate. I just want to make sure you know that."

"I appreciate that. I understand. Thanks for calling, Dr. Green."

"Wallace," he corrected her, inspiring her to be more casual.

"Wallace."

"So, Mrs. Wilson, tell me. Do you ever get a chance to get away and have lunch during the day?"

She stopped her typing and gave him her full attention. "Lunch?"

"Yes, I just thought we could get together soon and talk before it gets too late for Mattie to take the medicine."

"Why?"

"I know how it can be on the caregiving side. I was a caregiver to my dad, who died a few years ago. I wanted to give you a break from it."

"I've had a break. My brother-in-law has her now so we're all sharing the weight. I'm fine but thanks for asking."

"Are you sure?"

Mercedes paused before replying, swiveling her chair toward the high-rise view. She thought about her threats to Mason. And then she spoke. "Well, I'm sure there wouldn't be anything wrong with just one meal together."

He spoke with optimism. "Me neither. It might be just what you need."

She stood up and walked toward the glass sofa table. The arrangement of three dozen red roses stared back at her. She took the notecard and read it. *Through the years, you've never let me down. I'm sorry that I did. I love you.*

She tucked the card back in place and continued her conversation. "But, Dr. Green, I'm very sure there's no need for us to get together. I assure you."

"Just a friendly offer."

She took slow-paced steps back to her desk chair and sat down. "And I appreciate it. But don't forget, I'm a married woman and if we were to share a meal on a personal level, my husband would be there as well."

"Is that so?"

"Yes, it is. I have no problem with being friends. But, my friends are his friends."

His swallow could be heard. "I get it. I'll check on both of you soon, or my assistant will call to schedule a follow-up once the other lab results come back. It was nice talking to you."

"You, too. Thanks so much. I see Mattie is in good hands."

"The good hands doctor, that's me," he joked.

"I'll bet. Have a good day."

"And thanks for the lovely time at your home. You looked amazing."

Mercedes sat straight up in her chair. "Thanks," she said as she ended the call, enjoying the flattery but disconnecting while she still had strength. She gazed back at the roses. Still, she looked unfazed.

Vicky buzzed in over the intercom. "Mrs. Wilson, I know you asked not to be interrupted, but Colette is in the outer office. She is very upset and she refuses to leave."

"Let her in please. Thanks, Vicky." Mercedes exhaled with force.

Colette looked stressed, and she talked a mile a minute. "Mercedes, please tell me. Is Torino seeing Sequoia?"

Mercedes kept her focus on her computer screen. "If you're here to talk about work, I'm available. Otherwise I'm working on a project, Colette."

Colette stood over Mercedes's desk. "Mercedes, why are you suddenly treating me like a stranger?"

"Why are you acting like someone I don't know?" Mercedes looked at her, tilting her head as if trying to figure her out.

"You act like you've never had your heart broken."

"Colette, this is between you and Torino. He's my husband's brother. What do you expect me to do?"

"Just the fact that you're doing nothing answers my question."

Mercedes flipped through some papers. "Then why did you even ask me? I already know you've driven by the house."

"Yes."

"Why do you do that?"

Colette ignored her question, giving a nervous sigh like she had all of the evidence already. "I've seen that dark green Jaguar."

"What good does it do to drive by? It can only make you feel worse."

"It gives me the answer that he won't give me. Even you won't give it to me. I have to look out for myself."

"Have you asked him?"

Colette strode a trail from the window, back to Mercedes's desk, almost looking embarrassed to say it. "Yes. But he won't take my calls."

"Colette, it's over. You've got to get to the point where you can move on."

"I know, but I still love him."

Mercedes looked up at her. "It takes time. You can't expect the feelings to go away so soon. Have you thought about dating someone else?"

"Yes, that's one reason why Torino won't talk to me."

"Don't tell me he's jealous."

"Jealous, no—mad as hell, yes. I started seeing Kyle."

Mercedes sat back. "Kyle? Girl, you must admit that is pretty low. That's his best friend."

"Not anymore." Colette said faintly, moving closer to Mercedes, leaning her hands flat on the desk, pressing the weight of her body forward. "So you mean to tell me that your best friend didn't tell you about Kyle and me? Don't tell me she doesn't know."

Mercedes faced her stare. "Colette, like I said, this is between the two of you. I've gone beyond what I should have already." Mercedes picked up a piece of paper and pointed to a date on the spreadsheet. "I have an assignment for you tomorrow at Gucci in Beverly Hills."

Colette stood at attention, "I can't make it."

"Why not?"

Colette looked conflicted. "I have an abortion scheduled for tomorrow, Mercedes. Maybe."

Mercedes looked annoyed. "I don't condone abortion. I just want you to really take some time to think about your future and this baby. Don't allow Torino to be more important than your own life. And don't try to snag him by bringing a baby into the world either. A baby won't make a relationship better. If anything, it will add to the ton of responsibilities and pressure you had before. You have to be ready for that."

"I hear you," Colette said, almost sounding like she actually didn't hear a word.

Mercedes glanced back at her computer screen. "Now, I'm going to leave you on the schedule to appear in the show tomorrow." She spoke to Colette's face again. "You show up and I'll know what's up. Do you hear me? And eat a good meal. You look mighty scrawny to be pregnant."

"I will."

"Colette, I mean it. Take care of yourself."

"Mercedes, I held on too tight didn't I?" Colette spoke as if she had ignored Mercedes's statements.

"I don't know. Maybe so. But it is time to let go." Mercedes stood up to walk her out. "Now I've got to get back to work. Call me tomorrow morning to let me know you're okay." She placed her hand on Colette's upper arm.

"I will. Good-bye, Mercedes."

"Colette. I want to see you tomorrow."

"Take care," Colette said, walking out the door.

Mercedes closed her door and took a seat at her desk. She checked her daily horoscope which read, *Your sense of duty drives you, and you take great pains to provide security for your family. Your spiritual task is to live full in the present.* She did not react.

She began to type away on her keyboard.

*They say we learn where we are in the present from where we've been in the past and that our first love begins in our families. Well, mine sure did. The most pivotal moment in my life was when my father took me to dinner when I was fifteen years old. We sat in a booth at the Which Stand restaurant on Overhill. His mission was to take the time to explain what makes a woman secure about the love of a man. What makes a woman virtuous, and what makes a woman secure in herself.*

*I was never the same after that conversation. Even in the*

*tenth grade, I understood the roles of a man and a woman based upon the events I'd witnessed in my childhood. My parents were good at being feminine and masculine, and making sure the kids were the priority. They danced well together. He led and she followed. In the days when single parenting was becoming popular, I was blessed by having a loving, attentive father who made me feel worthy and valued. He taught me self-love. My most private moment was that day my dad told me I could do anything, that he would love me unconditionally, and that the true worth of a man can be measured by his love and protective nature for his family. Would he die for them?*

*Well, my father did die for my mother. He suffered a heart attack one year after she died from heart disease. His heart broke for her and now they are together.*

*I can't imagine the success of the last nearly two decades with Mason without knowing the love of a male at an early age. I pray that Star knows that love from her dad. It is an invaluable, priceless lesson. I love Mason as a husband, father and a man. He is human and allowed to make mistakes. Knowing that allows me to have unconditional love for him. He is the father of my children. I might require forgiveness from him one day. For now, by the grace of God, nothing is more important than forgiving him and making this work so that we might live the life that the Lord has intended for us to live as a family. But I am angry and I cannot see continuing on as his wife. I ask the Lord to come into my heart, my home and my life at this very moment, and bestow His blessings upon us. I pray for strength, patience and love in dealing with my husband's sins of the flesh. I ask this in the name of the Father, the Son and the Holy Spirit. Amen.*

Mercedes grabbed her purse, turned off her computer and flicked the light switch. "Vicky, I'm going home early. I'll see you on Friday."

Mercedes would soon discover that the doctor did not ask them to do their homework to share with him or each other. He'd assigned it as a personal exercise so they could hear themselves think. And she did indeed, think. As for Mason, well he never got around to doing his homework at all.

In Beverly Hills, Vicky and Mercedes were in fifth gear. It was two hours before the Gucci show for women and three models had not shown up yet. The Gucci store was shut down to the public. The show's assistant producer fell ill the night before and asked Mercedes to fill in as she'd done before. Only Gucci employees, designers, show staff, and security filled the back dressing room. One of the stylists walked in with a cream-colored satin gown with a corset look.

"This outfit is labeled for Colette," Vicky told Mercedes.

Mercedes looked over her clipboard list. "Colette would look great in that. But I think we need to focus on Alexis as a backup."

"Isn't she a size six? This dress is a size four. We don't have any size four models left. Unless we give it to one of the swimsuit models from the first portion of the show."

"Okay, then pull Wilette to model evening wear. I'll get Alexis to do swimsuits."

Vicky asked, "Where is Colette anyway?"

"She might be running late. We'll see what happens in the next hour or so."

"I'm ready to do makeup," yelled one of the artists who had set up her table near a corner with a full lighted mirror and open chair all ready to go.

"Fine. Vicky, go get the first model ready for makeup. Keep an assembly line going from face painting to hair like clockwork. That is after they get their fittings done."

"Will do."

Within thirty minutes of showtime, the room began to fill up. The mayor of Beverly Hills was in the front row with his wife. The media were all around, interviewing celebrities like Jodie Foster, Phylicia Rashaad and Ivanna Trump who gave their comments on what they expected to see as the new collection was unveiled. Before long the room was completely full and all was a buzz. Mercedes's nerves were evident as sweat beads built up over her lip.

"It's almost showtime," Vicky told her boss. "Any sign of Colette."

"She's a no-show. Let's just write her off."

Just as Mercedes completed her sentence, she noticed a face in the crowd. She looked away and then did a double take. A face not very familiar by sight, but very familiar by instinct. Mercedes's vision zoomed in to focus on the seated onlooker, and suddenly there were only two people in the room. The face in the audience was Natalie Glenn. Her husband's lover.

Stuck in her stance like glue, Mercedes began squinting her eyes. She could feel Vicky's breath in her face as Vicky talked to her, but without volume. The words just faded away into the air.

Mercedes's glance was interrupted by a towering figure on the catwalk. It was the first group of swimwear models doing their thing. Mercedes blinked for the first time in about forty seconds.

"Mercedes, did you hear me?" Vicky asked over the loud music.

"Yes. I mean no, what did you say?"

"Alexis needs a glue stick for her bikini top to cling along her neckline. Did you bring one?"

"Yes, look in my YSL garment bag in the back."

Vicky walked away but Mercedes still stared straight ahead. Natalie was looking up at the statuesque models, bouncing her head to the music of the Madonna CD. Mercedes cut her eyes and turned to walk backstage. She rubbed her sweaty forehead and shook her head. Never had she wanted to rip someone's head off so badly in her life. Her high quickly sank to a feeling of depression. She looked around at all of the hurried people working to pull off the big show. Yet she felt heavy, weighted, and discouraged. She was sharing the room with the woman who shared her husband.

Before long, the models had changed about three times each. It was time for the last group of women, the evening gown models. Wilette approached, wearing the glamorous cream-colored gown. She walked by Mercedes, prepared to hit the runway. Mercedes watched her long, elegant frame proceed, and then she followed behind her, only to exit to the right of the stage along the side row toward the audience. Mercedes found herself heading in the direction of Natalie. With every step, she took a deeper breath. She excused herself from the group of people behind the first row, and leaned in toward Natalie's back, right up close to her left earlobe.

Mercedes whispered closely and softly, "Excuse me, but I'm your lover's wife. We need to talk."

Natalie turned around and looked up at Mercedes's face. Without blinking, she took her tiny red bag from her lap and stood up. Mercedes led the way with Natalie less than two steps behind her. They exited the front door and stood out on Rodeo Drive under the lamppost. Natalie put on her dark Aviator lenses.

Mercedes started off. "First off, his name is Mason, and not Mace."

"Okay." Natalie was nonchalant.

"How dare you come on to my husband. You'd better be glad that I have too much class to curse you out and slap your face."

"Mrs. Wilson, I want to tell you how bad I feel about what happened. I don't even know how it happened. It just did."

"It just did, huh? And you feel bad? I'll bet it didn't feel so bad when Mason was inside of you, did it?"

Natalie sighed, glancing over Mercedes's shoulder toward the front door of the Gucci store as though she wanted to go back in.

"And take off your shades, Natalie. You need to be woman enough to look me straight in the eye."

Natalie pulled her glasses off with a subtle snatch.

Mercedes continued, "Let me tell you something. It's women like you who screw up the good things that women like me work so long and hard to build. You just simply come around and seductively toss your charms at any man who will catch them. You don't even have enough couth to at least hit on the single ones. Why do you have to go for the married men with lives and women at home? Were you once fooled around on and now you feel a need to pay back females in your own way. Didn't your mother ever tell you what goes around comes around?"

"Ummh, I believe she did."

"Then what in the hell happened? You can't go around doing this to families. Do you hear me? Families. It's not just about getting your freak on for a few minutes. It's about ruining relationships and trust. Your carefree affair cost me my ability to believe in a man I've known for more than half my life."

Mercedes paused to imagine what Mason saw in this woman. She looked her up and down, from her pretty red, rhinestone toes peaking from her strappy high heels, to her tiny waist cinched by a wide leather belt, to her perky little breasts showing their shape under a sheer black designer blouse, to the top of her upswept, bright red hair. She was pretty and sophisticated looking and that made Mercedes even madder.

Natalie clutched her bag. "With all due respect, you really need to check Mason too, Mrs. Wilson. He is a grown man and he's the one you need to get on."

"I need to get on you right now, Natalie. You were the one who seduced my man. If more women like you had more self-respect, women like me wouldn't have to worry about who we need to check. You're a nice-looking woman. Why can't you get a man of your own?"

"I can."

"Then do that and leave the taken ones alone. Or else I guarantee you that one day, you'll be in my shoes, trying to figure out why some woman destroyed your marriage. And I know that Mason called it off with you. Just make sure you don't even think about dialing his number or coming up to his room, or e-mailing him, or contacting him in any way. Because I will not only see to it that I have your job, I will have your ass."

Natalie looked defiant. "Is that a threat?"

"That's a promise."

"Okay."

"Okay. Turns out you weren't the prize this time around, huh?

I guess it never got that deep where he was willing to have you on a full-time basis, right?"

"We didn't bond. That's exactly how I wanted it."

"Oh, don't get it twisted. That's exactly how he wanted it. So are you moving on or not?"

"I've more than moved on."

Mercedes cringed away from her. "Probably to the next victim. You'd better watch your back. One day some woman isn't going to be as nice as me. You just might find yourself fighting for your life."

Suddenly, a man spoke. "Natalie, I was looking for you."

As the tall gentleman came toward them, Mercedes said to Natalie from the corner of her mouth, "Oh, so you're an athlete chaser, huh? Okay." Mercedes extended her hand once he reached them. "Hello, I'm Mercedes Wilson."

He extended his hand, too. "Hello. It's nice to met you. I'm Akrika Downing."

Mercedes looked up at his six-foot-ten-inch frame. "Oh, yes the basketball player who just got traded from Chicago to the Sacramento Kings."

"Yes."

Natalie took his hand. "Mercedes is Mason Wilson's wife."

"Oh, Natalie has told me so much about your husband."

Mercedes gave Natalie a snarl of a look. "I'll bet she hasn't told you nearly enough."

He seemed oblivious. "I saw you two walking out and wondered what was up. Is everything okay?" he asked his date.

"Yes."

Mercedes explained, "Sorry but I didn't see anyone but your little lady here when I walked up." Mercedes prepared to end the conversation. She took a step back toward the store. "You two enjoy the show now."

He replied. "We will. Nice to meet you."

"You, too."

Natalie gave a fake closing. "Yes, nice to meet you, Mrs. Wilson."

Mercedes spoke only to Akrika. "Take care, Mr. Downing. Good luck with the team. And keep an eye on her. After all, she sheds, you know."

He looked askance at Mercedes as if he didn't quite know what to make of that comment.

Natalie put her sunglasses back on and snuggled in close to her man's arm as he handed the valet the ticket. And then they kissed.

# chapter 20

Before Mason and Mercedes could return to their next therapy meeting, Mason left a message to cancel the sessions.

Mason spoke from his cell. "Dr. Little, it's Mason Wilson. You've been very helpful to my family and me. But with all due respect, I think I know how to get to my son so we're going to stop right here. We'll be using your tools to work through this, along with a lot of love. Please send me your bill for your services thus far. I'll send you a check in the mail upon receipt."

After Star's knee bandages came off, she and her dad spent a long, leisurely Saturday morning, hanging out, eating lunch, walking and talking, going to the mall, and to the music store. And they even had pedicures. They laughed and talked and renewed their connection.

Mason took her home and then picked up Rashaad. It was father and son time. By the afternoon, Rashaad was into the start of his second hour at the driving range tent at the Westchester park golf course. A group of golfers stared at Mason as he stood by his son. They whispered to each other and pointed his way.

Rashaad took a swing, looking like a pro, but the ball veered to the left, causing him to look frustrated.

Mason moved from standing behind him to standing beside him. "No, son. You have to keep your head down. Golf is about distance and location. Set up, grip, posture, and alignment are all so very important in order to hit the ball straight and get it where you want it to go. I keep telling you, you must remain focused. Don't let me or anyone else distract you. Otherwise you're not in full control. Mental imagery is key. Golf is a mind game, it has very little to do with the physical. And you'll never have the same game twice. Each game will always be different, with you focusing on different areas that you found kept you stuck on the previous hole. But just be consistent in what you say to yourself, remind yourself over and over."

Rashaad sneered at Mason as if his dad had been preaching. "Dad, you keep telling me all of that. But if I make a mistake, just let me make it. I know what you told me. I keep hearing you over and over again in my head."

"Then that's your problem. You shouldn't hear what I tell you over and over. It shouldn't be my voice. It should be your own voice, telling yourself over and over again."

Rashaad gripped his club tighter, shifting his weight to his other leg. "Whoever is telling me, I'm going to make mistakes."

"True, I still do. Golf is hard and you're not going to be an expert right away."

"Dad, please let me make my own errors. Give me a few cents but don't throw it at me."

"Don't throw it at you? Where in the hell did you hear that?"

"Some show, I don't know. Dad, I'll get the hang of this on my own."

"On your own, without me?"

"Maybe so." Rashaad set up another ball. "You know I played before when I was little. I still remember a lot from what you told me over the years."

"Okay, I'll leave you alone and I'll come back in an hour. No, better yet, I'm going to make a call. Your butt needs some dang lessons."

Rashaad got in position to take his swing as Mason stepped away and walked toward a nearby bench. He sat down, flipped open his cell, and placed a call.

"Troy Lyles? Hey man. How's it been going? It's been a while. Hey man. I need you to do me a favor. I need you to hook up my fourteen-year-old son Rashaad with some golf lessons. I'm about to kill that little dude, man. Yeah, he's pretty good. If not today, then as soon as possible. How soon could you have someone out here at the Westchester course? We'll be here. Thanks a lot. See you then."

Mason walked briskly back to his son. "Great news, son. Troy Lyles, himself, is coming over to teach you in about an hour."

"Who's he?"

"He's the son of the man who Tiger's dad referred me to years ago. He trains all of the juniors coming up. I don't know why I didn't think of this before. The first thing I learned in golf is to never teach someone you know. And especially someone you love. That's why I've never taught your mom. It gets too emotional and they get too defensive."

Rashaad focused, taking a couple of practice swings as his dad spoke. "Uh huh."

"Son, I'm going to be paying this man top dollar now so I want you to absorb his every word like a sponge and take advantage of this opportunity. Not every young man can have his dad just pick up the phone and get Troy Lyles to show up. Get all you can. I want to see a difference in your game."

"Can I practice until he gets here?" Rashaad asked as if his dad was still distracting him.

"Go right ahead."

Rashaad waited before resuming his practice. "Weren't you leaving for an hour?"

"All right already, dang." Mason took a step and then stopped. Rashaad looked at him as if he should continue walking away. "Remember your grip, Rashaad. Get that down and you'll notice a big difference."

"Good-bye," Rashaad said, looking annoyed yet grateful. "And thanks, Dad."

"You're welcome."

Rashaad yelled toward his father. "Hey, Dad."

"Yes," Mason yelled back as he stopped.

"You and Mom are okay, right?"

"What makes you ask that?"

"I just noticed . . . something. I don't know but you two seem different."

Mason felt concern on the inside but felt the need to assure his son. "We'll work it out, son. Don't you worry about it. You just keep your mind right."

"Okay, Dad. I will," Rashaad said, looking down as he placed his feet into position for his next swing.

Mason walked away, answering his ringing cell phone. It was Cicely.

She spoke plainly. "Mason I've sealed the deal in Atlanta and I think it's best if I go ahead and take that over and relocate."

"Oh, you think it's best?" Mason stopped in his tracks.

"Yes, I do. I also think it's best that you buy me out of Foreplay in Los Angeles and I go at it alone in Atlanta. I used to live there, you know."

"How would the investors feel about that? You going it alone."

"They'll be fine. They just want to make sure that one of us is involved in running the new club."

"But do they know that I would have no connection and no interest in it?"

"Actually, they've asked that it be that way."

"You've been negotiating this without letting me know?"

"Mason, they've been calling me ever since my meeting with them that you missed. I thought about it and I think it's best considering all that's happened. I haven't given them the final word yet."

"Considering what?" he asked.

Cicely sounded wounded. "That you refuse to allow me to be part of my own family. That you refuse to tell Mercedes and your brothers about me. That you keep me on the side like I'm some mistress of yours. My mom was your dad's mistress and you know what? He really loved her. He moved us here and he helped take care of us financially. But with your rejection of the truth, I've had a lot of stuff to consider, Mason."

"Cicely, I accept the truth. And so does Claude and Torino. But that's about as far as it goes."

"Whatever."

There was a few moments of dead silence.

"Is Heidi okay with you leaving?"

"She'll go, too. She's the closest thing to family I've got. Anyway, I no longer need the duplex in Leimert and she no longer needs the house on sixty-fourth. I'll have her advertise them both for lease if you'd like."

"No problem. I'll have Claude handle it."

"So we're cool then," Cicely suggested. "As far as you buying me out of the club."

"We're cool. I think you've done a great job. I knew you'd be good but not that good. But, I'll have my attorney draw up papers to buy you out of Foreplay here and maybe I'll let Torino go ahead and take over the other half."

"Good, so my own brothers will be going it alone without me. Why is it that you never answer my concerns about letting me live my life as your half sister, not even after all these years?"

"Because it would be a sign of disrespect to my mother, Cicely. I don't have a problem with you and I think I've done the best I could by you and for you. But I just can't do any more. I'm sorry."

Cicely sounded dejected yet ready to move on. "I'm sorry too, Mason. Please let me know when everything is set. I plan to leave by New Year's Eve so I can start over, new and refreshed."

"No problem, Cicely. Good luck."

"Good luck to you, too."

In deep thought, Mason hung up the phone.

After a while, short and stocky Troy Lyles came walking toward Mason wearing a Nike golf cap and a black nylon jogging suit.

"Hey Troy, that was fast."

"I live right around the corner, you know. This is my second home."

"Thanks for coming over. Rashaad is right over there," Mason pointed.

Troy looked over. "He's tall, just like you. And good-looking like his mom."

They both laughed. "You're right about that. You been cool?"

"I'm fine. How about you?"

"All is well."

They started to walk back toward Rashaad, but Troy paused as though a thought was brewing. "Brother, let me ask you a question. I've been thinking about this. You hired Kenny Rogers, man?"

"And?"

"To sing to a black woman on national television?"

"Oh, Troy. You and your radical ass. What's wrong with that, man?"

"A big no-no," Troy said with a warning.

"Mercedes and I like the damn song. It's been our song for years. What's the problem?"

Troy replied. "You, the poster child for down-home blacks not abandoning our own communities want to ask me what's the problem."

"Oh, so hiring Luther Vandross would have been the black thing to do? I don't know if I like where this is going."

"Mason, just examine your choices, that's all I'm saying. You can alienate any number of people to your detriment."

"True, but I won't alienate my self-respect. I will be Mason Wilson, black or not," Mason said definitively.

"Then why do you stick with the 'hood' and show allegiance to black designers? African-American groups honor you and you donate money to the NAACP and other black organizations. Man, you've already given the world an impression of just how black you are. Don't ruin it." They reached Rashaad's driving range section. "Hey Rashaad. I'm Troy Lyles. It's nice to meet you."

"Mr. Lyles."

"You can call me Troy."

Rashaad smiled. "Troy. Nice to meet you, too."

Mason excused himself, looking forward to ending the conversation. "Thanks man, I'll be back in what, one hour?"

"Make it two," said Troy as if willing to spend the time.

"See you both in two." Mason shook his head and walked away, emotionally twisted by the last few conversations.

In the distance he heard Troy tell his son, "If you want to be the best at what you do, you have to go beyond. You can't do what everyone else does—you'll just be average." Mason could have recited that code of excellence in his sleep. He chuckled.

His cell phone rang. Another conversation was about to begin.

"Mason, I can't believe you had the nerve to cancel our therapy sessions without consulting me."

"Cedes, I just think we can deal with this on our own."

"Who asked you to think for me? Coming from someone as selfish as you, that's a whole lot of nerve. It's always suggested that couples seek the counsel of someone they trust, and I trust Dr. Little implicitly."

Mason walked past a woman who gave him a wink. He ignored her and kept walking. "You know what, you're right. I should have asked you. But sometimes you can hear the same old thing over and over again. Now that we have the information, what do we do with it?"

"We keep going back until I say so. I have the veto right on this one. Not you. It's a process that takes time. It took you twenty years to clutter the room, it's not going to be uncluttered in two weeks."

"I know that."

"Mason, you go right ahead and back out on the one bright spot we have toward dealing with your penis problems. But I won't. I will continue to go on my own. Whether we share the same house or not. But I also suggest that you go and get some of your own therapy. Because you are the one with the problem. Your high and mighty selfishness has affected my life and the kids' lives."

"I'm working to correct that. I'm really trying here, Cedes. I'm committed to this relationship, woman. Do you hear me? I'll do whatever it takes to keep you."

Mercedes spoke at full volume. "Then you call Dr. Little back and tell him that you still need to continue so that you can become a better person, no matter what happens to us."

"Cedes."

"You heard what I said. It's up to you. And one more thing. I just know you're not at Starbucks, are you?"

"No."

"Keep your ass away from there." She hung up.

Mason stood still. His head was splitting from the weight of all of his interactions. He felt fifty pounds heavier and ten years older.

His cell rang again.

"And one more thing. I met your little groupie. She was definitely not worth all of this."

She hung up again, leaving Mason standing there with his mouth open. His thoughts were racing.

He dialed one more number and left a message.

"Dr. Little. Scratch what I said. We'll see you next week."

# chapter 21

Mason walked along the course in Ireland wearing his black skin, black pants, a black shirt, black shoes, a black golf cap, and with his new, male, white Titleist representative at his side. He passed a long line of fans behind the ropes who were applauding as he walked with pride, enjoying his moment.

"Look at that nigger." Mason Wilson heard the diseased word of hate coming from deep in the crowd. It rang out in his black ears in a reverberating, boisterous whisper, as if someone was too chicken to yell it out. But the volume of the words echoed in his head with jaw-tightening loudness. He missed a beat, turned, and his sight narrowed, praying to make eye contact with the perpetrator. It seemed all of the eyes that met his were sincere and joyful, basking in the moment of his landslide win. They were the eyes of his loyal fans.

"Did you hear that?" he asked the representative.

"Hear what?"

"Never mind," Mason said, knowing it was not his imagination. His irritation mounted and his enthusiasm dwindled a notch, looking out amongst the melting pot of faces, wondering how one is ever able to tell the racists from the supporters. Were people ever really going to be sincerely happy that he was exploring his God-given talents and raising the bar for all athletes, not just minorities?

It appeared as though the blue skies were suddenly cloudy,

playing tricks on him with imaginary rain clouds about to release their tears upon the course lined with fans. The moment brought sadness to Mason's soul for those who were not accepting of equal opportunities, so unable to handle the fact that all are God's children.

"Thanks," was his only response as he received his award and prize money.

He whisked past the fans and reporters, and got into his black limousine. The car pulled away, carrying a confused winner, suddenly feeling like a loser.

Mason sat in the lobby of the Howth Head hotel, sitting alone on a sofa, in deep thought. Atop the coffee table was an old English language issue of *Sports Illustrated* with Mason's face on the cover, smiling under the caption, "A Colorful Course." Instead of rereading the article, he picked up the day's newspaper in the Celtic language, opened it wide and shielded his face from his surroundings, not able to read the words, just glancing at the photographs, in a trancelike state.

A well-dressed, sophisticated white man approached Mason and introduced himself. He was fast-talking.

"Mr. Wilson, my name is Phillip Drummond and I work for the All-Pro Sports Marketing Association. We think you need to be promoted on a whole other level."

"Oh really?" Mason said, taking the man's card and giving it a quick once-over.

"Yes. See, we noticed that you're not the most popular golfer. I'm sure you don't cause a riot when you go into 7-Eleven. But we can boost your career. I see your entire image re-identified, rebuilt so that we switch up your sponsors, get you more money, upgrade your image and your persona and just elevate the entire package. Mind you, you're okay right now but we think we can take you to a certain level of success that America can relate to. You have to become more visible, Mr. Wilson."

"So, you're an agent?"

"I'm an image manager, so to speak."

Mason made it clear. "I've never had one and I don't need one."

"You have a business manager, don't you?"

"Yes, and he's the best." Mason resumed his perusal of the newspaper.

"Same thing. What I can do is manage your career, Mr. Wilson, not just manage you. You are a superstar but you're not shining like you could in my opinion. Your wardrobe, the Sean John thing, that's just not PGA quality."

Without looking up, Mason asked, "What is PGA quality exactly?"

"The Nike-, Reebok-, Adidas-type sportswear."

"I don't have a contract with them, so I don't wear them."

The man continued. "But you will. You need a more universal image. Less hip-hop."

Mason moved his paper to the side. "Sir, I am almost forty years old. I'm far from hip-hop. Do you even know what hip-hop means?"

"Let's just say that just because it's hip, doesn't mean it hops."

"What hops in your world, Mr. Drummond?"

"What hops is setting up an organization in your name where you travel as a role model and offer scholarships to our youth, appearing at schools and giving kids the impression that you're there for them."

"Impression?" Mason asked stiffly.

"It's all about having a bankable image and public perception. People love that kind of thing. And you need a commercial agent so you can do commercials like for cereal and energy bars. And also, we need you to relocate to the East Coast or down South, to a different type of neighborhood, maybe even to the exclusive South Beach section of Miami."

"Why? I'm raising my kids in Los Angeles."

The man spoke as though he'd done his homework. "The school system in South Beach is much better than where you live now. I know you lived in Ladera when you were a teen, but sometimes you need to stretch out beyond your comfort zone."

"So, you're saying once we Negroes make it, we should move away to the white world? Where should I have been living while in

California? In Bel Air, Malibu, Orange County, Beverly Hills?" Mason asked, seeking clarification.

"Even that would do wonders for your image."

"Mr. Drummond is it?"

He nodded his head yes.

"My image is just fine. I don't believe that my fans are thinking about what section of town I live in when I'm out there on the green. I just don't buy it. I have no desire to change anything."

"We call it zip-code recognition, Mr. Wilson. See, you're seen as a black golfer living a mid-level existence, without the savvy and leadership that comes from taking yourself to pro status. No one will take you seriously until you make a change. Get out of that 90056 mentality."

"I beg to differ. I let my game speak for itself. It's no one's business what I do away from golf or what my zip code might be."

The tone changed. "I guess so when you show up for a tournament smelling like Tanqueray, how serious do you expect to be taken? I know you don't want that to get out. Aren't you a member of Alcoholic's Anonymous?"

Mason was fast losing his patience. He put the paper on the coffee table and stood up. "I'm about to go up to my room."

"For a little private minibar nightcap?"

"Good night." Mason's jaw grew tense. "And if you come back around me . . . just good night." Mason walked away.

"Good night, Mr. Wilson. I see you put my card in your jacket pocket. Use it. Because you wouldn't want those photos of you and your lovely wife leaving a sleazy nudie bar to be circulated, now, would you? Or maybe the information about your chick on the side."

Mason reached inside of his coat pocket, pulled out the card and tore it in half. He dropped it on the marble floor just outside of the elevator. He pushed the up button and stood in front of the elevators, staring at the doors.

"And wasn't there a shooting in your neighborhood a couple of years ago?"

Mason balled up his fist just as the arrival of the up-elevator chimed. He took three steps in, turned around and pushed the button to the top floor. He faced the open door and locked sights on the revolting face of Mr. Drummond, giving him a killer look, squinting until the closing doors met to cut off his stare.

Mason headed back to his room and sat in silence in the dark. His mind drifted and his eyes fixed upon the view from the hotel window of the rugged landscape, green hills and rough blue ocean of the Irish land of Dublin City. His hotel room phone rang and his cell phone rang repeatedly, seemingly all at once. He ignored them both.

After an hour or so, he stood up, turned on the light and disrobed down to his boxers and socks. He decided to turn the television on just so he'd have company in the room.

He sat on the bed, took his briefcase from the nearby chair and looked inside to check his schedule for the next day. Tucked inside one of the business cards slots was a wallet size family picture of Mason, Mercedes, Rashaad, and Star. It had been taken a few years earlier. To him, the smiles were brighter and more carefree back then. He ran his middle finger across the photo and then brought it up to his lips, kissing it and then clutching it to his chest.

Also in his briefcase, to his surprise, conveniently slipped in front of his itinerary, was a note from Mercedes. It was handwritten on one of his formal note cards with the scripted initials, *MW.* He sensed her scent, sniffed it and smiled. It smelled of the gardenia fragrance she always wore. He broke the seal and began to read.

*Mason,*

*Our life is like a fairy tale. We have every convenience, and every need met, other than your fidelity, your honesty and your time. These are major issues. So the reality of it all is that this is not a fairy tale. In spite of how it may look, there are some things that money can't buy.*

*I tried to step back and examine how things must really look to other people, from the outside looking in. And I think they must see a king, a queen, a prince and a princess, living the fairy tale life in a castle. We prayed for a boy and a girl, and we got them. God blessed us in so many ways. But inside we're dancing to the song "Tears of a Clown." We can no longer go on together with these dysfunctions. We can only go on together without them.*

*You and the kids are all I have. I have no brothers and sisters. I have no parents. I cherish you all. I took a vow. And so . . . the real deal is that, you can no longer fool around on me. I will not have it. You can no longer lie to me. I will not tolerate it. And you can no longer put everyone before your family and still expect to have us. Because I will leave. No threats, just facts, Mason. Do it again, and we're gone for good. I forgive you.*

*Dr. Little told me you called him. Thanks. I'll be waiting when you get home.*

*Love,*
*Cedes*

Mason placed his briefcase back on the chair. He spoke out loud. "Now that is what unconditional love is all about." He put the note on the nightstand next to the bed and then knelt down on his knees. He pressed his palms together under his chin, closed his eyes, and began to pray.

*Thank you, Lord, for another chance with my family. I ask you to save me from the generational curses in my life and allow me to be the man you designed me to be. I know that I can change. I put my faith in you, dear God. I want to be the best man I can be. I ask this of you and know that it shall be done. You've blessed us dearly. I let go and let You do Your will. Amen.*

He then laid back and laughed out loud as *Girls Gone Wild* came on the cable channel. He turned off the television, no longer needing it. He no longer felt alone. He leaned over to reach into his briefcase again and pulled out the book that Star had given him on father-daughter relationships. He leaned back, turning to chapter one, reading along with a smile on his face.

* * *

The day Mason was to arrive back home, Mercedes decided to let an anxious Kailua run out onto the yard to get the morning paper. Her encouraging head nod, along with the word, "Fetch," sent him running at breakneck speed, overrunning his target. He grabbed the rolled-up morning edition and raced back to Mercedes, placing the paper at her feet and wagging his chocolate tail.

"Good boy," she said as Kailua jumped around her as if wanting his reward. "Just a minute," she said.

On the front page of the local edition of the *Laderian News* was a photo of her husband's face, and not a very flattering one at that. The article read as follows:

**Mason Wilson Selling His Home and Selling Out 90056 or 90210**

by Soledad Thompson

*Successful professional golfer, Mason Wilson, could be putting up more than a for-sale sign for his home. He might be putting up a for-sale sign for his soul, African-American soul, that is. Our sources indicate that recently, Mason Wilson has been spotted accompanied by a top-notch realtor in the Palm Beach Gardens area of Florida, eyeing a twenty-thousand-square-foot golf-course mansion with a private lake, nine-hole golf course and waterfall-like swimming pool.*

*Some say his seven-figure bank account can accommodate much more than what Ladera has to offer, and that knowledge is becoming more and more tempting, along with speculation that the support of African-American fans is waning after his decision not to hire an African-American performer to sing to his wife on their wedding anniversary recently, live, smack dab in the middle of the golf course while on tour in Mexico.*

*Mason Wilson has lived in Ladera Heights for a quarter century. Due to recent upgrades and additions, Mr. Wilson's seven-thousand-square-foot home is valued at 1.8 million, almost twice the price of most homes in the community. His brother Claude Wilson of Wilson Realty is both the selling and listing agent.*

*Several African-American stars called Ladera Heights home and then moved on when they outgrew their surroundings. But sources say that the move for Mason Wilson would be more for a change in image to surroundings with more of an upscale, less African-American feel. And in turn the move would allow him to cross over and appear . . . "less black."*

*Mr. Wilson could not be reached for comment. He was traveling back from a successful tournament out of the country. He is expected to resume his tour at the end of the month.*

"Who are they quoting when they say, 'less black'?" Mercedes ranted. She called him from the cordless phone. "Mason, where are you?"

"We're driving up Slauson now, from the 405. I'm so tired. It was an exhausting flight. I'll be there in five minutes."

"Okay," Mercedes said dryly. She clicked the off button and began looking out of the window, anticipating his arrival. Kailua sat at her feet waiting for his forgotten treat. Mercedes shooed him away toward the kitchen.

Mason's limousine made the right turn onto Bedford Avenue, and for the first time, he looked at the sprawling white house in a different light. It was almost as though the home itself was part of his problems in the first place. Part of his problems with his wife, with his kids, and with the fact that he was finally starting to grow weary of his career. It was also a reminder of Fatima's grisly death.

Mason's driver pulled up to his house, noticing the bold red and black Wilson Realty sign on his front lawn. His brother's face, name, and number were prominent, in big bold print.

"You're selling your home, huh?" the driver asked, looking at his famous passenger from the rear-view mirror.

"Yes, it's time to move on," Mason said, almost in a trance. The damaged sycamore tree from Star's little wreck stood tall on the strip of grass along the curb.

Mercedes opened the front door before he could find his key ring. She was full of questions. "What's this crap in the *Laderian* about you being a sellout? That you're talking about making yourself more visible to the white community?"

Mason stepped inside and gave her a hug. "Oh, that mess was actually printed already?"

She embraced him tightly. "Yes, on the front page of the newspaper. I know none of this is true, baby. You weren't looking at homes in Florida, were you?"

"Of course not. This agent approached me and then told his dumb-ass story to someone. Now I know the 'N' word I heard was not my imagination. It was a setup."

Mercedes's voice rose in pitch. "Someone really called you that?"

"Coincidence, huh?"

"Mason, I'm so sorry. How can people be so cruel?"

He shrugged his shoulders. "Your guess is as good as mine."

"What are you going to do?" she inquired, helping him take off his jacket.

"To react would mean to give in and stoop to his level just by trying to explain."

"Baby, if you live amongst your people, you at least owe it to them. I know you don't want people to have any doubts about you, especially when they see that for-sale sign outside on our lawn."

Mason asked, "What would be so bad if they did? Most athletes move the hell out and they're still on top."

"Yes, but they're already out. You're still in the game. Talk to your agent and see what he says, honey." She hung up his jacket in the hall closet. "I was wondering why he called three times between yesterday and this morning."

"I will."

"Baby, you've come too far for this type of bullshit." Mercedes encouraged, "Don't sit back and let them do this. Speak up."

Mason placed a call on his cell before he and Mercedes lay down. It was a call to his sports agent.

"Yes, go ahead and book *Sports Illustrated* and *Golf* magazine, but schedule a BET interview, *Jet* and local radio in Los Angeles as soon as possible. Thanks."

As they lay down fully dressed, Mercedes gave him a big hug. She placed her cheek on his back and held him tight.

"Cedes, I thought you were sick of the way you've been treated here in Ladera anyway."

"Mason, I was just talking off of the top of my head. I don't want to leave."

"You don't?"

She confirmed her answer for him. "No. The kids are in school and they're doing fine. What about you?"

"I don't know." He thought again, shifting his focus, feeling more relaxed. "Hey, I got your note, baby, thank you. It was right on time. I appreciate it." He turned around to face her, lying on his back as he kissed her forehead.

Mercedes kissed him on the lips, placing her forefinger under his stubble-ridden chin. "For better or for worse, Mason."

"Cedes, there's something else you need to know."

"What?"

Mason leaned up to face her more closely. "I need to come clean on a secret that I've been keeping from everyone except my brothers. Even you."

She squinted her eyes. "What, Mason?"

"Cicely is Dad's daughter."

"Cicely is what?" Mercedes put her hand on Mason's chest to back him away. She sat up.

"He had a long affair right after I was born. His lover had the baby but I didn't find out until my pre-teen years. Dad told me and swore me to secrecy. I didn't tell Claude and Torino until Dad died, and I didn't tell Cicely that I knew until a few years ago."

"Mason."

Mason scooted back and sat up, too. "I feel so bad about not telling you until now."

"Cicely is my sister-in-law?"

"Yes."

"And all this time I was insecure about your relationship with her. How could you watch me be so nervous about her and not tell me?"

"I'm sorry. The longer I waited to tell you, the more difficult it was to come clean."

"Mason, we never kept anything from each other. What happened to us?"

"I don't know. Revealing it made me feel like I was betraying my father."

Mercedes reflected back. "No wonder Mamma was so angry about her. Does she know?"

"Yes."

"Mason, your dad fooled around, too. How are you going to break that cycle?" Mercedes stood up and paced a trail to Mason's side of the bed. "You could very easily be just like him. How could he keep that going on for so long?"

"Apparently, she wasn't the only one from what Mom says."

"And here I was thinking your dad was so devoted and so into your mom. What happens now with Cicely? Can't she, I don't know, maybe get to know us better?"

"I'd like to leave it just as it is. She's moving on to Atlanta to run the club there anyway. I've tried to take care of her as best I can, but I just can't get past Dad's wishes. And Mom wants no part of her."

Mercedes sat next to her husband. "Cicely's leaving? Mason, I can't believe how many discoveries are coming about in this family. It's time to come clean about everything, right now. Anything else I need to know?"

"No, Cedes. Nothing." He rubbed his temple.

"I guess this is called the 'worse' times. Don't give me another reason to have to forgive you, Mason. We need to continue to still see Dr. Little. These secrets just can't continue."

"I don't want there to be a reason to lose you."

"You haven't. Thanks for telling me now as opposed to never telling me at all." Mercedes leaned over to hug him. He held her tight. "I hope you can live with your decision."

"I'll just have to. At least as long as Mom is on this earth."

* * *

"I'm Ed Gordon. Tonight, BET comes to you live from our studios in Burbank, California, with Mason Wilson, who overall is the sixth highest tour and money winner in PGA history. His wins cover every aspect of the golf world, with the exception of the Masters. Lately, a story broke that Mason Wilson decided to leave his roots behind, so to speak, and step out into the larger world of non-minority millionaires, bigger sponsors, and more diverse surroundings. Tell us about this, Mr. Wilson. First of all, welcome."

"Thanks, Ed."

"We've heard a lot of stories lately about you having been called the 'N' word while on tour and that it's been affecting your game and your life. Can you tell us about that, and whether or not that did indeed happen?"

"Yes it did. I've been hearing all of this nonsense and felt I owed it to my fans and those who support the game of golf to clear things up. While I don't feel compelled to answer to anyone except myself, I also believe that it is incumbent upon me to set the record straight on many topics that might be misconstrued out there."

Mason continued, "I'm living a dream come true. There have been overwhelming obstacles along the way, but now it's becoming personal and the 'N' word is definitely personal to me. And first of all, let me get this out now before anyone else does. I am a recovering alcoholic and always will be. I hit rock bottom years ago but I fought to overcome the addiction and I'm winning. So again I repeat the word, recovering. It's a lifelong process that I possibly inherited. And I'm not ashamed of that."

"Wow, you are laying it all out there tonight, Mr. Wilson. I don't believe we'd ever heard any buzz about that. If you don't mind, when was the last time you had a drink?"

"It's going on thirteen years. I gave it up because it was either the bottle or my family, and I chose my family. I remain devoted to my family and to where I grew up in Ladera Heights. See, I was born in Houston, Texas, but moved to Los Angeles in the seventies. Los Angeles has been my home for more than twenty-five years. We still own our parents' condominium in Fox Hills. I own property all over the country, Ed, but I choose to live in *my* neighborhood, amongst *my* people so that *my* kids can experience the richness and greatness I experienced when I was their age. My parents moved me here for an opportunity at a better life. How can I, in turn, move my kids away from the better life to a life that is what? Acceptable by the elitists who try to dictate who we should be? I refuse to make the very money that individuals spend on the game of golf, Titleist advertising, programming, et cetera, and put it into communities that don't need it. Ladera needs certain businesses and upgrades. Why not put my money into the youth that I've lived amongst? I'm not trying to impress anyone."

"You're to be commended for that. That's been a prevalent concern in our communities when those who make it to the top sell out. But tell me, where did this story come from?"

"From a poor excuse of an agent who propositioned me and got turned down flat. His plan didn't work. I'm not budging."

"How about exposing him so that this won't happen to anyone else?"

"This man used just the right words and just the right bit of information to raise a ruckus and everyone jumped on it. It's unfortunate that people love misery and scandal. But the truth is, he didn't do anything illegal."

"How about the fact that he slandered you."

"I'm after his job more than anything. I do plan on having my attorneys schedule a meeting with the owners of his company."

"Good for you. Tell me, is it true that you're fourth on the money list this year?

"Yes, it is."

"Mason, let me just ask you this question. First of all, it is reported that as young as Tiger is, he made *Fortune's* 40 Richest Men Under 40 list. Can you tell us how close you are to making that list?"

"Ed, I'm surprised at you."

"Hey, you've got to ask, you know?"

"First off, I'm approaching forty so time is running out as far as making that list. But Tiger is with Nike and he has an endorsement contract with them so that plays into his totals. I'm with Sean John and I'm totally happy with the contract I have as well. But, it's not about the money, Ed. I'm here to talk about the recent misunderstandings and I'm prepared to put it in the hands of the Lord. God's will is too powerful for the rumors and assumptions people are making. It carries no weight unless we give it power."

"And how about the speculation that you plan to abandon Sean Jean as far as wearing their fit exclusively? I know you're happy with them but could there be room for other endorsements? Also, they say you missed P. Diddy's fashion show last month."

"That's because I was working. Sean John has been good to me. They have a quality product and I've enjoyed introducing his line to the golf world. I say if it's not broken, don't fix it. So it stays the same as it's been, Sean John and Titleist."

"And I've heard that you and your wife are going through some sort of problems."

Mason's look was firm and strong. "That's between me and my wife."

"I hear you." Ed Gordon looked down at his note card. "So what's next on your schedule?"

"I'm not sure yet. I just might retire soon, since it sounds like that's what everyone thinks I'm ready to do anyway," Mason laughed.

"Oh, certainly not. I say stay in the game but know when to leave."

"I agree. That's the whole 'leave while you're on top' theory. I'll tell you my game is not suffering. But, who knows, I just might write a book on my life called *Shadow on the Green,* Ed. I've accomplished so much in the game of golf and missed so much time with my family, my kids, wife and elderly mother who my family, brothers and I have been caring for. I'm not sure. But I'll keep you posted."

"Well, you heard it here first, ladies and gentlemen. Mason Wilson could leave the game soon."

"And don't jump on that either. I said maybe. Don't hold me to that."

"We won't. But we will hold you to coming back here when you're sure about your future. Deal?"

"Deal. Thanks, Ed."

"Thank you, Mason Wilson. Join us next time on BET Tonight. I'm Ed Gordon. Have a good evening."

Mercedes was waiting for Mason when he arrived home. It was almost two in the morning. He walked into the dimly lit bedroom to find her wide awake, under the covers.

"You did a great job, Mason."

"Thanks, Cedes."

"Mason?" asked Mercedes. Her curly hair was flowing along the pale yellow pillowcase.

"Yes?" he said, stepping out of his pants and underwear, tossing them onto the settee.

"Come to bed. Now." Mercedes threw the covers back and exposed her totally nude, curvy body, awaiting upon the satin sheets. Without hesitation, he crawled in and lay down next to her. She pulled the covers up over them both and hugged Mason as he climbed on top, mounting his wife with an enormous erection. She parted her legs to accept him. Slow and steady, he eased himself inside of her, sliding in and out to her moistness, as his breathing deepened and their hearts beat in tune. She whimpered and shuddered as he entered her soul, while he felt her throbbing walls envelop him. She held him tight, inside and out. Their words remained hushed as she kissed his lips and closed her eyes, while feeling him all through her from head to toe. Their lips danced the entire time, as they spread their arms to each side and grasped each other's hands, interlocking fingers and squeezing tight to the groove of their syncopated bodies. Their rhythms were in synch.

That night, Mason and Mercedes enjoyed a night of lovemaking and expressing their love for each other without a word being said.

Mercedes found herself pulsating intensely, contracting into her peak, while Mason felt her rumble coming on, giving him permission to join her. He released his love and she accepted, unconditionally. They lay there for the night. Mercedes was amazed that her mind did not race. The only people in her bed and in her mind were her and Mason. She let out a deep breath and fell asleep, underneath her husband.

# chapter 22

The Sunday before Thanksgiving, Claude and Cameron rode along the streets of Ladera. This time Cameron was driving the car that was soon to be his.

Cameron seemed to be in a good mood. "Dad, I made the basketball team. Varsity."

"Congratulations, son. Is that what you want? To play basketball?"

"Yes. I've just got skills, I guess."

"Okay, so I guess you do." Claude chuckled for a split second. He then decided now was as good a time as any to have a one-on-one about a more serious topic. "Son, are you okay with not knowing who your real dad is?"

"Yes. Why do you ask that?"

"It's just that I can't imagine what it must be like for you to not know."

"I do know, Dad. You're my real father."

Claude looked over and smiled. "Wow, that makes me feel real good, son."

"Well, it's true. You adopted me when Mom died. You've been my parent." Cameron made a lane change.

"I just want you to know that . . . It's just that I can't imagine what it must feel like for you to be without your mother and then knowing that you've never . . . never met your real dad."

"Like I said, you're the realest a dad could be."

He smiled again. "But, you never wonder about whether or not you have any brothers and sisters?"

Cameron fidgeted with the radio, turning it down as he made the turn.

"Not so far, Dad."

Claude let it go, allowing Cameron to concentrate.

Cameron pulled up into the Holy Cross cemetery. It was November 23, the anniversary of Fatima's death and Claude's birthday. Cameron parked Fatima's Lexus along the curb, parallel to the row of plots near her graveside.

Claude watched Cameron's every move. From the moment he put the car in park to the moment he turned off the ignition. What a shame, he thought, that this young man he called son, has no idea that his own father killed his mother. Claude was startled from his deep thought.

"Dad, I think that's Venus, isn't it?" Cameron aimed his index finger toward the hill near his mom's gravesite.

"Yes, son. It is." They exited the car and walked over toward Venus who was arranging a few bunches of clove pink carnations in the graveside vase.

"Hey, Venus. How are you?" Cameron hugged her warmly.

Venus looked sleep deprived. She wore an old pair of jeans and a sweatshirt. "I'm good, Cameron. How are you?"

"I'm okay. Are you feeling better?" he asked.

"I'm much better, Cameron. Thanks for asking. Hey, Claude."

Claude put his hand on her back. "Hello, Venus. It's good to see you. I didn't expect to see you here."

"I'm about to leave actually. I've been here for a little while."

Cameron looked around. "Where's your car?"

"I sold it, Cam. It was acting up. I'd gotten tired of that bulky SUV anyway."

"Which one is yours?" asked Claude.

She bowed her head toward the car in front of Cameron's. "That Corvette over there. I just wanted a two-seater. Something fast. Plus I got a job at Make-A-Wish," she said, almost expecting Claude to react negatively.

He remarked, "You got a job already?"

"Yes."

"Why so soon?"

"Why not? I needed something to occupy my time. You know how much having a purpose is important to me."

"With me, you surely didn't need the money, Venus."

"It's not about the money. And considering everything . . ." She stopped herself.

He looked at her new car. "You're going to need to pay for that new ride so I suppose it's a good thing. I know the payments have got to be steep."

She did not reply.

He spoke nicely. "That's a real nice car. Congratulations."

"Thanks." Silence took over the air.

Cameron broke the uneasiness with a question. "Are you going to be able to make it to dinner today at Auntie Mercedes and Uncle Mason's house? All of the guys are cooking," he told her with excitement.

"Oh, really? I don't think so. I'm going to go back to my dad's apartment and hang out with him and his new girlfriend."

"Dad has a new woman, huh?" Claude asked.

"Yes, some pretty young thing he met at the Club Post on Slauson Boulevard. My dad, the player," Venus said as if it was old hat.

Claude smiled. "Tell him I said hello."

"I will."

"Venus, we miss you," Claude admitted, sounding as though it was uncomfortable. "Like I said in my messages, things just aren't the same without you."

Cameron told his stepmother, "He's right, Venus."

"Thanks for saying that, Claude. And you too, Cameron. That's nice to know."

"Did you get the flowers I sent you yesterday."

"Yes, I did. They were very beautiful. And I got your messages. I just . . . well, thank you."

"You know what they say. Sometimes you don't know what you've got 'til it's gone," Claude disclosed.

"How well do we know that," she said, glancing at Fatima's headstone. "But for now, I think it's best that we all sit back and take the time we didn't take before. Just to think about the decisions we've made. We'll always have Fatima in common. But maybe her shoes were just a bit too big for me to fill."

"No one expected you to fill them," Claude told her.

"Just fill in, huh?"

"Not even that."

Venus glanced over at the Lexus and noticed the letters TIMA on his license plate. She looked back at Claude and Cameron. "I'm going to go now. You two take care and tell everyone I said hello." She offered a happy face.

Claude spoke up. "We will. But if you change your mind, we'd love to have you over to the house today. Bring your dad and his girlfriend, too. Will you think about it?"

"I'll think about it, Claude."

"Good-bye, Venus. Take care," said Cameron, throwing his arms around her with a bear hug. "Te amo," he said in her ear.

She paused in the middle of returning his embrace. "Wow, that's nice, Cameron. I love you, too." She waited for the lump in her throat to subside. She swallowed and fanned her face with her hand. She looked toward Claude. "You take care now."

"See you later, I hope," Claude said as if it were a question.

"Good-bye, Claude," she said without even a handshake. She turned toward her car. "And happy birthday," she said from the corner of her mouth without glancing back his way.

"Thanks," he replied, wondering how she could wish him to be happy when she was walking away from him and Cameron.

She walked down the slight hill toward her new ride, taking careful steps, looking back at her ex-men, while they stared back at her. Her mind raced.

She strained to focus upon them through the slight buildup of wetness forming in her eyes and blew out a forced exhale while opening the car door. She got inside and closed the door. Venus sat for a few minutes, placing her left hand on the door handle, looking back toward Fatima's gravesite. She then turned the ignition, put her banana yellow sports car in first gear and drove off.

Claude watched as she drove away. "That was my wife, son. That was the wife Fatima wanted for me. And I've let her get away."

Cameron looked his dad's way. "Dad, I'm sorry if I had anything to do with it."

"You didn't. It was just too much for her to handle."

They turned toward Fatima's grave and knelt together, closing their eyes and praying in silence, hearing the Corvette purring its way down the winding hill. Cameron opened his eyes, noticing two tiny branches from the shady tree near his knee. He handed one to his dad. They each formed the stems into the shape of a heart and placed it on the headstone. They continued to kneel in silence.

Back at Mason's house, it was Real Men Cook Day and the guys were gathered in the kitchen. There was an aroma of a combination of nutmeg and smoked turkey circulating in the air.

"Torino, you should have seen my boy out there yesterday," Mason said. "Rashaad, go get that trophy and show your uncle."

"Okay, Dad," Rashaad said, rushing through the kitchen door to his room, doing about eighty.

"He seems pretty happy today," Torino commented, slicing the smoked turkey.

"My son left everybody in the dust with his game." Rashaad walked back though the door holding a golden, three-foot-tall loving cup with a ten-inch golfer at the top in mid-swing.

Torino looked impressed. "Dang, that thing is almost as big as you are. That's a huge trophy for a high school tournament."

"Yep."

"When are you gonna start getting paid?" Torino asked.

Rashaad replied, looking full of anticipation, "As soon as I enter in the junior tournament early next year."

Mason added, "My boy is on his way."

"Like father, like son," said Torino, looking at Mason after turning down the oven.

"I want Rashaad to be just like himself, not trying to be like anybody—right, son?"

"Right, Dad."

"Congratulations, Rashaad. I guess it runs in the family," Torino added.

"I guess so," he said, placing the enormous trophy on the kitchen sink.

Torino stopped him. "Now hold up. Take that nice, big trophy on out of here. We're not gonna have any place to put all of these dishes if that monster takes up half the kitchen."

"Oh, Uncle Torino, it's not that big."

"He's right, Rashaad. Take it into the living room so everyone can see it. Plus it won't get all smudged up," said Mason.

"Oh, okay, Dad. I'll just put it in the case with all of yours."

"Okay, son."

"And come right back so you can finish helping out," Torino warned him.

"I will."

An hour later, Mason, Torino, and Rashaad were nearly done with dinner preparations when Claude and Cameron arrived through the side kitchen door.

Torino was the supervisor. "You two need to get on in here and help us with the corn bread and potato salad. We set those aside for you. Where have you guys been?"

"We stopped at the cemetery and then by my dad's office. What goes in potato salad other than potatoes?"

"Just follow this recipe." Torino had printed out an Internet recipe for Patti Labelle's potato salad.

Cameron took the recipe in hand and stood at the counter. "What is celery seed?"

"A seasoning, boy. Everything is right here. And all of the potatoes are done already." Torino handed Cameron a knife.

"How do I cut them?" Cameron asked.

Mason told him, "Small cubes should work. Shoot, just slice and dice and whatever happens, happens."

Torino picked up the box of corn-bread mix. "This is all that's left after the potato salad. I can make this in my sleep."

Claude was not impressed. "It's just a couple of boxes of Jiffy. Any fool could make that."

"Fool that I am, I'll tell you how to hook it up. Just get me some honey and butter. And oh yes, you add a package of yellow cake mix."

Mason remarked. "I guess you were watching when Mom would cook after all."

Claude looked suspicious after eyeballing the spread. "You know you guys had all that meat catered from Aunt Kizzy's restaurant. Who are you trying to fool?"

Cameron laughed.

"We've been up all night cooking it ourselves. We excuse your absence," Torino commented.

Claude took a seat at the kitchen table. "Man, I can't tell you what has been going through my head lately. Venus is all I can think about."

"We saw her at the cemetery a minute ago," Cameron told them.

"That must have been awkward. Is she going to be able to make it?" Mason asked.

"She's cooking for her dad at his house," Claude said.

"Yeah, right. Her dad, huh?" Torino said snidely.

"What are you trying to say, Tito?" Claude was ready for his brother.

"Nothing. I just know that Venus isn't gonna be out there long. Somebody's gonna scoop her up fast, man. I say you'd better pull out your big guns. "

Mason added, "Yeah, a bunch of big gifts would do it. Buy her as much stuff as you can, and make sure one of the packages has a big old diamond in it. And I mean a big diamond in this case."

"Venus isn't like that," Cameron said, while slicing up the last couple of potatoes. "I don't think any of that would work with her. If you ask me she likes to give more than receive anyway." He spoke as if he were the Venus expert.

Mason asked, "So you and Venus have been cool, huh Cam?"

"Yeah, Venus is all right. She tried real hard."

"I know she did. But some things are just not meant to be," said Torino.

"I don't know about all of that. But life is funny, though," Claude responded. "One day you're taking a happy home for granted and the next you're looking back, appreciating all that you had."

Mercedes entered the kitchen. "What are all of you big strong men gossiping about?"

Mason replied, greeting her with a hug. "Men don't gossip. We discuss."

"You all talk about the same things we talk about. You just give fewer details and try to mix in some sports."

Rashaad walked back in. "By the way, is the Lakers game on yet?" he asked, sitting next to his Uncle Claude.

"What if it is? You can't watch it. You've got work to do in here. Anyway, we're watching HGTV. You know, the home decorating show."

"That's so unfair," said Rashaad.

"What's unfair is that you all haven't offered to do this before now." She leaned in to grade Cameron's cutting skills. "Don't cut those too big now."

Mason shooed her away. "Why don't you just get yourself back into the living room with the decorating crew."

"I'm going. You all make me nervous. Is Venus coming, Claude?"

"Not sure." He didn't bother to look her way.

Mercedes acted offended. "Well, excuse me. And you all make sure to clean as you go."

Mattie strolled into the kitchen as Mercedes exited. "Where's Jesse?" she asked, looking at Rashaad.

"Jesse's . . . go ask my mom, Grandma." Rashaad replied, pointing toward the door.

"Where is she?" Mattie asked, looking around at the overload of male hormones.

"She just walked past you going into the front room, Grandma," said Cameron.

"Why didn't you say so? And hurry up, I'm starving. You all need Jesse to show you how to clean as you go. He never would have had a kitchen looking like this."

Mason replied, "Okay, Mom. Mercedes is right out there. Go on ahead now."

She pointed to Cameron. "And you chopped those potatoes too big, boy." She walked out waving them off like they needed to get a grip.

"You know we never come in here telling them what to do. What's up with this?" Mason asked.

"I'll bet if they were in the garage working under the hood we would," said Cameron.

"That'll be the day." Mason gave him a fisted dap.

Claude said, "Shoot, they barely know where the gas goes."

Torino told them, "Sequoia knows. That lady is something else. She actually changed her own tire the other day."

"What?" Mason asked.

"Man, she called me from the side of the road and I told her to call Triple-A. She came back an hour later talking about how she did it herself."

"See, a woman like that is already showing you that she wants to wear the pants. You'd better watch out for her," Claude commented, sampling a bit of grated cheddar cheese.

"Why, because she can take care of herself?" Torino asked.

"Man, you need a woman who's a little bit more helpless than that. Otherwise, what does she need you for?"

"Claude you are so chauvinistic. No wonder Venus . . ." Torino stopped himself.

"Venus what? Go ahead and say it. No wonder Venus what?"

Torino knew when to stop. "Nothing."

"No, go ahead and say it. You trying to say she left me because I tried to control her or she was too strong for me? Man, you don't even know the facts so just shut the hell up."

Mason interjected, "Claude, hold on, man. The boys are in here."

"Man, those boys have heard us curse before. This brotha is

gonna just front me in front of my own son. My son needs to know that ain't cool."

"Man, I was just playing. I knew that would get you going," Torino said, trying to play it off.

"Well, I'm not playing along. You all let me know when you chefs are ready to serve dinner. I'll be in the backyard." Claude walked out through the sliding glass kitchen door and on into the backyard.

Torino looked surprised. "He's pretty sensitive about that, isn't he?"

"Uncle Torino, that was cold," Cameron said, having his dad's back.

Torino explained, taking the bowl of batter himself and mixing it with a wooden spoon. "Hey, I'm sorry man. I'm just a little nervous about Sequoia and a little touchy when she's spoken of. I've finally found someone who does it for me. I get tired of people talking other folks out of being with someone. I say let me see your relationship and if it's working, then I want to hear what you have to say."

"You know how Claude has always been. He's not a direct communicator but he will get in your butt. You deserved that," said Mason.

"I know I did. I'll fix it."

"Hey, baby," Sequoia said, walking in through the side door with a Saran-wrapped, two-layer pineapple upside-down cake in her hands.

"Damn, woman. You baked that?" asked Torino.

"Yes I did, baby. Oh, did I break the brothers'-only-cook-today rule?" she joked, giving him a peck near his ear.

"Heck no, you didn't even break nothin'," said Rashaad, rushing over to take the plate, smelling the aroma rising from the glazed icing.

" 'Cause you know we're tired of cheesecake, huh, Torino," she said to her man, turning her back to him with a wink.

"That's right, no more cheesecake for me," he replied, giving her two circled a-okay fingers while he headed into the backyard.

* * *

Claude was on the basketball court shooting around in third gear. Torino grabbed the basketball as it bounced off the backboard, dribbling it around Claude, signaling a one-on-one. Claude walked away, headed for a patio table. He took a seat.

Torino joined him. "Hey, man. I really don't know what's going on between the two of us."

"Torino, I'm going to try to be nice. Please let me be."

"Claude, I know you have a lot on your mind."

"Well, then you sure don't need to add to my load by making comments like that about my wife. You don't need to remind me what a great catch she is."

"Okay, so I admit that trying to add a little humor backfired. Mainly, I was trying to scare you into fighting for her."

Claude crossed his ankle over his knee and tapped his fingers on the glass tabletop.

"Claude, man, I don't know what it's gonna take for you to be happy. Even with all that you have going on in your life, money, homes, cars, your health, you act like you have the weight of the world on your shoulders."

"One day you'll find out that those things don't equate to happiness. More money, more problems."

"I get what you're saying, but I'm about to go deep on you bro. If you don't mind me saying so, you have to forgive Owen in your heart, or else you'll never be whole. You couldn't save Fatima from her fate. That was God's will."

"Man, I know that."

"At times, you seem so connected with Venus and Cameron. And at other times, it's like the sight of them reminds you of Fatima."

"At times it does. Anyway, since when does little brother whose had to deal with older brothers coming down on him suddenly give advice?"

"You know, I really can't give you advice, big bro. My game is still being strategized as it is. But I do know that you've got to let that whole thing go. I, for one, can understand how you found love in Venus. I don't knock you for that. But man, you've got to let the past go and hold on to your woman. A good woman."

"What can I really do, though? I told her I want her to come home. Am I supposed to show up like Owen did and force her."

Over their left shoulders, Claude and Torino heard a familiar female voice from the side walkway. "Or show up like me, right, Torino?"

The brothers sprang to their feet. Torino's eyed bugged just as his heartbeat skipped. "What the hell are you doing here?" It was Colette, tiny bulging belly and all. With dark circles under her eyes, she was wearing a pair of black, baggy sweat pants, a tight T-shirt, and a bulky sweater.

With agitation spelled out on her face, she pointed to the rear house and spoke in a low tone with slurred speech. "Torino, can we go on back there and talk?"

"No. Colette, you need to get out of here." Torino struggled to control the volume of his voice. "You're trespassing on my brother's property. I'm not in the mood to play this."

"I was never trespassing before when I'd come walking down this very pathway to spend time with you."

"Those days are over. You made your bed so you lay in it."

She repeated her request. This time standing within six inches of his face. "Torino, I want you to follow me to your place so we can talk."

Claude moved in and stood between them. "Hold up now, Colette."

"No, you hold up. No one was talking to you." She cut her eyes. "You never liked me anyway."

Claude explained with little patience. "You disrespected my wife, and I'm not having that. And now you're sweating my brother. You need to leave."

She cut her eyes again and dismissed Claude with her hand. "Torino, we need to talk. Alone. Now."

Torino spoke. "You should have considered the consequences the night you got with Kyle. It's too late to talk now."

Colette got louder. "The same night you were sniffing up behind Sequoia at the club?"

Torino put his forefinger to his lips. "Sshhh. You need to get out of here before I call the police."

"Torino, I'm not playing with you." She turned her back away from the brothers and began to walk away, toward Torino's front door.

"Where are you going?" Torino asked.

Suddenly, Colette ran toward the back house. The dog, Kailua, started barking loudly from the side of the house. Claude immediately ran after Colette. Torino turned to make sure no one in the front house was coming outside and he, too, ran up behind his brother who was struggling to grab Colette from behind.

Claude was sounding very impatient. "What are you doing? Put your hands down," he demanded.

Claude turned her around to find that she had a small, ivory pocket knife pointed toward herself at waist level.

She clinched her jaw as she spoke to Torino. "I will kill this baby and myself if you don't do what I say."

With panic in his eyes, Torino took over. "Okay, what do you want, Colette?" Kailua continued barking. Torino looked toward the dog run and back at Colette.

The pace of her breathing quickened. "I want you to make her—Sequoia—leave and I want you to spend the next couple of days with me so that we can work this out."

"I can't do that, Colette."

Colette's tightly clenched fist shook under her stomach.

Claude took a shot at trying to reason with her as she stared Torino down, forcing breaths through her nose. "Colette, try to take a deep breath and calm down now. Listen to me. You should know what can happen when people want something they can't have so badly, that they try to force fate and threaten their way into what they want. It only ruins lives and makes things worse."

She looked up at Claude's face. "You're referring to your little Fatima?"

He noticed her sarcasm. "Yes. You wouldn't want someone who doesn't want you, would you?"

"Torino wants me. He's just mad because I got with Kyle." Her sights returned to Torino. "You and Kyle were very close, huh, Torino? Is that the real problem? That you're mad at me for taking your friend away?"

Torino became defensive. "Kyle played you because he was mad at me, and you played him for the same reason. So, at this point, talking it out with me is not gonna get you what you want. You need to grow up."

Colette shook her head downward, looking at her feet. She still held on tight to the knife and did not budge from Claude's hold on her forearms.

Torino added with a snarl, "You need help."

Claude asked Torino to calm down and then spoke to Colette. "Do yourself a favor and listen to me. This is no way to solve this type of situation. You're going to do harm to your unborn child and yourself over a man. It's not worth it. Fight for your baby, but not this way. It's obvious you decided to keep this baby and that's a great thing. So I know you won't hurt that baby. Why ruin everything now?"

Colette again gave Torino focused eye contact. "Because I loved him like I've never loved anyone else. All I ever wanted was to have Torino to myself. He had more women coming into that club than he could even juggle. I put up with that for so long, just begging him to ignore all of those woman. Why wasn't I enough, Torino?"

Claude responded for his brother. "Then why would you want someone who treated you like that? Colette, sometimes it's not about being enough. We all have temptations in life. It doesn't mean we don't love someone. We're all human."

Again, Torino turned toward the house, almost expecting someone to come out to check up on Kailua, who continued to bark.

Colette continued, "But a man doesn't just turn off his feelings like a lightswitch. How can he just suddenly fall out of love with me? It's like he never loved me to begin with."

"Oh, he loved you all right. I know that for a fact, just by the way he'd stick up for you and he'd include you in as a part of the family. He was thinking about taking it one step further and you know it. But Colette, you ran straight to his best friend. That's a cardinal sin for a man."

Suddenly, Colette's vision was redirected to Claude. "And look at you. You're one to talk. You ran straight to Fatima's best friend. If that isn't the pot calling the kettle black? I might as well be dead like she is. Maybe then it would be okay to marry whoever's left behind to grieve. Does death make it okay, Claude? You ask yourself that."

Claude reflected in his own head. Pausing to think back. And then he continued. "No, it doesn't. But love is love. And I fell in love with Venus. It just happened. I hear what you're saying, and I deserve that. But I'm begging you, think about those who you'd leave behind. Be here so that you can raise that child. Don't do this to yourself, Colette. I'm begging you, please don't hurt yourself. That baby needs its mother."

Claude's eyes started to well up with tears. At the very moment that he removed his hand to wipe his eyes, Colette unexpectedly grabbed him. She burst into tears. Claude hugged her, patting her on the back as she dropped the knife, bawling in his arms. Torino, looking stunned and shocked, bent down to pick up the knife. He tucked it into his pants pocket.

Claude's eyes were red. He separated himself from Colette and looked her dead in the eyes. She continued to cry. "You're already dying inside, just like me. I have to let go, and so do you. If you don't, you'll die inside anyway. Colette, I know you don't want to die. Like me, you just want the pain to stop."

Colette nodded in agreement as she sniffled. She touched Claude's arm and backed away, using her long sweater sleeve to wipe her face with her wrist. She wiped her eyes. She wiped her cheeks. She wiped her eyes again.

Claude told her, "And it will stop, eventually. I promise."

Colette shifted her vision to Torino and shook her head at him. "Good-bye, Torino. Enjoy your new life."

"Good-bye Colette," he responded without missing a beat.

She took a couple of steps and then stopped again. "I just need to know one thing from you. Did you love me?"

"Yes. And I always will. And I am sorry that you're hurting." Torino spoke with an exhausted tone to his words. He took a step toward her and reached out his arms.

Colette backed away. "Sure you are." She glared at Claude and then back at her ex. "You need to be more like your brothers. Because one thing is for sure . . . you played on me and you'll play on her too, Tito." Colette looked right through him and then turned to walk away. She headed for the side gate, head hung low, and left. Claude and Torino stood at Torino's front door as the gate closed, amazed.

Claude spoke first. "Bro, that was a trip. I would never have predicted that."

Torino exhaled. He went over to the dog run and reached over the fence to pet Kailua. "Calm down, boy." The dog jumped up, wagging his tail and licking Torino's arm. "I guess your little brother could have handled that a little bit better, huh, Claude?"

"Man, she's just crying out for attention."

"Well, she got that."

"There's nothing like the look of the fear of losing in someone's eyes."

Torino still looked nervously toward the house. "I say we go on inside."

"I'm right behind you." Claude turned to look back toward Torino's porch and then looked up toward the sky. *Thank you Lord,* he said to himself while pursing his lips. He headed back toward the front house and stepped inside after Torino. Before he closed the door shut, he wiped his eye again and then looked around the corner just to make sure that the desperate woman who had confronted his brother was not coming back. He locked the door securely and returned to his family.

Rashaad stopped Torino as he walked into the kitchen. "What were you two doing to Kailua? Teasing him with the ball?"

"Something like that," Torino replied, turning off the oven as he opened it.

Rashaad looked serious. He spoke quietly. "Colette is pretty hurt, huh?" he asked toward his uncle's back.

Torino turned immediately. His shock was evident. "Ahh, yes, she is. You checked on Kailua, huh?"

"I did."

Torino hesitated, searching for words. "Thanks, Rashaad. I appreciate that. You're quite a young man."

They resumed their chef duties, taking the baking dishes from the oven and preparing to serve the family dinner.

# chapter 23

Mercedes, Sequoia, Star, and Mattie sat at the dining room table in every other chair, making room for the men. They looked toward the closed kitchen door.

"Where's Fatima?" Mattie asked out of the blue.

"She's not here, Mamma," Mercedes replied, then leaning in toward Sequoia. "It's a good thing Claude and Cameron didn't hear that."

"For sure," said Sequoia, blowing air though her lips.

"You made that cake?" Mercedes asked Sequoia, changing the subject. "That looks good. Coming up in here making what white girls make."

"That's not a white girl dish. You're trippin'. There's so much soul up in that cake it's not even funny."

Mercedes teased her. "I'll bet Torino made it."

"No, but he bakes my cake," Sequoia whispered, leaning into Mercedes.

"Uh, huh, I know he does." Mercedes raised her eyebrows.

Sequoia continued to whisper. "And just for the record, I'm glad you and Mason were able to work things out."

Mercedes replied, "Thanks." She then looked toward the kitchen yelling, "Come on, my brothers. Where's the grub?" She hit the table with her flat hand.

One by one, with Mason leading, the men walked into the dining room, each holding a platter in each hand. Torino followed

Mason and Cameron was followed by Torino. Claude, bringing in the other desserts, followed Rashaad.

Mercedes basked in the sight, smell, and variety of the spread. "Now this is what I'm talking about. Real women being served by their men. I'm in heaven." She rubbed her hands together.

"We're not gonna feed your greedy butts. We just cooked the food," Torino vexed.

"It smells delicious," Sequoia said, inhaling the soulful aroma of the garlic string beans.

Surrounding the twenty-two-pound smoked turkey were plates of beef ribs, fried chicken, and pork chops. Also yams, sage dressing, potato salad, mustard greens, black-eyed peas, and cranberry sauce were placed on one end, and corn bread and the store-bought sour cream cherry pie were placed next to Sequoia's pineapple upside-down cake at the other end.

"My goodness, guys. You went all out," said Mercedes.

"I'm impressed," Sequoia remarked.

Star asked her father, "Daddy, you sure you guys made all of this?"

"Yes, Star. Didn't know your daddy had it in him, did you?" Mason took his seat.

"No. Other than your super pancake skills," Star joked with her dad. "I thought Mom and Grammy were the only cooks in this house."

Mason told his daughter, "I got it from both of them."

"Please, we know Torino was the head chef today," Mercedes said.

"And I helped," said Cameron.

"Sure you did, baby," said Mattie to her grandson.

Mason looked to all of the males. "We all did it."

"Let's just say grace and dig in," Mercedes said, rubbing her belly.

Mattie bowed her head and began to pray. "Heavenly Father, we do give Thee thanks for all of your abundant blessings. Please bless this food we are about to receive for the nourishment of our bodies. Bless the magnificent cooks and caterers, I mean helpers. May the goodness of their labor grow and blossom inside of us. And may this family continue to grow in health and happiness forever and ever, amen."

"Amen," everyone said in unison.

"Now let's eat," said Mercedes.

An empty seat remained next to Claude for Venus.

Conversation was silenced while plates were passed and drinks were flowing, meat was sliced, butter was spread, and hot sauce was dabbed. Within thirty minutes, only the men remained at the table, still grabbing spoonfuls and slices of seconds and thirds.

Mercedes yelled from the sofa, "I thought the cook's appetite shrunk due to inhaling the food while cooking."

Mason replied, "No that's just because you all taste test your way into fullness. I knew better than that." Mason looked at his brothers. "This food is good, my brotha's."

"Ummh, huh," Torino hummed in agreement, biting his way into a fourth rib. "Oh my goodness, " he said. "I forgot." He wiped his fingertips with his lap napkin.

"What, is something still in the oven?" Mercedes asked.

He replied, "No. Hold up. Ladies, back to the table for a second."

"Oh, Lord," Mattie said with her eyes half closed, resting on one end of the sofa.

"Come here just for a minute," Torino requested. He took a swig of spiked eggnog and glanced around the table for a minute. "Where are your glasses, everyone?"

"Mine's empty," said Mason, looking around for something.

"Then fill them up." Torino whisked his hands in circular motion for them to hurry up.

"Here, Dad. Pour yourself some water or something before he has a stroke," Star said, passing around the pitcher.

Mason took the pitcher and poured.

"You have a post-dinner toast or something?" asked Mercedes.

"Hold up now," Torino said, looking around the table to make sure everyone had a glass in hand. "Mom, come on over here, please," he begged Mattie, noticing she was still attached to the sofa. "I'd just like to say that I love you all, each and every one of you. Mom, you are the backbone of this family. We are so blessed to have you here, keeping an eye on us in Dad's absence. But I know he's looking down from heaven, tripping off us yet guiding us, too." Mattie finally got up from the sofa and slowly walked over beside him.

"Claude, thanks for everything. Especially for having my back like you just did." The ladies gave each other question-marked looks. "And Mason. You've held me up like no one else. Even when I'd ask you for a loan and you'd tell me to leave you a-loan, you believed in me and financed me unconditionally for years, bro. You didn't have to. I appreciate you for having my back when I needed it. But I don't need it anymore. I worked out a deal with a company who wants to produce Lady Di, the female rapper from the club, so I'll be managing her. And I took out a loan to pay you off for Cicley's share of the club. I'm going to run it and make it even more of a success."

"Congratulations," said Mercedes.

"Where's the check?" Sequoia asked, looking pleased.

"It's coming, baby. And as Claude knows, I made an offer on the property on Halm Avenue, around the corner. I'll be in my own home within the next forty-five days."

Mason remarked, "Damn, bro, you're just full of good news. Have you been approved yet?"

"Like I said, within the next forty-five days." Torino repeated for his brother's benefit.

"Forty-five days, okay." Mason made note of the date on his watch and laughed.

"Anyway. And finally, Mercedes. I've watched you support and nurture and love my brother for almost twenty years. Mason, you and Claude have known real love. In a way I've envied that feeling, always feeling like a misfit for not having a family. But I hope that will change soon." He looked at Sequoia and so did everyone else.

"Sequoia. You have changed my life. You make me feel good about myself. You are on my mind from the moment I wake until the moment I go to bed at night. I even dream about you. I look at Star and Rashaad and Cameron, and it makes me want to know the feeling of having and raising my own kids, an extension of me who can enjoy this family's love, and their grandma's love."

Mattie chimed in, "You gonna finally have some kids, boy?"

"I hope to soon, Mom. Sequoia, I'd like to ask you if you would make my life complete by agreeing to be my wife. Sequoia, will you marry me?"

Sequoia's eyes almost projected right out of her head. She stood still, appearing stunned and surprised.

She looked around at Torino's family and they gasped, looking back at her as if they could take their next breath if she would only answer.

"Torino, I'm shocked. I had no idea," was Sequoia's only reply.

With sweat starting to build up under his armpits, Torino reached into his right pants pocket. The first thing he felt was Colette's knife. It was the wrong pocket. He felt everyone's waiting glances as he dug deep into his other pocket and pulled out a black satin pouch. He turned it upside down, and into his unsteady hand fell a yellow gold, pear-shaped diamond solitaire. He put it between his thumb and forefinger, turned to face her and asked again.

"Sequoia, will you marry me?"

Sequoia was rarely tongue-tied. She put down her glass and faced him, looking up at his wide eyes. "Yes, Torino, I will marry you."

His hand steadied as he put it on her ring finger, sliding it down. It fit perfectly, radiating its glow from the light of the fancy chandelier above.

"Dang, bro. You sure know how to make a toast," Mason said. "Here's to the happy couple." Mason held up his glass and everyone clanged them in unison. Torino kissed Sequoia on her cheek while she still stared at her rock. Everyone else took a swallow. All except Mercedes, who hugged Sequoia, admiring her new diamond.

"That is perfect with your long fingers and brown skin tone, girl," Mercedes said, turning Sequoia's hand from left to right for a better look.

Sequoia's eyes stayed fixed on her ring. "It is beautiful. I've always wanted a solitaire like this."

Mercedes looked to Torino and asked, "You didn't know which style she wanted?"

"No, I just guessed. It just looked like her." Torino said, looking proud of himself.

Mercedes whispered toward Sequoia, "So I guess you did meet a man in a club after all, and not in church, huh?"

"I guess so," Sequoia replied.

"Well, Sequoia Wilson, welcome to the family," said Mason, coming over to hug her. He gave his brother a high-five.

Claude grabbed Torino's hand and gave him a fisted handshake. He then took hold of him with strength, pulling him close to his chest, patting him on the back and saying, "Congratulations, Tito, my brotha. Way to go."

Torino replied, "Thanks, man. She's the one. No more breaking hearts, dude."

"There's nothing like the love of a good woman," Claude told his little brother. They both smiled.

Rashaad and Cameron lined up to hug Sequoia. "Congratulations, new Auntie," Cameron said.

"Thanks so much. And it looks like I'll have some handsome nephews, too." Sequoia received a straight on hug from Rashaad, squeezing his upper body into her chest. "Uuhph, that was a nice strong hug, Rashaad. You're getting so strong."

Torino playfully put Rashaad into a headlock, pressing his fist into his back. "Hey, watch out there, young fella. I was a teenager, too. I can see right through you, boy," he warned.

Mercedes watched them and shook her head.

Claude stood by watching the celebration, admiring his brother for taking that step and getting his life in order. He wondered what was up with the fact that the holiday fell on his birthday this year, but no one seemed to remember, except for Venus who mentioned it earlier at the cemetery. He walked toward the living room and then said, "I'll be right back. I'm going to get some Remy." He actually headed for the front door.

While the family continued to gather near the dining room table, Star made her way to her piano, guiding Mattie along the way to join her.

Mason asked aloud, "Some Remy?"

Star yelled out to her uncle, "Hey, Uncle Claude, wait a second."

Claude, almost as if in a trance, opened the front door, pulling the cold, brass doorknob toward him and taking a half step.

He stopped with a sudden jerk, almost realizing that he was about to get a knock upon his chest if he proceeded.

"Oh, I'm sorry, I was just about to ring the doorbell but I know how you guys don't hear it when you're all having fun, so I thought I'd knock. Where are you going?"

The keystrokes of the piano rang out a melodic introduction to the song Star chose to play on the piano, which was Stevie Wonder's "Happy Birthday To You." Mattie sang the words from memory, bolting out the soulful chorus, and Star accompanied her.

Still distracted, Claude stood stiffly, almost afraid to move as though the sight on the front porch might be a dream and he would awaken. But it was not. Venus stood awaiting his reply in an off-white, backless lace pantsuit, with her short, golden hair gelled back away from her hairline. He locked his eyes on her honey red face, unusually made up and highlighted with rose blush, platinum eye shadow and cherry red lipstick. "You look beautiful," was all he could say.

"I got a little dressed up what with it being your birthday and all. Claude, all this time I was waiting for you to come and get me. And you never did."

Claude stepped out onto the porch. As Venus backed up two steps, he held her along the sides of her waist and said, "Venus, I wanted to but I just couldn't force you."

"Claude," she said, only to be interrupted.

"I love you, Venus. I want my family back. Life is too short to waste time. No more drama, Venus. Let's just be together and love each other."

Venus gave him a smile. "That's why I'm standing here, Claude. That's why I'm here. I love you, too."

Claude pulled Venus to him. She placed her head along his chest almost as if slow dancing while taking in the piano serenade. He felt her breathe, he felt her heart beat, and he felt her warmth.

And on the front porch, in the dusk air with the illuminated light of the gold sconces shining along his back, he kissed her, leaning down for a long, passionate exchange that symbolized a new beginning, another chance, a new opportunity to be family again.

Venus peered around Claude's side, smiling toward the jovial family members who peeked from behind him just inside the open doorway.

Her wink was interrupted by a male voice from outside.

"Hey, is this house still for sale?"

"Yes, it is," Claude replied loudly as if that question was music to his ears as well. "I'm the realtor."

Venus turned to face the couple as Claude hugged her.

"I know it's a holiday and all," the young man said, "But can we come in and look at it. Do you mind?"

"Be our guest," Claude replied, walking from the front porch, back into his brother's house with his wife and the future residents of 5100 Bedford Avenue who shook their heads in approval and proceeded ahead of the Wilson family.

# epilogue

***Two years later***

The lunchtime crowd at Magic Johnson's Fridays in the Ladera Center gathered to eat. Some watched the huge overhead television screens of the golf tournament in Canada, which included their neighborhood hero.

This year for Thanksgiving, no one was cooking. This year the Wilsons decided to give all of the cooks in the family a break. Even though Thanksgiving didn't fall on Claude's birthday this year, they still got together to celebrate the occasion anyway. Claude gathered with Venus, along with their ten-month-old baby girl, Skyy, and her big brother, Cameron, now a college freshman at Cal State Long Beach on a basketball scholarship. He decided to major in business so he could go into real estate like his father. Gloria, the live-in housekeeper, was at their home with Mattie, who had become non-ambulatory since the previous year.

Torino, no longer the bachelor extraordinaire, came with his wife, Sequoia Wilson, and their newborn son, Torino, Jr. And Mercedes came, without her husband, Mason, who was in Canada with Star.

Through the television speakers, the announcer's voice rang with excitement during the interview. "The winner today is Rashaad Wilson, who is the youngest amateur player to ever win the Young Golfer's Association's Tournament title two years in a row. The son of veteran golfer Mason Wilson obviously has a bright future ahead of him. Mr. Wilson, tell us about your game today."

Rashaad wore his dark blue YGA golf cap and spoke like a pro. "Well, in my head, I just kept replaying what my father always told me. He said to grip it and rip it, and I did. I'm very happy to have played such a great game of golf today."

"Yes, you did rip it indeed. It was a pleasure watching you, Rashaad. Thanks for your time. We'll let you move along to the winners circle for your prizes. Congratulations and we hope you continue to do just as well in the future for many years to come."

"Thank you very much." Rashaad tipped his golf cap.

"That's my boy," said Mercedes, high-fiving Cameron as Rashaad walked away through the crowd.

Sequoia asked, "Where's Mason? I didn't see him on camera."

"I'm sure he's somewhere in the background, just enjoying the moment," said Mercedes.

"Or over there promoting his new book, you think?" asked Torino.

Mercedes smiled. "Knowing him, I think you're right."

"Hey, Mrs. Wilson," said the elderly lady who lived on their old street on Bedford, walking up with her adult daughter by her side. "Where did you all end up buying?"

"We're over in the new Harris Homes on Ladera Crest Drive. Just up the hill and around the corner. We've been over there for a while now."

"Oh, good. And how is Star? She's such a lovely girl."

"She's fine. She just got accepted to Howard University's School of Fine Arts on a music scholarship for next year."

"Wow. Now that's really something else. I knew that young lady would make something of herself." The lady's daughter motioned for her to come along. "Hey, look, don't forget to visit from time to time, now."

"We won't. We'll have to have you over soon."

"I'd like that."

"Okay, you take care now."

As she walked away, Mercedes overheard the lady talking to her daughter, "I was wondering when they were going to move. It's a shame what happened to that poor girl who died on their porch years ago."

As the waitress brought the check, Claude decided to open his gifts from the family. Mercedes and Mason gave him a gold charm in the shape of a house. Torino and Sequoia gave him his favorite cologne, Declaration by Cartier. And his wife Venus gave him a framed photo of Skyy and Cameron for his desk at work.

"Wow, all of this is so special to me. I don't know what I'd do without each and every one of you. Thank you for celebrating with me and for coming together after all of these years. I really do . . . love you all."

Skyy clapped as soon as her dad stopped talking. Everyone laughed while Claude put his hand up in front of her and little Skyy returned his gesture with a high-five. Venus topped it off with a kiss on his lips.

As the Wilson family stood up to leave the crowded restaurant, a rarely seen Colette walked in the door with Kyle. They put their name on the list for a table. They stood in the waiting area looking around for seats, but none were available.

"Wow, look at her, she's so big," Colette said to Venus as she walked by holding Skyy.

Venus replied, "And your son is big, too. How old is he now?"

"He's nineteen months old," Colette said, holding his hand as he took unsteady steps by her side.

"He's big for his age," replied Venus.

"He's gonna be tall like his daddy," Colette said, looking at Kyle. She looked over next to Venus as though she'd just seen two long-lost friends. "Hi, Torino. Hi, Sequoia."

"Hello, Colette," Sequoia said, holding her and Torino's newborn son. Sequoia had shock written on her face. But she looked relieved by the warmth of Colette's energy.

Colette simply stared at the baby.

Torino gave a handshake. "Hey, Kyle. What's up?"

"Nothing dude. Just looking forward to chasing away these hunger pangs."

"I heard that." Torino headed for the door.

"Have a good day," said Sequoia as she and Torino walked out the door with everyone else.

"Happy Thanksgiving," Claude said to Colette and her new family, holding the door open for everyone to exit.

"Same to you," she replied.

Colette gave Claude a wink and he returned one as well, smiling down at the couple's little son.

Once outside, Mercedes and Venus slowed down to walk together. "So, how's work going, Venus. Are your employees respectful of their new assistant vice president?"

"Yes, that's the least of my worries. I love that job. I'm able to give back to the kids and that's the best part."

"I still can't believe Claude is okay with you working. He's really changed. He just seems so much happier and more loving now."

"He definitely is. But the work thing was one he had to bend on. By the way," Venus said, looking back toward the restaurant door, "Colette looks really good. Is she still working for you?" she asked as Cameron took his little sister from her and carried her to the car.

"Thanks, honey," Venus said to her stepson.

"No problem." Cameron walked away tickling his sister as she giggled.

Mercedes shook her head negatively to answer Venus's question. "No, she gave up modeling for motherhood. I think they're living off of his fireman's salary."

Venus moved closer to Mercedes and remarked, "That's amazing. That boy looks just like Torino. He definitely didn't get Kyle's eyes."

"I was thinking the same thing." Mercedes's cell phone rang. It was Mason calling from Canada.

Mercedes greeted him. "Hey, baby. How's it going?"

Mason was energized. "Extremely well. Did you see the match?"

"Yes. We all did. And where is that son of ours?"

"He's still being interviewed. Star is with him, basking in his glory. Where are you?"

"We're just leaving Fridays after an early lunch. Me, Torino and Sequoia, Claude and Venus, and the kids."

"Uh oh, over there near Starbucks?"

"Yes."

"What are you doing hanging out over there?" he asked with sarcasm.

"Funny. Just enjoying spending time with our family, that's all." Mercedes looked at Venus as she began to walk away. "Good-bye, Venus. I'll talk to you later."

"Good-bye. Tell that man of yours we said hello." Venus headed off to Cameron's car as he strapped the baby in the back seat. The license plate now read CAM23.

"Venus says hello." Mercedes walked to her SUV, waving good-bye to everyone else.

"Tell her hey. So Cameron and Torino Jr. are there, too?"

"They all showed up."

"Looks like we all have a new generation of Hot Boyz coming up."

"Yes we do, and a couple of Hot Girlz, too."

"All right then. Cedes, I'm going to run now. But we'll see you when we get home tomorrow."

"Mason, hold on," she said after she got into her car and started the engine. She couldn't believe her ears. "Through the Years" was playing on the radio. "Listen."

She put the phone to the speaker to let Mason hear the words about when everything went wrong, together they were strong.

His response was, "I love you."

"Ditto."